英語閱讀技巧完全攻略 3

作者 Zachary Fillingham / Owain Mckimm
譯者 劉嘉珮／丁宥榆／黃詩韻／林育珊　審訂 Treva Adams / H

...ess With
...eading

U0033652

全英文學習訓練英文思維及語感
可調整語速／播放／複誦模式訓練聽力

◀ 全文閱讀

◀ 單句閱讀色底
表示單字級等

◀ 單句閱讀

單句循環　語速設定

- 標示高中字彙、全民英檢、多益字級，掌握難度，立即理解文章
- 設定自動／循環／範圍播放，訓練聽力超有感
- 設定 7 段語速、複誦間距及次數，扎實訓練聽力
- 設定克漏字比率學習，提高理解力、詞彙量及文法
- 睡眠學習，複習文章幫助記憶

快速查詢字義
理解文章內容

課後閱讀測驗檢驗理解力

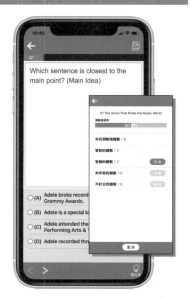

強力口說練習

錄下發音和原音比對辨識，精進口語能力。

單字分析掌握單字力

提供全書總單字量及單字表，掌握單字難易度，針對不熟單字加強學習。

目錄 Contents

目錄 Contents

簡介 Introduction

　　本套書共分四冊，目的在於培養閱讀能力與增進閱讀技巧。書中共有 100 篇文章，不僅網羅各類主題，還搭配大量閱讀測驗題，以訓練讀者記憶重點與理解內容的能力。

　　本書依不同主題劃分為四大單元。每單元主要介紹一種閱讀攻略。讀者不僅能透過本書文章增進閱讀能力，還能涉獵包羅萬象的知識，包括文化、藝術、史地、人物、科技、生物、經濟、教育等主題閱讀。

主要特色

• 包羅萬象的文章主題

　　本書內容涵蓋各類多元主題，幫助讀者充實知識，宛如一套生活知識小百科。囊括主題包括：

社會學		科學		其他主題	
	藝術與文學		動物／植物		體育
	歷史				
	地理與景點		健康與人體		
	文化				
	政治／經濟		網路或科技		神秘事件
	語言傳播				
	環境保育		科學		
	人物				
	教育				

• 全方位的閱讀攻略

　　本書以豐富的高效率閱讀攻略，幫助讀者輕鬆理解任何主題文章的內容。書中閱讀攻略包括：

1 閱讀技巧（Reading Skills）

幫助你練習瞭解整體內文的技巧。此單元涵蓋以下項目：

❶ 歸納要旨（Main Idea）

　　文章要旨代表的是文章想傳達的大意，有可能是一種想法或事實。文章要旨通常會以主題論述的方式表達。除了整體主旨之外，文章每段內容也有其中心思想，只要清楚每段內容的重點，即可了解整篇文章的意思。

❷ 找出支持性細節（Supporting Details）

　　支持性細節是作者用來支持文章主題句的說明，例如事實、直喻、說明、比較、舉例等，或是任何能佐證主題的資訊。一篇好文章，一定會以事實、統計數據和其他證據為基礎，堆砌出作者想要表達的主旨。

❸ 分辨事實與意見（Fact or Opinion）

　　大多數文章均含有事實和意見，因此分辨兩者間的差異相當重要。只要是能透過測驗、紀錄或文件來證明真實度的資訊，即屬於「事實」（fact）；「意見」（opinion）則代表作者的信念或主觀評判。有時候「意見」看似「事實」，倘若無法證明其真實性，該資訊還是得歸類為「意見」。

❹ 明瞭作者目的和語氣 (Author's Purpose and Tone)

　　作者寫作皆有目的，可能是提出論點、呈現重要議題，甚或只是想娛樂讀者。為了達到其寫作目的，作者會調整文中的字彙和資訊，來符合文章想呈現出的語氣。

❺ 釐清寫作技巧（Clarifying Devices）

　　釐清寫作技巧包括瞭解字彙、片語的應用，以及分辨作者用來讓文章大意與支持性細節更加清楚、更引人入勝的寫作方式。有時候，最重要的釐清技巧就是要能分辨「文章類型」和「作者意圖」。

❻ 進行推論（Making Inferences）

　　「推論」技巧意指運用已知資訊來猜測未知的人事物。舉例而言，如果朋友開門時看起來怒氣沖沖，你會猜測事有蹊蹺或有事發生。作者同樣會以推論方式，來提點讀者相似的情境。

❼ 理解因果關係（Cause and Effect）

事出必有因，所導致的行為或事件就是一種結果。因果之間的關係有時顯而易見，有時卻幾乎不著痕跡。為了更清楚理解因果關係，請仔細觀察具有因果意味的用字，例如「therefore」（因此）、「as a result」（所以）或是「consequently」（因而）。

❽ 瞭解譬喻性語言（Figurative Language）

作者會運用譬喻性的語言來觸動讀者的感受或令人在腦海中產生畫面，讓讀者留下深刻印象。本書會介紹下列幾種譬喻性語言：

明喻會以「like」（像）、「as」（如）或「than」（比……還……）等字比較兩者，例如「她的心比石頭還硬」。**隱喻**會更直接比較兩者，並且將兩者畫上等號，例如「她有一顆鐵石心腸」或「全世界就是一座大舞台」，因此表達效果比明喻更強烈。

擬人法意指將無生物的物體賦予人類特質，例如「太陽漫步於天空」。**成語**屬於不能照字面意思解讀的片語，其意義與拆解各字來看不同。例如「To let the cat out of the bag.」和貓一點關係也沒有，真正的意思為「洩漏祕密」。

誇飾法意指加油添醋的誇張表達方式，例如「我已經告訴過你一百萬遍了！」

❾ 明辨寫作偏見（Finding Bias）

作者有其本身的歷練、看法和信仰。混為一談時，就會形成偏見或特定觀點。雖然有時難以看出作者的偏見，但可從作者的用字以及是否公平陳述兩造論點來窺見端倪。

2　字彙練習（Word Study）

能幫助你練習累積字彙量與理解文章新字彙的技巧。本單元涵蓋以下項目：

❶ 同義字（意義相同的用語）（Synonyms: Words With the Same Meaning）

同義字是意義完全相同或非常相近的單字，例如 huge 和 gigantic 就是同義字。英語擁有將近一百萬個字彙，其中許多單字的意義相近。如果能夠辨識這些同義字，將是增進閱讀理解能力的一大利器。

2 反義字（意義相反的用語）（**Antonyms: Words With Opposite Meanings**）

反義字是意思相反的單字，good 和 bad、big 和 small、hot 和 cold，這幾組都是反義字。有時候我們很容易辨別反義字，有時候則需要費點力。記得務必要從前後文當中，尋找可能的線索。

3 依上下文猜測字義（**Words in Context**）

英文單字可能有許多不同的意思。當你遇到可能有爭議的單字時，一定要讀完上下文再決定字義。萬一你遇到完全陌生的單字，也可以從上下文來推斷字義。

3 學習策略（Study Strategies）

幫助你理解文意，並運用文章中不同素材來蒐集資訊，培養查詢資料的基本能力。影像圖表和參考資料等資訊，不會直接呈現出文章的含意，而是以圖片、編號清單、依字母順序編列的清單，和其他方法來展示資訊。本單元涵蓋以下項目：

1 影像圖表（**Visual Material**）

資料有許多種形式，有些難以用文字來表達，這時候就需要使用影像圖表來輔助說明。影像圖表運用了圖片和圖表來傳達資訊，包括了圖表、表格和地圖。運用得當的話，可以化繁為簡，使資料容易理解。

2 參考資料（**Reference Sources**）

百科全書、旅遊指南、網際網路、報紙、食譜等，都是知識的寶庫。但要在如此巨大的寶庫中找到特定的資訊，可不是件容易的事。此時，索引、搜索引擎、節目表等工具即可派上用場。只要學會如何瀏覽這些資料，即可大幅增進閱讀理解力。

4 綜合練習（Final Reviews）

以豐富的閱讀素材和推敲式問題，幫助你有效複習學過的內容。此單元目的在檢視你對本書所提供之學習資訊的吸收程度。為了檢測你理解內文的能力，請務必於研讀前述單元之後，完成最後的綜合練習單元。

• 最佳考試準備用書

本書適合初學者閱讀，亦為準備大學學測、指考、多益、托福及雅思等考試的最佳用書。

使用導覽 How Do I Use This Book?

全方位的閱讀攻略

每單元主要介紹一種閱讀攻略，幫助讀者更加輕鬆理解任何主題文章的內容。

包羅萬象的閱讀主題

內容涵蓋各類多元主題，包括藝術、地理、歷史、文化與科學，不僅能充實讀者的知識，亦可加強閱讀能力。

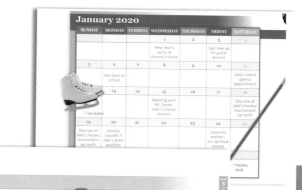

琳瑯滿目的彩色圖表

琳瑯滿目的彩色圖表,有助
於讀者學習使用圖表,幫助
快速理解文章內容,增加閱
讀趣味性。

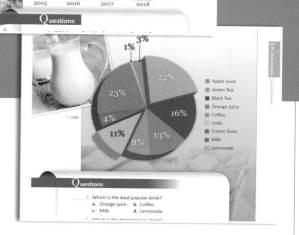

實用的主題式練習題

每篇文章後均附有五題選擇題,用以檢測
閱讀理解能力,並加強字彙認知力。讀者
可運用此類練習來有效評估自己的程度,
以作自我實力之檢測與提升。

Unit
1

Reading Skills

>>

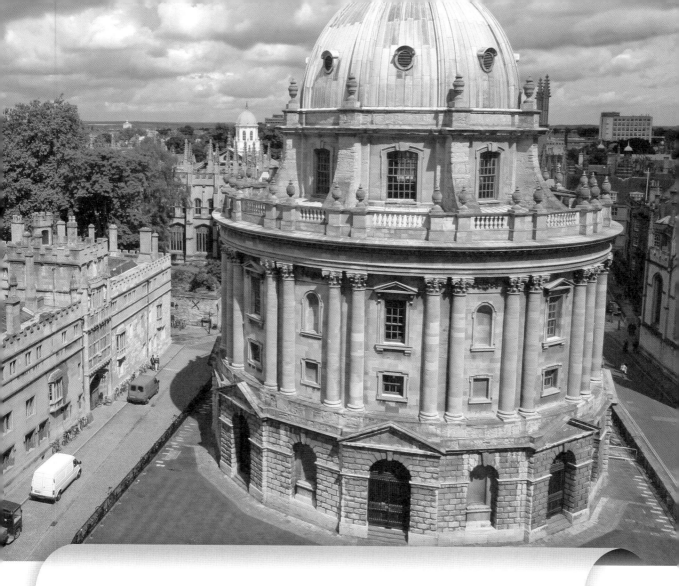

When it comes to understanding a text, knowing what the individual words mean is often not enough. It takes many different reading skills to truly understand what the author is trying to convey. Of course, understanding the literal meaning of a passage is an important first step, but you also need to be able to read between the lines; that is, you should analyze the relationships between ideas, recognize cause and effect, and predict the outcomes of stated events.

At an even more advanced level, you need to be able to recognize the author's persuasive techniques and bias and be able to distinguish between facts and opinions. The reading skills developed in this unit will help you do just that.

The **main idea** of an article is not always obvious, so when reading, don't forget to ask yourself, "What point is the author trying to make?" In addition to the article as a whole having a main idea, each paragraph will also have its own central idea. Once you know the point of each paragraph, you can use that knowledge to make sense of the whole piece.

≫ The California redwoods can reach up to 9 m in diameter.

1 I Feel Really Small: 🎧001
The California Redwoods

1 Visualize a place where the trees are so gigantic that you can't see the tops of them and so wide that a car could pass easily through a hole in their trunks. Standing in one of northern California's redwood forests, you don't need to use your imagination. There are trees there that have been alive for well over a millennium and tower above the ground at heights of over 90 meters. Many are taller than the Statue of Liberty.

2 California redwoods, also called coast redwoods, are evergreen trees that have a reputation as the tallest trees in the world. The tallest living example, a tree named Hyperion, has attained a height of over 115 meters. Reports have told of taller trees existing before they were cut down in the nineteenth century.

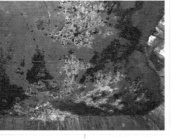

⌃ dried resin of a redwood tree
(cc by Sanjay ach)

3 The California redwoods can be found in a long, narrow strip of land that stretches about 750 kilometers along the coast of California, though since the 1850s, over 95% of the original forest has been cut down. The reason for this is that redwood is an incredibly desirable building material. It's light, durable, and largely resistant to fire. These qualities made it a must-have for the railroad industry, which once used it to build tracks.

4 Redwoods need an environment with high annual rainfall, abundant moisture, and temperatures of 10–16 degrees Celsius in order to grow. The area adjacent to the Pacific in which they thrive has ample rain, with fog and cool air from the coast keeping conditions damp all year long. The area's climate has also remained consistent for centuries, meaning that many of the

5

10

15

20

≫ The California redwoods tower above the ground at heights of over 90 meters.

giants have been able to continue to grow for many years; one specimen is thought to be 2,200 years old.

5 However, because of the abundant rainfall, nutrients are often washed 25 out of the soil, causing the redwoods to depend on the animals that live in and around them for adequate nutrition. Redwoods create great habitats for many forest animals, and the droppings of these animals help fertilize the soil and keep a redwood strong. When a redwood dies, its body is 30 completely recycled by the forest, revitalizing the soil that it once lived in.

>> The California redwoods have often been cut down for building material.

Questions

_____ **1.** Which of the following statements best expresses the main idea of the article?
   a. Many redwoods are taller than the Statue of Liberty.
   b. California redwood is a strong, light, durable wood.
   c. The California redwood is a magnificent natural phenomenon.
   d. Many of the original redwoods were cut down after 1850.

_____ **2.** What is the main idea of the second paragraph?
   a. The tallest tree in existence is called Hyperion.
   b. California redwoods are also called coast redwoods.
   c. There may have been taller redwoods before 1900.
   d. California redwoods are the world's tallest trees.

_____ **3.** What is the main point of the third paragraph?
   a. Much of the original redwood forest has been cut down over the years because of redwood's special properties.
   b. Redwoods can be found in a 750 km long strip of land along the coast of California.
   c. California redwood is an excellent building material, being light, durable, and resistant to fire.
   d. The railroad industry used California redwood to construct railroad tracks.

_____ **4.** The main idea of the fourth paragraph is that _____.
   a. because of their habitat's climate, redwoods can grow to a great age
   b. the east coast of California gets plenty of rain all year round
   c. the California redwood needs specific conditions in order to thrive
   d. the climate in which the redwoods grow hasn't changed in centuries

_____ **5.** Which of the following statements best expresses the main idea of the fifth paragraph?
   a. Redwoods are an essential part of the forest's natural balance.
   b. Redwoods provide habitats for many forest animals.
   c. When redwoods die, they are recycled by the forest.
   d. Heavy rainfall affects the amount of nutrients in the redwoods' soil.

2 The Conch Shell 🎧002

≫ conch shell

1   Hawaii is often called a tropical paradise. It's known for its white sandy beaches, its gorgeous weather, and its friendly, fun-loving people. Hawaiians love a party, and if you ever visit the island group, you're sure to find yourself attending one at some point or another. When you arrive at a Hawaiian party, called a luau, you'll often be greeted by a deep, sonorous sound similar to the cry of a medieval battle trumpet. This is the sound of the conch, or "pu" as the Hawaiians call it, and it's used to welcome guests and signal the start of the celebrations.

2   A conch is an entirely natural musical instrument. It's simply the large spiraled shell of a sea snail that has had a hole cut into the tip of the spire. These shells are often extremely elaborate and beautiful, with colors ranging from pearly white to a deep orange-pink, and are often used as decorations as well as musical instruments.

3   Aside from being used to herald the start of a party, the conch is also used in official settings, such as the opening of conferences held by the Hawaiian State Legislature and at certain events to present the royal court. A Hawaiian wedding is also incomplete without a conch, which is blown to signify the climax of the ceremony, when the bride and groom have been declared married.

4   Playing the conch effectively requires great skill, and most people are content to blow as hard as they can and make the loudest noise possible. The bulging internal chamber creates a sound so loud that it can be heard as far away as three kilometers. However, with the correct application of one's hands and fingers in the shell's opening, a surprising range of notes can be achieved, from high-pitched squeals to a booming bass. Playing these notes requires an

≪ Hawaiian reverend blowing a "pu" (conch shell)
(photo by U.S. Air Force staff Sgt. Mike Meares)

5

10

15

20

25

>> Korean military procession with conch trumpets (cc by Hachimaki)

excellent ear for pitch, as there are, of course, no set finger buttons or keys on a conch.

5   For those not keen on the conch's   30
earsplitting salutes, the musical shell holds
another more tranquil sound—a secret sound
that brings peace and calm to those who hear it.
Hold a conch to your ear and you'll hear, quite
clearly, the gentle crash of the ocean.   35

>> trombonist and seashell player Steve Turre (1948–) playing conch in 1976

Questions

_____ 1. What is the main idea of this article?
   a. The sound of a conch can be heard up to three kilometers away.
   b. The conch is a unique, natural instrument used in Hawaiian culture.
   c. You can hear the sound of the sea if you put a conch to your ear.
   d. Conches are often used as decorations as well as instruments.

_____ 2. Which statement below best expresses the main idea of the first paragraph?
   a. Conches are often used at Hawaiian luaus to welcome guests.
   b. The Hawaiians refer to the conch as a "pu."
   c. Hawaii is seen by many as a tropical paradise.
   d. The sound of the conch is deep and thundering.

_____ 3. The main idea of the third paragraph is that _____.
   a. at a Hawaiian wedding, the conch is blown when the marriage has been completed
   b. the conch is blown to signal the entrance of the Hawaiian royal family
   c. the conch marks the opening of the Hawaiian State Legislature's conferences
   d. the conch is used for official and formal occasions as well as social ones

_____ 4. What is the central idea of the fourth paragraph?
   a. When blown, the conch is able to produce a very loud noise.
   b. A conch's internal chambers are what produce the notes.
   c. It takes great musical skill to play the conch effectively.
   d. A conch has no set finger buttons or keys.

_____ 5. In the fifth paragraph, the main point the author tries to convey is that _____.
   a. a conch has more to offer than just loud music
   b. a conch may be called a musical shell
   c. some people do not like loud noises
   d. the sound of the ocean is considered peaceful

>> A trapdoor on the jungle floor leads down into the Củ Chi tunnels. Closed and camouflaged, it is almost undetectable. (Wikipedia)

(003)

3 The Củ Chi Tunnels

>> the camouflaged trapdoor, now open (Wikipedia)

1   Củ Chi, a suburban district of Ho Chi Min City, Vietnam, may seem like your average suburb—above ground, that is. For underneath the city lies another city, a secret city, a city made of tunnels.

2   With entrances invisible to those on the surface, these tunnels were first constructed in the 1940s during the French occupation of Vietnam and were expanded during the Vietnam War between 1955 and 1975. In fact, the 250-kilometer-long web of tunnels under Củ Chi was just a small part of a much larger network that stretched under much of the country.   5

3   For the Vietcong, the communist supporters in South Vietnam, these tunnels were the perfect hiding places, providing them with shelter, protection, and an effective place from which to ambush their enemies. Messages and supplies could also be delivered via the tunnels, and large amounts of food and weapons were accumulated in these secret places. In addition, aerial attacks, a tactic favored by the Americans and one that devastated the land aboveground, 15 had little effect on those hiding safely underground.   10

4   With aerial attacks and bombings becoming more frequent, more and more people retreated into the tunnels. Over time, the tunnels became their homes. The kitchens and wells could provide food for more than 10,000 soldiers and villagers. Hospitals were constructed to help the wounded, and schools were set 20 up to educate the children, some of whom had even been born underground.

The tunnels became a virtual city where whole populations would live and hide while the American troops marched aboveground, completely unaware that entire towns existed beneath their feet.   25

5   To protect their tunnels, the Vietcong built bamboo-stake booby traps, maiming or killing any

ʌ booby trap with bamboo stakes (cc by Phil Whitehouse)

>> local guide entering a tiny secret entrance, which can be easily camouflaged, at the Củ Chi tunnels (cc by Bencmq)

ʌ visitors entering the Củ Chi tunnels

« part of the Củ Chi Tunnels

American soldiers who came close to their underground
sanctuaries. But the Americans were not to be defeated
so easily. When they became aware of the network, they   30
trained special soldiers, known as "tunnel rats," to navigate
and map the tunnels and to set their own booby traps.
6 Nowadays, the Củ Chi tunnels are a part of a network
of war memorials around the country, and they remind
visitors of the incredible lengths that people will go to   35
in order to preserve an element of normality among the
horrors of war.

Questions

_____ 1. What is the main idea expressed in the first and second paragraphs?
  a. The tunnel network under Củ Chi stretches for over 250 km.
  b. During the Vietnam War, a vast network of tunnels was developed under Củ Chi.
  c. The entrances to the tunnels were almost invisible to those on the surface.
  d. The Vietnam War lasted for a period of 20 years, from 1955 to 1975.

_____ 2. Which statement best expresses the main idea of the third paragraph?
  a. The Vietcong used the tunnels to ambush American soldiers.
  b. Aerial attacks had little effect on the tunnels and those hiding in them.
  c. The tunnels provided the Vietcong with many benefits for fighting the war.
  d. The tunnels could be used to store weapons and food, as well as to hide.

_____ 3. Which statement from the fourth paragraph is closest to the main point?
  a. "American troops marched aboveground, completely
     unaware that entire towns existed beneath their feet."
  b. "The kitchens and wells could provide food for more than
     10,000 soldiers and villagers."
  c. "Over time, the tunnels became their homes."
  d. "Hospitals were constructed to help the wounded, and
     schools were set up to educate the children."

⌃ tour guide showing how
the Củ Chi tunnels work

_____ 4. What is the main idea of the fifth paragraph?
  a. The Americans had ways of fighting back against the soldiers in the tunnels.
  b. The soldiers who navigated the tunnels for the Americans were called "tunnel rats."
  c. The Vietcong built booby traps to kill the Americans they were fighting.
  d. The Vietcong built their booby traps out of bamboo stakes.

_____ 5. The main point of the final paragraph is that _____.
  a. there are a series of memorials in Vietnam commemorating the war
  b. it is possible for tourists to visit the Củ Chi tunnels
  c. war often brings terrible suffering and horror to ordinary people
  d. in war, people often go to extreme lengths to preserve normality

⋙ RSA Minimate, a new kind of educational video much shorter than RSA Animate (Source: https://www.thersa.org/discover/videos/rsa-animate)

⌃ People learn best when they learn visually.

4 A New Way of Learning From an Old Organization

(004)

1   Scientists tell us that we gain most of our sensory information from our eyes. Some also tell us that we learn faster and remember more when we learn visually. So it's no surprise that a new series of videos is challenging and changing many people's ideas about education. Ladies and gentlemen, welcome to the world of RSA Animate!

5

2   Based in London, the Royal Society for the Encouragement of Arts, Manufactures and Commerce (RSA) has existed for over 260 years. It calls itself a fellowship and currently has some 29,000 fellows, or members. Anyone can apply to join the RSA, though acceptance is not guaranteed. The organization is, it says, dedicated to changing and improving society. One way it aims to do that is by teaching people complex concepts in a simple way. That's where RSA Animate comes in.

10

3   All RSA Animate videos have the same basic structure. A lecture by an RSA fellow provides the soundtrack. A hand is seen copying the key points and rhetoric of this lecture at high speed as they are spoken. The hand also draws pictures, charts, graphs, and other visual aids—many of which appear to grow and change by themselves—to accompany the text. This is all done very quickly, forcing the viewer to pay attention for the full 10 or 11 minutes which most of the videos last.

15

20

4   It's important to mention that RSA Animate's videos deal with abstract concepts, not specific current events. The nature of motivation, changing educational priorities, and the relationship between language and human nature are among

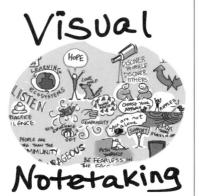

⌃ visual notetaking, a method widely applied in RSA Animate videos
(cc by Wesley Fryer, original image by Giulia Forsythe)

25 the topics addressed in the films. Particular individuals and situations are dealt with only as they relate to these larger ideas, which rarely happens.

5 In addition to the RSA Animate series, the RSA produces articles, speeches, and other standard videos, both animated and live-action. It also hosts various events throughout the world. The society
30 claims its goal is to create a 21st-century enlightenment, which is certainly an ambitious goal. No one is completely objective, however, so the question becomes whether the RSA's politics might
35 not compromise its educational value.

≪ RSA Animate videos deal with abstract concepts. (Pictured: The Power of Networks)
(cc by Duncan Hull)

Questions

_____ 1. What is the main idea of this passage?
  a. The RSA is a very old and distinguished organization.
  b. Most people are incapable of understanding abstract concepts.
  c. RSA Animate is a new method of teaching people things.
  d. People learn best when they learn visually.

_____ 2. Which statement from the second paragraph best expresses its main idea?
  a. "Based in London, the [RSA] . . . has existed for over 260 years."
  b. "It calls itself a fellowship and currently has some 29,000 fellows, or members."
  c. "The organization is, it says, dedicated to changing and improving society."
  d. "One way it aims to do that is by teaching people complex concepts in a simple way."

_____ 3. Which of the following best expresses the main idea of the third paragraph?
  a. Viewers have to pay close attention to RSA Animate videos.
  b. RSA Animate videos all share many similarities.
  c. Everything in an RSA Animate video happens very fast.
  d. RSA fellows give interesting lectures on many topics.

_____ 4. What is the main idea of the fourth paragraph?
  a. RSA Animate videos are more concerned with ideas than events.
  b. No particular individuals are mentioned in RSA Animate videos.
  c. The relationship between language and human nature is very complex.
  d. People should be more concerned about changing educational priorities.

_____ 5. What is the main idea expressed in the final paragraph?
  a. The RSA produces many different kinds of informative products.
  b. The RSA is involved in various events all over the world.
  c. The RSA wants to have an impact on the way modern people think.
  d. The RSA cares more about politics than it does about education.

5 🎧(005)
The Golden Flavor

1   In modern life we tend to take things for granted. Consider a vanilla ice cream cone for example. When we eat one, we only ever think about how delicious it is. It never occurs to us that the flavor—vanilla—actually comes from one of the most luxurious spices in the world.

2   Most vanilla is derived from an orchid that was originally native to Mexico. European powers introduced the crop to various colonies hundreds of years ago. Vanilla was first brought to Madagascar by France in 1793. The crop also came to be cultivated in Indonesia, Tahiti, India, and of course Mexico. Modern day vanilla production is still concentrated in these places. Madagascar and the tiny island of Réunion alone account for 80 percent of the world's natural vanilla.

3   Put simply, vanilla is a difficult flavor to produce. The plant takes anywhere from two to four years to mature, and the flowers open for just one day a year, which means they must be pollinated by hand. After the flowers are harvested, they must be processed over a period of months before they're ready for export. When all is said and done, it takes 600 blossoms to produce one kilogram of vanilla beans.

4   The long production process makes it hard for growers to respond to shifts in global demand. This can create major price swings, which is exactly what we're seeing right now. The cost of one kilogram of vanilla has increased by almost 20 times since 2011. In 2018, a kilogram of vanilla was more expensive than a kilogram of silver. Natural vanilla is now so valuable that a black market is emerging for the flavor.

5   There is a synthetic alternative to natural vanilla. In fact, that's probably what you're enjoying when you eat that ice

⌃ vanilla

⌄ vanilla beans, one of the most luxurious spices in the world

⌄ vanilla plant pollinated by hand

⌄ Vanillin, a synthetic alternative to natural vanilla, is widely used to keep costs down.

Vanillin.

⌄ vanilla plants and
green pods

≫ vanilla ice cream cone

cream cone. It's called "vanillin," and it's used in over 95 percent of vanilla-flavored foods. Vanillin can be derived from a variety of materials, most of which you probably don't want to be eating. Examples include paper waste, pine bark, cinnamon, and even coal tar. If you think that sounds gross, you're not alone. Part of the reason for the price surge is that people are avoiding synthetics in favor of natural options. The result has been a spike in demand that growers are still struggling to meet.

40

45

Questions

_____ 1. What's the main idea of the first paragraph?
    a. Vanilla is a popular ice cream flavor.   **b.** Ice cream cones are delicious.
    c. We take things for granted sometimes.   **d.** Vanilla is a spice.

_____ 2. Which statement from the third paragraph best expresses the main idea?
    a. Vanilla isn't an easy flavor to make.
    b. It takes a lot of flowers to make one kilogram of vanilla beans.
    c. Flowers need to be pollinated by hand.
    d. After being harvested, the flowers need to be processed for months.

_____ 3. What's the main idea of the second paragraph?
    a. European powers introduced vanilla to Madagascar.
    b. Vanilla is produced in a few countries around the world.
    c. Vanilla is produced on the tiny island of Réunion.
    d. The most popular vanilla plant was originally native to Mexico.

_____ 4. What's the main idea of the fourth paragraph?
    a. There's a black market for vanilla.   **b.** The price of vanilla has been surging.
    c. Vanilla takes a long time to produce.   **d.** Growers face some difficult challenges.

_____ 5. Which statement best expresses the main idea of the final paragraph?
    a. Lots of materials are used to make synthetic vanilla.
    b. Ice cream often contains synthetic vanilla.
    c. Synthetic vanilla is better tasting than natural vanilla.
    d. Most of the vanilla we eat is synthetic.

A good article is always built on a foundation of facts, statistics, and other kinds of evidence that help to develop the author's main idea. These are called supporting details, because they "support" the author's argument. So if you were to write an article on how cold it is in Russia, a good supporting detail would be temperature statistics.

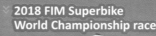

2018 FIM Superbike World Championship race

>> superbike

6 High Speed Fun: Superbikes

1   There is a certain type of motorcycle called a superbike, but people usually refer to it as a "crotch rocket." Why is that, you ask? Because these motorcycles are powerful, lightweight, and they put the rider in a hunched-over position for maximum speed. The ultimate result is the sensation of riding a rocket—hence the name "crotch rocket."   5

2   The rocket comparison is very apt, as superbikes can attain speeds of up to 400 kph. Some bikes, such as the Honda Fireblade, can accelerate to 100 kph in a mere three seconds. A specially designed helmet is a must at these speeds. Without one, a rider risks being distracted by the deafening torrent of wind against his face.   10

3   As they are with anything that moves quickly, people are particularly fond of superbike racing. The Superbike World Championship was founded in 1988, and it holds annual races at various exotic international locations, like Portugal, Italy, India, and Australia. Unlike the more renowned Grand Prix motorcycle racing (or MotoGP for short), the Superbike World Championship   15 allows only slightly modified production models. Viewers are thus able to go out and purchase the same superbikes they see the professionals use whenever they feel the need for speed—or perhaps just the need to spend.

4   Superbike stunt riding is also very popular. The raw power of the bike's engine allows riders to perform various tricks, like   20

« Honda CBR1000RR Fireblade SP1 (cc by Wilzz99)

popping a wheelie, which means tilting the bike back and lifting the front wheel off the ground. Riders can also try a **stoppie**, which is when the rider applies
25 the brakes at high speed and uses the bike's momentum to lift the back wheel while balancing on the front wheel. If these are too boring, a rider can always attempt a switchback burnout, which is when he sits backward and spins the rear wheel at full speed without going anywhere.

5 Neither crazy tricks nor wicked speed is generally
30 considered to be safe, so it should come as no surprise that people who ride superbikes are almost four times more likely to crash than regular motorcycle riders. If you still want to join the thousands of superbike fans worldwide, just remember to take it slow, if
35 that's even possible.

⌃ switchback burnout

Questions

_____ 1. According to the article, which of the following is NOT a race location in the Superbike World Championship?
   a. Australia.   **b.** Portugal.   **c.** Italy.   **d.** China.

_____ 2. Which of the following statements is NOT true?
   a. Superbike riders should always wear a helmet.
   b. Some superbike riders enjoy doing complex stunts.
   c. The Honda Fireblade can reach 100 kph in three seconds.
   d. Superbikes are considered safer than regular motorcycles.

⌃ stoppie
(cc by DaiFh)

_____ 3. According to the article, a **stoppie** is when _____.
   a. the rider brakes suddenly and balances on one wheel
   b. the rider goes off a jump while standing on the bike's seat
   c. the rider sits backward and spins the rear wheel
   d. the rider lifts the front wheel off the ground

_____ 4. Which of the following statements about the Superbike World Championship is true?
   a. It is a stunt-riding competition.
   b. It allows only production models.
   c. All the races take place in the United States.
   d. It was originally founded in 2005.

_____ 5. According to the article, why are superbikes good for performing stunts?
   a. They have excellent safety records.
   b. They have larger tires that absorb shocks.

⌃ popping a wheelie
(cc by AngMoKio)

   c. They have bigger engines that allow for stunts.
   d. They are made from indestructible materials.

Astro Boy

7 The Manga—Anime Craze

1   "Manga" is the name of a Japanese comic book style, one with a long and complex history dating back to the nineteenth century. "Anime" is an animation style adapted from Japanese manga. It dates back to the early twentieth century, when Japanese artists first started animating short films. That manga and anime are popular in Japan is not surprising. After all, it was Japanese culture that invented them. What's more remarkable, however, is that manga and anime have become worldwide phenomena.

2   In both cases, there were trailblazing works that made the early jump from Japan to overseas markets. Osamu Tezuka's *Astro Boy* is one such example. First published as a manga in 1952, *Astro Boy* came at a time when Japan was still coming to terms with the militant nationalism of World War II. The naïve yet powerful character of Astro Boy conquered Japanese hearts and became an overseas sensation as well, appearing in various comic and television series worldwide throughout the 1960s and 1970s.

5

⌃ Astro Boy theatrical release poster

10

15

3   On the anime side, *Akira* was a notable overseas success. Based on a manga series by Katsuhiro Otomo, *Akira* is a story about the grim consequences of unrestrained scientific experimentation. When the film was released overseas in 1989, it quickly attracted a fan following, and it is still regarded as one of the best anime films of all time.

20

4   The initially modest successes of *Astro Boy* and *Akira* went on to explode as a full-fledged cultural movement in the Internet Age. Nowadays, overseas fans of Japanese manga and

25

⌃ Akira

◯ crunchyroll
OFFICIAL SOURCE FOR ANIME & DRAMA

≫ Crunchyroll logo

anime engage in heated debates in online forums, compose their own translations of the latest series, and organize local clubs and anime viewings. New online distribution services like Crunchyroll are also making it so that anime can be distributed far and wide. 30

5 If you're not convinced, just pick up the latest issue of *Otaku* magazine in the United States. Inside you'll find information on upcoming cosplay conventions, events where fans dress up as their favorite anime characters. Some **cosplayers** are so dedicated that they start work on their costumes months before the big day. 35

6 Anime and manga have gone from eccentric Japanese fascinations to global cultural staples in the blink of an eye.

Questions

_____ 1. According to the article, a **cosplayer** is someone who _____.
   a. plays videogames professionally
   b. collects anime movies
   c. collects manga comic books
   d. dresses up like anime characters

_____ 2. According to the article, one of the first major anime movies to be successful overseas was _____.
   a. *Astro Boy*   b. *Akira*   c. *One Piece*   d. *Otaku*

_____ 3. Which of the following statements about manga is NOT true?
   a. It was first invented in Japan.
   b. It was invented in the nineteenth century.
   c. It is a style of animation.
   d. It is often discussed in online forums.

_____ 4. Which of the following statements about *Astro Boy* is NOT true?
   a. He was popular with post-war Japanese audiences.
   b. He was the subject of many TV series in the 1960s and 1970s.
   c. He first appeared in Japan in 1952.
   d. He was created by Katsuhiro Otomo, a popular manga artist.

_____ 5. According to the article, which of the following is NOT a reason why anime and manga have become popular overseas?
   a. Improved art and storylines.
   b. Online communities and forums.
   c. Local clubs and fan conventions.
   d. New forms of distribution.

⌄ cosplayer

⌃ the Akihabara neighborhood of Tokyo, a popular gathering site for *otaku*

⌄ carmine

⌄ female *(left)* and male *(right)* cochineal insects

8 (008)
The Insects
That Paint Your Food Red

1   If you were to ask someone: "Would you eat a bug?" They'd probably respond "no way!" Little do they know that they're probably already eating bugs all the time. Oh, and you are too whenever you eat or drink certain foods that are the color red.

2   This is the story of the cochineal insect, a tiny white bug that has   5 been giving us red luxuries for centuries. The cochineal is originally native to Mexico. The females have no legs or wings, and they spend most of their lives on cactus plants, eating red berries. When they're harvested, dried, ground up, and mixed with water, they produce an exquisite red color. The color can be used to dye clothes and—you   10 guessed it—color food products.

3   There's a long and fascinating history behind these tiny bugs. Cochineal insects were used by native populations to dye clothes for centuries. When the Spanish arrived in Mexico, they discovered that native dying techniques were superior to their own. They quickly   15 established a new industry and cornered the global cochineal dye market for nearly 250 years. Then, in 1777, a Frenchman smuggled a cactus out of Mexico, and soon people were producing cochineal dye in Haiti, Portugal, and India.

4   Following the invention of synthetic dyes in the 1900s, the usage of   20 cochineal declined. However, the insects have been making a comeback

⌃ Cochineal is mostly used in soft drinks and alcoholic beverages.

⌄ cochineal insects on cactuses (cc by Dick Culbert)

≫ Quechan woman making natural red dye out of cochineal insects, Cusco, Peru, 2017

Indian Collecting Cochineal with a Deer Tail (1777) by José Antonio de Alzate y Ramírez (1737–1799)

amid recent health concerns surrounding artificial colors. Many consumers now prefer natural colorants to scandal-plagued synthetics like Red Dye No.2, which have been linked to cancer in some studies.

5 People might not want synthetic colorants in their food, but they're still grossed out to learn the truth behind cochineal. Starbucks learned this the hard way in 2012, when a scandal broke out over its use of cochineal in strawberry Frappuccinos. The outrage forced the global coffee chain to switch to a different colorant.

6 If you're concerned about your own bug intake, just check the ingredients. Cochineal generally shows up as "carminic acid," "carmine," or "cochineal extract." It's mostly used in frozen meats, soft drinks and alcoholic beverages, canned soups and fruits, and candy. But keep in mind: most scientists agree cochineal is perfectly healthy. And if we've all been eating bugs this long and couldn't even tell, maybe they're not so bad after all . . .

25

30

35

Questions

≪ Starbucks' Strawberries & Crème Frappuccino, 2010
(cc by Jeff Gunn)

_____ **1.** According to the article, where did cochineal dye production first begin?
 a. India. **b.** Portugal. **c.** Mexico. **d.** Haiti.

_____ **2.** What caused the popularity of cochineal-based dye to bounce back in recent years?
 a. Health concerns over synthetic dyes.
 b. The high cost of synthetic dyes.
 c. The discovery of new bug grinding techniques.
 d. The invention of carminic acid.

_____ **3.** According to the article, what triggered a scandal for Starbucks in 2012?
 a. Customers were angry about Starbucks' use of synthetic dyes.
 b. Customers were angry about Starbucks' use of bug-based dyes.
 c. Customers wanted Starbucks to bring back the strawberry Frappuccino.
 d. Customers wanted Starbucks to offer cheaper drink options.

_____ **4.** Which of the following is NOT true about the cochineal insect?
 a. The female has no wings or legs.
 b. The female feeds on cactuses for most of its life.
 c. It is known to cause cancer in humans.
 d. It is actually a shade of white before being processed.

_____ **5.** Which of the following is most likely to contain cochineal-based dye?
 a. Soda pops. **b.** Starbucks Frappuccinos.
 c. Hamburger meat. **d.** Bread.

9 The Mediterranean Diet 🎧 009

1   In a world full of fast food, trans fats, and inactivity, nutritionists have increasingly turned their attention to Europe's Mediterranean coast, an area where people have lived long and healthy lives for thousands of years. What they discovered was a diet that can help reduce the chance of developing a host of diseases, including type-2 diabetes, high blood pressure, Alzheimer's disease, obesity, and heart disease. Perhaps best of all, you don't need to live in Europe to enjoy the benefits of the Mediterranean diet.

2   The Mediterranean diet refers to certain aspects of nutrition that have been derived from Italian and Greek cuisine. People following the diet should eat as many fruits and vegetables as possible while limiting their intake of red meat. Other types of food that should be scaled back include processed foods, salt, butter, and of course fast food. As for drinks, Mediterranean dieters should opt for plain water over sugary choices, and they're encouraged to have two or three small glasses of red wine during meals. Above all, the golden rule

5

10

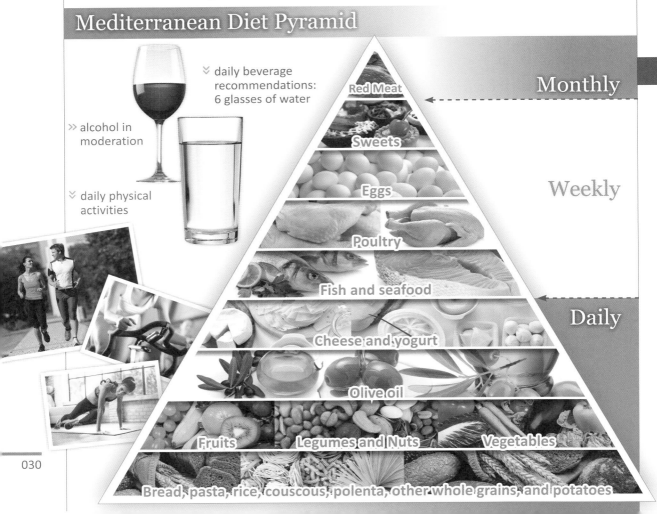

Mediterranean Diet Pyramid

⌄ daily beverage recommendations: 6 glasses of water

≫ alcohol in moderation

⌄ daily physical activities

Red Meat — **Monthly**

Sweets

Eggs

Poultry — **Weekly**

Fish and seafood

Cheese and yogurt — **Daily**

Olive oil

Fruits   Legumes and Nuts   Vegetables

Bread, pasta, rice, couscous, polenta, other whole grains, and potatoes

of the Mediterranean diet is variety. Dieters should mix and match 15
fruits, vegetables, chicken, and fish to provide their bodies with as
many nutrients as possible. And don't forget the extra-virgin olive
oil! Some nutritionists are convinced that this golden liquid holds the
entire Mediterranean diet together.

≪ The extra-virgin olive oil holds the entire Mediterranean diet together.

3   Diet isn't the only key to unlocking the health benefits of a 20
Mediterranean lifestyle. People living on the Mediterranean coast have
also traditionally worked outdoors and gotten a lot of physical exercise.
The modern equivalent might be to walk to work every day or take up
jogging in the park.

4   The Mediterranean diet isn't a fad that will fade away in a few 25
years; it works, and most people agree that it's incredibly delicious.
That's why it has consistently ranked among the top diets in North
America. The world seems to be coming around to a fact that people
living along the Mediterranean coast have known for a long time:
a nutritious diet and a healthy lifestyle help you lose weight, avoid 30
disease, and live longer.

Questions

_____ 1. According to the article, the Mediterranean diet is derived from _____.
    a. ancient Greek farming practices
    b. a certain kind of Mediterranean cheese
    c. Greek and Italian cuisine
    d. the top diets of North America

_____ 2. According to some nutritionists, the key ingredient of the Mediterranean diet is _____.
    a. cheese   **b.** nuts   **c.** fish   **d.** olive oil

_____ 3. Which of the following is NOT something that the Mediterranean diet calls for?
    a. Eating less fast food.   **b.** Trying to eat a variety of foods.
    c. Eating lots of butter.   **d.** Getting lots of physical exercise.

_____ 4. Which of the following is NOT considered to be beneficial in the Mediterranean diet?
    a. Sugary drinks.   **b.** Red wine.
    c. Water.   **d.** Fish.

_____ 5. According to the article, which of the following is NOT something that people are saying about the Mediterranean diet?
    a. It's unreliable.   **b.** It's popular.
    c. It's healthy.   **d.** It's delicious.

(010)

10 Living Freegan

1   How far would you go to save the planet? Would you be willing to sell your car or stop using air conditioning during the summer? For many people, these would be two extreme steps. But for a Freegan, they wouldn't be extreme enough.

2   Freeganism is a movement that seeks to save the planet by promoting a totally different kind of lifestyle. The name is a combination of the words "free" and "vegan" (someone who doesn't eat meat or animal products). Freegans believe that the capitalist system is causing environmental problems like climate change, farmland destruction, and ocean pollution. Therefore, Freegans try to undermine capitalist thinking and behavior whenever possible.

3   Take food waste for example. Freegans refuse to accept "throwaway culture" where huge volumes of edible food are discarded every day. So instead of buying new food at a supermarket, they go out and find the food that's being wasted. Freegans will often search dumpsters and trash bins for food that can still be eaten—a practice called "dumpster diving." It never takes too long to find something nice given the amount that's being thrown out. According to one study, around 40 percent of all food gets wasted in the United States.

4   "Dumpster diving" is the most well-known Freegan practice, but it's not the only one. Community gardens in public urban spaces are another popular method of undermining the modern food system. Freegans often plant gardens in city parks, using food waste

5

10

15

20

⌃ a freegan harvesting wasted edible food

« food collected from dumpster diving, Stockholm, Sweden (cc by Sigurdas)

25 as fertilizer. Then they'll either eat the harvest themselves, or share it with members of the community who are most in need.

5 Sharing is an important aspect of Freeganism, whether it's sharing skills, food, or transportation. Freegans will jump at any opportunity to engage in person-to-person exchange without using money. For example, you might help 30 fix someone's bicycle, and in exchange that person will help mend your winter jacket. The focus in these exchanges is always on fairness, local communities, and environmental sustainability.

6 The Freegan lifestyle is too excessive for many people, particularly "dumpster 35 diving," which they find disgusting. But given the serious environmental risks we now face, isn't it time to consider some more radical approaches?

Questions

_____ 1. Which of the following statements is true?
   a. Freegans will only engage in exchanges using money.
   b. Freegans reject the theory of climate change.
   c. Freegans believe that capitalism is destroying the planet.
   d. Freegans shop for animal products at a supermarket.

_____ 2. According to the article, what is "dumpster diving"?
   a. Exchanging skills with someone without using money.
   b. Sharing an urban space with the community.
   c. Searching through trash for edible food.
   d. Throwing out food that can still be eaten.

_____ 3. Which of the following is NOT a Freegan practice?
   a. Dumpster diving.   b. Sharing transportation.
   c. Selling food at the market.   d. Gardening in public spaces.

_____ 4. According to the article, what is a part of "throwaway culture"?
   a. The practice of wasting food.
   b. The practice of sharing cars.
   c. The practice of having a private garden.
   d. The practice of buying new clothes.

_____ 5. According to Freeganism, which of the following is NOT a negative effect of capitalism?
   a. Climate change.   b. Ocean pollution.
   c. Food waste.   d. Community gardens.

⌃ British advertisement promoting a freegan lifestyle
(cc by - HOGRE -)

Most pieces of writing contain a mixture of facts and opinions, and it's important to be able to differentiate between the two. Facts are things that can be proved to be true—whether it be through tests, records, or documents—while opinions express the author's beliefs or judgments. Sometimes an opinion may read like a fact, but if the truth of it cannot be proved, it remains only an opinion.

11 If a Picture Is Worth a Thousand Words, What Is *Yours* Saying?

011

1   Psychologists say people can often assess others' personalities with a glance. In an age when many people have more online friends than real ones, that means the profile photos we put on our social media pages are very important. And if researchers are to be believed, those photos say a lot more about us than we might think—or want.   5

2   A study of 66,000 Twitter profile photos, which divided users into five personality types, showed remarkably consistent results. Outgoing people, unsurprisingly, tend to post colorful photos of themselves that display positive feelings. They also post group photos more often than other people do. Neurotics, on the other hand, are unlikely to show their faces at all. If they do, they will   10
probably be staring at the camera with no emotion or hiding behind glasses.

3   Conscientious people often smile in their profile pictures, which tend to be of a good size and quality. This reflects their desire for order and planning. Agreeable people generally show positive emotions in their online photos. However, their photos tend to be less clear—and more colorful—than those of   15
other groups. Finally, those who are open to experience also tend to be creative. They often avoid showing faces in their profile photos, or do so in creative and unusual ways. This allows them to stand out from the crowd.

4   Other studies on the topic of profile pictures have also been done. According to some of the findings, people who post photos of dogs or cats instead of   20
themselves are less outgoing, conscientious or agreeable than others. They are also more neurotic. Sorry, pet-lovers!

« Profile photos reveal both open and hidden clues about people's personalities.

5   The battle of the sexes has its place in the world of profile pictures, too. Men dress more formally and smile less in their Facebook photos than women do. They
25 also like to display possessions such as cars and watches in their pictures. Women, however, are more likely to post pictures of their families. Some researchers believe this reflects Facebook's status as a mating and dating platform.

6   Like any other information we provide about ourselves, profile pictures offer both open and hidden clues about us.
30 We should be careful what we say through them.

« Twitter profile photo (cc by Wesley Fryer)

» Big Five personality traits (cc by Anna Tunikova for peats.de and Wikipedia)

Diagram: Personality — Openness, Conscientiousness, Extraversion, Agreeableness, Neuroticism

Questions

_____ **1.** Which of the following statements is a fact?
    a. People can always assess others' personalities with a glance.
    b. Profile photos say a lot more about us than we might think—or want.
    c. Men dress more formally in their Facebook photos than women do.
    d. Facebook is basically a mating and dating platform.

_____ **2.** Which of the following statements is an opinion?
    a. Outgoing people tend to post colorful photos of themselves.
    b. Neurotics often show no emotion in their photos.
    c. Conscientious people post the best profile photos.
    d. People who are open to experience are often creative as well.

_____ **3.** Which of the following is NOT a statement of fact?
    a. Many people have more online friends than real ones.
    b. Several studies of profile pictures and personality traits have been done.
    c. Agreeable people often show positive emotions in their photos.
    d. Men don't like to post pictures of their families on social media sites.

_____ **4.** The second-paragraph statement "A study of 66,000 Twitter profile photos, which divided users into five personality types, showed remarkably consistent results" is a(n) _____.
    a. fact   **b.** opinion

_____ **5.** Which of the following is an opinion about people who post profile photos of dogs or cats?
    a. They are less outgoing than other people.   **b.** They are all pet-lovers.
    c. They aren't usually conscientious.   **d.** Many of them are neurotic.

12 Why We Reject Rejection

012

1   Being rejected is painful for everyone, so much so that most people avoid it as much as possible. Science has provided some powerful insights into why being turned down stings so much. Studies of the brain show it reacts to rejection basically the same way it does to physical pain. That is,
5   the mental areas activated during times of physical and emotional aches are identical. It's almost as if the brain can't tell the difference.

2   Other research provides more proof of the connection between the two types of pain. When asked to recall a painful rejection experience, subjects given a pain medication beforehand felt less emotional discomfort than
10   those given a sugar pill. Thus, the question is not so much why we feel emotional pain when rejected. Rather, it's how we can best deal with it. Fortunately, psychologists offer the public some excellent tips on how to handle the hurt caused by someone's refusal of them. Here are some of the best tips:

15 **3**   One of the most important ways of coping is avoiding being too hard on oneself. Rejection is tough enough on a person's self-esteem. People shouldn't criticize or blame themselves for the other person's negative assessment. If they do, it only makes the pain deeper and longer lasting.

4   Similarly, people aren't doing themselves any favors by dwelling on
20   the negative aspects of being turned down. Instead, they should focus on something more positive, preferably a way to be more successful in the future.

« Being rejected is painful for everyone.

5   Don't try to totally block out all feelings after being rejected. Refusing to acknowledge the pain could actually make it worse, experts say. Many psychologists believe it's important to recognize the hurt and accept it. Indeed,
25 they consider a healthier way to deal with failure is to view it as a learning experience.

6   Perhaps all this advice could best be summarized in the following way. After rejection, people ought
30 to be kind to themselves. With that attitude, they can move on from the pain more quickly and lessen the pain of rejection.

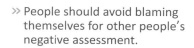
» People should avoid blaming themselves for other people's negative assessment.

Questions

____ 1. Which of the following is a fact about rejection?
  a. The tips on how to handle rejection are excellent.
  b. Physical and emotional pain activate the same brain areas.
  c. Dealing with rejection is difficult for many people.
  d. People shouldn't blame themselves when others reject them.

____ 2. Which of the following is NOT an opinion about being rejected?
  a. Blocking all emotions after rejection is not a good idea.
  b. People need to accept the pain associated with rejection.
  c. Medicine helped people feel less emotional pain.
  d. Avoiding being too hard on oneself is an important point.

____ 3. The statement "Thus, the question is not so much why we feel emotional pain when rejected" is a(n) _____.
  a. fact   **b.** opinion

____ 4. The statement "Many psychologists believe it's important to recognize the hurt and accept it" is a(n) _____.
  a. fact   **b.** opinion

____ 5. Which of the following is an opinion psychologists would likely have on dealing with rejection?
  a. People should reject those who reject them.
  b. Rejection should be avoided as much as possible.
  c. People's attitude towards rejection plays an important role.
  d. No matter what people do, they cannot reduce the pain of rejection.

13 Australian Aboriginals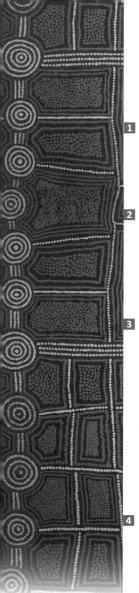

1   The Aboriginal Australian culture is the oldest continuous culture in the entire world. The ancestors of today's Australian Aboriginals arrived in Australia more than 40,000 years ago by crossing land bridges or island hopping by canoe when sea levels were low.

2   For the Aboriginals of old, the land they occupied was an unforgiving one, but they adapted ingenious ways of dealing with their environment. They altered the landscape using a technique called "firestick farming," burning unwanted vegetation to create grasslands that could sustain species they preferred to hunt.

3   Navigating the vast continent was also difficult, but the Aboriginals used special songs to find their way, sometimes across hundreds of kilometers of desert. The Aboriginals believed that they and the land they inhabited were created long ago during the Dreamtime. In the Dreamtime, the creator spirits wandered the land, creating as they went; the paths they took, along with the landmarks they created, were coded into songs. When an Aboriginal embarked on a journey, all he had to do was follow one of these paths, or songlines, singing the song as he went. This way he would never get lost.

4   In fact, songs and stories play a vital role in Aboriginal culture. Having no alphabet or system of writing, they have no written evidence of their existence. Their oral history, then, which has been passed down through generations by word of mouth, is not only significant to the Aboriginals but also incredibly useful to anthropologists.

⌃ Australian Aboriginal style of dot painting

5   Until Australia was colonized by the British in 1788, the Aboriginals of Australia possessed a way of life that had changed little in thousands of years. After colonization, much of the Aboriginal population was wiped out by foreign diseases to which they had no immunity, and those that survived were subject to racial prejudice for many years. They were displaced from their lands and their traditions, and, in a particularly dark period

5

10

15

20

25

30

« Australian Aboriginals playing the didgeridoo and wooden instruments

>> artwork depicting the first contact that was made with the Australian Aboriginals and the British

of Australian history, Aboriginal
35 children were taken from their
parents and forced to live with
nonindigenous families. Since the
1960s, however, the relationship
between the Australian government
40 and the Aboriginal community has
greatly improved. In 2008, the Australian
government officially apologized to the
Aboriginal people for their past mistreatment.

⌃ Aboriginal warrior throwing a boomerang

Questions

_____ 1. Which of the following is an opinion about the Aboriginal Australians?
  a. Their culture is the world's oldest continuous culture.
  b. Their ancestors arrived in Australia more than 40,000 years ago.
  c. They altered the land using a technique called "firestick farming."
  d. The methods they used to deal with their environment were ingenious.

_____ 2. The statement ". . . songs and stories play a vital role in Aboriginal culture" is an example of a(n) _____.
  a. fact   b. opinion

_____ 3. Which of the following is a statement of fact?
  a. Navigating the Australian continent was a difficult task.
  b. The Aboriginal's oral history has been passed down through generations.
  c. The taking of children from Aboriginal parents was a dark period in Australian history.
  d. The land the Australian Aboriginals inhabited was unforgiving.

_____ 4. The statement "In 2008, the Australian government officially apologized to the Aboriginal people for their past mistreatment" is one of _____.
  a. fact   b. opinion

_____ 5. Which of the following is an opinion?
  a. Before 1788, the Australian Aboriginals possessed a way of life almost unchanged for millennia.
  b. Much of the original Aboriginal population was wiped out by foreign diseases.
  c. Aboriginals were subject to racial prejudice for many years after colonization.
  d. The relationship between the government and the Aboriginal community has greatly improved.

14 Healing Plants

1   Plants have been used in medicine for thousands of years. Our ancestors used local plant life to treat a number of illnesses, and plants are still used today in many nonindustrial countries as a substitute for modern drugs, which are often prohibitively expensive.

≫ foxglove flowers

5

⌃ burdock

2   Many of the chemical compounds that occur naturally in plants, called phytochemicals, have beneficial medical effects when consumed by humans. By isolating and processing these phytochemicals, drug manufacturers have been able to create a wide range of complex and effective cures. In fact, 25% of all prescription drugs used today are based on phytochemicals found in plants.

10

3   Indeed, many plants hold the key to fighting incredibly serious diseases. Chemicals in foxglove, for instance, have been used to create a drug for treating patients with heart conditions. Similarly, the opium poppy has been used to create morphine, considered by many to be one of the world's most useful pain relievers.

15

4   So why is the use of herbal medicine often criticized as being ineffective or unreliable? One of the biggest factors might be that often great claims are made for plants that, while they may have medical uses, don't live up to the hype. Foxglove is a case in point. It was once used as a treatment for many illnesses, including epilepsy, for which it was completely useless. Burdock, a widespread, thistlelike plant, is another. Though it is an effective cure for minor skin irritations caused by stinging nettles and poison ivy, claims for it being able to cure cancer, AIDS, and diabetes are completely unproven.

20

25

≫ burdock roots

5   Medicinal plants may also contain side effects or dangers that are not always known to the recipient. Rosy periwinkle, which has been used in Chinese and Indian medicines for centuries and apparently heals

30

35

≫ opium poppy flowers

⌄ rosy periwinkle

ailments as diverse as diabetes and constipation, is in actuality highly toxic. In addition, due to varying environmental factors, two different specimens of the same herb may have widely different strengths— a factor that is difficult to predict and that can make prescribing the correct dosage a matter of perilous speculation. 40

6   This is not to say that taking herbal remedies cannot be effective. However, just as you would with prescription drugs, you should consult a medical professional before you take any. 45

Questions

_____ 1. The statement ". . . 25% of all prescription drugs used today are based on phytochemicals found in plants" is a(n) _____.
    a. fact
    b. opinion

_____ 2. According to the article, which of the following is an opinion?
    a. Morphine is made from the opium poppy.
    b. Foxglove has been used to create a drug for heart conditions.
    c. Morphine is one of the world's most useful painkillers.
    d. Rosy periwinkle is toxic.

_____ 3. The statement "One of the biggest factors might be that . . . [they] don't live up to the hype" is a statement of _____.
    a. fact
    b. opinion

_____ 4. Which of the following is a fact?
    a. Prescribing the dosage of a medicinal plant can be dangerous.
    b. It's vital to consult a medical professional before taking herbal remedies.
    c. The strengths of medicinal plants are difficult to predict.
    d. Plants have been used in medicine for thousands of years.

_____ 5. The statement "Many of the chemical compounds that occur naturally in plants . . . have beneficial medical effects when consumed by humans" is a statement of _____.
    a. fact
    b. opinion

Kitesurfing is a hybrid of surfing, kiting, paragliding, and gymnastics.

15 | The Sport of Kitesurfing

(015) **1**   Flying a kite is something to be done, often by children, on a relaxing summer's day in the park; surfing is a sport for cool people who love to catch a wave before partying hard on the beach. Who'd have thought that these two pastimes, as different as chalk and cheese, would be compatible?

2   Modern-day kitesurfing began in the early 1990s, when Bill Roeseler, an aerodynamics specialist for aircraft manufacturer Boeing, and his son Cory decided to hook a kite up to a pair of water skis.

3   Over the next few years, other designers refined the style and shape of the equipment, and the sport became a hybrid of surfing, kiting, paragliding, and gymnastics, requiring great skill and incredible athleticism to perform well.

4   The principles behind kitesurfing are simple. By exploiting the power of the wind, the kite is able to pull the surfer, whose feet are strapped to a surfboard, across the waves. A bar attached to the kite's lines gives the surfer something to control the kite with, and a harness around the surfer's waist connects them to the bar and takes the strain of the kite off their arms. Once the kitesurfer is able to competently control the board and the kite, he or she can start to learn stunts, like spinning, jumping, and board grabbing.

5   With good winds, some kitesurfers can reach speeds of around 100 kph as well as jump over 9 meters into the air and stay there for up to 22 seconds—an experience that must be as close to flying as one can get. However,

5

10

15

20

⌄ kitesurfing in Boracay, Philippines (cc by Anastasia Zhebyuk)

in areas with gusty, changeable winds, kitesurfing is potentially hazardous, especially for inexperienced kitesurfers. 25

6 It is highly recommended that individuals wanting to try out this sport enroll in a course where they can learn the techniques safely, without posing a risk to themselves and others. A good course should include basic operations, kite setup, equipment maintenance, weather planning, and (perhaps most importantly) emergency landings. 30 To find one of these courses, head to an area where kitesurfing is popular. Anywhere with consistent, strong winds and a large body of water is likely to be a magnet for kitesurfers. You might even be able to see kitesurfers on the beach nearest you!

« kitesurfer Alex Caizergues (1979–), world speed record holder since 2017 (cc by AlexAC21)

Questions

_____ 1. The statement "Flying a kite is something to be done, often by children, on a relaxing summer's day in the park . . ." is a(n) _____.
   a. fact   **b.** opinion

_____ 2. Which of the following is NOT the author's opinion?
   a. Surfing and kiting are as different as chalk and cheese.
   b. Kitesurfing began in the early 1990s.
   c. Kitesurfing requires great skill to perform well.
   d. The principles of kitesurfing are simple.

_____ 3. The statement "Anywhere with consistent, strong winds and a large body of water is likely to be a magnet for kitesurfers" is one of _____.
   a. fact   **b.** opinion

≫ kitesurfing kite

_____ 4. Which of the following is a fact about kitesurfing?
   a. Kitesurfing is as close to flying as one can get.
   b. Emergency landings are the most important skills to learn.
   c. Beginners should enroll in a course before kitesurfing.
   d. Kitesurfing exploits the power of the wind.

_____ 5. Which of the following is a fact?
   a. Kitesurfing is hazardous for inexperienced kitesurfers.
   b. Kitesurfers are attached to the control bar via a harness.
   c. You might see kitesurfers on a beach near you.
   d. Kitefurfing seems like a hybrid of many sports.

≪ jumping kitesurfer Jesse Richman (1992–) in 2016 (cc by Jimmie Hepp)

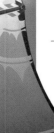

1-4 Author's Purpose and Tone

An author always has a goal in mind when he or she writes something. The goal might be to argue a point, to present an important problem, or even just to make the reader laugh. To achieve this goal, the author will adapt the vocabulary and the information presented, affecting the tone of the article.

16 Submarines (016)

1 Mankind has always wanted to explore the depths of the oceans, and this desire was brilliantly captured by Jules Verne's classic *Twenty Thousand Leagues under the Sea*. But even before the world was introduced in 1870 to the fictional Captain Nemo and his submarine, *Nautilus*, many were hard at work designing a real machine that could take us under the waves. 5

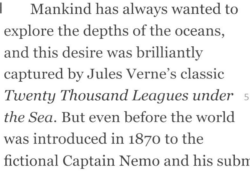

⌃ The *Alligator* was the first submarine purchased by the US Navy.

⌄ Ezra Lee (1749–1821), the *Turtle*'s operator

2 One of the first attempts at building a submarine took place in the United States, where David Bushnell built the *Turtle* in 1775. The *Turtle* was round and shaped like a nut, and it was meant to allow someone to attach explosives to British ships while they were anchored in the harbor. Despite several attempts, the *Turtle* never managed to sink a ship, and it was eventually destroyed during transport in 1776. 15 Given that the *Turtle* wasn't exactly waterproof, it's lucky that no one drowned in it! 10

⌄ Samuel Eakins (1825–1880), first commander of *Alligator*

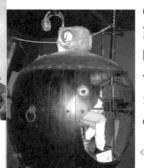

3 Another submarine that wasn't entirely waterproof was the USS *Alligator*. Launched in 1862, this submarine could reach awesome speeds of 7.4 kph. Its tour of duty lasted approximately one 20

≪ full-size model of the *Turtle* submarine (cc by Geni)

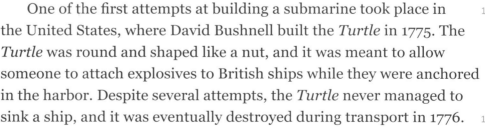

year, coming to an abrupt end when another ship had to cut it loose during some bad weather.

4 Submarines transitioned from a curiosity to a deadly tool in World War I, when the German Navy used submarines called "U-boats" to sink merchant ships that were supplying its enemies. In the early phase of the war, U-boats would surface before attacking in order to give passengers a chance to escape. It wasn't long before this policy was dropped and U-boats began to attack without warning. One of these attacks sunk a passenger ship called the *Lusitania*, tragically murdering 1,198 innocent people. The terrible injustice of the sinking of the *Lusitania* eventually brought the United States into the war on the side of the Allies.

⌄ *U-995*, a typical U-boat (cc by Darkone)

5 Nowadays, submarines are some of the most high-tech machines on Earth. A US *Virginia*-Class submarine is equipped with a nuclear-powered engine and can carry a crew of 134 people. It is also armed with Tomahawk missiles that can strike targets that are up to 2,500 km away. Apparently, submarine technology has come a long way from the days of the *Turtle*!

Questions

_____ **1.** It's obvious from this article that the author's purpose is to _____.
a. entertain readers with personal stories about submarines
b. inform readers about the history of submarines
c. explain to readers the dangers of submarines
d. state a problem about submarines

_____ **2.** When the author is discussing the *Turtle* and the USS *Alligator*, his tone is best described as _____.
a. serious b. cruel c. angry d. comic

_____ **3.** When the author is discussing German U-boats, his tone is best described as _____.
a. comic b. tragic c. joyous d. playful

_____ **4.** The author's tone in the final paragraph can best be described as _____.
a. playful b. sad c. disapproving d. upset

_____ **5.** Why did the author mention *Twenty Thousand Leagues under the Sea* in the first paragraph?
a. To support a statement. b. To disprove a statement.
c. To describe a submarine. d. To state a problem.

⌁ nuclear-powered attack submarine PCU *Virginia*

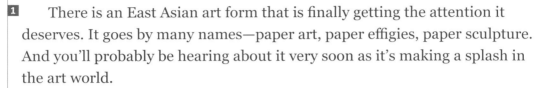

>> The beauty of East Asian paper art is in its fine craftsmanship and its temporary nature, which is destined for the flames.

17
Art for the Dead

1   There is an East Asian art form that is finally getting the attention it deserves. It goes by many names—paper art, paper effigies, paper sculpture. And you'll probably be hearing about it very soon as it's making a splash in the art world.

2   Paper craft is based on Chinese folk religion, particularly Taoism. Taoists believe that people go to another plane when they die. Those who are left behind can burn paper items to provide for loved ones on the other side. These items can be made to look like anything: money, tools, even houses. They tend to be quite beautiful, with vibrant colors and many complex folds.   5

3   The practice of burning paper for the dead is very old, dating back to the Han Dynasty. Those who made paper effigies in the past were masters who devoted their entire lives to the craft. Nowadays, a handful of factories produce many of the effigies used in Taiwan, Hong Kong, and elsewhere in East Asia. However, the old ways are still alive and well. Some young people have taken up their parents' trade and become skilled at paper craft. And during some funerals in Taiwan, the whole family will sit down and fold paper effigies for days on end.   10 15 20

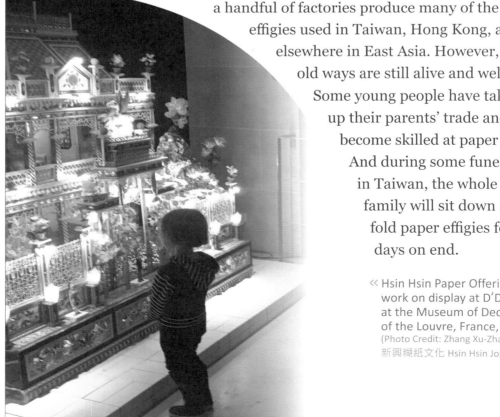

« Hsin Hsin Paper Offering Store's work on display at D'Days Festival at the Museum of Decorative Arts of the Louvre, France, 2016
(Photo Credit: Zhang Xu-Zhan / photo by 新興糊紙文化 Hsin Hsin Joss Paper)

↟ Paper craft continues to adapt to modern society.
(cc by ProjectManhattan)

↟ Chinese joss paper (shade/dark money) folded into lotus shapes and burned for the spirits of deceased ancestors

4 Part of the reason why paper craft has survived so well is that it continues to adapt to modern society. Any modern item you can think of is available in paper form: laptops, tablets, sports cars, even iPhones. There are also masters who can make more complex and personalized items. For example, one craftsman made a paper guitar for the family of a musician who died in an onstage accident.

5 The art world is now starting to take notice. In 2016, the Louvre held an international design event featuring items from Taiwanese artists. It's about time! The beauty of East Asian paper art isn't just in its fine craftsmanship, but also in its temporary nature, and the idea that these lovely objects are destined for the flames. Because if art exists to convey the human experience, what subject could possibly be grander than death?

Questions

_____ 1. What is the author's purpose in this article?
   a. To introduce a topic.   b. To state a problem.
   c. To present two historical examples.   d. To offer a solution.

_____ 2. Which of the following best describes the author's attitude toward paper art?
   a. Angry.   b. Indifferent.   c. Confused.   d. Inspired.

_____ 3. How can the author's tone best be described in the final paragraph?
   a. Comic.   b. Thoughtful.   c. Angry.   d. Sad.

_____ 4. From the final-paragraph question "Because if art exists to convey the human experience, what subject could possibly be grander than death?" we know the author wants to _____.
   a. suggest an alternative   b. state an opinion
   c. be funny   d. give a historical example

_____ 5. What does the author hope to achieve in the fourth paragraph?
   a. To introduce important facts.   b. To describe a problem.
   c. To set the tone for the article.   d. To provide a personal experience.

>> woman suffering from anorexia nervosa

<< starve

^ therapy program

18 Anorexia Nervosa

1 None of us expected to be spending Elizabeth's 22nd birthday there, assembled in silence around the frail form of my little sister on a hospital bed. The speed at which her anorexia nervosa had progressed was shocking. In just six months a young woman had gone from being healthy and full of life to being too weak to climb a set of stairs.

⌄ Anorexia nervosa is an eating disorder characterized by the irrational fear of gaining weight.

2 Her symptoms were relatively benign in the beginning. She spent a lot of time in front of the mirror, like most young women, and nothing could get onto her plate without being carefully checked for its caloric content.

3 It didn't take long for things to get worse. She started getting into screaming matches with Mom and Dad whenever they tried to get her to eat a little more. Then, when she actually started eating at the dinner table again, her weight continued to drop. We later found out why: she was going to the bathroom and throwing up after every meal.

4 When she started missing university lectures because of dizziness and exhaustion, we knew the situation had gotten out of hand. Anyone could see that her weight was dangerously low, and it was affecting her health. Even she realized something was wrong. She saw the fear and concern in our parents' eyes and felt the helplessness of being so frail. Despite our pleas for her

to seek help and her assurances that she would do just that, Elizabeth 25
continued to starve herself.

5   I don't know how my sister's body image got to be so distorted.
She was normal in just about every possible way before the anorexia
nervosa: normal friends, normal hobbies, normal TV shows, and
normal body weight. Yet I do know that if it can happen to her, it can 30
happen to anyone.

> Real beauty lies in health and happiness.

6   Back in the hospital room, holding my
sister's hand as she fights for her life, it's
impossible to ignore the fact that anorexia
nervosa can be a deadly disorder. But there 35
is still hope for its sufferers. When Elizabeth
wakes up, we are going to start a family-
based therapy program. Together, we will
help her rediscover what she once knew:
real beauty lies in health and happiness. 40

Questions

_____ **1.** The author's tone for most of this article is best described as _____.
    a. gross   **b.** comic   **c.** tragic   **d.** formal

_____ **2.** The author's tone in the final paragraph is best described as _____.
    a. annoyed   **b.** hopeful   **c.** angry   **d.** confused

_____ **3.** The author's purpose in this article is to _____.
    a. entertain readers with a story
    b. inform readers about a disorder
    c. make readers laugh
    d. defend a point of view

_____ **4.** Why did the author choose the setting of a hospital for this story?
    a. To emphasize the danger of anorexia nervosa.
    b. To emphasize the rareness of anorexia nervosa.
    c. To list the symptoms of anorexia nervosa.
    d. To show how to treat anorexia nervosa.

_____ **5.** What was the author's purpose in describing the process of how
Elizabeth ended up in the hospital?
    a. To show how to treat anorexia nervosa.
    b. To explore the causes of anorexia nervosa.
    c. To list the symptoms of anorexia nervosa.
    d. To present statistics on anorexia nervosa sufferers.

19 Sheep-Eating Plant ◀019▶

1   There are very few things that sheep truly fear. Thunder, lightning, and fire won't even get a reaction, and some farmers will tell you how they saw their sheep yawning calmly during a catastrophic earthquake. Even when faced with their own inevitable slaughter at the hands of humans, sheep approach death with a quiet dignity that is peculiar for an animal destined to become someone's 5 dinner.

2   Yet there is something that can strike fear into the heart of any sheep: the *Puya chilensis*, otherwise known as the sheep-eating plant. The *Puya chilensis* is a plant that's native to Chile. It has a lush green color, grows up to two meters in height, and most importantly (as far as sheep are concerned), the plant is 10 covered in long spikes.

3   This is where things get a little unpleasant. The spikes on the *Puya chilensis* are razor-sharp, and it uses them to ensnare sheep and other small animals. Its victims get caught on the spikes, and the more they struggle, the harder it is for them to get away. Ultimately, many of these animals either starve or bleed to 15 death right there on the *Puya chilensis* plant.

4   Of course, that's exactly what the *Puya chilensis* wants. Scientists believe that the plant has evolved these spikes to use the blood of dead animals as fertilizer. So basically, the *Puya chilensis* is a plant that 20 thrives on the blood and decomposing flesh of livestock. No wonder the sheep are so terrified!

5   Seeing a *Puya chilensis* in bloom outside of Chile can be quite a challenge, as it takes around 20 years for the plant to flower. One 25 plant bloomed in the United Kingdom in June 2013, a full 15 years after the Royal Horticultural Society (RHS) originally planted it. Workers at the RHS greenhouse claim that their *Puya chilensis* was raised on liquid 30 fertilizer, but it's always possible that some mischievous worker was sneaking in a few sheep snacks on the side. Needless to say, all local sheep shunned the entire exhibition.

《 The *Puya chilensis* is native to the mountains of Chile.
(cc by Stan Shebs)

Questions

_____ 1. The author's tone in this article is best described as _____.

    a. tiring   **b.** angry   **c.** disappointing   **d.** comic

_____ 2. Which of the following best describes the author's attitude toward how the *Puya chilensis* consumes sheep?

    a. Disgusted. **b.** Fascinated.   **c.** Indifferent.   **d.** Pessimistic.

_____ 3. It's obvious from this article that the author's purpose is to

    _____.

    a. tell a personal story   **b.** argue a point

    c. entertain the reader   **d.** state a problem

_____ 4. Why did the author introduce a specific example in the final paragraph?

    a. To make a point about the plant being rare.

    b. To encourage people to watch the plant.

    c. To argue why we should protect the plant.

    d. To compare it with another plant that eats animals.

_____ 5. The author's purpose in the fourth paragraph is to _____.

    a. offer a solution   **b.** defend an animal

    c. make a comparison   **d.** state a theory

⌃ The *Puya chilensis* grows up to two meters in height.

⌃ The *Puya chilensis* is covered in long spikes. (cc by Mokkie)

⌃ *Puya chilensis* in bloom (cc by Wvasco)

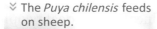

⌄ The *Puya chilensis* feeds on sheep.

20 | Sign Language

Charles-Michel de L'Épée (1712–1789), founder of the first public school for the deaf (Wikipedia)

1 Sign language refers to a language in which meaning is conveyed by hand motions and movements instead of sounds, which is the more commonly used method of human communication. Sign languages are favored by deaf people around the world because these individuals are unable to hear spoken words. ⁵

2 The evolution of sign language was stunted for hundreds of years because of a few irresponsible opinions that originated in ancient Greece. In the year 364 BC, the famous philosopher Aristotle ¹⁰ incorrectly declared that deaf people could not be taught because all learning occurred through hearing. This single ridiculous statement made Europeans assume for centuries that deaf people were inherently stupid.

hearing-impaired people signing

3 Attitudes began to change in France in the eighteenth century, ¹⁵ when a Catholic priest named Charles-Michel de L'Épée took an interest in two deaf street children who were able to communicate via hand signs. He went on to open a school that offered free education for deaf people. His students were encouraged to show him the signs they used ²⁰ at home, and L'Épée combined all these signs into a standard system. He used this system to teach his own students and educators from other countries. L'Épée eventually came to be known as the Father of the Deaf. ²⁵

sign language sculpture in Prague (cc by ŠJ)

4 Decades later, an American doctor named Thomas Hopkins Gallaudet wanted to teach his deaf neighbor how to communicate, so he traveled to Europe in search of advice. After consulting with many of L'Épée's successors, he returned to the United States and founded the American School for the Deaf, where his neighbor became one of   30 the school's first students.

5   Nowadays, there are many different sign languages around the world. American Sign Language (ASL), which was developed by Gallaudet's school, is the most popular dialect with anywhere between 250,000 and 500,000 users worldwide. ASL signs are somewhat like Chinese characters. They often   35 resemble the concept they are trying to convey, but they're not a direct match. Also, ASL is much more than just an alphabet, which is a common misconception.

6   Deaf people have come a long way since the days of Aristotle, and much of this progress is thanks to   40 the sheer will of people like L'Épée, as well as the development of educational tools like sign language.

≪ sculpture of *Thomas Hopkins Gallaudet and Alice Cogswell* in Washington, DC. Gallaudet is depicted teaching his pupil Cogswell how to sign the letter A. (cc by Mr. T in DC)

Questions

_____ 1. Which of the following best describes the author's attitude towards Aristotle's views on deaf people?
   a. Confused. **b.** Annoyed.   **c.** Sad.   **d.** Indifferent.

_____ 2. In the third paragraph, the author's tone can best be described as _____.
   a. angry   **b.** joyous   **c.** comic   **d.** serious

_____ 3. Why did the author discuss Aristotle in the second paragraph?
   a. To offer a solution.   **b.** To give historical background.
   c. To cite a specific example.   **d.** To tell a joke.

_____ 4. What was the author's purpose in mentioning Chinese symbols in the fifth paragraph?
   a. To make a comparison.   **b.** To argue a point.
   c. To present a statistic.   **d.** To tell a story.

_____ 5. What is the author's purpose in the final paragraph?
   a. To argue a point.   **b.** To make a comparison.
   c. To summarize the article.   **d.** To tell a joke.

1-5 Clarifying Devices

Writers strive to make their work both interesting and clear. They do this by using various techniques, words, and phrases that give the writing order and structure and that draw the reader's attention. To identify these devices, you'll need to be able to deconstruct a piece of writing structurally and recognize the tricks of the writer's trade.

FUNDS

21 Funds 🎧 021

1 Would you like to make money without having to lift a finger? Well, investing is one way to make your money work for you. The problem is that many of us just don't know where to start. 5

2 At the heart of it, what is investing? Put simply, investing is the act of committing money to something with the aim of obtaining a profit. Think of investing like betting on a 10 horse. Some investments are sure winners but won't earn you much money, while others are high-risk, high-yield wild cards that could 15 make you a fortune but could also lose you the lot.

3 What, then, is the best way to invest one's money? You could invest in stocks, but they can often be unstable, 20 their value fluctuating up and down like a yo-yo. Or you could invest in bonds, where you're virtually guaranteed to get your money back with interest. Consequently, though, the amount of interest you'll get is fairly low. 25

4 Additionally, investing independently requires good knowledge of the market economy. But what if the complexities of finance give you a terrible headache? If this is the case, a mutual fund is probably your best 30 option.

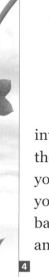

≫ Investing is the act of committing money in order to gain a profit.

≫ financial adviser

5   A mutual fund is a collective investment under the supervision of a professional. When you enter a mutual fund, you pool your money together with several other investors, and your investment manager coordinates your investments on your behalf. The result is lower   35 risk, as the collective investment can be spread over a wider range of options than would normally be possible.

6   There are many types of mutual funds to choose from. An equity fund is a fund that deals almost wholly in stocks, with the aim of multiplying the investment via capital growth. A balanced fund deals   40 in a mixture of stocks and bonds, balancing the potential losses of the stock market with the stability of bonds. A life-cycle fund initially deals in high-risk, high-yield stocks but becomes less risky as the investor ages, making it more suitable for a retiree. There are, of course, many more types of funds.   45

7   So which one to choose? Well, there's no right or wrong answer. It's important to choose a mutual fund that suits both your needs and your personality.

Stocks can often be unstable.

Questions

_____ **1.** The author develops the passage using a series of _____.
     a. tales   **b.** statistics and figures
     c. illustrative examples   **d.** questions and answers

_____ **2.** The author ends the article with a(n) _____.
     a. comparison   **b.** piece of advice
     c. famous saying   **d.** exaggeration

_____ **3.** In the second paragraph, the author uses _____ to explain investing.
     a. comparisons and metaphors
     b. a series of questions and answers
     c. quotations
     d. a logical argument

_____ **4.** The sixth paragraph is structured as a _____.
     a. step-by-step process   **b.** list
     c. series of causes and effects   **d.** chronological sequence

_____ **5.** The author starts the article with a question in order to _____.
     a. make the reader laugh
     b. shock the reader
     c. arouse the reader's interest
     d. make the reader sympathetic

22 Amazon Rain Forest 🎧022

1 The Amazon rain forest covers 5.5 million square kilometers of the South American continent in dense jungle and raging rivers. It is an immense hive of biodiversity, home to millions of species of plants and animals—some of which are still unknown to science. It is also the world's largest supplier of oxygen and a treasure chest for medical researchers who hope to find cures for diseases like ⁵ cancer and AIDS from the rain forest's diverse flora.

2 This rich rain forest, however, is at risk of being lost because of controversial deforestation caused by the actions of loggers, farmers, and settlers. Since the 1970s, 20% of the rain forest has been cut down. To get a comprehensive idea of the scale of the deforestation, consider the following: in the nine-year period ¹⁰ between 1991 and 2000, an area the size of Spain was cleared of trees.

3 Crop farmers clear the land using slash-and-burn farming, a method that involves cutting down forests and burning the land to make it suitable for agricultural purposes. The problem with doing this in the Amazon is that the soil is not rich enough to support multiple harvests. After a year, the nutrients in the ¹⁵ soil are exhausted, resulting in barren land where lush rain forests once stood. Meanwhile, the farmers move to other areas to clear yet more land.

4 Crop farming is not the biggest threat to the Amazon rain forest. That honor goes to cattle farming. Unlike crops, grass can grow in the infertile Amazon soil, and now 91% of all land deforested since 1970 is used for cattle grazing. ²⁰

5 Due to its role as the world's largest absorber and recycler of carbon dioxide into oxygen and clean air for us to breathe, the Amazon's continuous destruction increases the peril of global warming immeasurably. It's up to each individual to protest the destruction of the Amazon by refusing outright to purchase any food grown on lands that used to be rain forest and pressing political leaders to take ²⁵ decisive action against this environmental disaster. You may think that your voice will go unnoticed, but figures from 2011 showed the slowest rate of deforestation since records have been kept.

Deforestation in the Amazon rain forest threatens many species of tree frogs, which are very sensitive to environmental changes. (pictured: giant leaf frog) (cc by Cburnett)

Deforestation in the Amazon rain forest. In this image, intact forest is deep green, while cleared areas are tan or light green. (Wikipedia)

Questions

Effects of slash-and-burn farming can be devastating. (cc by Prashanthns)

_____ 1. In the first paragraph of this article, the author creates interest by _____.
    a. giving a vivid description   **b.** quoting a famous work
    c. giving a warning   **d.** presenting a contrast

_____ 2. A change of tone between the first and second paragraphs is signaled by the word _____.
    a. since   **b.** however   **c.** consider   **d.** because

_____ 3. The fourth-paragraph sentence "That honor goes to cattle farming" is an example of _____.
    a. listing   **b.** metaphor   **c.** sarcasm   **d.** exaggeration

top view of Amazon rain forest, July 2018 (cc by Alexander Gerst)

_____ 4. The author supports his claims mostly through the use of _____.
    a. statistics   **b.** first-hand testimonies
    c. expert opinions   **d.** logical argument

_____ 5. The final sentence of the article is intended to _____.
    a. make the reader laugh   **b.** summarize the content of the passage
    c. convince the reader   **d.** mislead the reader

slash-and-burn forest clearing along a river in Brazil

The Amazon rain forest covers 5.5 million square kilometers of the South American continent.

23 Fantasy Movies 🎧023

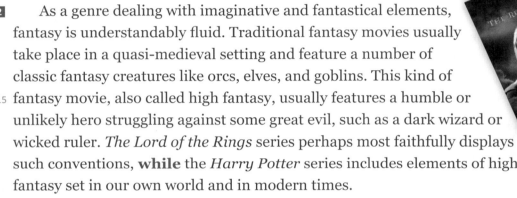

As children, we have all fantasized about going on adventures to far-off, magical lands, doing battle with wizards, or encountering bizarre and wonderful creatures. Even as adults, the secret thrill of entering these fantasy worlds often never diminishes. It is perhaps for this reason that fantasy films have dominated our movie screens for decades and achieved phenomenal commercial success.

As a genre dealing with imaginative and fantastical elements, fantasy is understandably fluid. Traditional fantasy movies usually take place in a quasi-medieval setting and feature a number of classic fantasy creatures like orcs, elves, and goblins. This kind of fantasy movie, also called high fantasy, usually features a humble or unlikely hero struggling against some great evil, such as a dark wizard or wicked ruler. *The Lord of the Rings* series perhaps most faithfully displays such conventions, **while** the *Harry Potter* series includes elements of high fantasy set in our own world and in modern times.

Certain movies, however, blur the boundaries between fantasy and other genres like science fiction, horror, or adventure. Take *Avatar* for example. Set on a faraway planet and featuring aliens and futuristic technology, this movie nonetheless displays elements of fantasy in its richly developed world and good-versus-evil plot. Needless to say, fantasy has an almost infinite number of subgenres, with fantasy adventure, romantic fantasy, and superhero fantasy being just a few.

Though fantasy movies did not really become popular until the 1980s, they have been made since the birth of moviemaking—*The Wizard of Oz*, chronicling the adventures of Dorothy in the strange land of Oz and the characters she encounters, being the most famous of these early endeavors.

With the development of special effects in the 1950s, fantasy took on a new dimension, but over-the-top acting and low budgets often meant that these early fantasy movies were looked on as cheap and rather unsophisticated. It was the invention of computer-generated imagery (CGI) in the 1990s that really fueled the fantasy revolution. With CGI, effects could be done safely, relatively cheaply, and, more importantly, they looked real. Today, the only limit to fantasy is the moviemakers' imagination.

Questions

« *The Hobbit*
series
(2012)

_____ 1. The information in the final paragraph is organized _____.
   a. in chronological order
   b. as a series of questions and answers
   c. as a series of contrasts
   d. in order of importance

_____ 2. The second and the third paragraphs are arranged as a series of
   _____.
   a. causes and effects   b. questions and answers
   c. explanations and examples d. statements and statistics

_____ 3. At the beginning of the article, the author engages the reader by
   _____.
   a. referring to a unique event
   b. appealing to the reader's sense of humor
   c. making an all-inclusive statement
   d. appealing to the reader's compassion

_____ 4. In the second paragraph, the word **while** indicates _____.
   a. the time something happened
   b. a contrasting example will follow
   c. the concept "although"
   d. a definition will follow

_____ 5. The final sentence of the third paragraph is an example of _____.
   a. exaggeration   b. comparison
   c. analogy   d. contradiction

⩔ Harry Potter
series (2001)

Classic
Fantasy Creatures

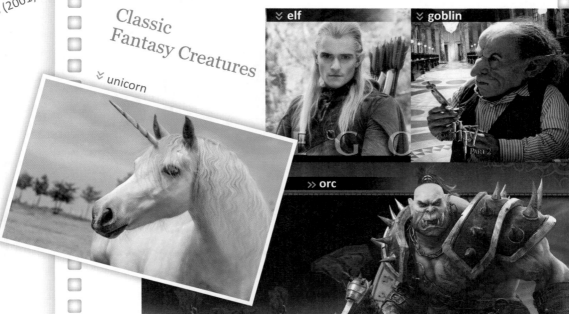

⩔ unicorn

⩡ elf

⩡ goblin

⩢ orc

>> Pins and other tools are used in *ikebana* to hold things in place.

>> The point of *ikebana* is to create something more beautiful than the materials themselves.

24 🎧024
The Way of Flowers

1   You might not think of arranging flowers as an art form, but the Japanese certainly do. *Ikebana* (giving life to flowers), or *kadō* (the way of flowers), is one of Japan's oldest and most popular arts. And its popularity is increasing both at home and throughout the world.

2   *Ikebana* is believed to date back to the sixth century AD, when Chinese monks   5 brought Buddhism to Japan. The monks made ritual offerings of flowers to the Buddha, inspiring their Japanese counterparts to decorate temples with flowers. Over the centuries, flower arrangement became an art in its own right, independent of religious associations. In 1462, the first *ikebana* school was established in Kyoto, teaching the very formal *Ikenobō* style which is still popular today.   10

3   But what makes *ikebana* so special? **Well**, unlike Western flower arranging, which focuses on large numbers of colorful blossoms, it is a very minimalist discipline. An *ikebana* arrangement might contain only a single flower, or even none at all. Branches, leaves, and other elements are as important as the blossoms themselves, which must be alive if there are any. Hidden stems, wires, pins, and   15 other tools are used to hold things in place. Flowers and leaves may be cut into odd shapes or even painted. Wood may be bent by soaking it in water. The point is

⌄ In an *ikebana* arrangement, branches, leaves, and other elements are as important as the blossoms themselves.

to create something more beautiful than the materials themselves, which reveals both their own and the artist's inner natures.

20

4 Traditional *ikebana* is based on religious symbolism. The tallest branch in an arrangement represents heaven. A second branch, one third shorter, represents man. A third, still shorter element, which may be a flower, a stem or something else, represents the earth. Up until relatively recently, nearly all "*ikebanaists*" observed these rules in creating their arrangements.

25

5 Like most other arts, however, *ikebana* changed a lot in the 20th century. Foreign flowers and plants were introduced, and artists began breaking the old rules. The *Sōgetsu* (modern) style challenged *Ikenobō*. At the same time, people outside Japan took up *ikebana*, experimenting with what had previously been an almost exclusively Japanese practice. As a result, the way of flowers is now an international art form with an unlimited range of schools and styles.

30

≪ *ikebana* on exhibition of *Sōgetsu* school, Moscow, Russia, 2017

Questions

_____ **1.** What is the function of the first paragraph of this passage?
   a. To make a comparison.
   b. To introduce the topic.
   c. To offer examples.
   d. To answer a question.

_____ **2.** What does the author do in the second paragraph?
   a. Give his own opinion of *ikebana*.
   b. Describe different styles of an art form.
   c. Explain what *ikebana* means to Japanese people.
   d . Provide some historical background.

_____ **3.** What is the function of the word **Well** in the second sentence of the third paragraph?
   a. To let the reader know that something is good.
   b. To show a contrast between two ideas.
   c. To introduce the answer to a question.
   d. To show that the author is impressed by something.

_____ **4.** How does the author end the third paragraph?
   a. By revealing something completely unexpected.
   b. By comparing *ikebana* to other art forms.
   c. By giving the reader a mystery to solve.
   d. By explaining the purpose of something.

≪ woman making *ikebana* in Sofia, Bulgaria, 2017

_____ **5.** How could this passage best be described?
   a. As an informative article.
   b. As a lesson in Japanese history.
   c. As a set of rules for an art form.
   d. As a humorous story.

Thaipusam is held in honor of Lord Subrahmanya.

25 Thaipusam— A Festival in Singapore

1   Though Singapore seems like any modern, prosperous city with its skyscrapers and high standards of living, the ancient traditions and customs of the three dominant ethnic communities—Chinese, Indian, and Malay—are still practiced with great passion. One of the most remarkable festivals is the Hindu festival of Thaipusam. A word of   5 warning, though: this festival is not for the faint of heart.

2   Celebrated during the full moon in the month of Thai—mid-January to mid-February in the Western calendar—Thaipusam is held in honor of Lord Subrahmanya, the Hindu god of war and victory. Devotees pay respects to him by parading from one temple to another, 10 carrying offerings of milk and flowers for the god. While this may not sound so bad, some devotees show their devotion through more extreme methods.

3   After putting themselves into a trance by chanting and meditating, they wound their own bodies, driving steel rods through one cheek   15 and out the other or attaching hooks to their backs, legs, tongues, or other body parts. They then use these hooks to drag around decorated weights, declaring their devotion to their deity while spectators and supporters play drums and sing religious chants to keep up morale. Some even carry around portable altars called *kavadis*, which are 20 attached to their skin by more than a hundred spikes. The devotees claim that Lord Subrahmanya protects them during these rites and ensures that little damage is done to his subjects.

⌃ worshipper carrying a *kavadi* during a Thaipusam festival celebration in Singapore

4 Devotees prepare for these feats a month in advance and spend a great deal of time starving themselves, praying, and meditating in order to make themselves spiritually strong enough to undergo the ordeal. Afterward, these people are considered to have encountered the deity through their acts of self-punishment, and **thus** receive favorable treatment from the community for the rest of the year.

5 Though this kind of spiritual devotion can seem extreme to most people, it is one of the most important religious rites of the Indian community in Singapore, and witnessing it enables an outsider to view something that is very sacred to these people.

⌃ A day of devotion—Thaipusam festival celebration in Singapore (cc by William Cho)

Questions

_____ 1. In the first and second paragraphs, the author uses dashes (—) to _____.
  a. ask the reader a question
  b. provide additional information
  c. introduce an exclamation
  d. reveal the author's opinion

_____ 2. At the beginning of the article, the author creates interest by using _____.
  a. a contrast
  b. a comparison
  c. statistics
  d. logical reasoning

_____ 3. The third paragraph is mostly made up of _____.
  a. statements giving advice
  b. questions and answers
  c. personal opinions
  d. a series of examples

_____ 4. The writer treats the subject matter with _____.
  a. seriousness
  b. humor
  c. disapproval
  d. fear

_____ 5. In the fourth paragraph, the word **thus** is followed by _____.
  a. an explanation
  b. an example
  c. a result
  d. a piece of evidence

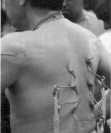

(cc by Nestor's Blurrylife)   (cc by Nestor Lacle)

1-6 Making Inferences

Inference is when we guess at something we don't know using the information we do know. For example, if a friend looks angry when she opens the door, you can guess that something is wrong or something bad has happened. Authors also use this kind of inference to make similar suggestions to their readers.

≫ Before you judge a person, walk a mile in their shoes.

26 Walk a Mile in Their Shoes 🎧026

1   Take a moment to consider everything you've ever heard about homeless people. It's usually negative, right? Maybe a family member called them too lazy to work. Or maybe you remember a news story about a secretly rich homeless person. Across the world, the stories are always the same. Homeless people aren't victims; they do it to themselves.   5

2   Of course these stories are almost always inaccurate. In reality, homelessness can happen to just about anyone—even you.

3   It can be as simple as losing your job. We never expect to be fired or downsized, and when it happens, it can take a long time to find a new position. And if you lose your apartment or house, then you lose your permanent address,   10 which can be a red flag on job applications.

4   Perhaps most surprising of all is the fact that many homeless are actually employed. They have full-time jobs yet still can't afford housing. By some estimates, anywhere between one-third to one-half of the US homeless population is employed. And it's a big population. New York City alone is home   15 to around 63,500 homeless people.

5   A personal or family tragedy can also result in homelessness. Divorce, medical bills, or a sudden expense can ruin family finances. In some cases, people are forced to flee for their own safety from an abusive spouse or family member. These individuals can end up in an entirely new place, with no job or   20

≫ There are a thousand different paths to homelessness.   (cc by Garry Knight)

support network to sustain them. Drugs are also a big problem, particularly opioid addiction. What starts as pain relief for a sports injury can end in a crippling habit that ends up costing your job and your home.

6 The truth is that there are a thousand different paths to homelessness.
25 And blaming the victims does nothing to solve the problem. Instead, we should extend a helping hand to friends, family, and community members when they need it the most. Timely assistance in the early stages can make a huge difference for someone faced with temporary homelessness.

7 We should try giving people the benefit of the
30 doubt. Next time you pass a homeless person in the street, remember the old saying: "before you judge a person, walk a mile in their shoes."

☆ lunch served to homeless veterans at the New England Shelter for Homeless Veterans, Boston, USA

Questions

_____ 1. What can we infer from the fifth paragraph?
   a. There are lots of networks out there to support homeless people.
   b. Suddenly losing a parent can increase your chances of homelessness.
   c. The problem of opioid addiction is slowly improving around the world.
   d. Homelessness is a leading cause of family tragedies.

_____ 2. What is likely true about New York City in the fourth paragraph?
   a. It has very high housing costs.
   b. It has a very good subway system.
   c. It has lots of high-paying jobs.
   d. It has the fewest homeless people in the United States.

_____ 3. Which of the following would most likely be the author's opinion?
   a. Homeless people are lazy and should get a job.
   b. Homelessness isn't a big problem.
   c. Homelessness is a very complex phenomenon.
   d. Homeless people should be put in jail.

_____ 4. What can we infer from the third paragraph?
   a. It will be easier to find a job in a big city than in a small town.
   b. Most international companies don't like to have too many employees.
   c. Always be cautious when you go for a job interview.
   d. Having a stable living situation is important when you need to get a job.

_____ 5. According to the article, which of the following is most likely another cause of homelessness?
   a. Graduating from school early.   b. Suffering a major personal injury.
   c. Working for a family business.   d. Renting out one's own house.

⌃ Temple of the Sun

» Incan ruins of Machu Picchu, Peru

27 The Inca of South America

⌃ The Intihuatana ("hitching post of the sun") is believed to have been designed as an astronomic clock or calendar by the Inca.
(cc by Jordan Klein from San Francisco, USA)

⌃ interior of an Inca building
(cc by Martin St-Amant)

1 When European sailors discovered South America around the turn of the sixteenth century, they encountered a land of many different languages, cultures, and political groupings. The Inca Empire was one such grouping—a 2,000,000 square kilometer area on the west coast of South America, which was home to between 6 million and 14 million 5 people.

2 The story of the Inca Empire begins in Cuzco, located in modern-day Peru, sometime around 1200. That's when a large family of nobles set about building the economic and administrative structures that would come to characterize Incan society. In 1432, the emperor 10 Pachacuti began to conquer the lands surrounding Cuzco, marking the birth of the Inca Empire. Thereafter, the empire flourished until it was toppled by a group of fewer than 200 Spanish soldiers in 1532.

3 The Inca can be considered a cultural and administrative superpower, if not a military one. People within the empire spoke a 15 universal language and practiced a religion based on the worship of the sun. Incan metalworks and medical technology were considered to be very advanced. Communication over long distances in the empire was made possible by an extensive 39,900 km network of all-weather

⌃ the residential section of the Inca building in Machu Picchu, Peru (cc by Christophe Meneboeuf – XtoF)

20 roads. Roads and other public works were built using a system by which citizens would labor for the emperor in exchange for food and clothing. The system seems to have worked, because most of these roads were so well built that they're still used to this day.

4   Perhaps the most remarkable aspect of Incan society is the splendor of their
25 castles and temples. Gold and silver was abundant in the Inca Empire, and it showed in people's homes. The first Spanish explorers to visit Cuzco spoke of gold relics, statues, pots, and jars, all inlaid with precious gems.

5   Any discussion about the Inca ultimately arrives at the question of how a small group of Spanish soldiers emerged victorious against a
30 mighty empire. The answer involves a mix of betrayal and bad luck. For one, the Spanish were ruthless, kidnapping the Inca emperor under a flag of truce and executing him even after he paid his own ransom. Then there was the disastrous effect of smallpox, a terrible disease that ravaged populations
35 across South America beginning in 1520.

≫ terraced fields in the upper agricultural sector of
Machu Picchu, Peru (cc by Christophe Meneboeuf – XtoF)

Questions

_____ 1. According to the third paragraph, which of the following statements is probably true?
   a. The Inca had advanced weapon technology.
   b. The Inca performed complex surgery.
   c. The Inca only traveled by horseback.
   d. The Inca's diet consisted of corn and rice.

≪ the Inca-Spanish confrontation
(cc by Lupo and Dynamax)

_____ 2. It's probably true that the Spanish _____.
   a. spoke the same language as the Inca
   b. taught the Inca how to survive in South America
   c. had better weapons than the Inca
   d. had a lot of respect for the Inca

_____ 3. Which of the following does the author believe of the Spanish?
   a. They tried to help the Inca.   **b.** They learned from the Inca.
   c. They deserved the Inca's gold.   **d.** They were cruel to the Inca.

_____ 4. Which of the following statements about smallpox is probably true?
   a. The Spanish brought it to South America.
   b. It was later cured by the Inca.
   c. It was spread by monkeys.
   d. It killed only old people.

_____ 5. It's most likely that the Spanish wanted to conquer the Inca because of their _____.
   a. religion   **b.** food   **c.** gold   **d.** temples

28 Recycling

« Taiwan's recycling symbol

⌃ international recycling symbol

1   You've probably heard what recycling is all about by now, but not all recycling programs are created equal. As public awareness grows and technology improves, some countries have begun to pull ahead in the war against waste.

2   Some of the most ambitious recycling programs are based on what is called   5
a "zero waste" approach. This calls on people and companies to stop producing waste by consuming less, reusing, and recycling. Recycling facilities play an important part in zero waste programs because the more materials that can be recycled, the fewer pollutants end up in landfills and incinerators.

3   Taiwan is a good example. In the 1980s and 1990s, waste piled up in landfills   10
across what was then nicknamed Garbage Island. In 1993, the *collection* rate for garbage in Taiwan was just 70 percent! People eventually got fed up and forced the government to adopt a zero waste policy in 2003. Since then, Taiwan has become a recycling role model for other countries. The Taiwanese government operates a recycling fund that pays private citizens and companies to collect recyclable   15
materials. These materials are then sent to facilities with sophisticated equipment that breaks them down into components that can be reused. These components are then sold to companies that can use them in their products. Perhaps the most important aspect of Taiwan's recycling fund is that it is financed by disposal fees placed on all consumer goods sold in the country, essentially making producers   20
responsible for the environmental impact of their own products. The harder the item is to dispose of, the higher the fee.

4   Germany is another country that is often cited as a recycling success story. As in Taiwan, people in

« recycle bins   ⌄ cycle sorters in Sims Municipal Recycling Facility, Brooklyn, USA (cc by JelloMistress)

25 Germany are expected to sort their own recycling. Neighborhoods have a colorful system of bins that take plastics, paper, glass, and household waste. The bin program is so successful that almost no waste is being sent to German landfills anymore.

5 German consumers also pay a deposit for glass and plastic

30 bottles. This is returned to them when they return the bottles to the shops where they bought them.

⌃ recycling

6 Recycling can even boost national economies and fight unemployment. In Germany, around 50,000 people are employed in the recycling industry, and German recycling

35 technology accounts for 24 percent of the global market share. That's not a bad bonus for saving the planet!

↗ people recycling plastic bottles at a reverse vending machine in Germany, 2018

Questions

crushed tin cans for recycling

⌃ paper waste at a recycling plant in Germany

_____ 1. Which of the following does the author probably believe about zero waste recycling programs?
   a. They are expensive and inefficient.
   b. Sometimes they work, and sometimes they don't.
   c. They improve the environment and the economy.
   d. They are possible only in developed countries.

_____ 2. What can be inferred from the third paragraph?
   a. There was an anti-landfill movement in Taiwan in the late 1990s.
   b. Recycling equipment is often extremely expensive.
   c. Computer makers don't need to pay into the recycling fund.
   d. Taiwan is often criticized for its recycling program.

_____ 3. According to the third paragraph, which of the following would likely pay the highest fees toward Taiwan's recycling fund?
   a. A paper bag company.   **b.** A clothing company.
   c. A home appliance company.   **d.** A restaurant.

_____ 4. Which of the following statements is probably true?
   a. Taiwan is the only country in the world with a recycling fund.
   b. Taiwan didn't have a recycling program before the 1990s.
   c. Germany's recycling program relies on Taiwanese technology.
   d. Large-scale recycling programs are usually very inexpensive.

_____ 5. Which of the following statements about Germany is likely true?
   a. It has one of the best recycling programs in the world.
   b. It does not have any landfills.
   c. Its recycling technology is not as good as Taiwan's.
   d. It does not believe that recycling is important.

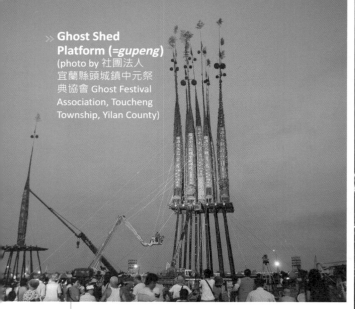

>> **Ghost Shed Platform (=*gupeng*)** (photo by 社團法人宜蘭縣頭城鎮中元祭典協會 Ghost Festival Association, Toucheng Township, Yilan County)

>> Toucheng Ghost Grappling Festival (photo by 社團法人宜蘭縣頭城鎮中元祭典協會 Ghost Festival Association, Toucheng Township, Yilan County)

29 (029)
A Spectacle Fit for a Ghost

1   Qianggu—"Grappling with the Ghost" pole can be traced back two hundred years in Taiwan. The purpose of the festival is to pay respect to the ancestors of the Taiwanese people who died in the new land or on the travel over from China. The ritual of the festival is to comfort the "wandering spirits" of their loved ones, who they believed could not find peace after dying away from home.   5

2   The festival takes place on the final day of Ghost Month, the seventh month of the lunar calendar. That's when people from all over Taiwan arrive in Toucheng Township in Yilan. Some visitors start off by making offerings to their ancestors, while others take part in special religious ceremonies. The crowds gather around a giant structure called a "*gupeng*," which towers into the night   10 sky. The *gupeng* is divided into two sections. The lower part has 12 thick poles that are almost 20 meters tall. The upper part consists of a large platform supporting another 13 towers made of bamboo. Altogether, the structure is a jaw-dropping 43 meters tall. And at the top   15 of each bamboo tower is a little red banner, called a "fair-weather flag."

3   As soon as the final hour of Ghost Month strikes, the contest can begin. Teams of five people

<< the last Ghost Grappling Festival during the period of Japanese rule in Toucheng, Yilan, Taiwan (1931–1933)

run to the base of the *gupeng* and start to scramble 20
up the tower. This is no easy task because the poles
have been greased with beef fat. Once the competitors
make it to the platform, they pause for a moment to be
connected to a safety line. Then they start climbing the
bamboo towers, which are covered in food offerings 25
and swaying in the wind. The first person to get a red
flag wins the competition, and they can expect a year of
good fortune. But it's not over yet. In one final custom,
the competitors will throw packaged food down from
the platform to the crowd below. 30

4   The crowds have been growing since a temporary
ban was lifted on the festival in 2004. What began as
a local religious ceremony to appease ghosts has now
turned into a major tourism attraction. In fact, many
say that the Ghost Grappling Festival is now one of 35
Taiwan's largest traditional events.

≫ competitors climbing the bamboo towers covered in food offerings (photo by 社團法人宜蘭縣頭城鎮中元祭典協會 Ghost Festival Association, Toucheng Township, Yilan County)

Questions

_____ **1.** What is the most likely reason the Ghost Grappling Festival was banned before 2004?
   a. It was too expensive.   **b.** It was too popular.
   c. It was too dangerous.   **d.** It was too crowded.

_____ **2.** What time does the final pole-climbing competition probably take place?
   a. 11 p.m.   **b.** 11 a.m.   **c.** 5 p.m.   **d.** 12 p.m.

_____ **3.** What does the final tradition of throwing food from the platform to the crowd below probably symbolize?
   a. Defeating your enemies.   **b.** Achieving wisdom.
   c. Comforting the ghosts.   **d.** Celebrating the victory.

_____ **4.** What can we infer from the first paragraph?
   a. The purpose of the festival is to avoid the ghosts.
   b. Life back then was harsh.
   c. Immigrant ancestors settled in China.
   d. People in China are superstitious.

_____ **5.** Based on the information in the third paragraph, what can we know about how the competitors feel about the contest?
   a. It is simple and time-consuming.   **b.** It is tense and important.
   c. It is effortless and dull.   **d.** It is ordinary and rewarding.

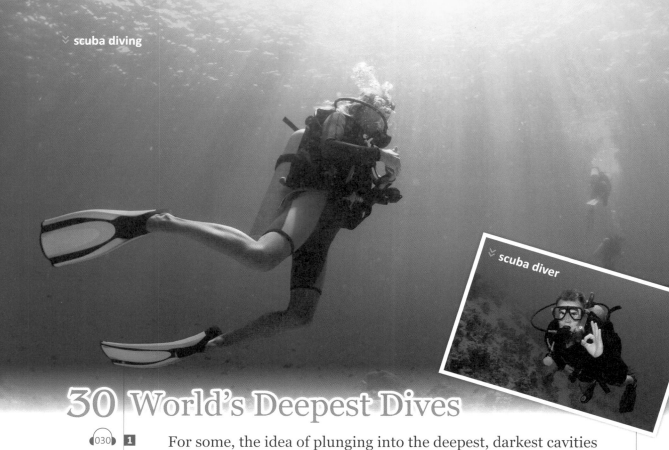

scuba diver

30 World's Deepest Dives

atmospheric
diving suit
in 1882
(cc by Myrabella)

(030) **1**   For some, the idea of plunging into the deepest, darkest cavities of the ocean is a thrilling prospect. For others, it's the stuff of nightmares. Depending on your own view, you might want to try scuba diving someday. If you work hard enough, you might even get yourself into the record books for the world's deepest dive!   5

2   "Scuba" is an acronym that describes the equipment scuba divers use to explore the depths. Of course, some divers go deeper than others. Normal recreational scuba divers are certified for depths of up to 30 meters, with anything deeper being considered dangerous. However, some of the deepest dives ever recorded make 30 meters   10 look like child's play. In September 2014, Ahmed Gabr became the Guinness World Record holder for the deepest scuba dive with a depth of 332 meters. It's possible to go even deeper using sophisticated equipment. A US Navy diver managed to descend to a depth of 610 meters using an atmospheric diving system suit.   15

3   Getting into the world record books for deep diving isn't just hard—it's downright dangerous. Most of this peril stems from how the human body reacts to extreme depths. For one, there's decompression sickness to worry about. Decompression sickness is caused by a buildup of nitrogen in the bloodstream. Its symptoms   20 range from mild headaches and nausea to life-threatening heart and lung problems. The deeper a diver goes, the more he runs a risk of developing decompression sickness. Oxygen levels can also pose a problem. The deeper a diver goes, the more his or her air is compressed by pressure and the faster it is consumed. Oxygen can also become toxic at depths of more than 66 meters, 25 which can lead to unconsciousness.

4   While most of these risks are problems only for professional divers who are trying to break world records, it's still a good idea to start slowly and always listen to your instructor when embarking on any scuba adventure.

Questions

_____ 1. Which of the following does "scuba" probably stand for?
  a. Safe Care Urgent Boat Animal.
  b. Sanitary Calm Uniform Bone Ankle.
  c. Self-Contained Underwater Breathing Apparatus.
  d. Self-Cleaning Used Bean Appliance.

_____ 2. What can we infer from the first paragraph?
  a. Most people like similar things.
  b. Everyone is different.
  c. Diving is an interesting activity for everyone.
  d. Diving is very easy.

_____ 3. Which of the following can be inferred about the atmospheric diving system suit?
  a. It is very inexpensive and easy to produce.
  b. It is available to the general public.
  c. It allows divers to breath liquid oxygen.
  d. It helps prevent decompression sickness.

_____ 4. Which of the following does the author believe?
  a. Scuba diving is easy, and anyone can do it.
  b. Scuba diving should be approached carefully.
  c. Scuba diving is too expensive.
  d. Scuba diving is boring.

_____ 5. This article suggests that _____.
  a. you need a certified license to scuba dive
  b. only US Navy divers can scuba dive
  c. all divers tend not to go deeper than 30 meters
  d. decompression sickness is a myth

⌃ US Navy divers training with an atmospheric diving suit at the deep submergence unit

» Surfacing divers must enter a decompression chamber for surface decompression, a standard operating procedure to avoid decompression sickness after long or deep dives. (Wikipedia)

1-7 *Cause and Effect*

A cause makes something happen, and an effect is the resulting action or event. The link between causes and their effects can sometimes be obvious; other times they are more subtle. To make identifying these relationships easier, look out for words that expressly imply a cause-effect relationship, such as "therefore," "as a result," or "consequently."

≫ Algae grow easily in almost any water body.

31 Going Green With Algae

(031)

1   Swimmers hate it, but the slimy, green organisms known as algae hold great promise as an energy source. This yucky-looking goo grows easily in almost any water body. All it needs is sunlight, water, and carbon dioxide to thrive. Most importantly, from an energy perspective, algae contain plant oil that can be transformed into biofuel. When processed, this fatty substance may be used as fuel for a wide variety of vehicles, even planes. As a biofuel, it burns much cleaner than petroleum, which is the main reason for its attractiveness.

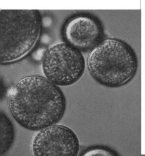

≫ Algae contain plant oil that can be transformed into biofuel.

2   The excitement over the development of algae as a source of energy is quite understandable. Some researchers believe algae could be up to a hundred times more productive than other plants in producing oil. Investors, corporations, and governments have poured in millions of dollars to develop algae biofuel over the years. However, to some, the results have been rather disappointing. This is mostly due to the challenges and technological obstacles related to using the aquatic material as energy.

3   The difficulties in producing large-scale algal fuel are related to growing the plant, extracting its oil, and processing it. Large amounts of water are needed to cultivate the quantity of algae required. Furthermore, huge sections of land, which could be used for other purposes, are also needed. Regarding the removal of the natural oil, there are various methods, but they are costly. Other costs include drying the algae and converting the oil into a usable energy source.

≫ photobioreactors in a laboratory transforming algae oil into biofuel

4   While some critics of this alternative energy have essentially given up on it, others are much more optimistic. The huge American

5

10

15

20

25

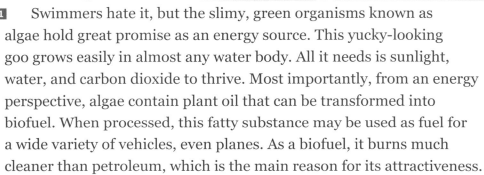

oil company Exxon Mobil has made a significant breakthrough in its research on algal fuel. Working with a bio-tech firm, Exxon has found a way to double the amount of oil algae produce. This has been achieved by
30 slightly changing one gene in a species of algae. Exxon believes it can produce 10,000 barrels of algae biofuel a day by 2025. That's a drop in the bucket compared to the tens of millions of barrels of petroleum produced today. However, it's an important step
35 towards ensuring a healthier, less polluted future for the world.

⌄ The difficulties in producing large-scale algal fuel are related to growing the plant, extracting its oil, and processing it. (photo by Bill Evans)

Questions

_____ 1. According to the article, which fact allows algae to be used as energy?
- **a.** The plant requires only sun, water, and carbon dioxide.
- **b.** The plant can grow in almost any water body.
- **c.** The plant is a hundred times more productive than other plants.
- **d.** The plant contains a natural type of oil.

_____ 2. Which of the following is a reason for the general interest in algae?
- **a.** Millions have been spent on development of algae as a fuel source.
- **b.** Exxon Mobil is doing research on algal fuel.
- **c.** Algae are a potential source for clean-burning fuel.
- **d.** Algae are found in oceans around the world.

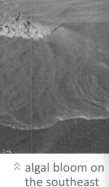

⌃ algal bloom on the southeast shore of Pelee Island, Ontario, Canada (cc by Tom Archer)

_____ 3. Which of the following has NOT caused a difficulty in using algae as a fuel source?
- **a.** Some people are critical of the idea.
- **b.** A lot of land is required to grow algae.
- **c.** Algae require large quantities of water.
- **d.** Processing algae into fuel is expensive.

_____ 4. What caused some people to be disappointed by algal fuel?
- **a.** Although it is good for cars, it's not suitable for other vehicles.
- **b.** It has been found to be more polluting than once thought.
- **c.** There are numerous problems associated with its development.
- **d.** Exxon Mobil has failed to develop algal fuel.

⌃ Researchers have been exploring the use of algae as biofuel. (photo by Elizabeth Andrews)

_____ 5. What is the effect of Exxon Mobil changing a gene in an algae species?
- **a.** It led to a partnership with an American bio-tech company.
- **b.** The amount of oil the algae produce increased by 100 percent.
- **c.** Exxon has been criticized for its slow development of algal fuel.
- **d.** It helped the company produce millions of barrels of oil per day.

>> combination of Japanese and Vietnamese cuisine: smoked salmon wrapped in rice paper, with avocado, cucumber, and crab (cc by Chensiyuan)

32 Fusion Cuisine 🎧032

⌃ Hawaiian broiled sushi tacos

1 Over the last few decades, the entire world has become a giant melting pot; instantaneous global communication has made cultural isolation a near impossibility. With the world's population looking for better situations, people are increasingly packing their bags and moving to new pastures, whether it be for jobs, marriage, or simply a better quality of life.

2 As a result of this widespread international immigration (of both cultures and people), fusion cuisine is becoming an ever more common phenomenon. When people settle in a new place, they often bring a piece of their culture with them. It should come as no surprise, then, that the food and cooking styles common to one particular place often mingle with those of another.

3 After a time, the new combination may even become the norm. Any restaurant that claims to make authentic Italian cuisine without using tomatoes is sure to be accused of fraud. But in fact, tomatoes are not native to Europe at all, but were brought there in the sixteenth century from South America.

4 Many Asian restaurants in the West use fusion cooking to generate dishes that are inclusive of an entire subcontinent. A restaurant focusing on Southeast Asian cuisine, for example, may combine in its dishes ingredients, spices, and cooking techniques from Vietnam, Thailand, China, and other countries in the region. In this way, it creates a distinctive Southeast Asian cuisine that is not quite Vietnamese, Chinese, or Thai, but something unique. This combination of styles also happens naturally, often in the border regions of two countries. As a result of their close proximity, a natural cultural exchange occurs; Tex-Mex cuisine, an ambiguous natural blend of Texan and Mexican food, is a good example.

⌃ Kaeng phet pet yang (Thai roast duck curry) is an example of early fusion cuisine combining Thai red curry, Chinese roast duck, and grapes originally from Persia. (cc by Terence Ong)

5   Sometimes, however, restaurateurs are more ambitious and try to 35
combine culinary styles from different continents. In the 1970s, the practice
of combining Asian and French cooking became popular among chefs in
the United States, and cross-continental cuisine has since become a feature
of many experimental restaurants. However, due to the fact that cross-
continental ingredients and cooking styles are often so different, this type of 40
fusion cooking is very difficult to do well, and the term "con-fusion cuisine"
has been used to describe the attempts that just don't blend.

Questions

⌄ Korean
tacos

_____ 1. What is named in the article as the immediate cause of the fusion
cuisine's increasing popularity?
   a. A rising global population.
   b. Instantaneous global communication.
   c. A shortage of jobs in certain areas.
   d. Widespread international immigration.

_____ 2. Which of the following is a reason why something that was
originally considered fusion cuisine sometimes becomes the norm?
   a. The passage of time.
   b. The trade of foods from other countries.
   c. The Italians' love of tomatoes.
   d. The desire to be authentic.

_____ 3. Which of the following sentences expresses the effect of good
fusion cooking?
   a. Many Asian restaurants produce dishes that represent an
   entire subcontinent.
   b. By combining different styles and ingredients, unique dishes
   are created.
   c. A restaurant may combine cooking techniques from many
   countries.
   d. Some Southeast Asian restaurants combine Vietnamese and
   Thai cuisine.

_____ 4. What is the effect of two countries bordering each other?
   a. The creation of cross-continental dishes.
   b. Accusations of fraud between the two.
   c. Natural cultural exchange between the two.
   d. Cultural isolation between the two.

_____ 5. What causes some food to be called "con-fusion cuisine"?
   a. The use of fusion cuisine in many experimental restaurants.
   b. Dishes that use ingredients that do not mix together well.
   c. Restaurateurs trying to combine styles from different continents.
   d. The combination of Asian and French cooking.

⌃ Tex-Mex
cuisine

33 The Advantages of Breast-Feeding

1   New parents have to make many difficult short-term choices that may significantly affect their baby in the long term. One of the first choices a new mother has to make is whether to breast-feed her child. To many, this may seem like a decision with no serious consequences either way. After all, a large percentage of adults in the United States were not breast-fed when younger (a phenomenon that has been put down to aggressive advertising by manufacturers of baby formula) and suffer no obvious ill effects. However, recent studies have shown that breast-feeding can affect children throughout their lives, even into adulthood. 10

2 The first major thing to be affected by breast-feeding is health. Because infants' bodies are not fully developed, they are more vulnerable to illness. Breast milk contains properties that help the infant resist infection, and so breast-fed infants are less likely to succumb to things like ear infections, respiratory illness, allergies, diarrhea, and vomiting. 15

3   Though formula can mimic many of its nutritional components, breast milk is not something that can be easily replaced. Breast milk is a remarkable source of nutrition that changes its composition as the baby grows, providing the exact combination of chemicals an infant needs at various stages of its growth. In fact, this early boosting of the child's development also reduces the risk of diseases such as diabetes, heart disease, and cancer 25 later in life.

4 One of the most surprising finds of recent years, though, is the positive effect that breast-feeding has on a child's future social class.

⌃ breast-feeding

⌃ new compact electric breast pump

>> The formula *(left)* is of uniform consistency and color, while the pumped breast milk *(right)* exhibits properties of an organic solution, separating into a cream layer of fat at the top, milk, and a watery blue layer at the bottom. (cc by Jengod)

⌃ manual breast pump

A study of 34,000 people in the UK compared each participant's social class with that of their fathers when they were growing up. Those that were breast-fed as children had a much higher chance of surpassing their fathers on the social ladder than those that were formula-fed.

5   The study seems to confirm earlier reports that the nutrients in breast milk actively improve brain development. Breast-fed individuals were also shown to have lower levels of emotional stress when they were children (a possible result of early skin-to-skin contact with their mothers), which could have also been a contributing factor to their success later in life.

Questions

_____ 1. Which of the following is NOT named as an effect of breast-feeding on children?
    a. A higher vulnerability to illness than other children.
    b. A higher resistance to infection when young.
    c. Less risk of getting diabetes when older.
    d. Less emotional stress when young.

_____ 2. Because the chemical composition of breast milk changes over time, _____.
    a. it decreases the risk of heart disease and cancer in adults
    b. it provides the specific nutrition the infant needs at different stages
    c. it allows babies to form a special emotional bond with the mother
    d. it causes the infant to pass his or her father on the social ladder

_____ 3. Which of the following is the cause behind the fact that many American adults were not breast-fed as children?
    a. A study of 34,000 people assessing the effects of breast-feeding.
    b. The difficulty of making a choice that affects long-term development.
    c. Ear infections, respiratory illness, allergies, diarrhea, and vomiting.
    d. Aggressive advertising campaigns by baby-formula manufacturers.

_____ 4. Breast-fed individuals showed fewer signs of emotional stress as children because _____.
    a. they were part of a research program examining breast-feeding
    b. they would have a lower risk of heart disease in later life
    c. they had early skin-to-skin contact with their mothers
    d. they had a good chance of being successful later in life

≪ public breast-feeding room in Taiwan
(cc by knittymarine)

_____ 5. Which of the following statements does NOT express a cause-and-effect relationship?
    a. Breast-feeding has a positive effect on a child's future social class.
    b. A UK study compared the participants' social class with that of their fathers.
    c. Breast-fed children have a higher chance of succeeding than formula-fed children.
    d. A study confirmed the nutrients in breast milk improve brain development.

Andy Warhol's Campbell's Soup I (1968)

>> Andy Warhol (1928–1987) (cc by Jack and Mitchell)

≫ Andy Warhol's famous Marilyn Monroe painting (1962)

34 Andy Warhol 🎧 034

1 Have you ever wondered who painted the famous paintings of Campbell's soup cans, or who depicted Marilyn Monroe as a multicolored celebrity on canvas? The artist behind these renowned paintings and of many others is Andy Warhol, the Pope of Pop. 5

2 Fascinated by the relationship between artistic expression and advertising, Warhol took well-known American objects such as Coca-Cola bottles, Campbell's soup cans, dollar bills, as well as celebrities, and manipulated them to create his art. This pop art—an experimental art form 10 based upon themes and techniques taken from popular mass culture—has been imitated by other artists ever since. While it may not seem unusual now, back in the 1960's this kind of art was groundbreaking, altering people's perceptions of what could be considered art.

3 Born in 1920s Pittsburg, Pennsylvania, Warhol was often sick and 15 confined to his bed as a child. Stuck at home, he filled his time by drawing, listening to the radio, and collecting pictures of movie stars. Warhol described this time in his life as being vital to the development of his personality, style, and interest in popular culture.

4 In addition to being an artist, Warhol was also a keen 20 businessman and, unlike many other artists, was not shy about benefiting financially from his creations. Warhol was obsessed with mass production, claiming that he wanted to become a machine, able to reproduce the same image over and over again. As a result of this fascination, he switched from 25 painting to screen printing, a technique that allowed him to

>> statue of Andy Warhol in Slovakia

« grave of Andy Warhol in Pittsburgh (cc by Allie Caulfield)

reproduce copy upon copy of identical images. After a time, he even stopped producing these works himself, employing assistants to create the prints for him. For Warhol, the business 30 of churning out these prints was as much a form of art as putting paint onto canvas. "Making money is art, and working is art, and good business is the best art," he wrote in one of his books.

5   Warhol's work foresaw much of what preoccupies us in the twenty-first century—fame, the media, and an insatiable appetite for mass-produced 35 products. Consequently, though he was criticized at the time for giving in to consumerism, Warhol's art has never gone out of fashion.

Questions

⌃ Andy Warhol's childhood home at Pittsburg, Pennsylvania (cc by Lee Paxton)

_____ 1. According to the article, why did Andy Warhol use well-known American objects to create his art?
   a. He struggled to find other forms of artistic inspiration.
   b. He thought that more people would buy his paintings.
   c. He was interested in the link between art and advertising.
   d. He thought that his art would remain famous for longer.

_____ 2. What was the effect of Warhol's groundbreaking art?
   a. It caused Warhol to become sick.
   b. It caused Warhol to employ assistants to mass-produce prints.
   c. It caused Warhol to become a keen businessman.
   d. It altered people's perceptions of what could be considered art.

_____ 3. What was the root of Warhol's interest in popular culture?
   a. His time stuck at home as a sick child.
   b. Being born in Pennsylvania.
   c. Being born in the 1920s.
   d. His artistic style.

_____ 4. As a result of Warhol's fascination with mass production, he _____.
   a. wanted to become a machine
   b. switched from painting to screen printing
   c. was not shy about making money from his creations
   d. became known as the Pope of Pop

_____ 5. Which of the following is cited as the reason why Warhol's art has remained so popular?
   a. Campbell's is still a popular brand of soup.
   b. Marilyn Monroe is as famous now as she ever was.
   c. His art expresses themes that are still relevant today.
   d. His artistic style has been imitated by many other artists.

35 Whale Shark: Gentle Giants

1   Growing to over 12 meters long and weighing more than 20 tons, the whale shark is the world's largest fish. Despite what its name implies, it is not a whale, but is named so because of its immense size and feeding habits, which are similar to some whales. The whale shark has dark gray skin, which can be up to 10 centimeters thick; a pattern of white spots unique to each shark marks 5 its surface. These shark fingerprints have allowed scientists to identify individual sharks and accurately count their population.

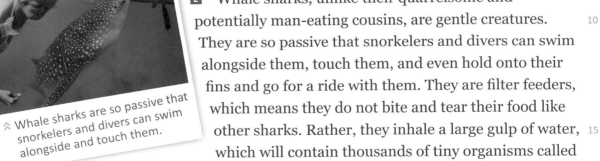

⌃ Whale sharks are so passive that snorkelers and divers can swim alongside and touch them.

2   Whale sharks, unlike their quarrelsome and potentially man-eating cousins, are gentle creatures. 10 They are so passive that snorkelers and divers can swim alongside them, touch them, and even hold onto their fins and go for a ride with them. They are filter feeders, which means they do not bite and tear their food like other sharks. Rather, they inhale a large gulp of water, 15 which will contain thousands of tiny organisms called plankton, and then filter out the water through their gills while the food is retained by filter pads. Though they do have 350 rows of tiny teeth, they aren't used in feeding, as the shark's diet of microscopic 20 creatures, along with millions of years of evolution, has rendered them useless. One danger divers should look out for, however, is being swallowed whole by one of these sharks—an experience that one diver in 25 Mexico narrowly escaped in 2011.

>> whale shark feeding

3   Preferring warmer waters, these gentle creatures can be found in tropical and subtropical seas. They are most often spotted along coastal regions and lagoons on tropical islands. Every spring, a large number migrates to the west coast of Australia, where the abundant supply of plankton near the area's coral 30 reefs proves too much of a draw for the sharks to resist. Another popular area for whale-shark migration is the sea around Donsol, a small fishing town in the Philippines. Between January and June of each year, whale sharks flock there to feed in the plankton-rich waters. Eager to swim with these amazing creatures, tourists are now rushing to Donsol, bringing much-needed development to 35 this small village. Human beings, it seems, just can't get enough of these serene giants of the ocean.

⌃ whale shark's size compared to an average human

Questions

_____1. What is the cause of the whale shark's potentially confusing name?
    a. Its size and feeding habits.   **b.** The area where it lives.
    c. The spots on its skin.   **d.** Its gentle nature.

_____2. Which of the following is cited as an effect of the shark's microscopic diet?
    a. The whale shark's skin has become very thick.
    b. Divers can swim alongside whale sharks and catch a ride.
    c. The whale shark's teeth have become useless.
    d. The whale shark population has been measured accurately.

_____3. Which of the following is the reason behind the whale shark's current choice of habitat?
    a. They are popular with tourists.   **b.** They filter water through their gills.
    c. They prefer warmer waters.   **d.** Their skin is dark and grey.

_____4. What is the cause of the spring migration to the west coast of Australia?
    a. Plentiful tourists.   **b.** The shark's mouth.
    c. The beautiful coral reefs.   **d.** Abundant food.

_____5. Which of the following sentences expresses the whale sharks' effect on the town of Donsol?
    a. Whale sharks flock to Donsol to feed in the plankton-rich waters.
    b. Tourists are rushing to Donsol, bringing much-needed development.
    c. The sea around Donsol is another popular area for whale-shark migration.
    d. People just can't get enough of these serene giants of the ocean.

« plankton

1-8 *Figurative Language*

Writers use figurative language to invoke feelings or create images that leave a deep impression on the reader. Here are some examples of the figurative language that you will encounter in this section.

Similes compare one object with another using the words "like," "as," or "than" (e.g., "Her heart is harder than stone."). Metaphors make more direct comparisons and usually equate one thing with another (e.g., "She has a heart of stone," or "All the world's a stage.") and are therefore more powerful than similes.

Personification is when a nonhuman object is given human qualities (e.g., "The sun strolled across the sky."). Idioms are phrases that should not be taken literally and have a meaning other than those of the individual words (e.g., "To let the cat out of the bag" has nothing to do with cats, but instead means "to reveal a secret.").

Finally, hyperbole is an exaggeration that is used for added effect (e.g., "I've told you a million times!").

036

36 Plato and His Thinking

1   Plato was one of Western philosophy's greatest thinkers. Born in 428 BC in Athens, Greece, Plato deserted a life of political power to pursue knowledge instead. This quest would, in the end, produce works on the subjects of morality, ethics, political philosophy, and justice that would be **guiding lights of wisdom** for millennia after his death.

5

⌃ Plato (428/427–424/423 BC)
(cc by Marie-Lan Nguyen)

2   Plato was a prolific writer, but his works are not dry, philosophical essays. In fact, they have a far more dramatic flavor: Plato's works take the form of dialogues, where several characters debate a topic, asking questions of each other, disagreeing, and proposing arguments and counterarguments. Though this would seem **to muddy the water**, in fact, it allows the reader to see all aspects of the argument and come to his own conclusions about which argument is the most valid.

10

3   The most important character in Plato's dialogues is Socrates. Socrates was not a fictional character, but a real person. In fact, he was the most revered thinker of the age. As a young man, Plato was one of Socrates's students, and in his dialogues Plato portrays a man who, through his combination of humility, logic, and critical thinking, often **hits the nail on the head**.

15

« Plato *(left)* and Aristotle *(right)*, a detail of *The School of Athens* (1509–1511) fresco by Raphael (1483–1520)

4   After the trauma of Socrates's death, Plato left Athens and   20
traveled throughout Europe for over a decade, visiting different
teachers and consuming knowledge like a man starving. During
his travels, he began writing his famous dialogues. Though Plato's
dialogues tend to feature Socrates as the main source of wisdom,
it is difficult to know how much of the dialogue is a true record   25
of Socrates's ideas and how much was actually Plato himself
speaking in the guise of his former master.

5   Perhaps the most famous of Plato's dialogues is the *Republic*,
in which Plato questions what is just not only for an individual but for a society
as a whole. He claims that the leaders of his era ruled not with their logic and   30
intellect but with their ego and power. Further, he argues that states
need to be governed by "philosopher kings," leaders who rule from logic
instead of greed, thereby bringing happiness to the people. For Plato,
logic and reason were the light at the end of the tunnel.

⌃ Plato's
The Republic

Questions

_____ 1. In the first paragraph, the writer describes Plato's works as "**guiding lights of wisdom**." This is an example of which kind of figurative language?
  a. Hyperbole.   **b.** Idiom.   **c.** Simile.   **d.** Metaphor.

_____ 2. In the second paragraph, the writer uses the idiom "**to muddy the water**." What do you think this idiom means?
  a. To make something confusing. **b.** To make something dirty.
  c. To make something useless.   **d.** To make something simple.

_____ 3. In the third paragraph, the writer says that in Plato's dialogues, Socrates often "**hits the nail on the head**." What does he mean by this?
  a. Socrates often performs a violent action toward others.
  b. Socrates often constructs elaborate and far-fetched arguments.
  c. Socrates often describes exactly what is causing a situation.
  d. Socrates often says things that make other people very angry.

_____ 4. In the fourth paragraph, the writer says that Plato consumed knowledge "like a man starving." This is an example of _____.
  a. a simile   **b.** a metaphor   **c.** personification   **d.** an idiom

_____ 5. Which of the following sentences contains an idiom?
  a. "Socrates was not a fictional character, but a real person."
  b. "For Plato, logic and reason were the light at the end of the tunnel."
  c. "Plato was one of Western philosophy's greatest thinkers."
  d. "Plato was a prolific writer, but his works were not dry, philosophical essays."

⌃ containing fragments
of Plato's *Republic*,
manuscript from the
third century AD

(037)

37 The Genocide in Rwanda

» photographs of genocide victims, Genocide Memorial Center in Kigali

1   Genocide occurs when one group of people want to terminate another group of people because of differences of race, religion, culture, or political views. The slaughter of the Tutsi by the Hutu in the East African country of Rwanda in 1994 is just one recent horrific example of genocide where, over a three-month period, nearly one million men, women, and children were butchered like animals in their homes and on the streets.

2   It is widely believed that the trigger for the genocide came when a plane carrying the Hutu president Habyarimana was shot down by the Tutsi-led Rwandan Patriotic Front. But the actual root of the Hutu-Tutsi conflict was a tradition of racial hatred as old as the hills.

5

10

15

3

⌃ the Hutu president Habyarimana in 1980

    The Tutsi had ruled over Rwanda since the fifteenth century, but the Hutu had always comprised a large majority (84–85%) of the population. The Hutu were generally considered peasants and were quite impoverished compared to the Tutsi ruling class (the word *Tutsi* actually means "rich in cattle"). As the Tutsi continued to strengthen their power and authority, they distributed land to individuals they favored—usually other Tutsi—instead of allowing it to be passed from generation to generation as had been done for centuries.

20

« displaced populations during the Rwandan Civil War in 1994 (cc by British Red Cross.)

» Five thousand Tutsi people seeking refuge in this church were killed by grenade, machete, rifle, or fire. (cc by Ntrama Church Altar)

086

4 This caused immense resentment among the Hutu, as they were forced by the Tutsi to labor on their own land in exchange for the right to inhabit it. Inevitably, a social revolution took place in 1959, and a Hutu was secured as president, causing many Tutsi to flee the country. The tables had turned on the Tutsi.

5 Still, after decades of Hutu rule, the Hutu and the Tutsi could not see eye to eye. It was agreed among many of the Hutu that the only way Rwanda could ever become a stable country would be if the Hutu drove out or killed all of the Tutsi people. The attack on President Habyarimana's plane was the spark that lit the gunpowder. The organization of the killings happened swiftly, as governmental forces sent radio broadcasts to Hutu citizens urging them to slay their Tutsi neighbors. The Hutu succeeded in wiping out 75% of the Tutsi race, and the Rwandan genocide became known as one of mankind's darkest moments.

⌃ Tutsi survivor of the Rwandan genocide
(cc by Seeds Scholars)

Questions

Rwandan refugee camp in east Zaire following the genocide, 1994

_____ 1. The expression "men, women, and children were butchered like animals" is an example of which kind of figurative language?
  a. A metaphor. **b.** A simile. **c.** An idiom. **d.** Hyperbole.

_____ 2. The phrase "a tradition of racial hatred as old as the hills" is an example of _____.
  a. a metaphor **b.** an idiom **c.** personification **d.** hyperbole

_____ 3. The idiom "The tables had turned on the Tutsi" means that the Tutsi _____.
  a. were in the opposite position to where they had been before
  b. had a secret advantage over their enemies
  c. would not agree to negotiate with their enemies, the Hutu
  d. were turning and fleeing from a bad situation

_____ 4. Which of the following sentences contains an idiom?
  a. "The Hutu succeeded in wiping out 75% of the Tutsi race."
  b. "The Hutu were generally considered peasants."
  c. "The Hutu and Tutsi could not see eye to eye."
  d. "The organization of the killings happened swiftly."

_____ 5. The sentence "The attack on President Habyarimana's plane was the spark that lit the gunpowder" is an example of _____.
  a. a simile **b.** a metaphor **c.** personification **d.** hyperbole

∨ The Star of David, the symbol of the Jewish faith and people

38 Judaism

🎧 038

1   The Jews are an ethno-religious group, which means that they are an ethnic group of people who are also unified by a common religious background. There are an estimated 14 million Jews in the world, most of them living in either Israel or the United States. They originated in the Middle East and settled in the land of Israel. From the sixth century BC onward, conquest, oppression, and exile forced them to **pull up stakes** and move to other areas of the world, mostly Eastern Europe, the Middle East, Africa, and more recently the United States. In 1948, after the reestablishment of the Jewish state in Israel, millions of Jews from around the world returned to their ancestral homeland to settle there and build up the country.

5

10

2   The glue that unites Jews is their religion, Judaism. Converts to Judaism, even if they are not ethnically Jewish, are considered Jews from the point of their conversion. Judaism is a monotheistic religion, meaning that it prescribes the belief in only one god, Yahweh.

15

3   Judaism and Christianity are closely linked; in fact, Judaism— one of the oldest religious traditions—gave birth to Christianity. The first half of the Christian Bible, the Old Testament, is a slightly reorganized (and occasionally mistranslated) version of the Jewish holy book, the Tanakh. But whereas Christians believe Jesus was the son of God (the Messiah), in Judaism it is believed that Jesus was an ordinary man and that the Messiah hasn't arrived yet.

20

⌐ It is customary to have two loaves of challah, braided bread, at the start of the Shabbat meal.

4   Another difference between the two religions is that the Jewish   25
day of rest, the Shabbat, falls on Saturday rather than Sunday.
Orthodox Jews take the Shabbat very seriously, and no deliberate
activity whatsoever is permitted on the Shabbat, not even turning on
electric lights, cooking, or driving a car.

It is a mitzvah for Jewish people to light Sabbath candles on Friday night.

5   In addition, there are many unique holidays and rituals that are   30
observed by Jews, such as Hanukkah, an eight-day celebration that
takes place around the same time of year as Christmas.
For it, candles are lit and sparkle like stars in every
window after dark, songs are sung, gifts are exchanged,
and delicious fried food is enjoyed by all. To adequately   35
explain every facet of this millennia-long religious
culture would itself, I fear, take millennia. This brief
taste, I hope, will satisfy you for now.

Questions

_____ **1.** In the first paragraph, the writer states that the Jews had to "**pull up stakes**." What does he mean?
  a. The Jews had to perform difficult manual labor.
  b. The Jews had to depend on income from gambling.
  c. The Jews had to abandon their homes.
  d. The Jews had to battle supernatural forces.

_____ **2.** The second-paragraph expression "The glue that unites Jews is their religion, . . ." is a(n) _____.
  a. hyperbole   **b.** metaphor   **c.** idiom   **d.** simile

_____ **3.** "In fact, Judaism . . . gave birth to Christianity" is an example of a _____.
  a. simile   **b.** metaphor   **c.** hyperbole   **d.** personification

_____ **4.** The simile in the statement "candles are lit and sparkle like stars in every window after dark" expresses which of the following?
  a. The Hanukkah candles are as beautiful as stars.
  b. The Hanukkah candles are as bright as stars.
  c. The Hanukkah candles are as far away as stars.
  d. The Hanukkah candles are as hot as stars.

_____ **5.** Which of the following sentences contains a hyperbole?
  a. There are an estimated 14 million Jews in the world.
  b. Converts to Judaism are considered Jews.
  c. To adequately explain Judaism would take millennia.
  d. The Jewish day of rest, the Shabbat, falls on Saturday.

⌃ Judaism is practiced in all parts of the world, for example in downtown Mumbai.
(cc by Conew)

39 Las Vegas: The Entertainment Capital of the World

>> Las Vegas sign

1   Where in the United States can you go and see the Eiffel Tower, the Egyptian pyramids, and a pirate ship with exploding cannons? Where can you ride roller coasters, watch an IMAX movie, go to a concert, enjoy a circus, stroll through a museum, lounge by a pool, get a spa treatment, eat until you can't take another bite, win a million dollars at a casino, and get married, all on the same day? If it's fun you're after, Las Vegas is willing and able to oblige.   5

2   Vegas is loud, brash, and unashamedly showy. Located in the middle of the Mojave Desert, Las Vegas is characterized by typical desert conditions of very hot, dry summers and mild winters. The consistent sunshine and little rainfall draw visitors 12 months a year; and its warts-and-all approach to tourism make it beloved by many who visit there year after year in search of a good time.   10

3   Las Vegas, which means "the meadows" in Spanish, was given this name because areas of the valley nearby the city used to contain lush, green areas, which provided relief to travelers in the desert heat. After the area was conceded to the United States by Mexico in 1848, Mormons moved into the area to attempt to convert the region's   15

≫ **Many of the largest hotel, casino, and resort properties in the world are located on the Las Vegas Strip.** (Wikipedia)

Paiute Indians. Their settlement was unsuccessful and was abandoned after only a few years. Who knows what Vegas would be like today if they'd stayed? 20

4 In 1931, gambling was legalized in the state of Nevada, and casino hotels, for which Vegas is now famous, began to spring up everywhere like mushrooms. During the 1940s, 1950s, and 1960s, people flocked to the city to see the nuclear bomb tests that were being conducted in the desert nearby, and developers (along with a fair number of gangsters) poured money into the city's 25 casino resorts, which light up the city like a Christmas tree every night of the

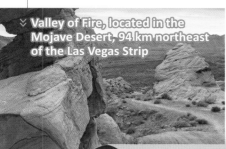

⋙ **Valley of Fire, located in the Mojave Desert, 94 km northeast of the Las Vegas Strip**

year. Thus, over time, Vegas grew to become the undisputed Entertainment Capital of the World.

5 Visitors to Vegas should remember just one thing: when you visit, don't be shy. **Jump** straight 30 **in at the deep end**, and Vegas will guarantee you a spectacular vacation you'll never forget.

Questions

⋀ **The Fountains of Bellagio is one of Las Vegas's most watched attractions.**

⋀ **The Fremont Street Experience (FSE) is a pedestrian mall and attraction in downtown Las Vegas.**
(cc by Tomàs Del Coro)

_____ 1. "Vegas is loud, brash, and unashamedly showy" is an example of _____.
   a. a simile
   b. hyperbole
   c. an idiom
   d. personification

_____ 2. The second-paragraph phrase "its warts-and-all approach to tourism" is an example of what kind of figurative language?
   a. An idiom.
   b. A simile.
   c. Personification.
   d. Hyperbole.

_____ 3. In the fourth paragraph, the author describes the city as being lit up "like a Christmas tree." What type of figurative language is used in this description?
   a. A metaphor.
   b. Personification.
   c. Hyperbole.
   d. A simile.

_____ 4. The fourth-paragraph phrase "began to spring up everywhere like mushrooms" suggests that _____.
   a. something happened that could not have been predicted
   b. something appeared rapidly and in great numbers
   c. something unwelcome and dangerous appeared
   d. something happened that was of great benefit to the area

_____ 5. Which of the following means the same as the final-sentence idiom "**jump in at the deep end**"?
   a. Burn the midnight oil.
   b. Let the cat out of the bag.
   c. Take the bull by the horns.
   d. Shoot the breeze.

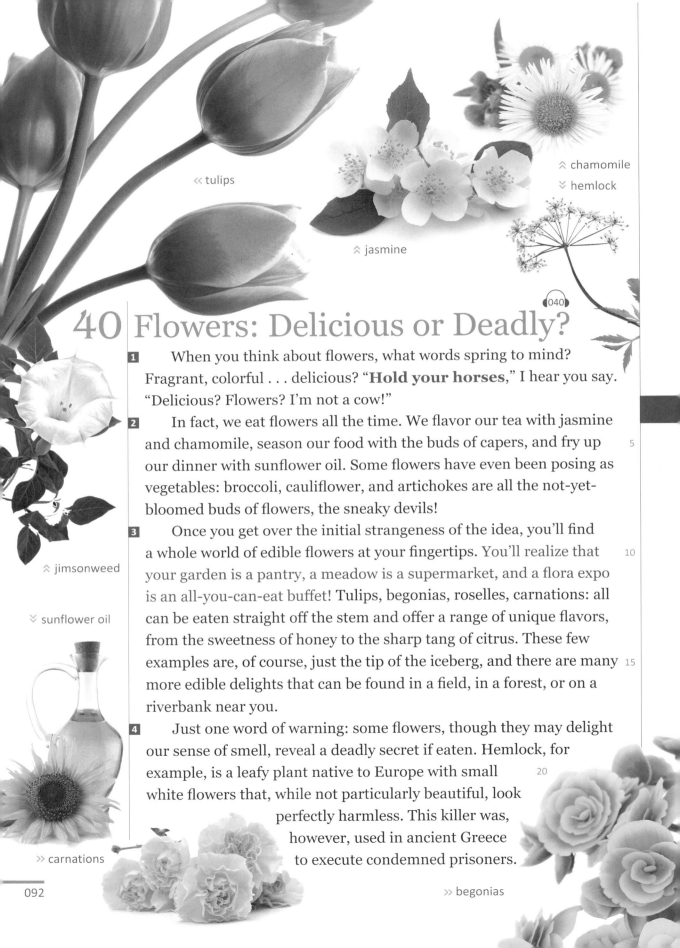

≪ tulips

≪ chamomile
≪ hemlock

⋏ jasmine

40 Flowers: Delicious or Deadly?

(040)

1   When you think about flowers, what words spring to mind? Fragrant, colorful . . . delicious? "**Hold your horses**," I hear you say. "Delicious? Flowers? I'm not a cow!"

2   In fact, we eat flowers all the time. We flavor our tea with jasmine and chamomile, season our food with the buds of capers, and fry up   5 our dinner with sunflower oil. Some flowers have even been posing as vegetables: broccoli, cauliflower, and artichokes are all the not-yet-bloomed buds of flowers, the sneaky devils!

3   Once you get over the initial strangeness of the idea, you'll find a whole world of edible flowers at your fingertips. You'll realize that   10 your garden is a pantry, a meadow is a supermarket, and a flora expo is an all-you-can-eat buffet! Tulips, begonias, roselles, carnations: all can be eaten straight off the stem and offer a range of unique flavors, from the sweetness of honey to the sharp tang of citrus. These few examples are, of course, just the tip of the iceberg, and there are many   15 more edible delights that can be found in a field, in a forest, or on a riverbank near you.

4   Just one word of warning: some flowers, though they may delight our sense of smell, reveal a deadly secret if eaten. Hemlock, for example, is a leafy plant native to Europe with small   20 white flowers that, while not particularly beautiful, look perfectly harmless. This killer was, however, used in ancient Greece to execute condemned prisoners.

⋏ jimsonweed

⋎ sunflower oil

≫ carnations

≫ begonias

« capers

Perhaps its most famous victim was the great philosopher Socrates. 25
Plato, Socrates's recorder, depicts how Socrates's feet first became
cold and numb. Then the sensation spread upward through his
body until it reached his heart.

5　　Jimsonweed, a bushy plant with foul-smelling, trumpet-shaped flowers,
has been administered for centuries in herbal medicine as a cure for asthma. 30
However, the fatal dose of this flower is only slightly higher than the medicinal
dose. A catchy little phrase describes the deadly effects of jimsonweed:
shortly before it stops your heart, you'll go "red as a
beet, dry as a bone, blind as a bat, and mad as a hatter."

6　　Don't be put off by **the black sheep of the** 35
family; edible flowers make an inspired addition to
any meal. Just remember to do your research before
digging in!

» cauliflower

Questions

_____ 1. "**Hold your horses**" in the first paragraph means "_____."
　　a. I don't understand　　　**b.** wait a minute
　　c. don't be stupid　　　　**d.** please be quiet

» broccoli

_____ 2. Which of the following statements from the article personifies flowers?
　　a. "We flavor our tea with jasmine and chamomile."
　　b. "In fact, we eat flowers all the time."
　　c. "Some flowers have even been posing as vegetables."
　　d. "Delicious? Flowers? I'm not a cow!"

» artichokes

_____ 3. "You'll realize that your garden is a pantry, a meadow is a supermarket, and
a flora expo is an all-you-can-eat buffet!" contains a series of _____.
　　a. metaphors　　**b.** similes　　　**c.** idioms　　　**d.** personifications

_____ 4. The purpose of the similes "red as a beet, dry as a bone, blind as a bat, and
mad as a hatter" is to _____.
　　a. make the symptoms of jimsonweed poisoning seem humorous
　　b. reassure people that the effects of jimsonweed aren't so bad
　　c. make the symptoms of jimsonweed poisoning more appealing
　　d. emphasize the powerful effects of jimsonweed.

_____ 5. What does the author mean when he refers to hemlock and jimsonweed as
"**the black sheep of the family**"?

» roselles

　　a. They are easy to spot despite being harmful.
　　b. They are terrible, but rare, exceptions.
　　c. They are prized and sought-after examples.
　　d. They are unpredictable and difficult to control.

Unit
1
Reading Skills

1-8
Figurative Language

093

1-9 *Finding Bias*

Writers have their own experiences, opinions, and beliefs. When you add all these together, they form a bias, or a particular point of view. Discovering a writer's bias can sometimes be difficult, but a good place to start is the language used and whether or not the writer portrays both sides of an argument fairly.

⌂041 41 Social Anxiety Disorder

1   Did you know that 7 to 13 percent of the population suffers from a disorder that can turn a public pool into a frightening hazard? It's called Social Anxiety Disorder (SAD). SAD is a condition that makes people feel humiliated around other people. SAD sufferers often feel like they're being judged by their peers. They can also have physical   5 symptoms, like accelerated heartbeat, blushing, and trembling. Sometimes, a SAD sufferer will even break out in a fit of excessive sweating.

2   Wait . . . doesn't that sound like a lot of people? All of us get nervous in social situations, so who can say when such a common   10 problem becomes an actual disorder? The experts will claim that the intensity of SAD symptoms greatly varies. Some SAD sufferers have a very subtle problem, like a tendency to sweat when they give a report at a business meeting. Others can't lead normal lives due   15 to an intense fear of social situations. But could it be that these people just have quirky personalities? Maybe SAD isn't much of a disorder at all.

≫ group therapy

≫ SAD is characterized by intense fear in social situations.

« Depression is considered the most prevalent
mental health problem in the United States.

3   The most common treatment for SAD is called "cognitive-behavioral
therapy." It's based on breaking the patient's mental associations, like   20
associating using a public toilet with being embarrassed, and replacing them
with more rational thoughts. After all of these associations have been broken,
SAD sufferers will often be able to do all of the social activities they previously
avoided, like speak in public, swim in a public pool, take a cooking class, or
simply go out for a meal with friends. If they're still not cured after cognitive-   25
behavioral therapy, the person in question might simply be a loser.

≍ alcoholism

4   Some people will tell you that SAD is the
third biggest mental health problem in the United
States behind depression and alcoholism, but that
seems a bit excessive. The older generation had a   30
different term for SAD. They called it "being shy."
After all, who's to say that SAD sufferers wouldn't
achieve the same results as cognitive-behavioral
therapy if they just went out and faced all of their
social fears head-on? Maybe it would help them   35
stop being so strange all the time!

Questions

_____ 1. In this article, the author shows bias against _____.
    a. the older generation   **b.** Social Anxiety Disorder
    c. cognitive-behavioral therapy   **d.** mental health disorders

_____ 2. Which of the following is NOT a biased word?
    a. Loser.   **b.** Therapy.   **c.** Strange.   **d.** Weird.

_____ 3. Which of the following from the article is NOT a biased statement?
    a. "Maybe it would help them stop being so strange all the time!"
    b. "The person in question might simply be a loser."
    c. "SAD sufferers often feel like they're being judged by their peers."
    d. "Maybe SAD isn't much of a disorder at all."

_____ 4. The author of this article creates a tone toward people suffering
from SAD that is _____.
    a. harsh   **b.** friendly   **c.** formal   **d.** poetic

_____ 5. "They can also have physical symptoms, like accelerated heartbeat,
blushing, and trembling." This is a statement of _____.
    a. opinion   **b.** bias   **c.** argument   **d.** fact

≍ psychologist

asthma

rheumatoid arthritis

hay fever

>> Chronic inflammation is the root cause of several diseases.

(042)

42 Foods That Fight Inflammation

1   Inflammation is part of the human body's protective response to harmful stimuli like viruses, bacteria, and other irritants. But sometimes this natural response can go too far and do more harm than good. Chronic inflammation, or inflammation that is too extreme, is the root cause of several diseases such as hay fever, rheumatoid arthritis, and asthma.   5

≫ foods that fight inflammation

papayas

2   Luckily there's a solution, and it starts right at your local grocery store. Certain foods contain vitamins and nutrients that help curb inflammation. Fatty types of fish like salmon, tuna, and mackerel are one example. These are high in omega-3 fatty   10 acids, which studies have shown reduce inflammation by a miraculous amount. In fact, omega-3 fatty acids are so amazing that most people skip the eating-fish step and take daily vitamin supplements instead.

cranberries

3   That's just the tip of the iceberg; there are lots of foods   15 that fight inflammation. Papayas contain high levels of vitamin C, E, and A, and they also have enzymes that reduce inflammation. Cranberries and blueberries are two other inflammation-fighting fruits. Nuts and whole grains are two other foods that can save your life. If you're cooking up a   20 stir-fry, be sure to include garlic and ginger because both are proven sources of anti-inflammatory chemicals. If everyone would eat these foods, there would be a lot less sickness in the world.   25

ginger

garlic

nuts

4   Of course, there are some foods that do more harm than good. These foods actually cause inflammation. They are sometimes referred to as the Three Ps, or processed, packaged, and prepared foods. No one should eat anything that falls under the Three Ps, not just because of the horrible inflammation they may induce, but in order to achieve the goal of a healthy lifestyle. These foods are incredibly dangerous. 30

5   Some ignorant people believe that medicine is a more powerful weapon than diet. For example, doctors often prescribe anti-inflammatory medications to patients suffering from inflammation. Most of the time, these doctors won't even mention the benefits of an anti-inflammatory diet. Worst of all, the prescribed medicine usually has worse side effects than the patient's inflammation in the first place! If doctors knew more about the healing power of fruits and nuts, they'd hesitate before reaching for their prescription pad. 35 40

⌃ Fish oil capsules are high in omega-3 fatty acids.

⌄ the Three-P foods

prepared food

processed food

packaged food

Questions

_____ **1.** In this article, the author shows bias against _____.
   a. fruits and nuts   **b.** inflammation
   c. prescription medicine   **d.** omega-3 fatty acids

_____ **2.** In this article, the author shows bias in favor of _____.
   a. doctors   **b.** certain foods
   c. asthma   **d.** vitamins and nutrients

_____ **3.** Which of the following is a biased word?
   a. Miraculous.   **b.** Fruits.   **c.** Certain.   **d.** Weapon.

_____ **4.** "Papayas contain high levels of vitamin C, E, and A, . . ." is a statement of _____.
   a. opinion   **b.** bias   **c.** argument   **d.** fact

_____ **5.** Which of the following from the article is NOT a biased statement?
   a. "These foods are incredibly dangerous."
   b. "No one should eat anything that falls under the Three Ps."
   c. "Cranberries and blueberries are two other inflammation-fighting fruits."
   d. "Some ignorant people believe that medicine is a more powerful weapon than diet."

43 Self-Cleaning Concrete

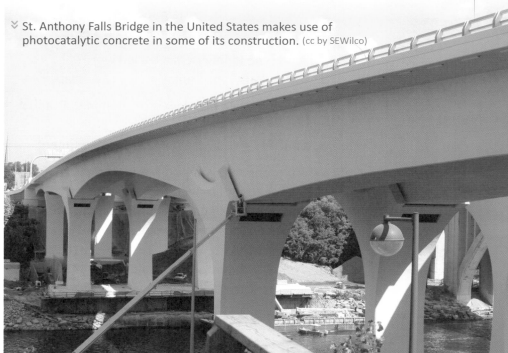

Photocatalytic concrete acts like a vacuum cleaner sucking up smog and air pollution.

1 Don't let the complicated name fool you; photocatalytic concrete is the greatest invention ever. It's a new type of concrete being developed by an Italian company, and it acts like a vacuum cleaner sucking up smog and air pollution.

2 The inventors of photocatalytic concrete originally set out to produce self-cleaning sidewalks. However, when they began to test their product, they stumbled upon a miracle. The self-cleaning titanium dioxide that destroys dirt and grime when exposed to sunlight doesn't just clean the sidewalk; it cleans the nearby air. The titanium oxide isn't used up as the photocatalytic concrete works, so it will theoretically keep on cleaning the air for decades to come. This is an invention that will surely change the world.

3 Photocatalytic concrete is still a cutting-edge invention, so it's only being used in a few pilot projects. Chicago became the first US city to try it out, and photocatalytic concrete has already been used to pave sidewalks in Italy and the Netherlands. Eventually, this revolutionary technology will be used to pave highways around the world. It will help make our urban sprawls greener and more sustainable, so that we can have the best of both worlds: cars and clean air.

5

10

15

20

↟ titanium dioxide

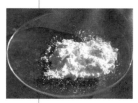

↟ photocatalysis (cc by University College London Faculty of Mathematical & Physical Sciences)

St. Anthony Falls Bridge in the United States makes use of photocatalytic concrete in some of its construction. (cc by SEWilco)

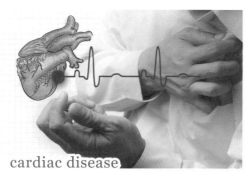

>> ⌄ Smog can cause lung cancer and cardiac disease.

cardiac disease

lung cancer

4   Even with such miraculous properties, photocatalytic concrete somehow doesn't excite certain fools out there. These people whine about the possibility of photocatalytic concrete being too ²⁵ expensive and difficult to maintain. Some people even complain about the invention of any green technology. They think we should stop using cars and go back to living in caves or something. ³⁰

5   Luckily, no one really listens to the sheer idiocy of these arguments. Most people are wise enough to know that smog is a serious issue. It contributes to several health problems such as asthma, cancer, and cardiac disease. If we can reduce the air pollution in our metropolitan areas by building roads and sidewalks with ³⁵ photocatalytic concrete, isn't that the shrewd way forward? After all, can we really put a price on our children's health?

Questions

_____ 1. The author of this article creates a tone that can best be described as _____.

    a. objective   **b.** ironic   **c.** opinionated   **d.** tragic

_____ 2. Which of the following best describes the author's bias in this article?
    a. Photocatalytic concrete is not really a big deal.
    b. Photocatalytic concrete is far too expensive.
    c. Photocatalytic concrete is going to change the world.
    d. Photocatalytic concrete does not exist.

_____ 3. Which of the following is a biased word?
    a. Fools.   **b.** Self-cleaning. **c.** Health.   **d.** Urban.

_____ 4. Which of the following from the article is a biased statement about photocatalytic concrete?
    a. "It's a new type of concrete being developed by an Italian company."
    b. "The inventors of photocatalytic concrete originally set out to produce self-cleaning sidewalks."
    c. "Chicago became the first US city to try it out."
    d. "Luckily, no one really listens to the sheer idiocy of these arguments."

_____ 5. Which of the following is NOT a biased word?
    a. Revolutionary.   **b.** Idiocy.
    c. Technology.   **d.** Whine.

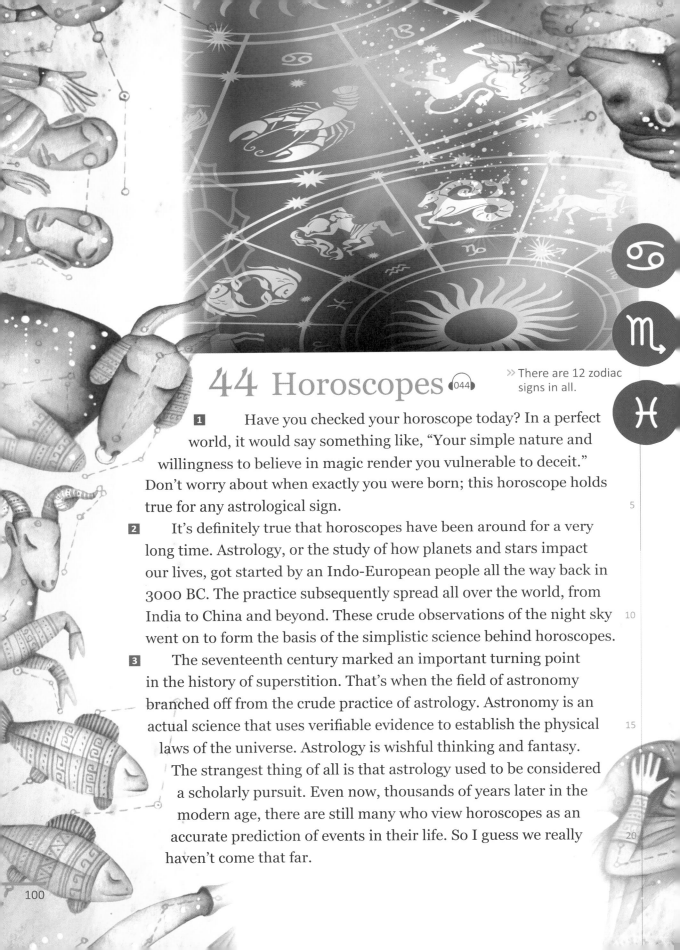

44 Horoscopes (044)

» There are 12 zodiac signs in all.

1 Have you checked your horoscope today? In a perfect world, it would say something like, "Your simple nature and willingness to believe in magic render you vulnerable to deceit." Don't worry about when exactly you were born; this horoscope holds true for any astrological sign.

2 It's definitely true that horoscopes have been around for a very long time. Astrology, or the study of how planets and stars impact our lives, got started by an Indo-European people all the way back in 3000 BC. The practice subsequently spread all over the world, from India to China and beyond. These crude observations of the night sky went on to form the basis of the simplistic science behind horoscopes.

3 The seventeenth century marked an important turning point in the history of superstition. That's when the field of astronomy branched off from the crude practice of astrology. Astronomy is an actual science that uses verifiable evidence to establish the physical laws of the universe. Astrology is wishful thinking and fantasy. The strangest thing of all is that astrology used to be considered a scholarly pursuit. Even now, thousands of years later in the modern age, there are still many who view horoscopes as an accurate prediction of events in their life. So I guess we really haven't come that far.

4   Most people in the West are familiar with horoscopes based on the Western zodiac, which includes signs like Virgo, Scorpio, and Capricorn. There are 12 zodiac signs

25 in all, and a person is assigned one based on the position of certain stars and planets on the day he or she was born. These zodiac signs aren't just used to predict the future via daily horoscopes. Some simpletons actually believe that their zodiac sign determines their personality traits. For example, someone who

30 is a Virgo (born between August 23 and September 22) is supposed to be analytical and observant. But let me tell you something: I'm a Virgo, and I wouldn't even know what country I lived in if it weren't clearly stated on my passport. There you have it: undeniable proof that horoscopes and the zodiac are a load of rubbish.

Questions

_____ **1.** The author of this article creates a tone that can best be described as _____.

    a. joking   **b.** objective

    c. tragic   **d.** skeptical

_____ **2.** Which of the following best describes the author's bias in this article?

    a. Horoscopes are an accurate prediction of the future.

    b. Horoscopes were really invented in China.

    c. Horoscopes are based on lies and superstition.

    d. Horoscopes are accurate only in the Western zodiac.

_____ **3.** Which of the following is a biased word?

    a. Rubbish.   **b.** Astrology.

    c. Load.   **d.** Impact.

_____ **4.** Which of the following from the article is a biased statement about astrology and horoscopes?

    a. "The seventeenth century marked an important turning point in the history of superstition."

    b. "It's definitely true that horoscopes have been around for a very long time."

    c. "Someone who is a Virgo . . . is supposed to be analytical and observant."

    d. "The practice subsequently spread all over the world, from India to China and beyond."

_____ **5.** Which of the following is NOT a biased word?

    a. Crude.   **b.** Wishful.

    c. Accurate.   **d.** Country.

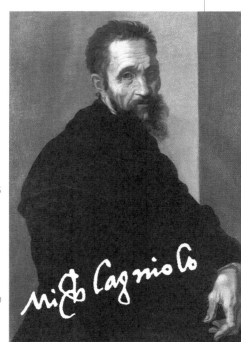

>> Michelangelo
(1475–1564)

45 Michelangelo

1   Michelangelo is a famous Italian painter who was born in Tuscany in 1475. As a young boy, he shocked his father by entering an art workshop instead of studying to become a merchant. There he spent several years refining his craft, and his artistic interests eventually narrowed to human anatomy and sculpture. Once Michelangelo emerged from his studies, he went on to produce some of the most famous masterpieces in the history of Western art. He is still considered by many to be one of the greatest artists who ever lived.

≫ *David*, completed in 1504, is proof of Michelangelo's mastery.
(cc by Rico Heil)

2   Does Michelangelo really deserve all of this credit? Take one of his most famous works for example. His best-known work *David* was carved in Florence from 1501 to 1504. Experts will tell you that it's proof of Michelangelo's mastery—a moving representation of the human form. But did you know that the sculpture's right hand is bigger than its left? Its eyes are also looking in two different directions. Where I come from, that's called "being sloppy." But since it's a work by Michelangelo, people are willing to overlook the obvious faults.

3   That's not the only instance where Michelangelo slipped up. His famous *Pietà* sculpture in St. Peter's Basilica is also distorted. The *Pietà* was completed before *David*. It depicts the Christian figure

≫ *Pietà*
(cc by Stanislav Traykov)

⌐ possible self-portrait of Leonardo da Vinci (1452–1519) (c. 1505)

of Mary holding the lifeless body of Jesus Christ. However, it fails in terms of historical accuracy and believability. Mary's face in the *Pietà* is unbelievably young and fresh, even though she would have been more than 40 years old at the time of her son's death. Even people living back in Michelangelo's time realized something was wrong. When his biographer asked him why Mary's face was so young, Michelangelo responded that she had led a blessed life. In truth, he should have just said he messed up.

30

4 It's sad that in everyone's rush to praise Michelangelo, a true hero of the classical art world gets missed: Leonardo da Vinci. Of all the words one could use to describe Leonardo—genius, visionary, master—sloppy isn't one of them. He even produced basic designs for a helicopter centuries before mankind achieved flight. Leonardo da Vinci is the true master here. Michelangelo is a mere pretender.

35

40

≪ Leonardo da Vinci's design for a helicopter (c. 1488)

Questions

_____ 1. In this article, the author shows bias against _____.
   a. art   **b.** sculpture   **c.** *David*   **d.** Michelangelo

_____ 2. In this article, the author shows bias in favor of _____.
   a. Italy   **b.** Leonardo da Vinci
   c. the *Pietà*   **d.** Jesus Christ

_____ 3. Which of the following is NOT a biased word?
   a. Pretender.   **b.** Hero.   **c.** Fault.   **d.** Figure.

_____ 4. Which of the following best describes the author's bias in this article?
   a. Classical art is not important in the modern age.
   b. One artist is better than the other one.
   c. Sculpture shouldn't be considered real art.
   d. Leonardo da Vinci is the real inventor of the helicopter.

_____ 5. Which of the following is NOT a biased statement?
   a. "Michelangelo is a mere pretender."
   b. "In truth, he should have just said he messed up."
   c. "As a young boy, he shocked his father by entering an art workshop."
   d. "However, it fails in terms of historical accuracy and believability."

>> Processed foods are addictive.

46 Quitting Junk Food Cold Turkey

(046)

1 Ever feel like you need just one more hit of bubble tea? Or maybe you're feeling sick and a chocolate donut is the only medicine that can cure you? Believe it or not, you might just be an addict.

2 Normally when we think of addiction, we imagine drugs, alcohol, or cigarettes. But it's not just the obviously harmful substances that can produce withdrawal effects. A study from the University of Michigan has shed some light on the shocking extent to which this is true.

3 The study found that people experience various negative symptoms when they give up processed foods like pizza and French fries. The symptoms included mood swings, intense cravings, anxiety, headaches, and insomnia. The effects surged immediately after the foods were eliminated from one's diet, but diminished and then disappeared within five days. The results suggest that going "cold turkey" on junk food is a lot like giving up cigarettes or marijuana.

4 The study adds to the growing body of evidence suggesting that processed foods are addictive. Various research has shown that our brains treat sugar like a drug. When we eat too much of it, our brain chemistry is altered to seek out even more sugar. Dopamine is

≫ processed food

5

10

15

20

25

104

released in our brain whenever we eat a donut or a bag of cookies, making us feel good. Eventually, it's not the food we're craving, but that feeling. But here's the worst part: like any drug, our body can build up a resistance to sugar. As a result,
30 it takes more and more sugar to achieve that dopamine release, so we eat more junk food. This cycle of over-eating can lead to serious health problems.

5   There are some valuable lessons to take from the University of Michigan research. First and foremost: junk food is a dangerous drug like any other. We should all limit the amount of processed foods that we eat. Obviously, this is
35 easier said than done, because no one wants to suffer from headaches or tossing and turning all night. But just remember that these symptoms will only last for a few days. It'll all be worth it when you're living clean
40 and sugar-free.

>> The cycle of over-eating caused by addiction can lead to serious health problems.

Questions

_____1. What is the main idea of this article?
    a. Our body can build up resistance to any drug.
    b. Processed foods are addictive.
    c. Our brains treat sugar like a drug.
    d. Giving up French fries can lead to negative symptoms.

_____2. What is the author's tone in the final paragraph?
    a. Comedic.   **b.** Serious.   **c.** Tragic.   **d.** Angry.

_____3. What is the function of the first sentence in the article?
    a. To relate to the reader.   **b.** To provide an important detail.
    c. To tell a personal story.   **d.** To make a comparison.

_____4. What can we infer about the fourth paragraph?
    a. Processed foods tend to be high in sugar.
    b. Dopamine is a dangerous chemical.
    c. Some people have a high resistance to sugar.
    d. Most types of junk food contain dopamine.

_____5. According to the article, which of the following is NOT a negative effect of eating junk food?
    a. Possible over-eating.   **b.** Insomnia.
    c. Anxiety.   **d.** Laziness.

ful medames, one of Egypt's nationa dishes, served with hard-boiled eggs (cc by Abdullah Geelah)

47 Egyptian Culture 🎧047

1   Ancient Egypt is one of the oldest civilizations in human history. Its advanced development and exotic trade goods lured merchants from the **four corners** of the ancient world. These merchants would often remain in Egypt and mingle with the locals. Perhaps this is why modern Egyptian 5 culture is such a cosmopolitan mix of old and new.

2   Take how an Egyptian will respond to a tourist in need for example. If someone is wandering around the streets of Cairo looking lost, it's not abnormal for a local to come up and offer to help. In mere minutes, a few more locals might appear and 10 start passionately discussing the best way for the tourist to get to where he's going. Maybe one will invite the tourist in for a cup of tea. They might even offer a plate of *ful medames*, which is an Egyptian staple dish consisting of fava beans, onions, and sometimes hard-boiled eggs. Egypt has been hosting travelers 15 for so long that the local population can't help but be friendly.

3   One thing that has changed since the days of ancient Egypt is religion. The population of Egypt is between 85 and 95% Muslim, and the day-to-day cultural life of many Egyptians is influenced by their religious beliefs. For example, since Muslims are prohibited from 20 eating pork, it can sometimes be hard to find it on the menu in restaurants. Egyptians also tend not to drink a lot of alcohol, which is prohibited in the Muslim faith as well.

« Muslim

106

4　Egypt's diverse history is also on display during its popular holidays. Its　25 two biggest holidays are the Muslim celebrations of Eid al-Fitr, which ends

the month-long fast of Ramadan, and Eid al-Adha. However, there are several folk festivals that have been celebrated for thousands of years as well. One such festival is sham el-Nessim,　30 or "smelling of the breeze," a day when many Egyptians will go out on a picnic. Christmas is also celebrated by Egypt's Christian population, who are also known as Coptic Christians. These Christians have lived in Egypt since AD 451, and　35 their customs include going on long pilgrimages to far-off places in order to worship the saints.

« Eidal-Fitr celebration (cc by Steve Evans)

Questions

≪ Eid al-Adha prayers
(cc by M. Tawsif Salam)

≪ ancient Egyptian hieroglyphs

_____ 1. What can be inferred from the third paragraph?
   a. The ancient Egyptians were not Muslims.
   b. The Muslim faith was invented in ancient Egypt.
   c. Egypt has the most Muslims in the world.
   d. Beer is regarded as the Egyptian national drink.

_____ 2. "Its advanced development and exotic trade goods lured merchants from the **four corners** of the ancient world." In this sentence, **four corners** is an example of a _____.
   a. simile　　　b. comparison
   c. idiom　　　d. personification

_____ 3. The author's tone in this article can best be described as _____.
   a. tragic　　b. angry　　c. comic　　d. formal

_____ 4. It is hard to find pork on a menu in Egypt because _____.
   a. pork is very expensive in Egypt
   b. Egyptians don't like the taste of pork
   c. eating pork is prohibited by the Muslim faith
   d. Egyptians are scared of diseases in pigs

_____ 5. "Egypt has been hosting travelers for so long that the local population can't help but be friendly." This sentence is an example of a(n) _____.
   a. fact　　　b. opinion

>> Green tea is a miracle drink.

>> green tea leaves

48 Green Tea

1   In the modern scramble to improve our health, we might be overlooking something that has been **right under our nose** all along. It's a drink that was first brewed in 2737 BC by the Chinese emperor Shen Nung, and its subsequent popularity in Asia has persisted to this day. It's inexpensive, plentiful, and scientists are discovering new health benefits linked to it every   5 year. It's green tea, and it truly is a miracle drink.

2   Illuminating all of the health benefits of green tea is no easy task because they are numerous and extensive. For one, studies have shown that green tea fights cancer and heart disease. One study in particular showed a 46% to 65% reduction in high blood pressure in green tea drinkers. Other limited studies   10 have shown that green tea can lower cholesterol and burn fat. Some experts even believe that green tea can help prevent diabetes, strokes, and dementia in the elderly.

3   The benefits of green tea don't stop at a healthy lifestyle. This miracle drink can make you look great as well. Want hair that is truly radiant? Just   15 steep some green tea, let it cool overnight, and then pour it over your freshly-washed hair. For the best results, be sure to use shampoo and conditioner once more   20 afterward. Green tea can also be used as a chemical-free alternative to hair dye. And your feet won't remain sweaty and smelly for long if you soak them in a nice tub of   25 cooled green tea. That's because green tea also has proven antifungal and antibacterial properties.

>> green tea fields

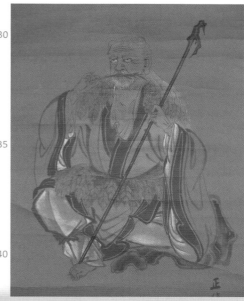

⩒ Some say the Chinese emperor Shen Nung discovered green tea. (cc by nagualdesign)

4   With so many obvious benefits, the next question becomes, "How much green tea should 30 I drink?" The most common answer seems to be around three cups a day. That's how much it takes to absorb a beneficial amount of the antioxidants in green tea. Another question you might have is, "Are black tea and white 35 tea as healthy as green tea?" Expert opinion is a little mixed on this one. Some say all teas have similarly beneficial health properties, and others maintain that green tea is the premier choice. Either way, everyone knows that green 40 tea is the best-tasting tea of all.

Unit **1** | Reading Skills   1-10   Review Test

Questions

_____ **1.** This passage focuses on a _____.
    a. study   **b.** sickness
    c. beverage   **d.** Chinese emperor

_____ **2.** "Everyone knows that green tea is the best-tasting tea of all." This statement is an example of a(n) _____.
    a. fact   **b.** joke
    c. metaphor   **d.** opinion

_____ **3.** Which of the following is a biased word?
    a. Miracle.   **b.** Common.
    c. Antioxidant.   **d.** Amount.

_____ **4.** It's obvious from this article that the author's purpose is _____.
    a. to tell a personal story   **b.** to offer a solution
    c. to inform the reader   **d.** to state a problem

_____ **5.** In the sentence "We might be overlooking something that has been **right under our nose** . . .," **right under our nose** is an example of a(n) _____.
    a. metaphor   **b.** simile
    c. personification   **d.** idiom

⩒ black tea

≫ white tea

109

49 | Rio Carnival

1   I will never forget my first assignment as a foreign correspondent in Brazil. It was a week-long gig in Rio de Janeiro to cover the city's Carnival. I hadn't heard about the
5 holiday before, so I did some research before arriving. Apparently, it begins on the Friday 40 days before Easter, and it carries on for five days until Wednesday. Some people say it has roots in the ancient Roman festival of
10 Saturnalia, when rich and poor people would swap clothes and party hard for days on end. Others argue that this is just empty rhetoric. They say that Carnival truly began when ordinary citizens began marching through Rio playing their drums and tambourines back in the mid-nineteenth century. Either way, everyone can agree on one
15 thing: Carnival is now a big deal. It is one of Brazil's largest cultural events, drawing up to two million tourists to Rio every year.

2   I was out on the streets on the first Friday of Carnival, armed with my camera and notebook, ready to do some work. Being there was a constant assault on my senses. Brazilian samba music filled the
20 air, coming from all directions and mixing into a chorus of thumping beats. Hundreds of people were singing and dancing. The air smelled like roast chicken, sweat, and occasionally vomit. I wandered for

⌄ 2018 Rio Carnival

hours on end, from one block party to another. At one point, I think it might have been around three in the morning, someone offered to trade me an alcoholic beverage and a golden feathered headdress for my camera. I'm still 25 not sure why, but I agreed to the swap. It was probably a question of getting swept up in the Carnival spirit. Unfortunately, my boss did not accept this explanation, and I had to pay for a new camera in the end.

3 It was worth it, though. I still have 30 that golden headdress, as it reminds me of just how spectacular those few days were. The Rio Carnival is something that everyone should add to his or her bucket list. It's a far better 35 experience than some of the trashy and boring affairs that pass for cultural events where I come from.

« **Carnival dancer**

Questions

1. Which sentence below best expresses the main idea of this article?
   a. Carnival is full of danger and areas that should be avoided.
   b. Carnival is full of music, dance, singing, and fun.
   c. Carnival was invented back in the time of ancient Rome.
   d. Carnival draws up to two million tourists to Rio every year.

2. Which of the following statements is an opinion?
   a. Everyone should add the Rio Carnival to his or her bucket list.
   b. Carnival begins on the Friday 40 days before Easter.
   c. Some people say Carnival has roots in an ancient Roman festival.
   d. Carnival is one of Brazil's largest cultural events.

3. Which of the following is considered to be a biased word?
   a. Roast.   b. Trashy.   c. Cultural.   d. Constant.

4. Which of the following statements about Carnival is NOT true?
   a. It begins around 40 days before Easter.
   b. It lasts for two weeks.
   c. It involves singing and dancing.
   d. It takes place in Rio de Janeiro.

5. This article can best be described as a(n) _____.
   a. timeline   b. example
   c. biography   d. personal narrative

⌄ samba dancers

« Carnival began when ordinary citizens began marching through Rio playing drums and tambourines back in the mid-nineteenth century.

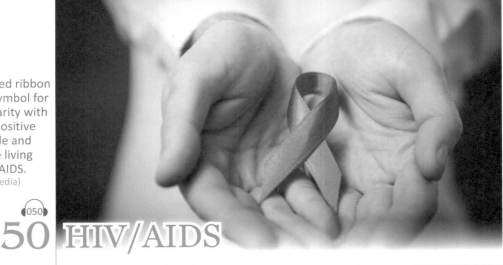

>> The red ribbon is a symbol for solidarity with HIV-positive people and those living with AIDS. (Wikipedia)

50 HIV/AIDS

1   HIV/AIDS refers to two diseases called the human immunodeficiency virus (HIV) and the acquired immune deficiency syndrome (AIDS). It is thought to have originated either in chimpanzees in West Africa or in monkeys   5 during the late 19th or early 20th century. Either way, HIV jumped to humans at some point, and cases began to appear in the United States in the early 1980s. Since then, it has become a global epidemic, and there are now   10 thought to be around 36.9 million people living with HIV/AIDS worldwide.

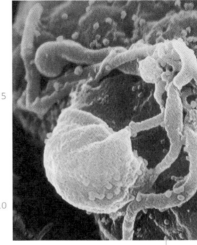

2   A person is infected with HIV by coming in contact with bodily fluids from a carrier of the virus. Once infected, HIV begins to destroy the body's CD4 cells. These are the cells that help our   15 bodies fight off disease. Once a certain number of CD4 cells have been lost, the patient is then diagnosed as having AIDS. AIDS patients have compromised and weak immune systems. They are at high risk of catching an opportunistic infection that can end up being a **death sentence.**   20

⌃ >> HIV/AIDS is thought to have originated either in chimpanzees in West Africa or in monkeys during the late 19th or early 20th century.

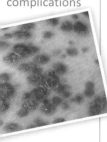

Kaposi's sarcoma, one of the HIV/AIDS complications

⌄ HIV-1 budding (in green)

3 Back in the 1980s and 1990s, HIV/AIDS meant certain death, likely within 13 years of contracting the disease. Nowadays, HIV has become a manageable chronic disease. A 20-year-old diagnosed with HIV can expect to live another 53 years. Infection rates are also dropping fast. According to the United Nations, new HIV infections 25 globally have dropped 47%, from 3.4 million in 1996 to 1.8 million in 2017. These victories have come thanks to new antiviral drugs that stem the advance of HIV. National education campaigns have also helped to end popular misconceptions and inform people about how to protect themselves from infection. However, there is still a lot of 30 work to be done. Antiviral drugs are often too expensive for the most vulnerable people to afford. There is also a lot of misinformation about HIV/AIDS that persists to this day, like the dubious and harmful myth of someone catching HIV from a toilet seat.

4 If there is a moral to the story of HIV/AIDS, it is that mankind 35 can beat a terrible disease. All it takes is some cooperation, education, research, and perhaps most importantly, understanding.

Questions

≫ abacavir, an HIV/AIDS treatment drug

_____ 1. What has caused global HIV/AIDS infection rates to drop?
     a. A new vaccine.   b. Changes in global weather.
     c. New drugs and education.   d. Widespread lifestyle changes.

_____ 2. In the final paragraph, the author's tone can best be described as _____.
     a. hopeful   b. angry   c. tragic   d. comic

_____ 3. The article mentions that opportunistic infections can be a **death sentence** for AIDS patients. **Death sentence** is an example of _____.
     a. personification   b. metaphor
     c. simile   d. hyperbole

_____ 4. How many people are now thought to be living with HIV/AIDS worldwide?
     a. About 1.8 million.   b. About 53 million.
     c. About 36.9 million.   d. About 3.4 million.

_____ 5. Which of the following statements would the author most likely agree with?
     a. More education is crucial in fighting HIV/AIDS.
     b. HIV/AIDS isn't a big problem.
     c. Scientists should research where HIV/AIDS originated.
     d. CD4 cells aren't very important.

Back in the 1980s and 1990s, HIV/AIDS meant certain death, likely within 13 years of contracting the disease. Nowadays, HIV has become a manageable chronic disease. A 20-year-old diagnosed with HIV can expect to live another 53 years. Infection rates are also dropping fast.

Unit 2

Word Study

>>

With so many words in the English language (nearly a million by some estimates), memorizing the meaning to every single one is an almost impossible task. But as your knowledge of English grows, you'll notice that many words share similar meanings. In addition, you'll see that clues to the meaning of any problematic word can be found in the sentence or paragraph that surrounds it.

By the end of this unit you'll have the skills to tackle any difficult word you come across. Being able to identify and use these words will make you not only a fluent reader but also a better writer and speaker.

⌄ kangaroo

2-1 *Synonyms*

Synonyms are words that have the same or almost the same meaning. Take "huge" and "gigantic" for example. English has nearly a million words, with many of them sharing a similar meaning. Being able to identify these words is a vital skill for improving your reading comprehension.

(051)

51 | Is It a Wallaby or a Kangaroo? It's a Wallaroo!

>> kangaroo crossing sign in Australia

1   An animal may get its name for all kinds of reasons. It may be named for its call, like the chiffchaff (a small European bird whose song is a simple chiff-chaff sound), or for its appearance, like the camelopard (the old name for the giraffe, which was thought to resemble a cross between a camel and a leopard). Similar to the camelopard, the wallaroo, an Australian marsupial, got its name because it seems to be stuck halfway between a wallaby and a kangaroo.   5

⌄ wallaby

2   Marsupials are a group of mammals that are almost **exclusively** native to Australasia. The female marsupial has a pouch called a marsupium, in which the young are kept through early infancy. A female wallaroo gives birth to a blind, hairless infant no more than an inch in size, which will remain in its mother's pouch for the next 237–269 days. Kangaroos, wallabies, and wallaroos are all types of marsupials that are found in Australia.   10   15

3   The color of a wallaroo depends on its **habitat**. Those that **inhabit** the rocky hills

>> baby kangaroo in its mother's pouch

✵ wallaroo

✵ Wallaroos that inhabit the rocky hills of eastern Australia are usually black or dull grey.

of eastern Australia are usually black or dull grey, while those living in the deserts of the west are reddish to better blend in with their surroundings. In addition, they are the only marsupials that have a bare, black snout, which makes it easy to **differentiate** them from their two look-alikes. 20

4 Wallaroos like to hide from the sun under granite boulders during the day. Water is a rare commodity in the harsh, dry deserts of Australia, so when wallaroos aren't hiding, they can be found digging holes that are a meter deep in an attempt to find groundwater. They are extremely agile and use their furry padded feet to navigate the rocky, uneven ground with great **precision**, feasting on grass and shrubs that they find along the way. 25 30

5 Most wallaroos are solitary beings, wary of contact with other animals and especially with humans. But if you do see one burrowing for water or napping under a rock, you'll know that though it may look like a wallaby or a kangaroo, it's neither. It's a wallaroo! 35

Questions

_____ 1. "Marsupials are a group of mammals that are almost **exclusively** native to Australasia." Which of the following is a synonym of **exclusively**?
a. Peculiarly. **b.** Oddly. **c.** Entirely. **d.** Differently.

_____ 2. "In addition, they are the only marsupials that have a bare, black snout, which makes it easy to **differentiate** them from their two look-alikes." A synonym for **differentiate** is _____.
a. distinguish **b.** mistake **c.** allow **d.** associate

_____ 3. "The color of a wallaroo depends on its **habitat**." Which of the following words has the same meaning as **habitat**?
a. Species. **b.** Lifestyle. **c.** Nutrition. **d.** Environment.

_____ 4. In the fourth paragraph, the author writes that wallaroos are able to "navigate the rocky, uneven ground with great **precision**." Which of the following is a synonym of **precision**?
a. Specialty. **b.** Exactness. **c.** Carelessness. **d.** Ignorance.

_____ 5. "Those that **inhabit** the rocky hills of eastern Australia are usually black or dull grey." A similar word to **inhabit** is _____.
a. depart **b.** enhance **c.** populate **d.** exploit

52 Lip-Reading

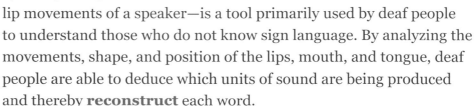

1   Lip-reading— the technique of understanding speech by interpreting the lip movements of a speaker—is a tool primarily used by deaf people to understand those who do not know sign language. By analyzing the movements, shape, and position of the lips, mouth, and tongue, deaf people are able to deduce which units of sound are being produced and thereby **reconstruct** each word.

2   In fact, those of us who do not suffer from impaired hearing also use lip-reading, albeit unconsciously. When we speak to someone, we use facial clues as well as the shape of someone's mouth to aid comprehension, particularly in environments with loud background noise.

3   One of the biggest **drawbacks** to relying solely on visual cues for lip-reading is that many sound units, or phonemes, are created by very similar lip movements. In reality, only about 30% of sounds in English can be definitely distinguished by sight alone. This is why understanding the context of a conversation is often vital to effective lip-reading. The words "meat," "beat," and "peat," for example, all have the same visual cue; however, if encountered in the sentence "The Chicago Bulls [blank] the Knicks last night," only one of these three words is possible.

> ⩔ Watch the news and focus on how people's lips move when they talk.

4   Needless to say, for people who were born deaf, learning to lip-read is a far bigger challenge than it is for those who are already familiar with these sounds. That being said, lip-reading is still not an easy skill to learn, and even when mastered, its effectiveness can be **compromised** by something as small as a mustache or a shadow.

5   If you're interested in learning to lip-read, here are some tips to get you started: Practice focusing on other people's lips while they're talking; watching the news is especially good for this as **anchormen** and anchorwomen tend ⁣ ⁣35 to speak more clearly than normal people. When you start to feel comfortable with this, watch a favorite movie or TV episode with the sound on **mute**. Try to follow the dialogue just by lip-reading. If the movie has subtitles, you can turn them on to give you a hand if you get stuck!

How to Read Lips

« Watch other people's lips while they're talking.

⌄ Watch TV on mute with the subtitles displayed. Pay attention to how people's mouths move to form the words displayed. (cc by James Morrison)

⌃ Watch TV with it on mute. Follow the dialogue by lip-reading.

Questions

_____ **1.** In the third paragraph, the writer discusses "the biggest **drawbacks** to relying solely on visual cues for lip-reading." Another word for **drawbacks** is _____.

    a. benefits   **b.** dangers   **c.** disadvantages   **d.** freedoms

_____ **2.** In the final sentence of the first paragraph, which of the following words could replace **reconstruct**?

    a. Recreate.   **b.** Remove.   **c.** Revise.   **d.** Renew.

_____ **3.** In the fourth paragraph, the author writes that the effectiveness of lip-reading "can be **compromised** by something as small as a mustache or a shadow." A synonym for **compromised** is _____.

    a. aided   **b.** protected   **c.** weakened   **d.** tested

_____ **4.** The author observes that "**anchormen** and anchorwomen tend to speak more clearly than normal people." Which of the following is closest in meaning to **anchormen**?

    a. Senators.   **b.** Pitchers.   **c.** Princes.   **d.** Newscasters.

_____ **5.** To practice lip-reading, the author suggests that you "watch a favorite movie or TV episode with the sound on **mute**." Another word for **mute** is _____.

    a. delicate   **b.** silent   **c.** immense   **d.** crooked

53 Ludwig van Beethoven

↑ 13-year-old Beethoven (c. 1783)

↑ young Beethoven

↑ Beethoven in 1803

↑ Beethoven after his loss of hearing in 1815

1   Ludwig van Beethoven was born in Bonn, Germany in 1770. His father, Johann Beethoven, was also a musician and wanted his son to be a child prodigy. Consequently, he motivated Ludwig to develop his musical talents.

2   Johann's resolution to make his son into a successful musician was so extreme that he would pull poor Ludwig out of bed in the middle of the night and force the young boy to practice piano until the early hours of the morning. 5

3   At the age of 11, Ludwig received professional piano and composition training in Bonn under the royal court's organist, and by the mid-1790s he had made a reputation for himself as a master pianist in Vienna, the musical capital of the age. By the end of the century, he was becoming known as the most important composer of his generation. 10

4   A huge turning point in Beethoven's life occurred in 1798, when his hearing started to become **impaired**. He was plagued by a constant ringing in his ears, which made it difficult for him to hear music. This caused him to **shun** company and become depressed. He even contemplated suicide. 15

5   Battling both depression and his loss of hearing, Beethoven continued to produce music with a special **adaptation** to his piano. By attaching a rod to the soundboard of his piano and biting the rod, he was able to detect vibrations of sound. The music that he created during this period expressed heroism and struggle and went on to become some of his most famous compositions. 20 25 30

6   The battle against deafness began to take its toll on the brilliant composer. After the 35

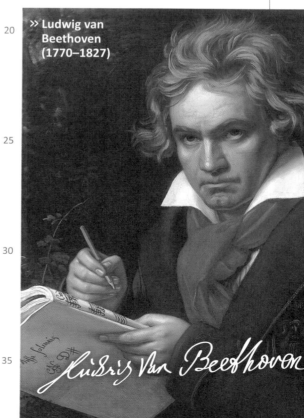

>> Ludwig van Beethoven (1770–1827)

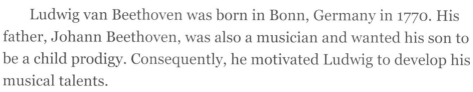

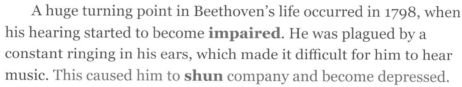

« statue of Beethoven in Central Park, New York City

» house of Ludwig van Beethoven's birth
(cc by Sir James)

performance of his *Ninth Symphony*, he turned around to see the **ecstatic** applause of the audience but broke down in tears when he realized that he couldn't hear them.

7   After a long illness, Beethoven died at   40 the age of 56 on March 26, 1827. The true cause of his death was unknown for a long time, but later analysis of his hair and skeleton suggests that he was accidentally poisoned by his doctors, who prescribed **excessive** doses of lead-based medicine. Whatever the cause, the death of the great   45 man shocked Vienna. Twenty thousand people attended his funeral procession, paying their respects to a true musical genius of their time.

Questions

_____ **1.** In the fourth paragraph, the author writes that Beethoven's hearing began to become **impaired** in 1798. Which of the following is a synonym for **impaired**?
  a. Complicated.   **b.** Damaged.   **c.** Improved.   **d.** Recovered.

_____ **2.** "This caused him to **shun** company and become depressed." **Shun** is another word for _____.
  a. reject   **b.** tackle   **c.** ambush   **d.** beckon

_____ **3.** In the fifth paragraph, the author writes that "Beethoven continued to write music with a special **adaptation** to his piano." Which of the following words is a synonym for **adaptation**?
  a. Model.   **b.** Viewer.   **c.** Adjustment.   **d.** Antique.

_____ **4.** "After the performance of his *Ninth Symphony*, he turned around to see the **ecstatic** applause of the audience." A synonym for **ecstatic** is _____.
  a. bored   **b.** common   **c.** overjoyed   **d.** doubtful

_____ **5.** Beethoven died because of "**excessive** doses of lead-based medicine." A synonym for **excessive** is _____.
  a. brisk   **b.** moderate   **c.** disastrous   **d.** extreme

≫ page from Beethoven's manuscript of the *Ninth Symphony*

≫ Beethoven Monument in Bonn, Germany
(cc by Sir James)

54 Spontaneous Human Combustion

1 On February 18, 2013, the badly burned **corpse** of 65-year-old Danny Vanzandt was found in his home in Muldrow, Oklahoma.

2 According to the county sheriff, Ron Lockhart, Vanzandt's body had been almost completely reduced to ashes except for, **bizarrely**, his head, hands, and feet; no obvious external ignition source was detected. Stranger still, there was very little damage to the house; no furniture was burned, and even objects within just three feet of the body were unharmed.

3 In order to explain these factors, it was proposed that Vanzandt had fallen victim to a strange phenomenon called Spontaneous Human Combustion (SHC), whereby a human being, with no apparent external spark or flame, simply bursts into flames and burns from within.

4 There have been around 200 documented cases of SHC over the last 300 years. Incidents are often **characterized** by the almost complete destruction of the torso, but often not the hands, feet, or head. In addition, very little fire damage happens to the room itself. Though there are many theories that propose supernatural forces as causes, a scientific explanation is, in fact, on hand.

5 The first thing to address is the reason why the person caught fire. In most cases of supposed SHC, the victim was a smoker. In addition, most victims were often either overweight, disabled, or **alcoholics**, making it difficult for them

⌃ Spontaneous human combustion refers to the death from a fire with no obvious external ignition source.

alcoholic

⌄ Most SHC victims were often either overweight, disabled, or alcoholics.

overweight disabled

5

10

15

20

25

to move quickly enough to escape a fire. The fact that no obvious source of external ignition was found can be put down to the fact that after hours of burning, this would also have been destroyed. Mr. Vanzandt, for example, was both a smoker and an alcoholic.

6   What about the other strange factors such as the undamaged   30
limbs and the enclosed nature of the fire? Well, if a person's clothes catch on fire and the person is unable to move, soon the body fat starts to melt from the heat and begins to fuel the fire. Much like a

candle, the person's clothes will keep burning slowly but with an intense but centralized heat   35
until the fuel—the fat—runs out, sometimes many hours later. This explains why the fire damage does not spread to any nearby furniture and why the person's hands and feet (not covered by clothes) remain largely **intact**.   40

« In most cases of supposed SHC, the victim was a smoker.

Questions

_____ 1. "On February 18, 2013, the badly burned **corpse** of 65-year-old Danny Vanzandt was found in his home in Muldrow, Oklahoma." Another word for **corpse** is _____.
   a. vehicle   **b.** housewife   **c.** body   **d.** human

_____ 2. "Vanzandt's body had been almost completely reduced to ashes except for, **bizarrely**, his head, hands, and feet." Which of the following is a synonym for **bizarrely**?
   a. Grossly.   **b.** Brutally.   **c.** Concisely   **d.** Peculiarly.

_____ 3. "Incidents are often **characterized** by the almost complete destruction of the torso." A synonym for **characterized** is _____.
   a. disclosed   **b.** documented   **c.** declared   **d.** distinguished

_____ 4. "In addition, most victims were often either overweight, disabled, or **alcoholics**." The word **alcoholics** could best be replaced by _____.
   a. drunks   **b.** celebrities   **c.** frauds   **d.** bachelors

_____ 5. In the final paragraph, the author explains why, in certain cases of death by fire, a person's hands and feet "remain largely **intact**." Another word for **intact** is _____.
   a. faultless   **b.** undamaged   **c.** undefeated   **d.** nontoxic

55 Deadly Space Junk

(055)

1   We often think of space as an unexplored frontier, a dark and endless stretch of emptiness. But did you know that there are literally tons of random junk just floating around up there?

2   This material is called space debris, or more informally: "space junk." Some of it is natural, like **chunks** of floating rock or metal, which are called meteoroids. The rest of it is man-made, like old satellites or rocket parts that are no longer **functional**. But make no mistake: all space debris is a danger to astronauts and satellites alike.

3   The risk comes from the high speeds that space debris can travel at while in orbit. Imagine a tiny screw floating in space. Not terribly threatening, right? Now imagine that screw traveling at a speed of 17,500 mph (about 28,000 kilometers per hour). At that speed, it could easily pierce an astronaut's space suit or even the walls of the International Space Station.

4   All space debris can be dangerous under the right circumstances, and there's no shortage of the stuff. NASA estimates that there are over 20,000 pieces of space debris, each larger than a softball, and another 500,000 pieces larger than a marble, orbiting the planet. According to European Space Agency (ESA), there are 166 million more that are too small to track. As if that wasn't bad enough, space junk can multiply on its own. When one piece of space junk hits another one, both can **shatter** into thousands of new pieces.

5   There's still no easy way to clean up space debris, though new experimental methods are being developed. One is the University of

⩔ U.S. Air Force reservist on a NASA mission to retrieve space debris (fallen satellite parts) from Mongolia, 2011 (photo by Master Sgt. Linda Welz)

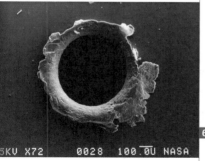

⌄ bullet hole caused by a piece of space debris

5KV X72   0028   100.0U NASA

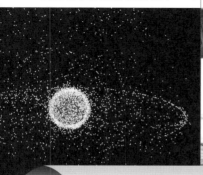

⌄ illustration of objects in Earth's orbit that are currently being tracked. Approximately 95% of the dots are orbital debris. (NASA)

Surrey's RemoveDEBRIS project, which aims to deploy 25 a giant sail to collect space junk. Until a clean-up solution can be found, NASA will focus on tracking the space debris that's already out there. NASA maintains a **catalogue** of over 21,000 tracked pieces of space debris. Whenever one of these pieces threatens a ship, NASA 30 will make sure that the ship changes its position.

6   So long as there's untracked space debris, human activity in space will face deadly risks. Space programs around the world have been lucky so far. There have only been a handful of **collisions** in the past few decades. 35 But how long until our luck runs out?

« U.S. Air Force reservists retrieving fallen space debris (a 480-pound rocket part) from Mongolia, 2011 (photo by Master Sgt. Linda Welz)

Questions

_____ 1. In the second paragraph, the author writes that "Some of it is natural, like **chunks** of floating rock or metal, . . ." Which of the following is a synonym for **chunk**?

    a. Container.   **b.** Lump.   **c.** Outline.   **d.** Shape.

_____ 2. Which of the following is closest in meaning to **functional** in the second paragraph?

    a. Old.   **b.** Expensive.   **c.** Working.   **d.** Dangerous.

_____ 3. Which of the following is a synonym for **collision** in the final paragraph?

    a. Direction.   **b.** Crash.   **c.** Equipment.   **d.** Agreement.

_____ 4. "NASA maintains a **catalogue** of over 21,000 tracked pieces of space debris." Which of the following is closest in meaning to **catalogue**?

    a. Index.   **b.** Technology.   **c.** Program.   **d.** Type.

_____ 5. "When one piece of space junk hits another one, both can **shatter** into thousands of new pieces." A synonym for **shatter** is _____.

    a. miss   **b.** exchange   **c.** resemble   **d.** break

56 (056)
Body Language

1   My grandfather always used to say, "Words can lie but bodies always tell the truth." He was a **firm** believer in the importance of body language, or how our   5 posture, movements, and facial expressions often provide hints about our moods and personality. Initially, I found these lectures on body language to be extremely boring. Years later, however, they turned out to be invaluable.   10

2   My first big job interview provided a lesson on the importance of body language. I remember sitting in the waiting room and eyeing my nearest **competitor**. He was **slouching** in his chair with his arms crossed in front of him. If my grandfather were there, he would have politely told him that his body language implied a lazy, antisocial personality. When it came time   15 for my interview, I abided by all the rules of positive body language: I maintained good eye contact and posture to convey **self-confidence**, and I made sure not to fidget with my hands or feet. The interview ended up going so well that I was hired on the spot.

⌄ Eye contact and posture convey
  self-confidence.

3 After that, I applied my grandfather's theories of good body language to every aspect of my life. When out on a date, I knew if the girl was interested in me. If she always moved closer, kept her hands and arms open, and smiled and maintained eye contact, I knew she was a keeper. However, someone who tilted her body backward, looked off to the side a lot, or fiddled with her hands wasn't worth much of an emotional investment.

>> Good body language can open doors in someone's professional and personal life.

4 There was even one time when I knew a breakup was coming months in advance, all because I noticed a few telltale signs that my partner was lying. According to my grandfather, liars will often touch their face or hands, cross their arms, and lean away from you. As much as I didn't want to believe it at the time, it turns out he's totally correct.

5 I owe a great deal to my grandfather for the insight into body language he gave me. Good body language can open doors in someone's professional and personal life, and bad body language can be a considerable **handicap**.

Questions

☆ Liars will often cross their arms.

_____ **1.** Which of the following means the opposite of **competitor** in the second paragraph?
   a. Boss.   **b.** Child.   **c.** Teammate.   **d.** Opponent.

_____ **2.** "He was **slouching** in his chair with his arms crossed in front of him." The opposite of **slouching** is _____.
   a. crouching   **b.** straightening   **c.** bending   **d.** lounging

_____ **3.** When someone has a lot of **self-confidence**, he or she is NOT _____.
   a. timid   **b.** fearless   **c.** assured   **d.** brave

_____ **4.** The author describes his grandfather as being a **firm** believer in body language. The opposite of **firm** is _____.
   a. solid   **b.** weak   **c.** strong   **d.** fixed

_____ **5.** The opposite of **handicap** in the statement "bad body language can be a considerable **handicap**" is _____.
   a. clue   **b.** burden   **c.** communication   **d.** benefit

>> Pluto

⌄ computer-generated impression
of the Plutonian surface
(cc by ESO/L. Calçada)

⌃ rough comparison of the
sizes of Earth and Pluto

57 Is Pluto a Planet?

1 August 24, 2006, is a day that will stand out in the minds of science teachers and planetarium fans worldwide. That's the day when Pluto lost its status as a planet, forcing a mad **rush** of revised lesson plans, new textbook printings, and incorrect trivia answers. 5

2 Pluto's reclassification resulted from shifts in standards within the scientific community. The International Astronomical Union (IAU), an international organization in charge of naming practices in space, held a vote on adopting new criteria to dictate what makes a planet. After several **vigorous** debates, new criteria were voted through by a 10 majority of the IAU's members. A planet was **subsequently** defined as a celestial body that orbits the sun, exceeds a certain threshold of generating its own gravity, and has cleared the orbit of its immediate neighborhood.

3 Although Pluto passes the planet test for the first two criteria, it fails on the third. Pluto has not cleared out its own neighborhood. In fact, it's located 15 in the middle of a large field of space debris called the Kuiper belt. The Kuiper Belt is located beyond Neptune, and it has several **celestial** bodies of **comparable** size to Pluto. Had the competing argument won out in the 20 2006 IAU debate, these bodies would be considered planets along with Pluto, and the Solar System would have 12 planets.

>> protest and counter-protest of Pluto
de-planet controversy

>> solar system

4   We all know what actually happened, however. Pluto was kicked out of   25
the planet club and a new classification was invented: the "dwarf planet."
Dwarf planets refer to any **celestial** body that fulfills the first two criteria of
the IAU planet rules, but not the third. Now, these dwarf planets have only
two paths back to astronomic credibility: either several asteroids or other
rocks crash into them, allowing them to increase their overall mass and   30
regain planet status, or they wait until the scientists of the IAU change the
definition of what constitutes a planet again. Until then, Pluto stands as the
sole example of a celestial body that experienced the highs of being a planet
and the lows of being on the outside looking in.

Questions

_____ **1.** Which of the following means the opposite of **rush** in the first paragraph?
    a. Surge.   **b.** Factor.   **c.** Angle.   **d.** Delay.

_____ **2.** Which of the following means the opposite of **vigorous** in the second paragraph?
    a. Confused.   **b.** Feeble.   **c.** Defensive.   **d.** Intense.

_____ **3.** The word with the opposite meaning to **subsequently** in the second paragraph
phrase "A planet was **subsequently** defined as . . ." is _____.
    a. forever   **b.** never   **c.** afterward   **d.** previously

_____ **4.** If two things are NOT **comparable**, they are _____.
    a. disordered   **b.** planetary   **c.** rounded   **d.** dissimilar

_____ **5.** Which of the following means the opposite of **celestial**, as it is used several times
in the article?
    a. Heavenly.   **b.** Earthly.   **c.** Ancient.   **d.** Technical.

>> Angkor Wat

58 Angkor Wat

1 The largest religious monument in the world isn't Vatican City in Italy, the Kaaba in Mecca, or Jokhang Temple in Lhasa. It's Cambodia's Angkor Wat, a place that was perhaps best described by one of the first Westerners to see it. He said, "It is of such **extraordinary** construction that it is not possible to describe with a pen, particularly since it is like no other building in the world." 5

2 Angkor Wat is a temple that was originally built for the Hindu god Vishnu, only later to be converted into a Buddhist place of **worship**. It was built by King Suryavarman II sometime between AD 1113 and AD 1150. There is one 65-meter tower on the top of the 10 temple, surrounded by four smaller towers. This is how the original builder visualized Mount Meru, which is where the gods are believed to reside in Hindu mythology. It's also surrounded by a large moat that's roughly four meters deep. Thus, the temple has all of the important elements comprising a memorable picture: **exquisite** 15 architecture, lush vegetation, and the reflective surface of the moat. Unsurprisingly, tourists usually flock to Angkor Wat at sunrise in order to capture that perfect shot with their camera.

3 Some people refer to Angkor Wat as the "jungle temple." This is because it's located in a **vast** complex of ancient **ruins**, some of 20 which are being slowly consumed by giant banyan trees. The 400 km² complex is called Angkor, and it's home to the various capital cities of the ancient Khmer Empire that dominated Southeast Asia from AD 802 to AD 1431. Whenever a new ruler took over, he would build a new city. Some of these cities would have had hundreds of thousands 25 of people living in them back in the glory days of the empire.

⌃ Cambodia's Angkor Wat is the largest religious monument in the world.

4   Angkor Wat is now one of the most popular tourist destinations in Asia. People who are interested in visiting should fly to Siem Reap, which is about 5.5 km south of Angkor Wat. From there it's possible to organize tours of the entire Angkor temple complex, but don't forget: there are lots of different ruins 30 to explore, so give yourself a few extra days in the area.

⌄ Some people refer to Angkor Wat as the "jungle temple."

⌃ Suryavarman II depicted in a bas-relief at Angkor Wat

Questions

_____ **1.** Which of the following is the opposite of **extraordinary** as it is used in the first paragraph?
    a. Special.   **b.** Extensive.   **c.** Normal.   **d.** Ancient.

_____ **2.** Which of the following means the opposite of the word **worship** as it is used in the second paragraph?
    a. Adoration.   **b.** Respect.   **c.** Criticism.   **d.** Religion.

_____ **3.** Which of the following means the opposite of **exquisite** in the second paragraph?
    a. Plain.   **b.** Precise.   **c.** Colorful.   **d.** Striking.

_____ **4.** The author writes that Angkor Wat is "located in a **vast** complex of ancient ruins." When something is **vast**, it is NOT _____.
    a. enormous   **b.** gigantic   **c.** tiny   **d.** extensive

_____ **5.** Which of the following is NOT an example of **ruins** as the word is used in the third paragraph?
    a. A house burned down in a fire.
    b. The remains of a lost city.
    c. A palace decorated with gold and silver.
    d. A town destroyed by an earthquake.

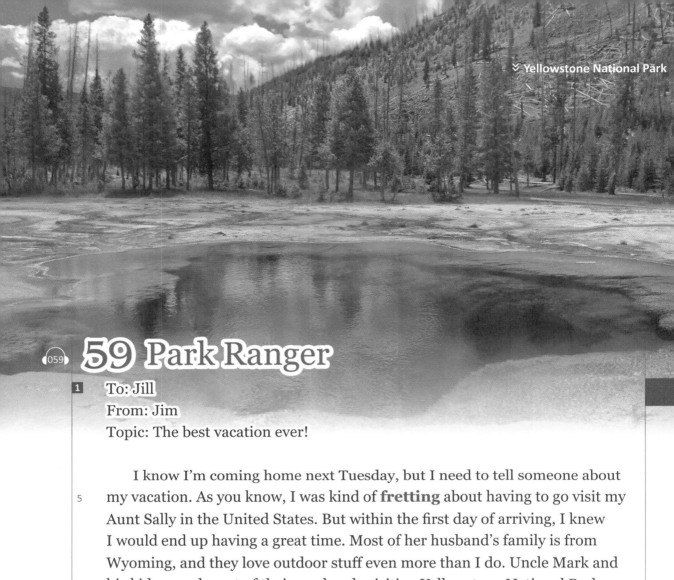

🎧059 59 Park Ranger

1 To: Jill
From: Jim
Topic: The best vacation ever!

5   I know I'm coming home next Tuesday, but I need to tell someone about my vacation. As you know, I was kind of **fretting** about having to go visit my Aunt Sally in the United States. But within the first day of arriving, I knew I would end up having a great time. Most of her husband's family is from Wyoming, and they love outdoor stuff even more than I do. Uncle Mark and his kids spend most of their weekends visiting Yellowstone National Park,
10 where they go on treks through the **wilderness**.

2   But that's not even the half of it. I've also discovered the coolest job in the world, and I totally know what I want to be when I graduate from university now. Uncle Mark's sister Betty works as a park ranger at Yellowstone National Park. I had never heard of
15 a park ranger before, but they're kind of like a mix between outdoor cop and scientist. They work in national parks in the United States, and they have lots of different duties. For example, Betty told me that last month she tracked down some thugs who
20 were on the prowl for rare **endangered** species. She actually jumped out of a car with some local cops and yelled, "Hands up!" How cool is that?

» park ranger

3   Park rangers also do a lot of nature stuff. Sometimes, Betty is sent out to make sure that certain **vulnerable** habitats are being preserved. There's even the odd time when she takes visitors out on   25 a tour and introduces them to the local ecology. I guess a park ranger is actually part cop, part scientist, and part teacher!

4   Betty said that the only qualification necessary to become a park ranger is a love for the natural world. I told her that sounds slightly **absurd**, and she laughed and got a bit more specific. Supposedly,   30 it's a good idea to have a bachelor's degree in a scientific or an environmental field. I heard her loud and clear. I'm already looking up science programs at the local universities. I'm positively destined to be a park ranger!

Questions

≫ park ranger leading visitors on an educational tour

_____ **1.** Which of the following means the opposite of **fretting** in the first paragraph?
- **a.** Relaxed.
- **b.** Worrying.
- **c.** Crying.
- **d.** Bothered.

_____ **2.** Which of the following means the opposite of **wilderness** in the first paragraph?
- **a.** Mountains.
- **b.** Lightning.
- **c.** Indoors.
- **d.** Nature.

_____ **3.** When something is **endangered**, it is NOT _____.
- **a.** at risk
- **b.** thriving
- **c.** threatened
- **d.** rare

_____ **4.** In the fourth paragraph, the author mentions that Betty said something **absurd**. Which of the following has the opposite meaning of **absurd**?
- **a.** Crazy.
- **b.** Rational.
- **c.** Loony.
- **d.** Ridiculous.

_____ **5.** Which of the following means the opposite of **vulnerable** in the third paragraph?
- **a.** Dangerous.
- **b.** Complicated.
- **c.** Protected.
- **d.** Overgrown.

≫ Park rangers are like a mix between outdoor cop and scientist.

133

60 Easter Island

1 There is an isolated island in the vast stretch of the Pacific Ocean, somewhere between Chile in South America and Tahiti in Polynesia. The history of this island highlights some of the best and worst aspects of human civilization. You might have heard of this place before. It's called Easter Island, and it's a UNESCO World Heritage Site.

≫ Easter Island is covered with moai statues shaped like humans.

2 Easter Island was first settled around AD 300 by a Polynesian people with a Stone Age level of technological development. They called the island Rapa Nui, and their culture evolved in total **isolation** until the Europeans arrived in 1722. But the most interesting thing is where these people originally came from. According to some theories, the original inhabitants of Easter Island **migrated** from somewhere in Polynesia in search of a better life. These early explorers managed to cover thousands of kilometers of ocean in little canoes.

3 Of course, Easter Island is best known for the stone statues that the locals built. The island is covered with moai statues shaped like humans. Experts still disagree over how the locals were able to move such heavy slabs of stone. Experts also aren't sure about what the statues were used for in the first place, though most believe they were used in some form of religious rites or ritual. Whatever the intention of their original creators, the moai statues stand as a **timeless** reminder of the best in creative endeavor.

≪ Easter Island moai

5

10

15

20

25

4 However, there are a few **disturbing** chapters in the story 30 of Easter Island. For one, the island experienced a disastrous environmental transformation sometime in the sixteenth century. The trigger for this disaster is anyone's guess. Some believe it was the result of overpopulation and environmental destruction, and others think that the introduction of an invasive species caused vegetation on the island 35 to wither and die. The crisis caused the population to split into two different groups, one of which ended up pushing over all of the moai statues on the island. Thus, when the Europeans arrived, they found a **bleak** place with a population of 2,000–3,000 people; far fewer than the 15,000 people who are thought to have been living on the island 40 a century before.

⌃ *A View of Monuments of Easter Island, Rapanui* (c. 1775–1776) by William Hodges (1744–1797), the first known painting of Easter Island

Questions

_____ 1. Which of the following situations has the opposite quality of **isolation** as it is used in the second paragraph?
   a. Sleeping in a treehouse.
   b. Riding a bike on a mountain path.
   c. Riding the subway during rush hour.
   d. Going on a hike alone.

_____ 2. If someone **migrated**, then he or she definitely did NOT _____.
   a. stay
   b. wander
   c. leave
   d. shift

_____ 3. Which of the following means the opposite of **disturbing** in the fourth paragraph?
   a. Nervous.
   b. Ancient.
   c. Pleasant.
   d. Painful.

_____ 4. Which of the following descriptions means the opposite of **timeless** as it is used in the third paragraph?
   a. Something that keeps the time.
   b. Something that can't be understood.
   c. Something that is very valuable.
   d. Something that doesn't last long.

_____ 5. Which of the following means the opposite of **bleak** in the final paragraph?
   a. Heavy.
   b. Cheerful.
   c. Dangerous.
   d. Beneficial.

English words can have a variety of different meanings. For example, the adjective "fine" can be used to mean "acceptable," "thin," or "attractive." When you come across a potentially confusing word, it's important to examine the context to determine its meaning. Looking for context clues can also help you deduce the meanings of words that you are completely unfamiliar with.

⌃ the tam-tams in Montreal
(cc by Genséric Morel)

61 The Montreal Tam-Tams

🎧 061

1 Every Sunday afternoon in a park bordering the progressive Le Plateau neighborhood of Montreal, thousands of people of all ages, nationalities, and economic backgrounds gather to play instruments, sing, and dance. These weekly summer events, hosted at the Sir George-Étienne Cartier Monument in Mount Royal Park are known as "tam-tams"—a name that refers to a type of African drum—and have become a tradition among Montreal's **bohemians**. 5

2 Drummers cluster around the statue, trading rhythms, elaborating on each other's **beats**, improvising riffs, and lulling the hordes of spectators into a trance. A circle is cleared in front of the drummers for dancers— mostly hippies dancing without any shyness, though you'll be surprised how quickly even the most conservative viewers lose themselves to the beat. 10

3 Le Plateau is one of Canada's most culturally diverse districts, and many artists, musicians, and writers inhabit this area because of the cheap rent for apartments and studios. In the 1960s, it became known as the avant-garde area of Montreal, and the stores began selling clothing, music, and books that catered to the funky **tastes** of its residents. 15 20

⌃ The Montreal tam-tams are a drum circle based in Montreal, Canada.

4   In the 1970s and 1980s, Mount Royal Park was where many of these artists and musicians would meet to have lunch or just spend an afternoon together. Musicians—namely drummers—brought   25 instruments, and eventually spontaneous jam sessions got started, subsequently attracting poets who recited their works to the music being performed.

5   Word got out about these gatherings, attracting even more people, until it was decided that these gatherings would happen every Sunday   30 afternoon. Not only did people have a great time at these gatherings, but it was also an excellent opportunity for musicians to network and schedule further meetings in order to work together on musical projects.

6   Tam-tams have now become a sort of Montreal **institution**, attracting thousands of people every week and representing freedom   35 and creativity. The events **commence** around noon on Sunday and end at sunset. Everyone is invited to attend a tam-tam, but it is recommended that you bring an instrument, for it's the crowd participation that makes every tam-tam the distinctive occasion that it is. So head over, go with the flow, and give in to the inevitable; the   40 rhythm is definitely going to get you!

Questions

_____ **1.** In the first paragraph, the writer states that tam-tams have become a tradition among the city's **bohemians**. From the context of the article, the word **bohemian** most likely refers to a(n) _____.
   a. first-time visitor to a foreign city
   b. artist or musician who lives freely
   c. teacher who specializes in teaching drums
   d. descendant of immigrants

_____ **2.** The word **beat**, as it is used in the second paragraph, means _____.
   a. defeat   **b.** hit   **c.** rhythm   **d.** heart

_____ **3.** In the third paragraph, the word **tastes** most likely means _____.
   a. preferences   **b.** flavors   **c.** samples   **d.** senses

_____ **4.** "Tam-tams have now become a sort of Montreal **institution**, attracting thousands of people every week and representing freedom and creativity." The word **institution** here means _____.
   a. organization   **b.** institute   **c.** society   **d.** custom

_____ **5.** "The events **commence** around noon on Sunday and end at sunset." From the context of this sentence, we can infer that **commence** means _____.
   a. conclude   **b.** start   **c.** continue   **d.** pause

137

062 62 The Hum

1   Listen carefully. Can you hear it—a low rumbling, constant and rhythmic? If so, what you're hearing might be the Hum. Described as a persistent, low-frequency buzzing akin to a drill or car engine, it is heard by people in towns and cities all over the world, from New Zealand to Scotland. But not everyone can hear it. In the places where it appears, on average only about 2% of the population is aware of its existence. But those who are aware claim that it **disrupts** sleep, causes headaches, and sometimes even induces nosebleeds.   5

2   Tinnitus, a condition that causes the sufferer to hear a constant, high-pitched ringing sound in his ears, has been cited as a possible cause. However, the Hum is more of a low **drone** than a high-pitched ringing. Further, some   10 people are only able to hear the Hum in certain places—their homes, for example. Others say that the sound is much louder indoors than outdoors, and still more claim that they can feel the vibrations of the sound in their bodies.

3   Many **skeptics** insist that the Hum is simply normal background noise generated by traffic, power lines, wind farms, and the like. Power plants,   15 aircraft, industrial fans, and a Hawaiian volcano have all been found to be sources of the Hum that, once shut down, provided welcome relief for hundreds. The fact that the Hum is identified as a low-frequency sound is also   20 significant, as low-frequency noises travel farther and through more materials than high-pitched ones and may even be **amplified** by walls or enclosed   25 spaces, such as houses.

4   But what, then, is the cause when no single source can be identified (around two-thirds of the cases)? According to Dr. David   30 Baguley of Addenbrooke's Hospital in Cambridge, UK, the Hum can be explained by a natural human defense mechanism: oversensitive hearing.

⌄ The Hum is more of a low drone than a high-pitched ringing.

⌃ The Hum can be a very disturbing phenomenon.

5   Our hearing has evolved to become especially sensitive at times of   35
extreme danger or stress. For some people, this becomes a vicious **cycle**
where the more they focus on normal background noise, the more anxious
they get; the more anxious they get, the more their ears turn up the volume.
Though it may seem laughable, the cure for the Hum could just be to relax.

⌃ The hum disrupts sleep, causes headaches,
and sometimes even induces nosebleeds.

Questions

____1. In the first paragraph, the author writes that the Hum "**disrupts** sleep, causes
headaches, and sometimes even induces nosebleeds." The word **disrupt** most likely
means to _____.
   a. make it difficult for something to continue normally
   b. cause or encourage something to happen
   c. make something seem less important than it actually is
   d. keep something working well and in good condition

____2. From the context of the second paragraph, the word **drone** most likely means _____.
   a. an aircraft without a pilot   **b.** a lazy person who does not work
   c. a continuous deep noise   **d.** a stingless male bee

____3. Considering the information given in both the second and third paragraphs, what does
the word **amplified** in the third paragraph likely mean?
   a. Made quieter.   **b.** Made higher-pitched.
   c. Made louder.   **d.** Made lower-pitched.

____4. "Many **skeptics** insist that the Hum is simply normal background noise generated by
traffic, power lines, wind farms, and the like." The word **skeptics** describes people
who _____.
   a. always expect good things to happen
   b. doubt that strange claims are true
   c. are able to imaginatively plan the future
   d. live solitary and lonely lives

____5. In the final paragraph, the author describes a "vicious **cycle**." In the context of the
paragraph, what does **cycle** mean?
   a. A bicycle or motorcycle.   **b.** A set of creative works.
   c. A long period of time.   **d.** A repeated series of events.

63
In Vitro Meat

1   Hamburgers are a great comfort food. They're tasty, juicy, and satisfying, but no one would argue that they're healthy. But one day, perhaps not too far in the future, hamburgers that taste great but have the same fat **profile** as salmon could be on the market. This is just one of the possibilities that growing meat in vitro (in a lab), rather than killing an animal for it, is set to offer us in the twenty-first century.   5

2   Currently, meat production is one of the major causes of environmental damage threatening the stability of our global ecosystem. As much as 18% of global greenhouse gas emissions come as a result of meat production, and with human population expected to **rocket** to over 9.8 billion by 2050,   10 scientists worldwide have suggested that in vitro meat may be a crucial part of the solution to the feared global food shortage.

3   Animal rights organizations have hailed recent developments in the field as a major step toward reducing animal cruelty and saving the environment. Investors seem to agree, and have been lining up to help this   15 new technology succeed. Even the major chicken producer Tyson has gotten in on the action.

4   In vitro meat is grown by soaking stem cells in a nutrient-rich soup and then manipulating them to grow into muscle tissue. This has been successfully done with chicken, duck, and beef, though opinions seem to   20 vary on the **issue** of taste.

5   Oddly enough, one of the biggest problems for scientists is not how to grow the meat in the first place; it's getting the feel right. Real meat is composed of a **myriad** of textures that tickle the taste buds in just the right   25 way. Blood vessels, pockets of fat, and stringy tendons are all things that make meat feel like meat, and give scientists a real headache to recreate.

>> In the future, hamburgers that taste great but have the same fat profile as salmon could be on the market.

6 One team of Dutch scientists may have come the closest to achieving **this goal**. By growing 20,000 strips of muscle tissue and painstakingly assembling them one by one, they managed to produce a hamburger that tasted "reasonably good," according to one member of the team.

7 That hamburger cost a cool $325,000 when it was created in 2013. The price is now down to lower than $12. Whenever lab meat makes it into restaurants, affording it will be no problem for hungry meat eaters.

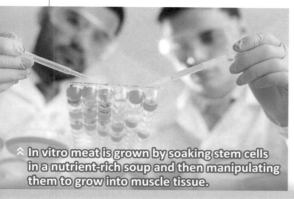

↟ In vitro meat is grown by soaking stem cells in a nutrient-rich soup and then manipulating them to grow into muscle tissue.

Questions

_____ **1.** In the first paragraph, the writer says that one day, hamburgers that "have the same fat **profile** as salmon" could be on the market. What does the word **profile** mean in this context?
   a. The outline of a person's face when observed from the side.
   b. A paragraph or short article giving someone's biographical information.
   c. Data expressing a thing's significant features.
   d. The outline of something that you see against a background.

_____ **2.** What does **rocket** mean as it is used in the second paragraph?
   a. To move quickly in a special machine.
   b. A firework that explodes with colored lights.
   c. To increase rapidly and suddenly.
   d. A craft capable of reaching space.

_____ **3.** "This has been successfully done with chicken, duck, and beef, though opinions seem to vary on the **issue** of taste." What does **issue** mean here?
   a. A particular edition of a magazine.   **b.** A thing that comes from a particular place.
   c. A problem or difficulty.   **d.** A topic of discussion.

_____ **4.** "Real meat is composed of a **myriad** of textures that tickle the taste buds in just the right way." What does **myriad** mean as it is used in the fifth paragraph?
   a. A large number.   **b.** A shortage.   **c.** A gradual decline.   **d.** A tiny speck.

_____ **5.** "One team of Dutch scientists may have come the closest to achieving **this goal**." What does **this goal** refer to here?
   a. Making an affordable in vitro hamburger.
   b. Reproducing the complex structure of real meat.
   c. Making in vitro hamburger with the same fat profile as salmon.
   d. Reducing greenhouse gas emissions.

∧ People are 30 times more likely to laugh if they are with others.

» Babies laugh a lot more than grown-ups.

64 Teenager's Blog: The Magic of Laughter

1   Hi, everyone. Welcome back to my daily blog, where I write about the interesting stuff that I find online each day. Today's entry is a bit science-y, but I hope you'll enjoy reading it anyway. I'm sure you're all familiar with the phrase "laughter is the best medicine." I always thought it was just a saying, but I read an article online today that explained that laughter actually has genuine medical **benefits**.   5

2   First, though, let me tell you some facts about laughter. Apparently, we laugh a lot more when we're babies than we do after we grow up. On average, babies laugh 300 times a day, while adults laugh only 17 times a day; for my math teacher, Mr. Reginald "Chuckles" Savage, this figure is probably more like 17 times in his whole life!   10

3   In addition, according to the **encyclopedia** app on my phone, people are much less likely to laugh if they're alone. In fact, you're almost 30 times more likely to laugh at something if you have company. Next time you watch a sitcom by yourself, pay attention to how many times   15 you laugh out loud—I mean big belly laughs (the kind that makes you spray potato chips everywhere). Then compare that to when you're watching TV with a friend. I guarantee you'll laugh a lot more with your buddy than you do all by your lonesome. Why? Because laughing makes the social   20 **bond** between two people stronger, see?

« Laughter is the best medicine.

142

4   So, now we're done warming up. Let's get down to business: laughter as medicine. OK, no one's claiming that we should replace all doctors with clowns or that people should throw their pills away and buy a Simpsons box set instead. Let's keep things in perspective here. But studies have shown 25 that laughing actually causes your blood vessels to **dilate**, increasing blood flow and protecting you against heart trouble. Laughter also causes the brain to release endorphins, natural feel-good chemicals, which help reduce stress and can relieve physical pain. On top of that, laughing increases the production of infection-fighting antibodies, making you more resistant to 30 disease. So the next time you feel a bit under the weather, read a comic book or watch a stand-up comedian. You'll **feel right as rain** before you know it!

« People are much less likely to laugh if they're alone.

» Laughing causes your blood vessels to dilate, increasing blood flow.

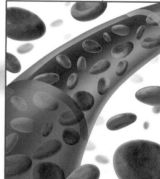

Questions

_____ 1. In the context of the first paragraph, **benefits** means _____.
a. acts of kindness
b. charity events
c. useful effects
d. insurance payments

_____ 2. "In addition, according to the **encyclopedia** app on my phone, people are much less likely to laugh if they're alone." The word encyclopedia most likely refers to a(n) _____.
a. book of famous sayings
b. medical journal
c. collection of information
d. instruction manual

_____ 3. In the final paragraph, the writer says that laughing "causes your blood vessels to **dilate**, increasing blood flow." Which of the following is the most likely definition of **dilate**?
a. To make something narrower.
b. To make something move more slowly.
c. To stop something working.
d. To make something more open.

_____ 4. In the context of the third paragraph, the word **bond** means _____.
a. a written, legal agreement
b. an emotional connection
c. a rope or a chain
d. a sum of money

_____ 5. What does **feel right as rain** in the final paragraph mean?
a. Feel sweaty.
b. Not feel very well.
c. Feel perfectly fine.
d. Feel homesick.

>> Viking warrior

65 The Vikings

1 The Vikings were fierce warriors and invaders who conquered much of Europe between the eighth and eleventh centuries. They lived in what is now modern-day Scandinavia and had a reputation for being cruel, vicious 5 killers. Their skills in warfare were unsurpassed, as was their aptitude for **seafaring**.

>> Viking warrior carving in Scandinavia

2 The Vikings were extremely tough individuals who endured many hardships such as cold and hunger due to the extreme northern latitudes of their countries. But dealing with such a harsh climate 10 instilled in them an ability to **brave** anything that nature could throw at them, even terrible storms that raged during long winter months at sea. And it wasn't just warriors who braved these dangers, either. Owing to their desire not to be separated from their families, the Vikings often took their wives and 15 children on ships and sailed off into uncharted waters.

>> Viking longship

3 Famed for their **navigation** skills, the Vikings mastered the oceans with their sleek, **versatile** longships, which could carry enough provisions to enable travel over 20 vast distances while remaining agile enough for combat. Their courage and spirit of exploration resulted in the discovery of Iceland, Greenland, 25 and the Faroe islands; they even made it as far

<< statue of Leif Eriksson (c. 970–1020) in the United States

>> *Leif Eriksson Discovers America* (1893) by Christian Krohg (1852–1925)

west as the Americas. The first European to actually set foot in the Americas was the Viking Leif Eriksson in the eleventh century. One story goes that he was on his way to Greenland when he sailed off course and found himself, by accident, 30 on a whole new continent. He called it "Vinland" (wine land) because of all the grapes growing there.

4   What of the Vikings now? Well, true to the Vikings' fighting spirit, their culture could not be defeated by something as feeble as time. The hammer-wielding god of thunder, Thor; the shape-shifter and mischief maker, Loki; 35 and many other mythical beings from Viking **mythology** will probably already be familiar to you from the 2011 blockbuster *Thor* and the series of comics it was based on. But the influence of the Vikings goes even deeper. Not many people know that we get the names of our weekdays from Viking gods. Thursday is Thor's day, and 40 Wednesday is named after Woden (or Odin), Allfather of the gods. Friday is the day of Freya, the Viking goddess of love.

>> *Thor* series movie posters

Questions

_____ **1.** The word **brave**, as it is used in the second paragraph, means _____.
  a. excellent or splendid   **b.** to be willing to do dangerous things
  c. to endure with courage   **d.** a Native American warrior

_____ **2.** "Their skills in warfare were unsurpassed, as was their aptitude for **seafaring**." Considering the content of the article, **seafaring** probably means _____.
  a. the use of the sea for travel   **b.** political debate and argument
  c. preparation of magnificent feasts **d.** the conducting of fair criminal trials

_____ **3.** In the third paragraph, the author says that the Vikings were "famed for their **navigation** skills." The correct definition of **navigation** is _____.
  a. the practice of buying and selling goods
  b. the science of getting from place to place
  c. the art of composing poetry
  d. the science of constructing buildings

_____ **4.** In the final paragraph, the author mentions some characters from Viking **mythology**. Considering the context of the paragraph, **mythology** most likely refers to _____.
  a. modern entertainment   **b.** ancient stories
  c. factual reports   **d.** medical knowledge

_____ **5.** In the third paragraph, the author describes the Viking longships as **versatile**. **Versatile** means _____.
  a. elaborately decorated   **b.** poorly constructed
  c. difficult to recognize   **d.** having many uses

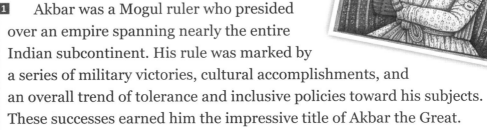
>> Mogul emperor
Akbar (1542–1605)

66 | Akbar

1   Akbar was a Mogul ruler who presided over an empire spanning nearly the entire Indian subcontinent. His rule was marked by a series of military victories, cultural accomplishments, and an overall trend of tolerance and inclusive policies toward his subjects.   5 These successes earned him the impressive title of Akbar the Great.

2   Akbar's success was never a sure thing. When Akbar was born in 1542, his father was poor and living in exile. His father regained power in 1555 only to die soon after and leave Akbar in control at the age of 14. At the time, the kingdom was small and **insignificant**, but Akbar   10 and his regent would soon change all that. Together they organized a successful military campaign to **seize** control of northern India from the Afghans. In 1560, Akbar dismissed his regent and took full control.

⌃ Akbar leads his armies during an attack.

3   Subsequent events helped Akbar to eventually earn a celebrated place in the history books. He immediately set about reorganizing   15 the military and instituted the mansabdari system, which increased efficiency and rewarded soldiers for their service. Akbar also took advantage of technological innovations involving cannons, defensive structures, and the use of elephants. These innovations   20 combined with Akbar's natural abilities as a general to produce a **string** of military victories that expanded the borders of the Mogul Empire.   25

⌃ Akbar leads the Mogul army during a campaign.

4   Akbar didn't just expand the state, but strengthened its administration as well. Most of the people who lived in lands he conquered weren't Muslims like   30

>> the Mogul emperor Akbar depicted training an elephant

Akbar. Instead of taxing these people more than Muslim citizens, as was normal at the time, he adopted a fair rate across the board. He also appointed Hindus to important positions within the government. Some people even believe that the tolerance displayed by Akbar **set the stage** for the multiculturalism that exists in modern India. 35

5 This was a period when the arts also thrived. Akbar developed the Mogul style of architecture during his reign, which combined Persian, Hindu, and Islamic elements. He was also a **patron of the arts**, and his court was said to be populated by artists, poets, philosophers, and musicians. Akbar truly was a ruler of many talents. 40

⌃ Akbar holds a religious assembly of different faiths.

⌃ Fatehpur Sikri, India, a city built by the great Mogul emperor Akbar

Questions

_____ **1.** What does it mean in the fourth paragraph that Akbar **set the stage** for multiculturalism in India?
  a. He was a passionate fan of the theater.
  b. He helped prepare for multiculturalism.
  c. He discovered multiculturalism.
  d. He hated multiculturalism.

_____ **2.** In the third paragraph, the article mentions that Akbar achieved "a **string** of military victories." In this example, the word **string** refers to a _____.
  a. piece of rope **b.** line   **c.** series   **d.** few

_____ **3.** The final paragraph mentions Akbar was a **patron of the arts**. A **patron of the arts** is someone who _____.
  a. cannot understand art   **b.** supports artists
  c. fears art   **d.** is an artist

_____ **4.** What is another word for **seize** as it is used in the second-paragraph sentence "Together they organized a successful military campaign to **seize** control of northern India from the Afghans"?
  a. Take.   **b.** Find.   **c.** Explore.   **d.** Befriend.

_____ **5.** Which of the following has the opposite meaning of **insignificant** in the second-paragraph statement "At the time, the kingdom was small and **insignificant**"?
  a. Immense.   **b.** Organized.   **c.** Peaceful.   **d.** Important.

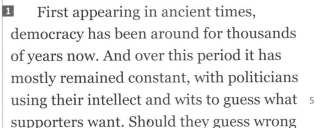

67 Technology vs. Democracy

1 First appearing in ancient times, democracy has been around for thousands of years now. And over this period it has mostly remained constant, with politicians using their intellect and wits to guess what ⁵ supporters want. Should they guess wrong or ignore the will of the people, then they won't be in power for long.

2 But that's all changing now. Technology is transforming democratic politics worldwide, and it's doing it by removing the guesswork. The shift is being driven by two major developments. First is the **advent** ¹⁰ of platforms like Facebook, which hold huge amounts of data about the public. Second is the invention of new AI and machine learning techniques that can process the data.

3 These tools allow political parties to scan **massive** amounts of data for behavioral and voting patterns. For example, a party can use these ¹⁵ techniques to identify groups of potential supporters. Then they can directly target their advertising resources on these groups using social media platforms, ignoring other groups. Given that most elections are decided by a narrow margin of votes, these targeting methods can be **decisive**. ²⁰

4 New technologies have already affected the outcome of elections around the world. In 2016, a data firm called Cambridge Analytica used a quiz application to scrape voter data from Facebook. The information was used to create psychological **profiles** for tens of millions of

>> New technologies have already affected the outcome of elections around the world.

American voters. These profiles helped the Trump campaign target advertising at ₂₅ likely supporters. The same strategies were used in the 2016 British referendum on membership to the European Union. In both cases, the side using advanced AI techniques ended up winning the vote. The same can't be said for the 2017 French presidential election. In that contest, an unknown party used thousands of fake Twitter accounts to spread false information about Emmanuel Macron. ₃₀ Macron still went on to win the election by a wide **margin**.

5 It's clear that democracy faces a challenge from these new technologies. However, we should remember that it's not the technology itself that's bad, but rather how it's used. AI might destroy democracy, but it also might restore it by helping voters engage with politicians in new ways. The choice is entirely up ₃₅ to us.

>> Brexit campaign whistle-blower Christopher Wylie speaking at the Fair Vote rally outside the House of Commons on Parliament Square, central London, March 29, 2018 (cc by Jwslubbock)

Questions

_____ 1. Which of the following is a synonym for **advent** in the second paragraph?
   a. End. **b.** Organization. **c.** Arrival. **d.** Return.

_____ 2. Which of the following has the opposite meaning to **massive** in the third paragraph?
   a. Tiny. **b.** Old. **c.** Missing. **d.** Dangerous.

_____ 3. **Decisive**, as it is used in the third paragraph, means _____.
   a. original **b.** annoying **c.** obvious **d.** significant

_____ 4. "The information was used to create psychological **profiles** for tens of millions of American voters." From the context of the fourth paragraph, a **profile** most likely means _____.
   a. a short description of someone or something
   b. a list of potential consequences from a decision
   c. a new technology that changes how something is done
   d. a contest that is very competitive

_____ 5. What does the word **margin** mean in the fourth-paragraph sentence "Macron still went on to win the election by a wide **margin**"?
   a. An unexpected occurrence. **b.** A degree of difference.
   c. A person contesting an election. **d.** A type of political system.

68 Confucius

1   Confucius was born in 551 BC in a
time of tyranny and **chaos** in China. As
a result of this instability, society began
to break down. Confucius observed
that people were becoming more and   5
more immoral and saw it as his duty to
reinforce the old ideas of compassion and
self-discipline in the troubled society of
which he was a part. One of Confucius's
most famous teachings is known in   10
English as the Golden Rule: "What you
do not want done to yourself, do not
do to others." According to Confucius,
if rulers acted in this way, they would
be **charitable** and kind toward their   15
subjects, and the common people
would be good to each other. Confucius
practiced his own ideals during his
lifetime and remained open to teaching
anyone, regardless of class or social   20
background. This is how he came to earn
affectionate titles such as the Great Sage and First Teacher. His method
was often not one of preaching, but rather one in
which students would be encouraged to arrive at
great truths through their own reasoning.   25

2   Confucius believed that for society to function,
there must be a hierarchy in place. He deemed
filial piety to be crucial in fulfilling these roles. That
means a son must honor his parents, a young person
must honor his elders, and the population must   30
honor the emperor, who in turn will rule them with
wisdom and kindness. This filial piety, however, was
not to be abused and exploited for personal gain.
In Confucius's words, "The mind of the **superior**

⩘ The *Analects* of Confucius

« Tomb of Confucius in Kong Lin cemetery,
  Shandong Province, China

≽ Confucius temple in Taipei, Taiwan

man is conversant with righteousness; the mind 35
of the mean man is conversant with gain." To
put it another way, the **righteous** person will
heed his role in society and perform his duties
well, while the inferior person will think only
of his own personal benefit. It was important to 40
challenge those who were behaving poorly, even
if they were higher up in the social hierarchy. In
short, Confucius saw human civilization as a kind
of puzzle, one in which peace would prevail if the
puzzle pieces were in their proper place. 45

Questions

_____1. The word **righteous** in the final paragraph means _____.
    a. musically talented   **b.** personally unhappy
    c. morally good   **d.** physically attractive

_____2. According to Confucius, if rulers followed the Golden Rule, they would be **charitable** and kind toward their subjects. A person who is **charitable** is _____.
    a. silly   **b.** generous   **c.** cruel   **d.** harsh

_____3. The first paragraph mentions that Confucius earned **affectionate** titles. The word with the opposite meaning of **affectionate** is _____.
    a. friendly   **b.** uncaring   **c.** heavenly   **d.** imperial

_____4. The first paragraph mentions that Confucius was born "in a time of tyranny and **chaos** in China." A word with a similar meaning to **chaos** is _____.
    a. arrangement   **b.** harmony   **c.** affection   **d.** disorder

_____5. "The mind of the **superior** man is conversant with righteousness; . . ." A word with a similar meaning to **superior** as it is used in this sentence is _____.
    a. exceptional   **b.** destructive   **c.** contemporary   **d.** ordinary

« Confucius temple in Nagasaki, Japan

69 Swing Music

» bandleader (photo by Johnny Saldivar)

⌃ Benny Goodman (1909–1986)

1 Swing music, one of the most celebrated styles to emerge from the United States in the twentieth century, got started back in the Great Depression in the early 1930s. During this time of high unemployment and widespread poverty, large African American jazz bands started to form. Some of these bands began to experiment with rhythm and instrument composition. Tubas and banjos were replaced with guitars and string basses, and the rhythm was switched from 2/4 to a 4/4 time signature. The role of the bandleader also changed from being a mere conductor to being a **skilled** musician who took the lead for the rest of the band.

2 These changes occurred in relative obscurity until 1935, when Benny Goodman and his band began to conquer radio **transmissions** across the United States. In the years that followed, Goodman would come to be referred to as the King of Swing and the Raja of Rhythm. In 1938, Benny Goodman played the legendary Carnegie Hall in New York City. He was the first jazz bandleader to ever play there, and the concert's success helped to usher in the swing era in the United States.

3 The swing era lasted from 1935 to 1946. It was a time when young people across the country would gather to listen to large jazz bands. Many people would dance to the music, and several dance steps were in vogue during this period. **These** included the Lindy Hop, Balboa, Collegiate Shag, and the jitterbug. Several **legendary** jazz artists were pulled into the spotlight during the swing era, such as Louis Armstrong, Billie Holiday, and Ella Fitzgerald.

« Swing music is well known for its use of brass instruments such as saxophones.

5

10

15

20

25

30

» jitterbug

⌃ Lindy Hop (cc by Frankie Manning)

4   Swing music began to decline in popularity during World War II. For one, it was hard to keep a large jazz band going when many of its members were overseas fighting a war. There were also several recording bans instituted after 1942, and it was very difficult for bands   35 to travel around the country because of wartime travel restrictions. Ultimately, the spotlight was **wrenched** away by bebop, another type of jazz that became popular through the 1950s and 1960s.

Questions

⌄ Billie Holiday
(1915–1959)

_____ **1.** The second paragraph mentions that "Benny Goodman began to conquer radio **transmissions** across the United States." What is another thing that might send or receive **transmissions**?
    a. A building.   **b.** A window.
    c. A dog.   **d.** A television.

_____ **2.** The third paragraph states, "Several **legendary** jazz artists were pulled into the spotlight during the swing era." A word with a similar meaning to **legendary** is _____.
    a. unimportant   **b.** worthless
    c. famous   **d.** trivial

_____ **3.** The final paragraph mentions that "the spotlight was **wrenched** away by bebop." Another word for **wrenched** is _____.
    a. taken   **b.** given
    c. sought   **d.** organized

_____ **4.** What does **these** in the third paragraph refer to?
    a. Dance steps.   **b.** Musicians.
    c. Jazz music.   **d.** Concerts.

_____ **5.** The first paragraph mentions that swing bandleaders tended to be **skilled** musicians. A word with the opposite meaning of **skilled** is _____.
    a. experienced   **b.** clumsy
    c. expert   **d.** trained

70 The Icy Finger of Fate 🎧070

1   It's amazing to consider how many species of animals are able to survive in the near-freezing waters of the Arctic and Antarctic seas. After all, no human being could **last** there for even a minute without a whole lot of special clothing and equipment. But even some of the icy deep's toughest residents should fear one thing: the phenomenon known as the brinicle. 5

2   In the polar winter, sea ice forms from water molecules, which lose their salt in **the process**. (Salt, of course, lowers the freezing point of water, which is why people sprinkle it on icy roads.) The salt left behind by the now-frozen water forms pockets of brine inside the solid ice. Brine is water with a much higher amount of salt in it than ordinary seawater. 10

3   Because it is so salty, brine can become much colder than seawater without freezing. It is also heavier and denser than seawater. So when the ice cracks, the brine in it quickly drops into the sea. There, its low **concentration** of water molecules attracts water, which naturally moves from higher to lower concentrations of itself. This water is instantly frozen by the extremely cold 15 brine. It then begins forming an ice tube which can stretch all the way down to the ocean floor.

≫ When the ice cracks, the brine in it quickly drops into the sea.

≫ Brinicle is captured on camera for the first time by BBC filmmakers in 2011.
(Source: http://www.bbc.com/earth/story/20161219-brinicle-finger-of-death)

By Matt Walker
31 December 2016

Watch the amazing moment when Sir David Attenborough and BBC filmmakers recorded a deadly underwater icicle form.

Even better, you can watch a further 1000 more memorable moments, for free, anytime, on your smartphone or tablet, via **Attenborough's Story of Life** app, which is now available to download via Google Play, or Apple's app store.

4   Once a brinicle reaches the sea floor, it begins to **spread**, forming a carpet of ice. This is where things start to get scary. Slow-moving, bottom-dwelling creatures such as starfish and sea urchins cannot escape the brinicle's path. 20 They are captured by the ice and frozen solid within it. A single brinicle, if it lasts long enough, can kill countless thousands of animals in this way.

5   But don't worry. The brinicle is not considered dangerous to larger species such as people. Even if it were, how many of us are likely to go scuba diving in Antarctica anytime soon? Still, much about the brinicle remains **a mystery**, 25 as this phenomenon was only fairly recently discovered. Who knows what else might be down there in the coldest seas on Earth, waiting for its next victim?

⌃ Slow-moving, bottom-dwelling creatures such as starfish may be frozen solid within a brinicle.

⌃ Brine is water with a much higher amount of salt in it than ordinary seawater. (cc by Rhode Island Institute for Archaeological Oceanography)

Questions

_____ **1.** The third paragraph mentions that brine's "low **concentration** of water molecules attracts water." Which of the following words is most similar in meaning to **concentration**?
     a. Quality.   **b.** Depth.   **c.** Movement.   **d.** Amount.

_____ **2.** "In the polar winter, sea ice forms from water molecules, which lose their salt in **the process**." What does **the process** refer to?
     a. Water molecules losing their salt.   **b.** The formation of sea ice.
     c. The creation of a brinicle.   **d.** Lowering the freezing point of water.

_____ **3.** What does the word **last** mean in the first paragraph?
     a. Swim.   **b.** Live.   **c.** Die.   **d.** Grow.

_____ **4.** Which of the following words means the opposite of **spread** in the fourth paragraph?
     a. Shrink.   **b.** Grow.   **c.** Kill.   **d.** Enjoy.

_____ **5.** Which of the following means the opposite of "**a mystery**" in the last paragraph?
     a. Unknown.   **b.** Dangerous.   **c.** Well known.   **d.** Thought about.

Unit
3
Study Strategies

In this unit, we will introduce you to two important strategies: interpreting visual material and using reference sources. Visual material graphically represents data such as statistics and figures in a way that is easy to understand. Reference sources, on the other hand, are things that help us locate information quickly and efficiently. This unit will give you the skills you need both to analyze graphical representations of data effectively and to find desired information quickly.

By the end of this section, your reading comprehension will no longer allow you merely to understand, interpret, and criticize a text; it will also allow you to effectively navigate the vast world of information that is out there.

3-1 *Visual Material*

Information comes in many forms, and sometimes it can be difficult to convey using words. This is where visual material can come in handy. Visual material uses pictures and graphics to convey information. It includes charts, tables, and maps. If used properly, it can make complex information easy to understand.

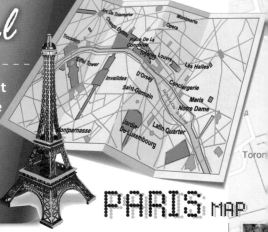
⌄ tourist map

PARIS MAP

71 Map: Find Out Where You're Going With Google Maps

(071)

1   It used to be easy to get lost while traveling. There was no Internet and no smartphones—just paper maps. Well not anymore! Now whenever we visit a new place, we have useful tools that can help
5   us get to wherever we want to go.

2   Take a look at the Google Map on the next page. It contains a lot of useful information. For example, at the bottom right is the scale, which tells you the distances that the map represents.
10   The streets are all clearly labeled, and the map also contains symbols for important landmarks like museums, restaurants, hotels, stores, and gas stations. It also shows metro stations, which are
15   represented by a little "M" symbol.

3   Please use the map on the next page to answer the following questions.

⌄ GPS navigation on a map application

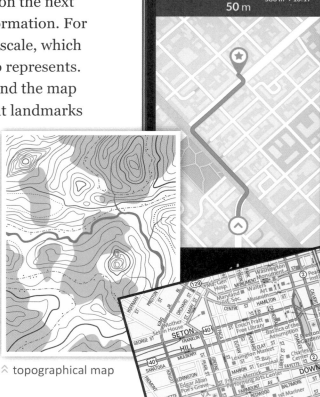

≫ Google Map

⌃ topographical map

(Source: https://www.google.ca/maps/@43.6542703,-79.3785653,16.71z)

Questions

_____ 1. Which of the following is NOT a street that borders Toronto Old City Hall?
   a. Shuter St.   **b.** Queen St. E.
   c. Bay St.   **d.** James St.

_____ 2. Which street is the Carbon Bar on?
   a. Jarvis St.   **b.** Queen St. E.
   c. Church St.   **d.** Dalhousie St.

_____ 3. Where is Massey Hall located?
   a. On Richmond St. E.   **b.** On Queen St. E.
   c. On Yonge. St.   **d.** On Shuter St.

_____ 4. Where is the Queen metro station?
   a. The intersection of Queen St. E. and Church St.
   b. The intersection of Queen St. E. and Yonge St.
   c. The intersection of Queen St. E. and Jarvis St.
   d. The Intersection of Queen St. E. and Bay St.

_____ 5. What's across the street from the Urban Outfitters store?
   a. CF Toronto Eaton Center.
   b. The Queen metro station.
   c. The Carbon Bar.
   d. Holiday Inn Express.

« street map

159

72 Calendar: Canada's Sport

1   Ice hockey is a sport in which two teams compete on ice and to try to get a puck into the other team's net. Player equipment includes ice skates, protective padding, a hockey stick to handle the puck, and a helmet. The sport was invented in Canada in the nineteenth century. Now it's popular worldwide,
5 particularly in countries with cold climates.

2   An ice hockey tournament is one appointment that appears on the calendar below. Calendars are a visual tool that people use to organize time. The most common type of calendar divides the days of a month into individual boxes. This allows us to write down important appointments and see what day of the
10 week a particular date is. It's a good idea to use a calendar and check it every morning so that you never miss an important event.

3   Now, use the calendar below to answer the questions on the next page.

January 2020

SUNDAY	MONDAY	TUESDAY	WEDNESDAY	THURSDAY	FRIDAY	SATURDAY
			1 New Year's party at Joanne's house	2	3 Sign Jake up for guitar lessons	4
5	6 Jake back to school	7	8	9	10	11 Jake's talent agency appointment
12	13	14	15 Meeting with Mr. Foster, Jake's science teacher	16	17	18 Day one of Jake's hockey tournament up north
19 Day two of Jake's hockey tournament up north	20 Hockey playoffs if Jake's team qualifies	21	22	23	24 Leave for mother–son spiritual retreat	25
26 Brunch with Lily and Alice	27 Meeting with lawyer	28	29 Begin cleaning out the basement	30	31	

≪ ice skates

≪ hockey stick

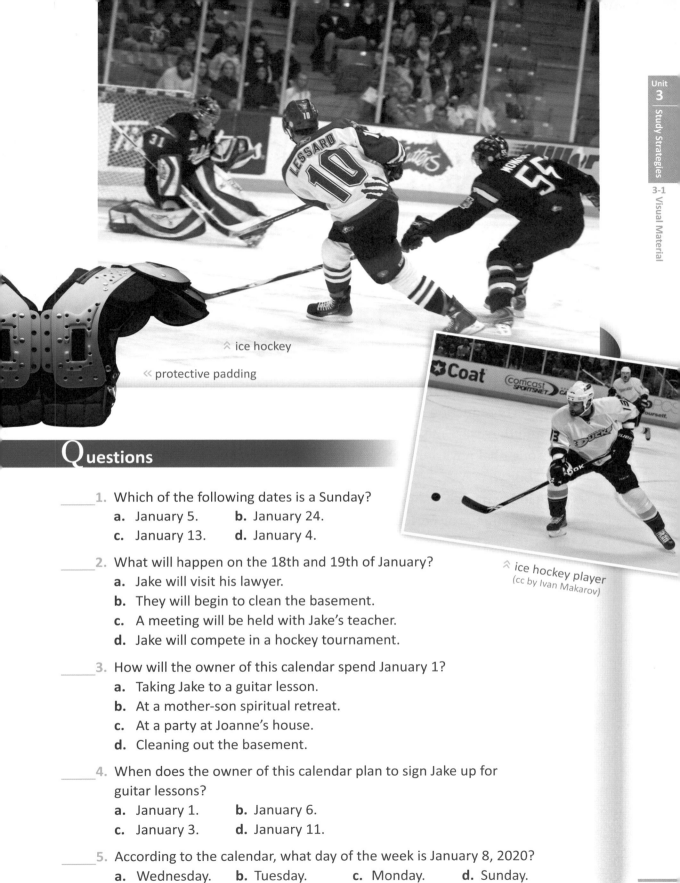

ⵉ ice hockey

« protective padding

ⵉ ice hockey player
(cc by Ivan Makarov)

Questions

_____ 1. Which of the following dates is a Sunday?
   a. January 5.   b. January 24.
   c. January 13.   d. January 4.

_____ 2. What will happen on the 18th and 19th of January?
   a. Jake will visit his lawyer.
   b. They will begin to clean the basement.
   c. A meeting will be held with Jake's teacher.
   d. Jake will compete in a hockey tournament.

_____ 3. How will the owner of this calendar spend January 1?
   a. Taking Jake to a guitar lesson.
   b. At a mother-son spiritual retreat.
   c. At a party at Joanne's house.
   d. Cleaning out the basement.

_____ 4. When does the owner of this calendar plan to sign Jake up for guitar lessons?
   a. January 1.   b. January 6.
   c. January 3.   d. January 11.

_____ 5. According to the calendar, what day of the week is January 8, 2020?
   a. Wednesday.   b. Tuesday.   c. Monday.   d. Sunday.

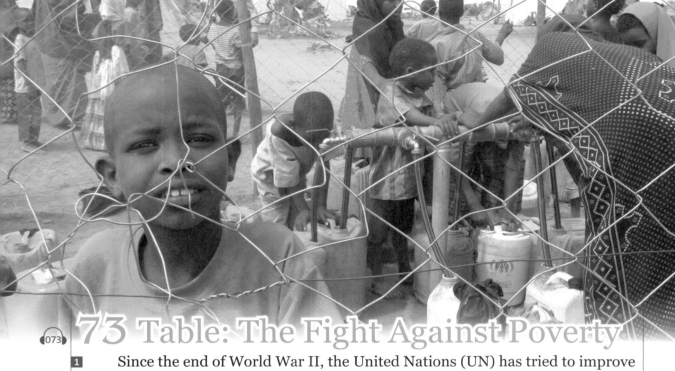

73 Table: The Fight Against Poverty

1   Since the end of World War II, the United Nations (UN) has tried to improve the state of the world. In the year 2000, all 189 UN member states agreed to a set of poverty reduction goals. They were called the Millennium Development Goals, and they were meant to be achieved by 2015. They targeted different
5 aspects of global poverty, such as education, health, hunger, and environmental sustainability.

2   The following table shows the largest individual donations towards these goals over a nine-year period. It also shows the countries that received them. A table can be a great visual aid for presenting information in a way that is easy
10 to sort through and understand. Most tables are divided into vertical columns and horizontal rows, each of them displaying a specific kind of data. People often use tables in office presentations, personal records, and budgets. Please answer the
15 following questions using the table on the next page.

⌄ poster at the United Nations Headquarters, showing the Millennium Development Goals

⌃ UN logo. The Millennium Development Goals are a UN initiative.

>> poverty

Year	Name of Biggest Donor	Amount Raised	Country
2005	Tom Green	$10,245	India
2006	Lisa Brill	$56,980	Malawi
2007	Mark Heasley	$7,985	Tibet
2008	Tom Green	$210,120	India
2009	Ike Jones	$14,980	Ethiopia
2010	Mark Heasley	$100,600	Indonesia
2011	Mary Smith	$9,750	Uganda
2012	Lisa Brill	$18,765	Panama
2013	Mark Heasley	$86,900	Indonesia

Questions

_____ 1. How many times did Tom Green record the highest donation?
   a. Once.   **b.** Twice.   **c.** Three times.   **d.** Four times.

_____ 2. In what year did Mary Smith record the highest donation?
   a. 2005   **b.** 2009   **c.** 2011   **d.** 2013

_____ 3. According to the table, what was the lowest donation ever recorded?
   a. $7,985   **b.** $9,750   **c.** $6,500   **d.** $10,245

_____ 4. According to the table, what was the highest donation ever recorded?
   a. $56,980   **b.** $86,900   **c.** $100,600   **d.** $210,120

_____ 5. Who recorded the highest donation the most times?
   a. Tom Green.   **b.** Lisa Brill.   **c.** Ike Jones.   **d.** Mark Heasley.

74 Bar Graph: Yoga—In Search of Spiritual Tranquility

1   Yoga is a spiritual well-being trend that is sweeping the world. It refers to a set of physical and spiritual practices that originated in ancient India. Yoga has meant different things to different people over the years. In the past, yoga practitioners retreated from civilization to lead a life of
5   fasting, self-denial, and simplicity. Nowadays, it's not abnormal to see a yoga practitioner throwing an empty coffee cup out the window of a new sports car.

2   The bar graph on the next page tracks male and female admissions to the Universal Yoga School
10   from 2014 through 2018. A bar graph is a handy visual tool for presenting changes in data over time. The vertical axis often represents quantity, and the horizontal axis often shows time. This allows us to see how quantities of something have risen or
15   fallen over a certain period. Occasionally, there are multiple bars on the same graph. Now, please answer the following questions using the bar graph on the next page.

>> Yoga is a set of physical and spiritual practices.

downward-facing dog

crow pose

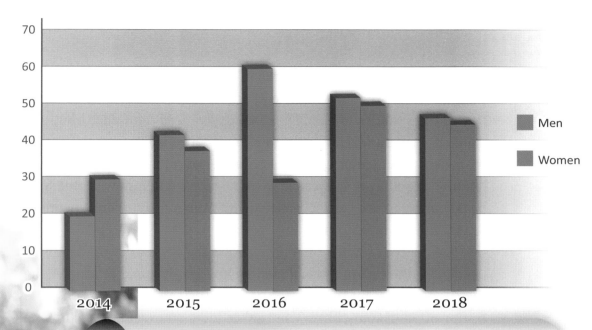

Questions

_____ 1. Which year had the fewest enrollments?
    a. 2014   **b.** 2015
    c. 2016   **d.** 2017

_____ 2. Which year had the fewest female enrollments?
    a. 2015   **b.** 2016
    c. 2017   **d.** 2018

_____ 3. Which year had the most male enrollments?
    a. 2015   **b.** 2016
    c. 2017   **d.** 2018

_____ 4. Which year had the fewest male enrollments?
    a. 2014   **b.** 2015
    c. 2016   **d.** 2017

_____ 5. From 2017 to 2018, total enrollments _____.
    a. increased   **b.** decreased
    c. stayed the same   **d.** stabilized

bridge pose

75 Pie Chart: The Spice of Life

1 Variety is a miracle of modern life. Whereas people used to have very few choices about what to eat, drink, or buy, there are now endless possibilities thanks to global trade and advanced manufacturing. Take drinks for example. Have you ever gone to a convenience store and marveled at the seemingly endless shelves of colorful, thirst-quenching liquids? Probably not, because we're all so used to it now. But it sure beats having to use your hands to drink from a dirty river as people did thousands of years ago.

2 The pie chart on the next page shows the popularity of various drinks. Pie charts are a visual aid like line graphs and bar graphs, but they don't represent the passage of time. Instead, they focus on the composition of something. This makes them an excellent tool to break down complex concepts or systems into smaller parts. Now, use the pie chart on the next page to answer the following questions.

≫ soda

≫ apple juice

≫ orange juice

⌃ cream soda

≪ lemonade

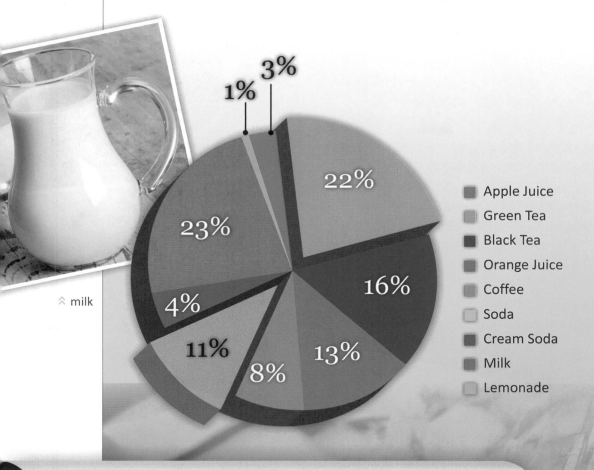

22%

23%

1% 3%

4%

11%

8% 13%

16%

Apple Juice
Green Tea
Black Tea
Orange Juice
Coffee
Soda
Cream Soda
Milk
Lemonade

⌃ milk

Questions

_____ 1. Which is the least popular drink?
   a. Orange juice.   **b.** Coffee.
   c. Milk.   **d.** Lemonade.

_____ 2. Which is the most popular drink?
   a. Orange juice.   **b.** Milk.
   c. Coffee.   **d.** Green Tea.

_____ 3. Apple juice is almost as popular as _____.
   a. soda   **b.** cream soda
   c. coffee   **d.** black tea

_____ 4. According to the pie chart, what percentage
   of people prefer to drink soda?
   a. 8%   **b.** 11%
   c. 16%   **d.** 22%

_____ 5. According to the pie chart, what percentage
   of people prefer to drink coffee?
   a. 3%   **b.** 4%
   c. 8%   **d.** 23%

We live in a world of boundless information. Encyclopedias, travel guides, the Internet, newspapers, cookbooks—all are valuable warehouses of knowledge. But finding specific information in such vast repositories can be tricky. That's where indexes, search engines, listings, and similar tools come in handy. By learning how to navigate these collections, a world of information will soon be at your fingertips!

>> Terry Herbert
(cc by Portable
Antiquities Scheme
from London, England)

76 Schedule: England's Buried Treasure

1   Buried treasure—the phrase conjures up images of one-legged pirates, lost islands, and maps where X marks the spot. Seldom, if ever, would anyone associate a piece of farmland near the sleepy village of Hammerwich in central England with such a romantic notion. But on July 5, 2009, a man named Terry Herbert, armed with 5 only a metal detector, found the mother lode: a collection of 3,500 gold and silver items from the Anglo-Saxon period that had lain buried in the English countryside for more than 1,300 years. The treasure, estimated to be worth $5.3 million, is the largest hoard of Anglo-Saxon treasure ever found. 10

2   To find out why the treasure was buried and by whom, you may be interested in watching a TV documentary on the subject. Check out the local TV listings on the next page to find out when and on which channel a 15 particular show will be broadcast.

(Source: http://www.tvguide.com/Listings/)

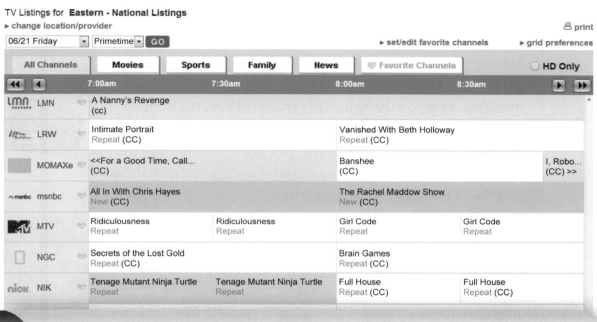

TV Listings for **Eastern - National Listings**
▶ change location/provider   🖨 print
06/21 Friday ▾ Primetime ▾ GO   ▶ set/edit favorite channels   ▶ grid preferences

All Channels	Movies	Sports	Family	News	♥ Favorite Channels	☐ HD Only

⏪ ◀	7:00am	7:30am	8:00am	8:30am	▶ ⏩
LMN	A Nanny's Revenge (cc)				
LRW	Intimate Portrait Repeat (CC)		Vanished With Beth Holloway Repeat (CC)		
MOMAXe	<<For a Good Time, Call... (CC)		Banshee (CC)		I, Robo... (CC) >>
msnbc	All In With Chris Hayes New (CC)		The Rachel Maddow Show New (CC)		
MTV	Ridiculousness Repeat	Ridiculousness Repeat	Girl Code Repeat	Girl Code Repeat	
NGC	Secrets of the Lost Gold Repeat (CC)		Brain Games Repeat (CC)		
NIK	Tenage Mutant Ninja Turtle Repeat	Tenage Mutant Ninja Turtle Repeat	Full House Repeat (CC)	Full House Repeat (CC)	

Questions

_____ 1. Which of the following shows do you think is about the Anglo-Saxon treasure?
   a. *Brain Games.*   **b.** *Intimate Portrait.*
   c. *Teenage Mutant Ninja Turtles.*   **d.** *Secrets of the Lost Gold.*

_____ 2. On what channel does the show air?
   a. MTV.   **b.** NGC.   **c.** NIK.   **d.** LMN.

_____ 3. How long does the show last?
   a. Two hours.   **b.** 30 minutes.
   c. One hour.   **d.** One hour and 30 minutes.

_____ 4. Which show could you NOT watch if you wanted to watch the show about the Anglo-Saxon treasure?
   a. *All In With Chris Hayes.*   **b.** *Girl Code.*
   c. *Banshee.*   **d.** *Vanished With Ben Holloway.*

_____ 5. Which of the following is NOT true about the show?
   a. It airs on a Friday.   **b.** It's showing for the first time.
   c. It's followed by *Brain Games.*   **d.** It's shorter than *A Nanny's Revenge.*

(077) **1**   Macau, a special administrative region of China, was governed by Portugal. It is known for its gambling industry, which has surpassed even Las Vegas in scale and grandeur.

2   If you visit Macau, you'll probably need a tourist map
5 to find your way around the city's many sights, restaurants, hotels, and casinos. Maps are designed to be easy to navigate and are often presented as a grid, with letters along the top (A, B, C . . .) and numbers down the side (1, 2, 3 . . .). The map's index will give you the names of notable places, the number
10 or symbol that represents each of them on the map, and a grid reference (e.g., A1 or C3) to guide you to the relevant square.

3   Now, answer the following questions using the map index below and the map on the next page.

⌄ Macau

Central Macau

Eating

Alfonso III	1	E3
Fat Siu Lau	2	D2
La Bonne Heure	3	E2
Margaret's Café	4	F3
New Yaohan	5	E4
Ou Mun Café	6	E2
St Dominic Market	7	E2

Sleeping

Augusters Lodge	8	F3
East Asia Hotel	9	D1
Hotel Sintra	10	E4
Hou Kong Hotel	11	C2
Ole London Hotel	12	C3

Entertainment

Corner's Wine Bar	13	E1
Crazy Paris Cabaret	14	F4
Emperor Palace Casino	15	E4
Grand Lisboa Casino	16	F4
Macau Soul	17	E1

Sights

Church of St Augustine	18	D3
Church of St Dominic	19	E3
Hong Kung Temple	20	D1
Macau Cathedral	21	E3
Monte Fort	22	F1
Museum of the Holy House of Mercy	23	E3

Na Tcha Temple	24	E1
Ruins of the Church of St Paul	25	E1
Sam Kai Vui Kun Temple	26	E2
Treasury of Sacred Art	27	E2

Shopping

Flea Market	28	E1
Koi Kei	29	D2
Pun Veng Kei	30	E2
Traditional Shops	31	E1

Information & Services

Bank of China	32	E3
Main Post Office	33	E3
Portuguese Consulate	34	F2

Questions

_____ **1.** You're currently in square E3 on the map. Which of the following sights is furthest away?
   a. Macau Cathedral.
   b. Hong Kung Temple.
   c. Museum of the Holy House of Mercy.
   d. Treasury of Sacred Art.

_____ **2.** You're staying at the East Asia Hotel. Where is it on the map?
   a. In square E3.   **b.** In square F1.
   c. In square C2.   **d.** In square D1.

_____ **3.** You want to visit the Grand Lisboa Casino. Which heading should you look under in the index to find it?
   a. Entertainment.   **b.** Sights.
   c. Eating.   **d.** Information.

_____ **4.** You want to go to Margaret's Café for lunch. The café is represented by the number _____ in square _____.
   a. 6; F3   **b.** 4; E2   **c.** 4; F3   **d.** 6; E2

_____ **5.** What can you do at the place on the map represented by the number 33?
   a. Gamble.   **b.** See a show.
   c. Send a postcard home.   **d.** Withdraw money.

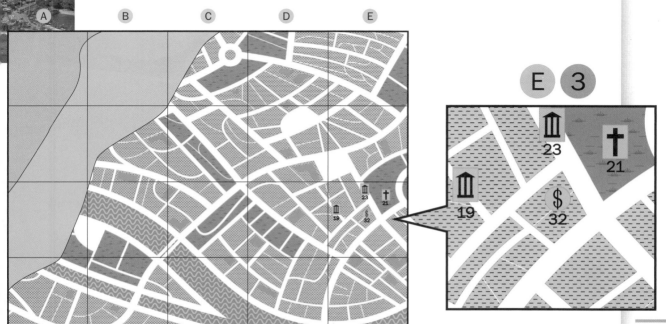

78 Recipe: Pancakes

1 Quick and easy to make, pancakes are eaten all over the world. They can be enjoyed sweet or savory, as breakfast or as dessert, and with a mind-boggling array of toppings.

2 Different countries have their own unique styles of preparing and enjoying pancakes. In Europe, for example, pancakes are usually thin and are often served with fruit or ice cream, while in South America, ground meat and vegetables are favorite fillings.

5

⌃ North American hotcake

⌄ flour

⌄ baking powder

Fluffy American Pancakes

Serves: 4-6 people

Ingredients:
- 135 g plain flour
- 1 tsp baking powder
- ½ tsp salt
- 2 tbsp sugar
- 135 ml milk
- 1 large egg, lightly beaten
- 2 tbsp butter, melted, plus extra for cooking

To serve:
- Butter
- Maple syrup

⌄ batter

Instructions:

1. In a large bowl, mix together the flour, baking powder, salt, and sugar.
2. In a separate bowl, lightly whisk together the milk and egg, and then whisk in the melted butter.
3. Pour the milk mixture into the flour mixture and, using a fork, beat until you have a smooth batter.
4. Heat a frying pan over a medium heat and add some butter.
5. When the butter has melted, add a scoop of batter to the frying pan.
6. Wait until the top of the pancake begins to bubble, and then turn it over and cook until both sides are golden brown and the pancake has risen to about 1 cm thick.
7. Repeat until all the batter is used up.

≫ butter

3 The most well-known version of the pancake, though, is perhaps the North American hotcake, which is thick, fluffy, and commonly eaten for breakfast with powdered sugar or syrup.

10

4 Learning how to make pancakes is easy—just find a recipe online or in a cookbook. A recipe contains a list of ingredients (along with how much of each ingredient is needed) and step-by-step instructions on how to prepare the dish. Before you know it, you'll have a plate of hot, delicious pancakes ready to enjoy.

15

5 Now, answer the following questions using the provided recipe on the previous page.

≫ frying pan

« pancakes

Questions

_____ 1. With this recipe, you can make pancakes for a maximum of _____.
   a. two people   **b.** four people   **c.** six people   **d.** eight people

_____ 2. How much sugar do you need to prepare for this recipe?
   a. Two teaspoons.   **b.** 135 grams.
   c. Two tablespoons.   **d.** One teaspoon.

_____ 3. Which of the following is NOT used to cook the pancakes?
   a. Butter.   **b.** Milk.   **c.** Flour.   **d.** Maple syrup.

_____ 4. After melting some butter in the frying pan, what should you do next?
   a. Add a scoop of batter.
   b. Pour the milk mixture into the flour mixture.
   c. Turn the pancake over.
   d. Mix together the flour, salt, and sugar.

_____ 5. According to the recipe, what should you use to beat the flour and milk mixtures into a batter?
   a. A knife.   **b.** A spoon.   **c.** A fork.   **d.** A frying pan.

ᐱ sumo wrestling

79 Search Engine: Sumo Wrestling

1   Two giants collide in the ring. Bare-skinned except for a silk belt covering their modesties, they grab, push, and heave each other to the edge of the circle until one finally loses his footing and stumbles over the edge. It's over in less than 10 seconds.

2   Unique to Japan, sumo wrestling can be explosively exciting. When the two wrestlers clash, glory can be won or lost in an instant. But sumo is not just about the thrill of the competition. Its origins, history, and traditions all offer an intriguing insight into Japanese culture.

3   You can find information about all aspects of sumo wrestling on the Web. Type "sumo wrestling" into a search engine, and you're likely to be faced with lots of options. Each result consists of a title, a Web address, and a summary or extract from the page. Use the following search results to identify which website is most likely to have the information you're looking for.

5

10

≫ Sumo Nobori flags

ᐁ sumo wrestlers

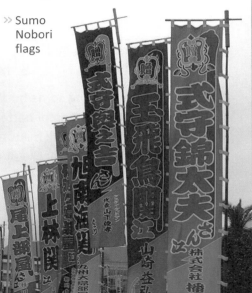

Sumo - Virtual Culture - Kids Web Japan - Web Japan 🔲Norton
web-japan.org › Kids Web Japan › Virtual Culture ▾
Learn how wrestlers win at sumo. The History of Sumo: How did sumo evolve? A
Day in the Life of a **Sumo Wrestler**: Follow a **sumo wrestler** for an average day.

Behind the Scenes With the **Sumo Wrestlers** of Japan 🔲Norton
www.slate.com/.../paolo_patrizi_gentle_giants_examines_the_daily_lives... ▾
Apr 17, 2013 – The stables where **sumo wrestlers** practice their sport in Japan are
places where tradition reigns and only glimpses of the modern world creep ...

Tokyo: 10 Things to Do — 2. **Sumo** - TIME 🔲Norton
www.time.com › Time.com › Travel › City Guides › Tokyo ▾
Forget kabuki; **sumo** is better theater. If you happen to be in Tokyo during one of the
three grand tournaments — 15-day events in January, May and September ...

USA SUMO - **Sumo Wrestlers**, Sumo Models, US Sumo Open, Sumo ...
🔲Norton
www.usasumo.com/ ▾
Contains overview of **sumo** within the United States and the sport's bid to become
an Olympic sport. Also, features news, events calendar, history, photo gallery, ...

Nihon **Sumo** Kyokai Official Grand **Sumo** Home Page 🔲Norton
www.**sumo**.or.jp/eng/ ▾
News, interviews, and records from the world of **sumo**.

Questions

_____ 1. Which websites would you visit if you wanted information on the daily lives of sumo wrestlers?
   a. *www.slate.com* and *web-japan.org*
   b. *www.time.com* and *www.usasumo.com*
   c. *www.sumo.or.jp/eng/* and *web-japan.org*
   d. *www.usasumo.com* and *www.slate.com*

_____ 2. On which website would you most likely find a list of past tournament winners?
   a. *www.time.com*   **b.** *www.sumo.or.jp/eng/*
   c. *web-japan.org*   **d.** *www.usasumo.com*

_____ 3. If you visited *web-japan.org*, which of the following would you NOT be likely to find?
   a. Information on the origins of sumo wrestling.
   b. The basic rules of sumo wrestling.
   c. A typical sumo wrestler's diet.
   d. The results of the latest sumo-wrestling tournament.

_____ 4. On *www.usasumo.com* you'd definitely find _____.
   a. interviews with famous sumo wrestlers
   b. pictures of sumo wrestlers
   c. information on sumo wrestling in Europe
   d. the average cost of a ticket to a sumo tournament

_____ 5. How many times a year does a grand sumo tournament happen in Tokyo?
   a. Once a year.   **b.** Twice a year.
   c. Three times a year.   **d.** Four times a year.

80 Endnotes: Annie Oakley

[080] **1**   Annie Oakley was a shooter from the Wild West whose skills with a gun were so legendary that some have called her America's first female superstar.[1] From a distance of 90 feet, she could hit a playing card edge on,[2] hit a coin as it was tossed into the air, and shoot the ash from the end of a cigarette.[3]

2   Oakley started learning to shoot at a young age. By age eight, she was an accomplished hunter and supported her widowed mother by killing and selling wild animals.[4] In 1885, she joined Buffalo Bill's Wild West Show[5] and spent the next 17 years traveling the world performing her feats for emperors, kings, and queens.[6]

5

- -

3   Notes

* ANNIE OAKLEY, *
(LITTLE SURE SHOT.)   208 BOWERY, N.Y.

OOD. PHOTO.

⌃ cabinet card of Annie Oakley

    1. Connie Fields, *The Legendary Annie Oakley* (New York: Penguin, 2009), 12.

    2. She would put several more holes in it before it touched the ground.

15

    3. T. J. Stone, *Annie Oakley: Sharpshooter Extraordina*ire (London: Random House, 1998), 71-73. Oakley once shot the ash from the end of the cigarette of Kaiser Wilhelm II of Germany— the man who would later be responsible for starting World War I.

    4. Phyllis Mathews, *Little Sure Shot: The Early Years of Annie Oakley* (New York: New York University Press, 1994), 89.

20

    5. The show's original champion marksman, Captain Bogardus, had left the show after only a year, creating a lucky break for Oakley.

    6. Jeremy Wilde, *Buffalo Bill's Wild West Show: A History* (Cambridge: Cambridge University Press, 1987), 123. Even the reclusive Queen Victoria of England came to see Oakley perform when the show visited London in 1887.

4   When writing an informative piece like this, an author will often cite his or her sources in notes that come at the end of the chapter or book. Endnotes also give the author the chance to provide any extra information he or she feels is interesting but not immediately relevant. Try to answer the following questions using the endnotes above.

30

« Annie Oakley (1860–1926)

Questions

_____1. From which book did the writer get his information about the particular tricks Annie Oakley could perform with a gun?
   a. *Buffalo Bill's Wild West Show: A History.*
   b. *Annie Oakley: Sharpshooter Extraordinaire.*
   c. *The Legendary Annie Oakley.*
   d. *Little Sure Shot: The Early Years of Annie Oakley.*

_____2. Who wrote the book *Buffalo Bill's Wild West Show: A History*?
   a. T. J. Stone.   b. Connie Fields.
   c. Jeremy Wilde.   d. Phyllis Mathews.

_____3. What extra information does the writer give about the fact that in 1885, Annie Oakley joined Buffalo Bill's Wild West Show?
   a. The original marksman, Captain Bogardus, had left the show after only a year.
   b. Oakley once performed a trick for the man who started World War I.
   c. Oakley could hit a playing card edge on and shoot it many times as it fell.
   d. Queen Victoria of England came to see Oakley perform in 1887.

_____4. On what page of the book *Little Sure Shot: The Early Years of Annie Oakley* would you find the information cited in the article.
   a. 94   b. 123   c. 12   d. 89

_____5. In which of the works cited would you probably find the most information about the modern-day perception of Annie Oakley?
   a. *Buffalo Bill's Wild West Show: A History.*
   b. *Annie Oakley: Sharpshooter Extraordinaire.*
   c. *The Legendary Annie Oakley.*
   d. *Little Sure Shot: The Early Years of Annie Oakley.*

Unit

4

Final Reviews

>>

Now that you're familiar with a variety of reading and word skills, not to mention some important study strategies, it's time to put them to the test. Unlike in previous units, you'll no longer be faced with just one type of skill per article; now you'll be faced with the challenge of having to apply several different skills to each individual text.

Use these review units to see how much you've progressed and how much you've learned from the study units. Try to do these tests under exam conditions, and then analyze your strengths and weaknesses. This will give you a good idea of which areas you need to work on in the future.

>> DuoSkin enhances the aesthetics of existing metallic jewelry-like tattoos by embedding LEDs in silver leaf traces. (Photo: Jimmy Day / photo by Cindy Hsin-Liu Kao)

⌃ DuoSkin and control devices from DuoSkin 2D trackpad (Photo: Jimmy Day / photo by Cindy Hsin-Liu Kao)

081 # 81 Tattoos With Tech

⌃ DuoSkin's fabrication process (Photo: Microsoft Media/ MIT Media Lab / photo by Cindy Hsin-Liu Kao)

1 Suppose you could choose songs from your music player just by sliding a finger along your arm. Or read reviews of the latest movies by holding your smartphone near the back of your hand. Well, now you can, and the best part is that you'll look good doing it. Welcome to the world of DuoSkin, the technological breakthrough that's also a fashion statement. 5

2 Developed at the Massachusetts Institute of Technology, DuoSkin isn't actually a product, but a method. It allows almost anyone to create his or her own unique electronic tattoos cheaply and easily. Technology has never been this personal before! 10

3 The magic ingredient in DuoSkin is gold leaf, an electro-conductive material that is cheap, strong, and safe for the skin. After drawing a pattern with graphic design software, the user cuts it onto tattoo paper with a vinyl-cutter. The gold leaf is then applied directly to the cut paper and pressed onto the skin like a temporary tattoo. Sound easy? Well, 15 apparently it is!

4 DuoSkin tattoos currently come in three varieties. The first type senses touch for input purposes. These tattoos can control devices just like a touch pad or screen. One elementary school class even made a tattoo that takes selfies whenever someone taps it! 20

5 The second type is for display, or output. Heating elements against the skin enable these tattoos to change color when they detect changes in body temperature. Others contain LEDs that light up when the wearer experiences strong emotions. These sorts of tattoos first appeared before the development of DuoSkin, but were used only for medical purposes. 25

↳ DuoSkin allows users to create three types of user interfaces: input on skin through capacitive touch sensing *(left)*, output on skin through thermochromic resistive heating circuitry *(right)*, and wireless communication through NFC *(center)*. (Photo: Jimmy Day / photo by Cindy Hsin-Liu Kao)

6   Finally, there are tattoos that can store and transmit data. Using near-field communication (NFC) chips, these designs can communicate with nearby devices much
30 like a key card communicates with a lock. Unlike a key card, however, they can receive as well as send information, making them kind of like tiny, wearable hard drives.

7   While the technological aspects of DuoSkin are
35 remarkable, its creator, Cindy Hsin-Liu Kao of Taiwan, is also proud of its more stylish side. By giving the wearer control over both its look and function, DuoSkin brings human and machine together in a whole new way. But once our gadgets are actually on our skin, where will they go next?

≪ Cindy Hsin-Liu Kao, creator of DuoSkin
(Photo: Jimmy Day / photo by Cindy Hsin-Liu Kao)

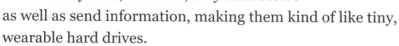

Questions

_____ 1. What is this article mostly about?
  a. The history of tattoos.
  b. A new type of technology.
  c. Different uses for gold leaf.
  d. MIT researchers.

_____ 2. How does the author introduce the reader to the idea of DuoSkin?
  a. By describing the process of its creation.
  b. By relating his personal experience with it.
  c. By asking the reader to imagine something.
  d. By quoting one of DuoSkin's creators.

_____ 3. Which of the following can be inferred from the fourth paragraph?
  a. More types of DuoSkin tattoos may be available in the future.
  b. Touch pads and screens are too inconvenient for people to use.
  c. DuoSkin is very popular with elementary school students.
  d. Only three types of DuoSkin tattoos will ever be available.

_____ 4. Which of the following statements is NOT true?
  a. DuoSkin tattoos can store data just like a computer's hard drive.
  b. DuoSkin is the first type of technological tattoo ever created.
  c. DuoSkin isn't something you can walk in and buy at a store.
  d. DuoSkin is readily available to a wide variety of people.

_____ 5. How could you describe the author's tone in this article?
  a. Humorous.   **b.** Angry.   **c.** Confused.   **d.** Interested.

>> Istanbul

˄ Bosporus Bridge

>> catamaran

82 Istanbul

082

1   Istanbul, Turkey, is undoubtedly one of the world's most vibrant cities, where the ancient and modern blend together almost effortlessly, where Europe meets Asia, and where hospitable, generous, and charming locals always have a story to tell.

2   Istanbul is the only settlement in the world that sits on two continents. The Bosporus, one of the world's busiest waterways, divides the city in two: the western part being the European side and the eastern part being the Asian side. Because there are many monuments and other things of interest, taking a boat ride down the Bosporus Strait is the best way to see Istanbul.

3   The ideal way to see the city in the shortest amount of time is to hire a catamaran—a fast sailing boat with two hulls—or if you can't afford to hire one, you can also book a seat on a catamaran tour. On a catamaran, you can travel the length of the Bosporus to either the Black Sea or the Sea of Marmara, seeing all that Istanbul has to offer. A catamaran is very convenient, but it has one big shortcoming—it doesn't allow you to mingle with the local residents, perhaps the most intriguing part of this unique city. To get a taste of the native culture, you should take

5

10

15

20

˄ Topkapı Palace

˄ Turkish Tea

˅ ferry

>> Bosporus Strait, where Europe and Asia meet

one of the many ferries that are used for public transportation and are more affordable than catamarans. Though they don't go as far as the
25 catamarans, you can still see many of the highlights of Istanbul, and the ferries allow you to mix with Turkish people and see how they live.

≪ Eminönü is heaving with shoppers.

Ferries start running early in the morning; they leave the west side of Istanbul regularly from the main downtown port of Eminönü and continue running throughout the day until early evening. It's
30 quite an experience to sit in the tea shop located in the middle of the ferry, watching jewels like the Topkapı Palace and the Hagia Sophia float by. Waiters in embroidered velvet jackets and fezzes bring you "cay"—Turkish tea—in tulip-shaped glasses
35 with a cube of sugar on the side. Sightseeing on the Bosporus as you sip on your tea is a magical way to witness the
40 beauty of Istanbul.

≪ the interior of Hagia Sophia

≪ Hagia Sophia

Questions

_____ 1. What is the main point that is conveyed by the article?
   a. Tea is served on the ferries that run across the Bosporus.
   b. Istanbul is a magnificent city best taken in by boat.
   c. Istanbul is a city that is half in Europe and half in Asia.
   d. The Bosporus is one of the world's busiest waterways.

_____ 2. The statement "The ideal way to see the city in the shortest amount of time is to hire a catamaran" is a(n) _____.
   a. fact   b. opinion

_____ 3. Which of the following do you think the author likes best about Istanbul?
   a. The sights.   b. The tea.   c. The river.   d. The people.

_____ 4. The author writes that on one of Istanbul's ferries, you can watch "jewels like the Topkapı Palace and the Hagia Sophia float by." This is an example of _____.
   a. a metaphor   b. a simile   c. hyperbole   d. personification

_____ 5. From the article, we can infer that hiring a catamaran is perfect for someone with
   _____.
   a. a lot of money and a lot of time   b. lots of money and not much time
   c. a lot of time and a little money   d. no time and no money

183

83 All Apologies

083

1　Having lived in ten East Asian countries over the past 26 years, I consider myself pretty familiar with the region's cultures. Two things I still
5　find occasionally surprising, however, are the manner in which Asians apologize and the frequency with which they do so. What exactly is the engine driving the Far East's "apology culture"?

2　Japan is perhaps the country most
10　associated with excessive apologizing, so it seems like a good place to start. With at least 20 different verbal apologies and

⌃ apologizing

many apologetic gestures, the Japanese are ready to say sorry for almost
15　anything, and they do. Or at least, they *seem* to.

3　By far, the most common "apology" heard in Japan is *sumimasen*, a word which translates not as "I'm sorry" but rather "excuse me." This humble statement can be used in all sorts of situations, from moving past someone on a bus to showing up five minutes late. It's also a more
20　common way of saying "thank you" than *arigatō*, as it recognizes that someone has gone to some sort of trouble for you. So the next time you're in Japan and someone holds a door for you, don't thank him; excuse yourself!

4　It's not surprising that Japan's apology culture was brought to
25　Taiwan during the colonial period. *Bùhǎoyìsi* (bad feeling) is the island's equivalent of *sumimasen*, with an even wider range of uses. In addition to an apology, a thank-you, a request to be excused and so on, this flexible term can even start a conversation.

5　Taiwan's culture, like Japan's, values politeness, modesty, and
30　harmony. The group is considered more important than the individual,

and people are expected to put society's interests first. The extremely crowded and stressful conditions in which most Taiwanese and Japanese live make this especially important. Almost any interaction is viewed as an intrusion on another person's space and must be acknowledged as such.

35

6   Nevertheless, all this apparent apologizing may have the effect of taking any actual sense of regret out of the real thing. Like many other foreigners in Asia, I've heard countless automatic, meaningless "I'm sorry"s over the years, for everything from undone homework to stepping on my foot. It could just be that the more people say it, the less they mean it.

40

« The humble statement *sumimasen* is also a common way of saying "thank you."

⌃ The extremely crowded and stressful conditions in Taiwan and Japan make apology culture especially important.

Questions

_____ 1. What is the main idea of this article?
   a. Japanese people are too polite.
   b. Foreigners in Asia have a hard time.
   c. Taiwanese people don't apologize enough.
   d. Apologies are not always what they seem.

_____ 2. Which of the following is NOT a reason why the Japanese use the word *sumimasen* so much?
   a. Their culture values politeness, modesty, and harmony.
   b. They have no other words for "thank you" or "I'm sorry."
   c. It shows appreciation for other people's time and trouble.
   d. They live in a crowded, stressful society.

_____ 3. How does the author finish the article?
   a. With a personal observation.
   b. With some historical information.
   c. With a funny story that he heard.
   d. With a question for the reader.

_____ 4. How would you describe the author's tone in this passage?
   a. Apologetic.   b. Humorous.
   c. Skeptical.   d. Sentimental.

_____ 5. In the first paragraph, the author asks, "What exactly is the engine driving the Far East's 'apology culture'?" What is this an example of?
   a. Exaggeration.   b. A simile.
   c. A metaphor.   d. Poetry.

84 Temples in Kyoto

1   Kyoto is a city in the middle of Japan that is known for its beautiful temples. It was the capital of Japan from 794 to 1868, and now it is a major tourist destination and a wonderful place to explore for its temples, gardens, and traditional Japanese culture, which can sometimes be hard to find in the country's bigger cities.

2   Unlike the **ornately** decorated and painted Chinese temples, the Japanese places of worship are simpler and use natural colors. The Japanese temples are still considered beautiful and are known for their elegance rather than their ornamentation. The Enryakuji complex of temples is one sight not to be missed in Kyoto. Built in AD 788 on top of Mt. Hiei, it consists of 120 temples and three pagodas and offers hiking opportunities and stunning views of all of Kyoto. Further, if you want to glimpse some living history, in the Primary Central Hall there are lamps that have been kept alight non-stop for over 1,200 years!

3   Another worthwhile visit is to Nishi Honganji in the center of Kyoto. It contains five buildings that are examples of the most beautiful artistic and architectural achievements of the Momoyama period—the period when Japan was ruled from Kyoto. This temple is still the

Kinkaku-ji
(Golden Pavilion Temple)

Ginkaku-ji
(Temple of the Silver Pavilion)

Kiyomizu-dera

other famous temples in Kyoto

^ Nishi Honganji   ^ The Sanmon Gate, the main gate of Nanzen-ji   ^ Primary Central Hall at Enryakuji
                      (cc by hiro)

headquarters of the Jodo Shinshu religious school, an organization with over 12 million followers worldwide.

4

25 Located at the base of Kyoto's Higashiyama mountains is the Nanzen-ji. At one point the retirement **villa** for Emperor Kameyama, the temple is now one of the most famous Zen temples in the world. If you visit it, you can see people meditating and practicing Buddhist religious **rites**. The Sanmon Gate stands at the entrance to the temple and is impressive in both its immense size and the beautiful hand-painted **murals** that decorate its

30 ceiling.

5

Visiting gardens is another pastime in Kyoto, and the Leaping Tiger Garden is a classic Japanese garden and a wonderful one to visit. With a waterfall to watch and straw mats to sit on, it's an ideal place to partake in the Japanese tea ceremony—the perfect way to

35 **attain** inner peace at the end of a long day of temple viewing.

» Nanzen-ji

Questions

_____ **1.** In the second paragraph, the writer describes Chinese temples as being "**ornately** decorated." Which of the following is most likely the meaning of **ornately**?
   a. Having a strong local flavor or identity.
   b. Plain and simple, with no unnecessary additions.
   c. Covered with small, complicated designs.
   d. Having something to do with religion.

_____ **2.** In the fourth paragraph, the author mentions "Buddhist religious **rites**." Which of the following is a synonym for **rites**?
   a. Rituals.   **b.** Prayers.   **c.** Vices.   **d.** Symbols.

_____ **3.** An antonym of **attain**, as it is used in the final paragraph, is _____.
   a. condense   **b.** lose   **c.** astonish   **d.** ban

_____ **4.** In the fourth paragraph, the author mentions the **murals** that decorate the Sanmon Gate. What does the word **murals** most likely mean?
   a. Edible treats.   **b.** Sound recordings.
   c. Large paintings.   **d.** Traditional stories.

_____ **5.** Nanzen-ji was once "the retirement **villa** for Emperor Kameyama." Which word could replace **villa** in the passage?
   a. Mansion.   **b.** Cemetery.   **c.** Temple.   **d.** Prison.

187

85 | Quantum Physics

1 According to pioneer physicist Niels Bohr, "Anyone who is not shocked by quantum theory has not understood it." Quantum physics is the study of matter and energy at subatomic levels. It has caused a great deal of **controversy** since its formulation not only challenges the classical laws of physics but also offers new possibilities and **breakthroughs** in science that were once thought to be possible only in science fiction.

2 Quantum physics is a relatively new field of study and was developed in the early twentieth century in order to attempt to explain the results of several experiments that did not **conform** to, and even seemed to contradict, the classical laws of physics (those proposed by Isaac Newton and Galileo Galilei, among others, several hundred years ago).

3 For any student of quantum theory, truly coming to grips with the principles that it suggests is an incredibly difficult task. This is because quantum theory is almost stubbornly **counterintuitive**. The subatomic world that quantum theory aims to illustrate operates on a dramatically different set of rules to the physical world we experience every day: elementary particles behave as both particles and waves; it is impossible to know the position and momentum of any particle at the same time; and subatomic particles, such as electrons, exist as an expression of probability, collapsing into reality only when measured. Even Einstein, who contributed to the development of quantum theory, had serious doubts about some of the claims that were being made and tried for years, though unsuccessfully, to refute them.

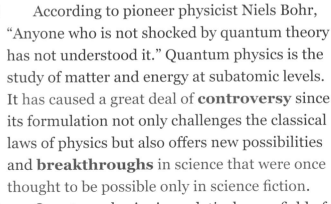

⌃ Niels Bohr (1885–1962) as a young man

⌃ beam of electrons moving in a circle in a magnetic field

4 As it is such a complex **field**, there are many interpretations of quantum theory possible, and different physicists support different interpretations. One interpretation suggests that subatomic particles can move backward as well as forward in time and appear in all possible places at once. Another suggests that at each moment the universe splits into billions of parallel universes, meaning that an almost infinite number of versions of you exist. Still another interpretation suggests that our very consciousness affects the behavior and even existence of subatomic particles.

5 Confused yet? Well, don't feel too bad. To quote another famous quantum theorist, Richard Feynman, "If you think you understand quantum mechanics, you do not understand quantum mechanics."

« Richard Feynman
(1918–1988)
(cc by briola giancarlo)

40

45

50

Questions

_____ 1. As it is used in the fourth paragraph, the word **field** means _____.
   a. an area of land used for growing crops
   b. a subject or activity, usually academic in nature
   c. part of a database in which similar information is recorded
   d. a region in space where a particular force exists

_____ 2. In the first paragraph, the author claims that quantum physics "has caused a great deal of **controversy**." Which of the following words could replace **controversy** here?
   a. Debate.   b. Gratitude.   c. Agreement.   d. Dismay.

_____ 3. Which of the following is an antonym of **conform** as the word is used in the second paragraph?
   a. Predict.   b. Convert.   c. Oppose.   d. Support.

_____ 4. In the third paragraph, the author describes quantum physics as "stubbornly **counterintuitive**." What is the meaning of **counterintuitive**?
   a. The opposite of what is morally right.
   b. Under-researched and lacking evidence.
   c. Supported by evidence and widely understood.
   d. The opposite of what one would expect.

_____ 5. The author claims that quantum physics offers "**breakthroughs** in science that were once thought to be possible only in science fiction." Another word for **breakthroughs** is _____.
   a. investigations   b. advancements   c. vocations   d. losses

⌃ blue tears in Matsu, Taiwan (cc by ynes95)

86 The Glorious Glow-in-the-Dark Beaches of Matsu

(086)

1   In this age of smartphones, flying robots, and the Internet, it can sometimes seem like you've seen it all. But then nature shows you something truly remarkable, something that makes you feel like a little kid again. These experiences are as scarce as they are special. And luckily, you don't always need to go very far to find them. 5

2   One natural wonder is waiting at the Matsu Islands, a tiny archipelago administered by Taiwan. The beaches there can literally emit a bright, neon glow at night. The phenomenon is called "blue tears" and it's caused by the harmless algae *noctiluca scintillans*. On some nights, the entire coast is engulfed in a mysterious blue tide. **It** can be 10 an awe-inspiring sight and, for many tourists, make for unforgettable social media posts as well.

3   You might be wondering: What's causing the blue glow? First off, there's a lot of algae out there. A single drop of water can contain thousands of tiny *noctiluca*. 15 Scientists believe that the glow itself is a natural reaction meant to scare off the algae's predators.

⌄ *noctiluca scintillans* (cc by Maria Antónia Sampayo, Instituto de Oceanografia, Faculdade Ciências da Universidade de Lisboa)

» The blue glow is caused by the harmless algae *noctiluca scintillans*.

190

« The calmer the sea is, the better your chances are to see the blue tears.

4 A little luck is required to witness blue tears in all its neon glory. Though the effect can appear from April to September, it's at its height from April to June, so those months are the best time to visit. Weather is also a **crucial** factor. Aim for a night when there's a dark sky and it's hot out—that's when the blue-tears effect is most **vibrant**. Also, the calmer the sea is, the better your chances are to see it. Ideally, waves will be under 20 inches high without any whitecaps.

5 In terms of location, the phenomenon can appear in all of Matsu's islets, including Dongyin, Nangan, and Beigan. However, the less light pollution there is nearby, the more likely you are to see the blue tears. Local hotel and tour group operators can really **come in handy** here. They can assist in finding the lesser-known dark spots and even **forecast** when the best conditions for viewing will occur.

6 Anyone visiting Matsu should accept the possibility that they might be unlucky and not see the blue tears. But that's just one of many natural wonders the islands have to offer, so get out and get exploring!

Questions

_____ 1. What does the word **It** refer to in the second paragraph?
   a. Matsu.   **b.** Blue tears.   **c.** Beaches.   **d.** Tourists.

_____ 2. What does **come in handy** mean in the fifth paragraph?
   a. To be useful.   **b.** To be hard to find.
   c. To be unexpected.   **d.** To be expensive.

_____ 3. Which of the following words has the opposite meaning of **vibrant** in the fourth paragraph?
   a. Annoying.   **b.** Dangerous.   **c.** Flashing.   **d.** Dim.

_____ 4. The author says that weather is "a **crucial** factor" in the fourth paragraph. What's another word with the same meaning as **crucial**?
   a. Unpredictable.   **b.** New.
   c. Important.   **d.** Violent.

_____ 5. What does **forecast** in the fifth paragraph mean?
   a. To predict or estimate a future trend.
   b. To share secret knowledge no one else has.
   c. To join an exclusive club of only a few people.
   d. To arrange an event or party.

« molecular gastronomy dessert

87 Playing With Your Food

1   For those with a passion for cooking, creating delicious dishes is like being a painter or sculptor. They love to experiment with flavors and textures, relying on creativity and intuition as much as recipes. Followers of molecular gastronomy, however, take a more scientific approach. This doesn't mean their creations lack originality, though. On the contrary, molecular gastronomy has opened the door 5 to a new world of amazing cuisine.

2   What exactly is molecular gastronomy? Simply put, it examines cooking mainly from a scientific perspective. More specifically, it focuses on the physical and chemical changes that occur during the culinary process. The term was coined by two Oxford University scientists, Nicholas Kurti and Hervé This in 1988. The 10 pair studied the chemical composition of foods and how they interacted. Hervé This even devised a mathematical formula to help people analyze food according to molecular gastronomy. In one sense, food science was nothing new then. However, it had been limited to large-scale food manufacturing, items bought in supermarkets, for example. Molecular gastronomy introduced a type of food 15 science to a new audience: chefs and ambitious home cooks.

3   Kurti and This's work led to some astounding—even bizarre—food combinations. Who would have thought that snail porridge or smoky-bacon ice cream could taste so good? According to molecular gastronomy, they contain just the right mix of ingredients. Moreover, using the principles of this fairly new 20 discipline, entirely new dishes are possible. These include what's been called "apple

>> liquid nitrogen, used for flash freezing in molecular gastronomy

⌃ molecular gastronomy dish

caviar," which doesn't use fish eggs at all. A syringe is required, though, to help add apple juice to a mixture so that it bubbles. Another apple dish tastes like meat with the help of the scientific principles of molecular gastronomy. How about delicious, creamy, homemade ice cream? No problem with liquid nitrogen! 25

4 Those wanting to get a taste of molecular gastronomy have a few options. Adventurous cooks can scan the Internet for recipes and try them at home. Alternatively, people can try to find a restaurant that offers this exclusive—and very expensive— 30 cuisine. Most people, though, will likely find those choices either too tricky or costly. Feasting their eyes on photos of molecular gastronomy will likely be the closest they ever get to it.

⌃ A syringe is required to make "juice caviar."

Questions

⌃ molecular cocktail Mojito with mint caviar and sugar cloud, foam made from sugar and carbon dioxide

_____ 1. What is this passage mainly about?
   a. The author explains how to make delicious dishes.
   b. The reader is introduced to the use of science to influence cooking.
   c. The types of food that scientists like the most are explained in detail.
   d. The difficulties of making new, interesting meals are presented.

_____ 2. What is the focus of molecular gastronomy?
   a. The creation of bizarre food combinations.
   b. The production of food in more safe and efficient ways.
   c. The artistic side of cooking, including intuition.
   d. The chemical changes that occur during cooking.

_____ 3. In the first paragraph, what does the author compare those passionate about cooking to?
   a. Artists.   **b.** Scientists.   **c.** Doctors.   **d.** Manufacturers.

_____ 4. Which of the following can be inferred about molecular gastronomy from the passage?
   a. It will become more popular around the world soon.
   b. It was started by people who used to be painters and sculptors.
   c. It is too difficult to even try to make at home for some people.
   d. It creates food with a taste that only a few people will like.

_____ 5. What is the purpose of the third paragraph?
   a. To show how unusual molecular gastronomy dishes can be.
   b. To explain the most common food molecular gastronomy cooks create.
   c. To encourage readers to try molecular gastronomy cuisine.
   d. To demonstrate how terrible molecular gastronomy recipes are.

⌃ stage musical
The Lion King

⌃ *Les Misérables* (2012)
movie poster

⌃ *Mama Mia* (2008)
movie poster

88 Listing: Musicals

1   The phenomenal success of *Les Misérables* at the 2013 Oscars introduced musicals to a whole new generation of fans. Although at their core a stage genre, many stage musicals have been adapted into films (e.g., *Mamma Mia!*, *The Sound of Music*, *Les Misérables*) since the dawn of cinema, and some films have even been adapted into stage musicals (e.g., *The Lion King*, *Billy Elliot*).   5

2   Musicals are easily confused with opera. However, though these two genres both use song to convey a story, there are some essential differences between them. Operas usually have no spoken dialogue, while musicals do have some sections where the dialogue is spoken rather than sung. Musicals also use dance, have a variety of different musical styles, and tend to be more   10 lighthearted than operas.

3   If you're ever in the United States or the United Kingdom on vacation and you'd like to see a stage musical, head to New York's Broadway district or London's West End. To find out what's on and where, you can check the listings section in a newspaper or check out a listings website online. Listings provide   15 information about local performances and events. There, under each show's name, you'll find information like performance dates, venue, ticket prices, and a short description of the show.

4   Now, use the listings on the next page to answer the following questions.

» London's
West End

(Source: https://www.visitlondon.com/)

The Book of Mormon at the Prince of Wales Theatre

Musical

 Add to list

Read More

From 26 February 2013 to 3 May 2014
Prince of Wales Theatre W1D 6AS [map]
This comedy musical follows the plight of a pair of teenage Mormon missionaries sent to convert a village in a dangerous part of Uganda.

The Lion King at the Lyceum Theatre

Musical

Add to list

Read More

From 23 February 2010 to 20 July 2014
The Lion King is a hugely popular London musical set against the majesty of the Serengeti Plains, to the evocative rhythms of Africa. The show brings the characters from the animated Disney film to life with imaginative costumes and amazing special effects.

We Will Rock You at the Dominion Theatre

Musical

Add to list

From £25.00
(TWD 1,228.11)

Read More

From 2 January 2012 to 26 October 2013
Dominion Theatre W1T 5AQ [map]
Ben Elton and the remaining members of the rock group Queen bring you this vibrant musical. Set in a futuristic world where rock music has been banned, it's up to Galileo to save the world!

Les Misérables at the Queen's Theatre

Musical

Add to list

From £20.00
(TWD 982.49)

Read More

From 17 July 2013 to 26 April 2014
Queens Theatre W1D 6BA [map]
Cameron Mackintosh's legendary production of Boublil and Schönberg's Les Misérables is a global stage sensation. Seen by more than 60 million people in 42 countries and in 21 languages around the globe, it is still breaking box-office records everywhere in its 28th year.

≈ stage musical
Billy Elliot

Questions

_____ 1. Which musical was playing at the Lyceum Theatre?
  a. *We Will Rock You.*   b. *Les Misérables.*
  c. *The Book of Mormon.*   d. *The Lion King.*

_____ 2. When was your last chance to see *We Will Rock You*?
  a. January 2, 2012.   b. July 17, 2013.
  c. October 26, 2013.   d. February 8, 2014.

_____ 3. What was the cheapest price for a ticket to see *We Will Rock You*?
  a. £10.00   b. £20.00   c. £25.00   d. £27.50

_____ 4. Which of the musicals would you go to see if you wanted to see a comedy?
  a. *We Will Rock You.*   b. *Les Misérables.*
  c. *The Book of Mormon.*   d. *The Lion King.*

_____ 5. What was the earliest you could go to see *Les Misérables*?
  a. February 23, 2010.   b. February 26, 2013.
  c. July 17, 2013.   d. April 26, 2014.

>> broken heart

89 Dying of a Broken Heart

1   Most of us have had our hearts broken at some point. It might have been a school crush that went sour or a **betrayal** by a close friend. At the time it can feel like the end of the world, as if you're in **excruciating** physical pain. But eventually you get past it and life goes on.

2   If you're lucky, that is.

3   In some cases, a figurative broken heart can lead to a literal heart attack, severe depression, stroke, or even death. Such is the conclusion of a new study from Rice University. The team there uncovered **compelling** evidence that major grief episodes can have very real consequences for your health. Their study tracked widowers who had recently lost their spouses. The results were alarming: grief sufferers have on average 17 percent more body inflammation than normal people. Increased inflammation has been linked to a number of health conditions, including diabetes, cancer, and heart disease.

4   Then there's the mysterious "broken heart syndrome." The illness is also called *Takotsubo* because it makes the heart look like a pot used to catch octopuses in Japan. It was first noticed as a **novel** type of heart defect in 1990. But when doctors discovered that many sufferers had recently lost a loved one, it got the nickname "broken heart syndrome." Symptoms include chest pain and shortness of breath, which are often mistaken for a heart attack. Some doctors suspect that broken heart syndrome can even be **terminal** in extreme cases. For proof, they point

>> takatsubo, a pot used to catch octopuses in Japan

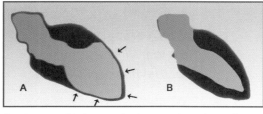

⌃ scheme of left ventriculogram in Takotsubo cardiomyopathy (A) and normal (B)
(cc by JHeuser)

↟ Debbie Reynolds (1932–2016) *(left)* is believed to have died from broken heart syndrome.

to the tendency of a person to die almost immediately 25 after their spouse passes away. Some believe that Debbie Reynolds, mother of *Star Wars* star Carrie Fisher, died from it after her daughter passed in 2016.

5   Formal research into broken heart syndrome is still lacking. But is it the least bit surprising that 30 there's a link between our mental and physical health? It's not for doctors working on the frontlines of the health sector. They've seen how people with chronic physical conditions are at higher risk of developing mental health problems. They've also seen how mental 35 health contributes to physical health. In the end, it's impossible to separate body and mind. So if you're going through a break-up, remember to take it easy and not to be too hard on yourself.

≪ In some cases, a figurative broken heart can lead to a literal heart attack.

Questions

_____ 1. What's another word for **excruciating** in the first paragraph?
   a. Mysterious.   **b.** Extreme.   **c.** Loud.   **d.** Expected.

_____ 2. Which of the following has the opposite meaning of **compelling** in the third paragraph?
   a. Joyous.   **b.** Controversial.   **c.** Boring.   **d.** Expensive.

_____ 3. What does **betrayal** in the first paragraph mean?
   a. The act of tricking or hurting someone who trusts you.
   b. The process of growing close with someone after years spent together.
   c. A surprising but positive turn of events.
   d. A sudden development that results in intense confusion.

_____ 4. What does **terminal** mean in the fourth paragraph?
   a. Easily treated if identified early.
   b. Incurable and likely to result in death.
   c. Hard to know where it came from.
   d. Easily spread to other patients.

_____ 5. "It was first noticed as a **novel** type of heart defect in 1990." The opposite of **novel** is _____.
   a. deadly   **b.** suspicious   **c.** common   **d.** rare

90 | Bar Graph: Living Abroad

🎧 090

1   Everyone should live abroad at some point in his or her life. Being completely immersed in a way of life that's different from your own is a character-building experience, but moving abroad is not a simple thing. It can be tough surviving on your own in a country where you have no family or friends and don't speak the local language. 5

2   Moving to another country, then, is not a decision that should be made lightly. It might be a good idea to do some traveling first to see if moving abroad would suit you. Perhaps first take a holiday to the country you're considering moving to in order to check it out. Will it be easy to get a job there? Does the climate suit you? Does the food 10 seem delicious or does it turn your stomach? Is it somewhere you could see yourself living long term? There are, of course, many reasons for living in another country. Check out the bar graph on the following page to learn the reasons given by 1,000 foreigners for their move to Taiwan and then answer the following questions. 15

Questions

_____1. What percentage of foreigners moved to Taiwan to learn Chinese?
   a. 10%   **b.** 15%   **c.** 20%   **d.** 30%

_____2. What was the least popular reason for moving to Taiwan?
   a. Earning money.   **b.** Gaining life experience.
   c. Pursuing further education.   **d.** Pursuing a better quality of life.

_____3. How many of the 1,000 foreigners asked moved to Taiwan to pursue further education?
   a. 10   **b.** 20   **c.** 100   **d.** 200

_____4. Which of the following statements is true?
   a. More people moved to Taiwan to earn money than moved there to gain life experience.
   b. More people moved to Taiwan to pursue further education than moved there to learn Chinese.
   c. The same number of people moved to Taiwan to earn money as moved there to gain life experience.
   d. The same number of people moved to Taiwan to earn money as moved there to find a better quality of life.

_____5. What percentage of foreigners moved to Taiwan to visit family, volunteer, marry, etc.?
   a. 9%   **b.** 10%   **c.** 11%   **d.** 20%

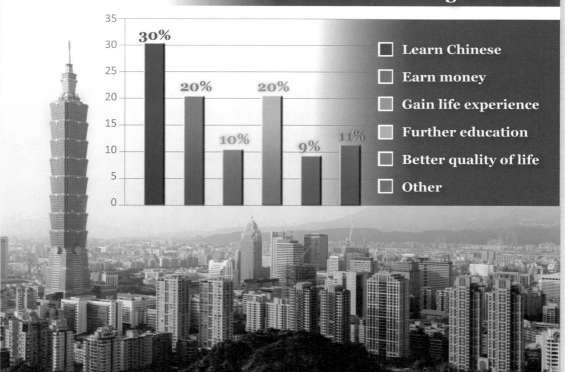

Reasons for Moving to Taiwan

□ Learn Chinese
□ Earn money
□ Gain life experience
□ Further education
□ Better quality of life
□ Other

>> Maria Montessori
(1870–1952)

91 Maria Montessori

(091)

1   Maria Montessori was born in Italy on August 31, 1870. Growing up, she was heavily influenced by her mother, who was both highly educated and an avid reader. This might be why Maria refused to compromise when it came to her own education. At first she wanted to study engineering, a controversial choice given the social conventions of her time. Then she switched to medicine, which was even more contentious to those misguided people who believed a woman's place was in the home. Ultimately, Maria's hard work paid off when she became the first woman ever to be admitted into the University of Rome's Faculty of Medicine.

2   That Maria Montessori was an intelligent, brave, and capable woman is undeniable. But these admirable traits are not exclusively why she is still remembered today. It is the field of education where her greatest legacy resides.

3   Later in life, Maria began to work with children, and she established her first Casa dei Bambini, or "children's house," in 1907. Maria was convinced that, given a suitable environment, children would take the lead in their own education. In other words, they would start learning themselves not because they were told to, but rather because they wanted to. To Maria, the real challenge was figuring out the right educational environment.

4   Maria's theories are popular to this day, and many schools around the world offer a Montessori education. These schools attempt to cater to certain elements of

5

10

15

20

25

⌃ Italian 1000 Lire banknote representing Maria Montessori (cc by Flanker)

>> Montessori phonograms

human psychology, such as communication, work, order, and abstraction. In doing so, their aim is to allow students to build up their own conceptions and self-motivate, instead of being told they're wrong by a figure of authority. When it comes to the actual teaching, Montessori schools use an approach that includes all five of the senses, not just listening and watching. 30

5   Advocates maintain that the Montessori approach prepares students to conquer the challenges of adult life, whether emotional, academic, or professional. There are also several examples of highly successful people who received a Montessori education, including Jeff Bezos, the founder of Amazon.com. However, if Maria Montessori were still around today, she would 35 likely emphasize that her system is based on developing a life-long love of learning, not a massive bank 40 account.

⌃ Jeff Bezos (1964–), the founder of Amazon.com (cc by Steve Jurvetson)

⌃ The Edward Harden Mansion housed the first American Montessori school in 1911. (cc by Daniel Case)

Questions

_____ 1. Which statement below best expresses the main idea of this article?
   a. Maria Montessori invented an educational approach.
   b. Maria Montessori was the first woman to study medicine in Rome.
   c. Maria Montessori loved teaching children.
   d. Maria Montessori established her first "children's house" in 1907.

_____ 2. What can be inferred from this article about the time in which Maria Montessori lived?
   a. Children were not educated.   **b.** Newspapers hadn't been invented.
   c. Schools focused on independence. **d.** There weren't many female doctors.

_____ 3. Which of the following is NOT true about the Montessori approach to education?
   a. It employs all five senses.
   b. It helps students develop a love of learning.
   c. It corrects students whenever they make an error.
   d. It caters to elements of human psychology.

_____ 4. This article is best described as a _____.
   a. folk tale   **b.** documented incident
   c. myth   **d.** descriptive essay

_____ 5. According to the article, what made Maria prioritize her own education?
   a. She loved to read books.   **b.** She loved children.
   c. She had an educated mother.   **d.** She wanted to get rich.

92 *The Art of War*

» statue of Sunzi
(cc by 663highland)

1 Sunzi was an important Chinese military strategist who was born in 544 BC. He is best known for writing *The Art of War*, an essay that describes how to win battles and conquer opposing countries. It is divided into 13 chapters, each focusing on a certain aspect of war. These include "Waging War," "Maneuvering," and "Variation of Tactics."

2 Although Sunzi's strategies are based on ancient warfare, there are still people who turn to his writings for advice in the present day. For example, Sunzi wrote that "all war is deception." This was true back in Sunzi's time, and it is still true now. In fact, there was an Allied strategy in World War II called Operation Fortitude, which was based solely on deception. The Allied powers set up fake armies, including inflatable tanks, to make their enemies think that they were about to launch an attack. In the end, Sunzi's observation turned out to be correct—Operation Fortitude was a success.

3 Another heavily favored quote from *The Art of War* is "The general who advances without coveting fame and retreats without fearing disgrace is the jewel of the kingdom." Radio, television, and the Internet help make this quote very relevant in modern times, since it can be hard for military planners to act strategically because there are so many people judging their actions from the sidelines.

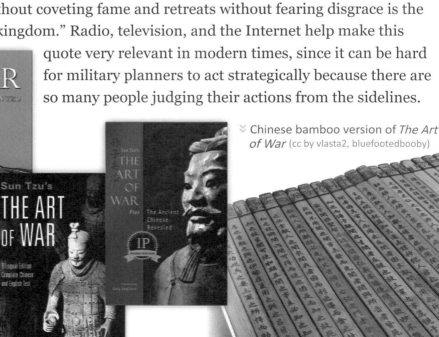

≫ Chinese bamboo version of *The Art of War* (cc by vlasta2, bluefootedbooby)

⌃» *The Art of War* has been published worldwide in English.

4   Businessmen around the world also turn to *The Art of War* in search of an advantage over their peers. They believe that the traits identified by Sunzi as being ideal in a general are also good for a manager. For example, Sunzi believed that cowardice, recklessness, and a bad temper are all weaknesses in a military leader. Obviously, they would also be weaknesses in the world of business. Two other Sunzi quotes that businessmen are particularly fond of are "Know thy enemy," and "Exploit your enemy's weaknesses and avoid his strengths." 30

5   Having come up with so many wise and pertinent observations over two thousand years ago, Sunzi was obviously a true genius. But even the great tactician himself might raise an eyebrow at how his wisdom is now showing 35 up in useless self-help books like *Use the Art of War to Save Your Marriage.*

≫ Sunzi
(544 BC–496 BC)

Questions

_____ 1. What is closest to the main point the author wants to make?
    a. People have largely forgotten the works of Sunzi.
    b. *The Art of War* was the bloodiest essay ever written.
    c. People consult Sunzi's writings to this day.
    d. Sunzi wrote the very first self-help book.

_____ 2. Which of the following is NOT a quote attributed to Sunzi?
    a. "All war is deception."
    b. "Never do battle without a thick coat on."
    c. "Know thy enemy."
    d. "Exploit your enemy's weaknesses and avoid his strengths."

_____ 3. Which of the following is an opinion?
    a. Sunzi was obviously a genius.
    b. Sunzi is known for writing *The Art of War*.
    c. Operation Fortitude used a deception strategy.
    d. Sunzi was born in 544 BC.

_____ 4. In this article, the author showed bias against _____.
    a. Sunzi   **b.** self-help books
    c. World War II   **d.** war

_____ 5. The author's tone in this article can best be described as _____.
    a. depressed   **b.** excited   **c.** loving   **d.** serious

93 Finland's Education System

1   Global rankings consistently place Finland as having the best education system in the world, which is quite an impressive accomplishment. But what's even more interesting is *how* Finland is coming out on top, especially since it's doing so using the opposite **approach** of most other countries.   5

2   There are several fascinating aspects of Finland's **superb** education system, one of which is how teachers are treated. Teachers in Finland must possess a Master's degree, and they are all selected from the top 10% of their graduating class. This means that all Finnish teachers are highly   10 qualified. In addition, teachers are treated as professionals. They're given a lot of space with which to craft their own education strategies. This includes being granted two hours a week of professional development time, apart from the four hours a day they teach,   15 and they thereby have time to tutor struggling students privately if need be.

3   This brings us to another interesting fact: students rarely fall through the cracks in the Finnish education system. They are not   20 divided into "smart" and "slow" student groups, but are rather treated as being at different stages of development. If a student is struggling in class, his teacher will try various personalized approaches to rectify the problem. This is a very common situation, as nearly 30% of Finnish students receive   25

⌃ Finnish students rarely do homework or take exams until their teens.

≫ Finland

204

specialized help during their first nine years of school. It must
be working though, because Finland has some of the highest
graduation rates in the world.

4   What people might find most shocking is Finland's approach
to testing. Unlike the "test early, test often" approach favored   30
by most countries, Finnish students rarely do homework or take
exams until they're teens. There is no testing whatsoever for the
first six years of a student's education. On top of all this, students
get a total of 75 minutes of **recreational** time every day.
Students in the United States get only 27 minutes on average.   35

5   In conclusion, the success of Finland's education system seems to
be the **triumph** of quality over quantity. Instead of going by numbers,
whether in test scores or student admissions, Finland emphasizes the
human element. The results speak for themselves.

≪ A teacher in Finland must possess a Master's degree.

Questions

_____ 1. What does the author mean when he says that "students rarely fall through the cracks"?
  a. Schools are kept in good condition.
  b. Students are accepted regardless of background.
  c. Students are supported so they don't lag behind.
  d. Schools make sure that every student has a teacher.

_____ 2. "Students get a total of 75 minutes of **recreational** time every day." Which of the following is an example of a **recreational** activity?
  a. Playing.   **b.** Studying.   **c.** Working.   **d.** Packing.

_____ 3. "There are several fascinating aspects of Finland's **superb** education system." A word with the same meaning as **superb** is _____.
  a. modern   **b.** magnificent   **c.** boring   **d.** ordinary

_____ 4. Which of the following sentences uses **approach** in the same way as it is used in the first paragraph?
  a. His test score approached perfection, but not quite.
  b. Tim approached the door slowly.
  c. The approach to the landing strip was sand.
  d. John's approach to studying was very complicated.

_____ 5. In the final paragraph, the author states, "Finland's education system seems to be the **triumph** of quality over quantity." The word with the opposite meaning of **triumph** is _____.
  a. battle   **b.** competition   **c.** defeat   **d.** celebration

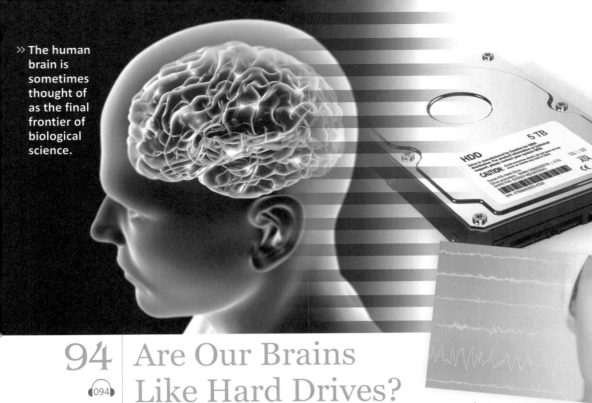

» The human brain is sometimes thought of as the final frontier of biological science.

94 | Are Our Brains Like Hard Drives?

(094)

1   The human brain is sometimes thought of as the final frontier of biological science. While scientists have steadily increased their knowledge of other parts of the human body, the brain's function remains somewhat of a mystery. But given the pace of modern research, the true nature of 5 the brain might be illuminated before long.

2   Psychologist Giulio Tononi of the University of Wisconsin-Madison has **formulated** a new theory that might change the way we look at not just the human brain, but sleep as well. Professor Tononi believes that the brain resets itself during sleep, breaking existing 10 neural connections so that new ones can be formed.

3   His theory helps answer a question that has puzzled scientists for a long time: Why is the brain so active while we sleep? What is it up to? Unlike the rest of our body, which remains in an almost **paralyzed** state during sleep, our brain maintains a level of activity that's nearly 15 the same as when we're awake.

4   Until now, scientists have assumed that the brain was busy building new neural connections while we sleep. These connections are formed by learning or remembering an 20 experience. But according to Professor Tononi,

⌃ Our brain maintains a level of activity while we sleep.

⌄ Our brain is working like a computer hard drive while we sleep.

the opposite might be true. He believes that the constant building of these connections would consume too much energy and overwhelm our brains with pointless details. Instead, our brains break down these connections while we sleep. Their removal creates space for new connections to be made the next 25 day when we learn or experience something new.

5   If our brain is working like a computer hard drive while we sleep, **deleting** memories so that new ones can be properly stored, this raises a number of interesting questions. For example, how does our brain know which memories are of little consequence and thus worthy of deletion? Perhaps with a bit 30

more research, scientists will discover how we can control the process. Wouldn't it be great if we all had **the final say** over what we remember and what we forget? It would certainly be a lot easier to pass English exams if that were the case. Someone 35 who suffered a traumatic episode would also have an opportunity to forget it and move on.

« Someone suffering trauma may have an opportunity to forget it with brain science.

Questions

____ 1. The article mentions having **the final say** over something. If someone has the **the final say**, that means he or she can _____.
   a. avoid a danger
   b. speak many languages
   c. decide on something
   d. understand an issue

____ 2. If someone is **paralyzed**, as the word is used in the third paragraph, then he or she _____.
   a. is awake
   b. is thinking hard
   c. cannot move
   d. is tired

____ 3. The author compares our brain to a computer hard drive **deleting** memories while we're asleep. A word with a similar meaning as **deleting** is _____.
   a. sorting   **b.** observing   **c.** remembering **d.** destroying

____ 4. What does **the opposite** mean in the fourth paragraph?
   a. Something important.
   b. Something that occurred earlier.
   c. Something that is longer.
   d. Something that is completely different.

____ 5. The second paragraph states that psychologist Giulio Tononi "has **formulated** a new theory." Which of the following has the same meaning as **formulated**?
   a. Developed.   **b.** Rejected.   **c.** Arranged.   **d.** Encountered.

95 Insider Trading

1 There are two types of companies: public and private. If a company is private, it is wholly owned by a limited number of people. If a company is public, on the other hand, anyone is able to invest in it. All you need to do is buy its **stock** at a stock exchange.

2 This stock will rise or fall in value depending on what's happening in the market. Maybe that company posted earnings that were higher than everyone expected, and the stock price spiked. But earnings could also go down, which would cause the stock price to fall. Whatever the case, the important thing is that sensitive information is made available to everyone at the same time, allowing them to decide whether to buy or to sell stock.

3 What happens when people attached to the company hear something before the public does? Maybe they discover that corporate earnings are down, so they sell off their own stock while the price is still high, before everyone else gets a chance to. This is called insider trading, which is the practice of using nonpublic information to make stock purchasing decisions. This is not just a case of being unfair—insider trading is illegal in most countries.

4 You don't need to be a high-level executive in a company to engage in insider trading. If you overheard a corporate executive discussing companies that were about to **merge** and then went out and bought stock, you could be arrested for insider trading. The key criterion for insider trading is using nonpublic information to make a trade, not the existence of any personal connection to the company involved.

5

10

15

20

25

⌃ Insider trading is the practice of using nonpublic information to make stock purchasing decisions.

5   Insider trading arrests can often be big news because **they** tend to involve very wealthy and well-connected people. In 2004, Martha Stewart, a **celebrated** television personality in the United States, was found guilty of **conspiracy** and sentenced to five months in prison after selling her shares of ImClone on an inside tip from her friend. In 2003, an Australian banker named Rene Rivkin was imprisoned for nine months after an inside trade that earned him less than $3,000. These are just a few of the hundreds of insider-trading scandals that make it into the news headlines every year.

≫ stock exchange

>> If you overheard insider information and then bought stock, you could be arrested for insider trading.

Questions

_____ 1. "If you overheard a corporate executive discussing companies that were about to **merge** . . ." Which of the following is something else that can **merge**?
   a. People.   **b.** Highways.   **c.** Dogs.   **d.** Windows.

_____ 2. "All you need to do is buy its **stock** at a stock exchange." The word **stock** means _____.
   a. a share of investment in a company
   b. a history of a company
   c. the founder of a company
   d. a product created by a company

_____ 3. In the final paragraph, the author mentions that Martha Stewart was found guilty of **conspiracy** and was imprisoned. Which of the following is an example of a **conspiracy**?
   a. A plan to rob a bank.   **b.** A vacation.
   c. A speeding ticket.   **d.** A home renovation.

_____ 4. Which of the following means the opposite of **celebrated** as the word is in the final paragraph?
   a. Profitable.   **b.** Dirty.   **c.** Unknown.   **d.** Priceless.

_____ 5. What does **they** in the final paragraph refer to?
   a. Rich people.   **b.** Famous TV personalities.
   c. Insider trading arrests.   **d.** International companies.

96 Left Wing and Right Wing

1   Anyone who reads the newspaper or tunes into political talk shows will undoubtedly have heard the **talking heads** touch down on left-wing and right-wing political parties before. But what do these statements mean, and where did they come from?

2   The answer can be found within the pages of French history. Back in 1789, during the early phases of the French Revolution, members of the National Assembly followed a very specific seating plan. It was customary for supporters of the king to sit to the right and supporters of the revolution to the left. The press eventually got into the habit of identifying each faction by their position in the assembly: left and right. And so an important part of our modern political vocabulary was born.

3   Although these labels were invented over 200 years ago, their original meaning is still relevant to their modern usage. Take the left, or left-wing, for example. During the French Revolution, these people believed in a radical change for France's political system. To them, the old political structures were unfair and ineffective, and they needed to be eliminated before the country could make progress. Nowadays, someone who is left wing tends to believe in trying new political strategies in order to improve society. They are also biased toward higher taxes and welfare programs that aim to redistribute wealth to poor and vulnerable people. Left-wing people also

5

10

15

20

⌃ French Revolution

⌃ In the meeting of the Estates General, 1789, supporters of the king sat to the right and

≫ Left-wing people tend to stress peace and nonviolence.

tend to stress peace and nonviolence, which is ironic given 25 the chaos of the latter stages of the French Revolution.

On the other side of the National Assembly, there were the right-wing politicians. These people would hold on to tradition even if it meant hundreds of thousands of their fellow citizens starved to death. Right-wing politicians 30 already had money and power, so they feared change because they had the most to lose. Nowadays, right-wing politicians still favor tradition. They tend to believe that people should succeed or fail based on their own personal merit, without any help from the government. What they 35 find difficult to understand, however, is differences in individual circumstances. Questions of merit aside, it's a lot harder for someone to excel in life if he or she had to drop out of school in order to put food on the table.

≪ Right-wing people favor tradition.

Questions

_____1. Which statement below best expresses the main idea of this article?
   a. Left and right are two old labels still used to this day.
   b. The French Revolution was an important historical event.
   c. Right-wing politicians favor tradition over change.
   d. Left-wing supporters tend to favor welfare policies.

_____2. In this article, the author showed bias against _____.
   a. left-wing politics   b. newspapers
   c. the French Revolution   d. right-wing politics

_____3. Which of the following can be inferred from the third paragraph?
   a. The French Revolution became very violent.
   b. The French Revolution lasted over 30 years.
   c. The French Revolution was started by right-wing people.
   d. The French Revolution failed to achieve change.

_____4. In the first paragraph, the writer mentions **talking heads**. What does this refer to?
   a. Lawyers.   b. Political commentators.
   c. Schoolchildren.   d. Doctors.

_____5. What caused two different French political movements to be labeled as **left** and **right**?
   a. Their headquarters.   b. Their leaders' names.
   c. Their flags.   d. Their seating plan.

97 Encyclopedia: Humans and Cats— A History of Friendship

097

1   Scientists now believe that cats and humans have been living side by side for up to 12,000 years. That's the amount of time that has passed since humans first
5 started farming on a substantial scale. Farming meant having to store grain for the winter, and that's where cats came in. Cats helped kill rats and other animals that would eat the grain stored in silos. What began as a useful partnership for both sides eventually turned into cats and humans living under the same
10 roof.

2   That still hasn't made cats dependent on us. Unlike dogs, which have lost many of their survival skills over time, cats still have most of their natural instincts intact. Many cat owners can personally attest to this, as
15 cats are still in the habit of going outside, killing something, and bringing it back as a "gift."

3   Please answer the following questions about the encyclopedia entry
20 about cats on the next page.

CAT

Cats are agile, hunting mammals with keen senses and sharp teeth and claws. Domestic cats make some of the most popular pets.

The longhaired Persian needs regular grooming to keep its coat sleek.

The hairless sphinx was bred in the 1960s from a kitten born without fur.

The Manx cat from the Isle of Man, in the U.K., is famous for its lack of a tail.

The blue shorthair has copper eyes and a quiet, affectionate nature.

The Cornish rex has a curly coat of short, thin hair and large, open ears.

The Siamese has long been one of the most popular pedigreed (purebred) cats.

HUNTER IN THE HOME

Even a domestic cat, like this tabby, has the hunting instincts of its wild relations. Cats often toy with their prey, rather than killing it immediately. They hunt mostly at night, catching mice, small birds, and insects.

Large, sensitive ears pick up sounds too faint for human ears to hear

Pupils open wide to let in a maximum amount of light. A mirrorlike layer at the back of the eye intensifies the light

Whiskers are modified hairs with nerves at their base and are ultra-sensitive to touch

THE CLAWS

Extended

Retracted

Cats retract (pull back) their claws to keep them sharp when not in use. Each claw is attached to a toe bone. It is retracted by ligaments, which are worked by muscles.

(Source: *The Kingfisher Children's Encyclopedia*)

The cat family is divided into two main groups, based largely on size. The first group is made up of big cats such as tigers, lions, and leopards. The second includes cougars, bobcats, and lynxes, as well as the many small wild cats and the domestic cat. In all there are about 37 species of cat.

PET CATS

It is thought that the domestic cat was originally a small wild cat living in Africa. By 2000 B.C. it had been tamed by the Ancient Egyptians, who used it to protect their stored food from mice and rats. Today, there are many breeds of domestic cat, including longhaired Persians and Angoras and the shorthaired Manx and Siamese.

CAT CHARACTERISTICS

Domestic cats resemble their wild relatives in many ways. They are excellent hunters, strong and agile, with a keen sense of hearing and very good eyesight. They have curved claws, strong jaws, sharp teeth, and whiskers that are sensitive to touch. Cats are naturally inquisitive and are expert climbers and jumpers. Their flexible backbones allow them to swivel their bodies into a wide range of positions.

CAT BEHAVIOR

Cats spend at least an hour a day grooming their fur by licking it with their rough tongues. This helps to keep their fur in good condition and keeps them cool in hot weather. Cats sleep, on the average, twice as long as other mammals, spending up to three fourths of the day asleep, usually in short intervals—hence "catnaps."

HUNTING TACTICS

Although most domestic cats do not have to catch their own food, their instinct (inborn behavior) is to hunt. A cat's sensitive nose quickly picks up the scent of its prey. With its soft, padded paws, a cat can stalk its prey without being noticed until it is close enough to pounce. Then it grabs the prey with its claws and kills it with a powerful bite—usually at the back of the head, breaking the victim's neck.

SEE ALSO

Animal, Mammal, Sight, Tiger

68

Questions

_____ 1. What type of encyclopedia is this entry likely taken from?
- **a.** A farming encyclopedia.
- **b.** An animal encyclopedia.
- **c.** A business encyclopedia.
- **d.** A computer encyclopedia.

_____ 2. A cat's grooming habits would likely appear in which section?
- **a.** Hunter in the Home.
- **b.** Pet Cats.
- **c.** Hunting Tactics.
- **d.** Cat Behavior.

_____ 3. How a house cat kills a mouse would likely appear in which section?
- **a.** Hunter in the Home.
- **b.** Pet Cats.
- **c.** Cat Behavior.
- **d.** The Claws.

_____ 4. Which of the following does NOT appear in the encyclopedia entry?
- **a.** Cat types.　**b.** Cat claws.　**c.** Hunting facts.　**d.** Cat noises.

_____ 5. Which of the following encyclopedia entries would appear AFTER this one?
- **a.** Cactus.　**b.** Badger.　**c.** Aye-aye.　**d.** Centipede.

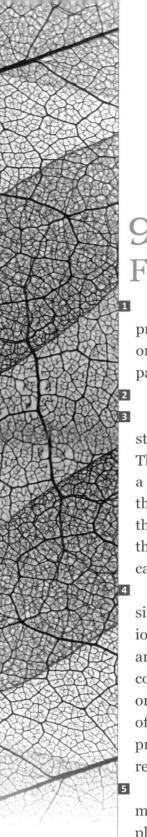

>> leaf veins (sometimes referred to as nerves)
(cc by Curran Kelleher)

98 (098)
Fight Like a Plant

1   Have you ever felt guilty for stepping on a plant? The answer is probably "no." After all, most of us think of plants more as decorations or food rather than as living things. Plants can't move around or feel pain, so we view them as objects.

2   But what if we're wrong?   5

3   Scientists at the University of Wisconsin-Madison have made a stunning new discovery that could change the way we view plants. The experiment began by applying glutamate to a plant. Glutamate is a substance that improves communication between neurons. Then, the scientists used a glowing green protein to track the flow of calcium   10 throughout the plant. Finally, they cut a section of leaf off and observed the reaction under a microscope. What they saw was shocking: glowing calcium pulsed through the entire plant as if to respond to the threat.

4   The results suggest that plants have their own nervous system similar to ours. Instead of nerves, plants appear to rely on calcium   15 ions to send signals throughout the body. Some human functions are also regulated with calcium ions, such as heart beats and muscle contractions. In the case of plants, these signals can be used to switch on defense mechanisms. And perhaps most interesting of all: the extent of the damage determines the amount of calcium released. A small cut   20 produces a small response, but if the entire leaf is crushed, the calcium release surges.

5   You might be wondering: What kind of defense could a plant mount? There are actually many possibilities. For example, some plants release acids that harm insect digestion, causing insects to flee.   25 In other cases, plants can harden their cell walls, making it impossible for would-be attackers to eat them. Sometimes a plant defense can even be deadly. Such is the case with jasmonates, which release toxic compounds when they're damaged by an attacker.

6 The University of Wisconsin-Madison experiment merely confirms what 30 we already know: human and plant cells have some common biology. Maybe we should begin to keep that in mind when dealing with our **green friends**. So next time you're out for a hike, please be careful where you step!

⌄ Some plants, such as sweet pea *(Lathyrus odoratus) (left)* and *Gastrolobium polystachyum (right)*, defend themselves by releasing acids that harm insect digestion.

Questions

⌄ Jasmine oil extracted from *Jasminum grandiflorum* led to the discovery of the molecular structure of jasmonates.

_____ 1. According to the experiment, what substance allows a plant to send signals to other parts of its body?
   a. Jasmonates.   **b.** Neurons.   **c.** Calcium ions.   **d.** Cells.

_____ 2. What was the author's purpose in the first paragraph?
   a. To provide a list of examples to the reader.
   b. To ask a question and get the reader thinking.
   c. To tell a personal story.
   d. To tell a funny joke.

_____ 3. How does the author present information in the article?
   a. By showing contrasts.   **b.** By using a dialogue.
   c. By describing a process.   **d.** By giving personal opinions.

_____ 4. Which of the following is probably true?
   a. Humans are much older than plants.
   b. Humans and plants share some similarities.
   c. Most plants are toxic to consume.
   d. Plants can't react to their surroundings.

_____ 5. What does the term **green friends** refer to in the final paragraph?
   a. Scientists.   **b.** Calcium.   **c.** Insects.   **d.** Plants.

99 Say Bye-Bye to Baldness —and Smell Good, Too!

[099]

1   New research has scientists thinking a possible cure for baldness is not far away. Even more amazingly, the study suggests parts of the body besides the nose have the ability to "smell." Are you confused yet? Don't worry; the details are complicated, but not complex enough to make you pull your hair out! They are also fascinating, even if you aren't going bald.

⌃ Our nose has 400 different types of receptors, which allow us to detect one trillion odors.

2   To **appreciate** the research and its implications, it's necessary to know what receptors and Sandalore are. Our nose has 400 different types of receptors, which allow us to detect one trillion odors. Sandalore, meanwhile, is a chemical that artificially produces the fragrance of sandalwood. If you've never experienced the smell of sandalwood, do yourself a favor. It has a wonderful woody and somewhat flowery scent.

3   A team led by a University of Manchester scientist named Ralf Paus soaked scalp tissue in Sandalore. Incredibly, in a short period of time, **significant** changes in hair development in the tissue were noted. Not only did Sandalore slow down loss of hair, it stimulated hair growth after just a short time. Researchers said it did this by increasing a hormone in the scalp by up to 30 percent. The **astounding** results were beyond the researchers' expectations. "To be honest, I did not

⌄ sandalwood

≪ scalp

really expect this to happen," Paus told a journalist. The better-than-expected results mean that an effective treatment for hair loss may be **just around the corner**. It will likely be on the market sooner than later. Testing with human volunteers has

30   already begun.

⌄ An effective treatment for hair loss may be just around the corner.

4   If you aren't impressed enough by all of this, consider this next point. The researchers made this discovery because they knew of one particular receptor's role in healing wounds. They assumed the receptor—named OR2AT4—could also help with

35   hair growth. Smell receptors are not **limited** to the nose; in fact, they are all over our body. In theory, smell receptors could be stimulated to help other body areas, not just the scalp. In this way, the study has done more than just help men and women with hair loss. It has opened the door to an entirely new

40   field of skin research and possibly the prevention of diseases.

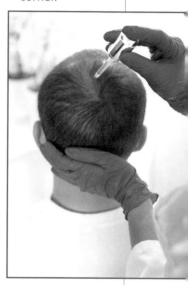

Questions

_____ 1. In the first sentence of the second paragraph, which word could replace **appreciate**?
    a. Understand.   **b.** Recommend.   **c.** Thank.   **d.** Describe.

_____ 2. Which of the following means the opposite of **significant** in the third paragraph?
    a. Unusual.   **b.** Encouraging.   **c.** Unimportant.   **d.** Mistaken.

_____ 3. "The **astounding** results were beyond the researchers' expectations." What does **astounding** mean?
    a. Expected.   **b.** Definite.   **c.** Surprising.   **d.** Confusing.

_____ 4. If something is **just around the corner** as in the third paragraph, that means _____.
    a. it is difficult to find   **b.** it will happen soon
    c. it cannot be seen   **d.** it has been forgotten

_____ 5. In the context of the last paragraph, another word for **limited** is _____.
    a. restricted   **b.** useful   **c.** organized   **d.** abundant

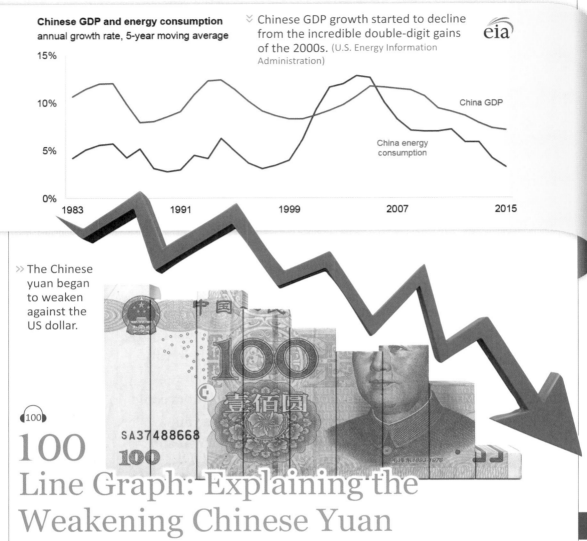

Chinese GDP and energy consumption
annual growth rate, 5-year moving average

⌄ Chinese GDP growth started to decline from the incredible double-digit gains of the 2000s. (U.S. Energy Information Administration)

eia

15%

10%

China GDP

5%

China energy consumption

0%

1983   1991   1999   2007   2015

>> The Chinese yuan began to weaken against the US dollar.

(100)

100
Line Graph: Explaining the Weakening Chinese Yuan

1   After a decade of appreciating in value, the Chinese yuan began to weaken against the US dollar in 2014. The trend continued in the years that followed. Why is this? For one, Chinese GDP growth started to decline from the incredible double-digit gains of the 2000s. Another reason is the trade war that was launched by Donald Trump at the end of 2017. China exports a lot of goods to the United States, so tariffs can be very damaging to the Chinese economy.   5

2   The line graph pictured on the next page shows the value of the Chinese yuan against the US dollar from 2005 to 2018. The y-axis on the left side shows the amount of yuan that one US dollar buys. The horizontal x-axis represents time. The graph gives us a longer-term view of the Chinese yuan. It tells us that   10 even though the currency is weakening, it's still far off from 2005 levels.

>> High tariffs on exports from China to the United States can be very damaging to the Chinese economy.

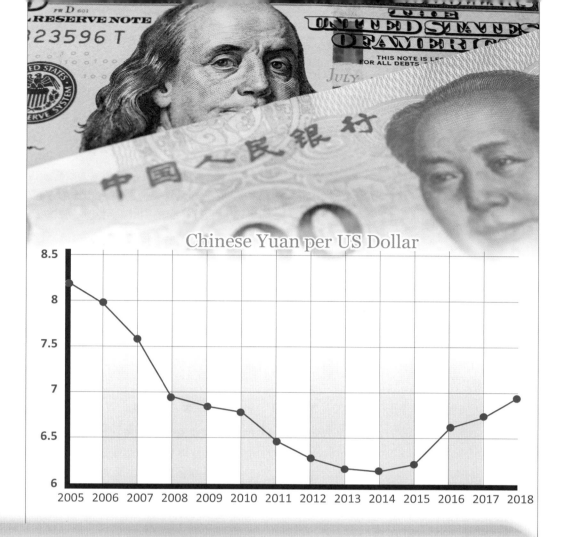

Questions

_____ 1. What was the strongest year for the yuan?
   a. 2014   **b.** 2013   **c.** 2018   **d.** 2005

_____ 2. Which period saw the biggest change in the yuan's value?
   a. 2005–2006   **b.** 2014–2015
   c. 2007–2008   **d.** 2016–2017

_____ 3. How many more yuan did one US dollar buy in 2017 compared to 2016?
   a. 0.5   **b.** 1   **c.** 0.1   **d.** 0.8

_____ 4. What happened to the value of the Chinese yuan against the US dollar between the years 2013–2016?
   a. It went up and then down.
   b. It went down and then up.
   c. It went down and stayed the same.
   d. It stayed the same.

_____ 5. In what period was there a severe drop in the value of the Chinese yuan?
   a. 2007–2008   **b.** 2015–2016   **c.** 2014–2015   **d.** 2010–2011

TRANSLATION

Unit 1 閱讀技巧

關於理解內文的技巧，光是瞭解各語詞的意義仍稍嫌不足。必須具備各種不同的閱讀技巧，才能真正讀懂作者試圖傳達的訊息。當然，看懂一段文章的字面意義是重要的起步，但除此之外，還要能領會字裡行間的弦外之音，也就是分析各觀點之間的關係、理解因果關係，以及預測文中所述事件的結果。

更進一步來說，你必須要能看出作者遊說的技巧和其本身的偏見，還要能明辨事實與意見。本單元所介紹的閱讀技巧，將有助你培養上述能力。

1-1 歸納要旨

文章主旨並非總是顯而易見，因此當閱讀時，別忘了在心裡提問：「作者想要傳達的重點是什麼？」此外，文章除了具有整體主旨，每段內容也有其中心思想，只要清楚每段內容的重點，即可藉此了解整篇文章的意思。

1. 擎天巨木：加州紅杉林　P. 014

想像一下，你走進一片高不見頂的森林，樹木的碩大程度，甚至能讓汽車輕鬆穿越樹幹的樹洞。當你站在加州北部的紅杉森林裡，就會發現想像中的景象竟是如此真實地呈現在眼前。這裡的林木樹齡均超過上千年，以超過 90 公尺的高度俯瞰著大地，許多紅杉甚至比自由女神像還高。

加州紅杉亦稱海岸紅杉，屬於常青樹的一種，且為世上最高聳的林木。現存最高的紅杉名為「海柏利昂」，其高度超過 115 公尺。更有研究報告指出，19 世紀大肆砍伐之前，紅杉高度甚至超越現有紀錄。

加州紅杉生長於加州海岸大約 750 公里長的狹長林地，不過自 1850 年代以來，已有超過 95% 的原生紅杉林遭到砍伐。原因在於紅杉是一種極為搶手的建材，擁有輕盈、耐用且防火的特性，也因此成為當年鐵路業用以建造軌道的必備材料。

紅杉需生長在年雨量與濕氣豐沛，且溫度約為攝氏 10 度至 16 度的環境。加州紅杉生長繁盛的地區鄰近太平洋，雨量充沛，海岸所帶來的霧氣與冷風，能維持全年潮濕的狀態。數世紀以來，該地區的氣候維持不變，許多巨人般的紅杉得以長命百歲，有的樹齡甚至能到 2,200 歲。

然而，由於雨量充盈，容易沖刷帶走土壤中的養分，使得紅杉必須仰賴棲息於樹上和周遭環境的動物來獲取足夠養分。對於許多森林動物而言，紅杉是絕佳的棲息地，而這些動物的排泄物為土壤施肥，幫助紅杉成長茁壯。紅杉枯亡後，遺木完全回歸大自然，再次豐沃了曾經孕育紅杉的土壤。

2. 海螺殼　P. 016

大家常稱夏威夷為熱帶天堂，夏威夷以雪白沙灘、舒適氣候，與濃厚人情味聞名。當地人很喜歡舉辦派對，到此處觀光的時候，你絕對有機會參加派對。夏威夷人的派對現場（亦稱「魯奧宴」（luau）），會以近似中世紀開戰時所吹奏的響亮號角聲來迎接賓客，這就是海螺的聲音，夏威夷人則稱海螺為「普」（pu）。他們通常會以海螺聲來迎賓與示意慶典正式開始。

海螺是純天然的樂器，它其實就是海蝸牛所居住的大型螺旋外殼，尖端處有個開口。海螺殼的外觀十分精美，從珍珠白到深粉橘的色系皆有，可做為裝飾品或樂器。

除了做為派對開場的道具之外，正式場合同樣會運用到海螺，例如夏威夷州議會所舉辦的座談會，以及特定花車遊行活動，均以海螺聲揭開序幕。海螺亦為夏威夷婚禮不可或缺的要角，一宣布新郎新娘成為合法夫妻後，就會有專人吹奏海螺，意味著儀式進行到最高峰。

海螺要吹奏得好必須擁有高超技巧。大多數人都會使出吃奶的力氣，盡可能吹出最響亮的海螺聲。海螺內部渾圓的共鳴空間所產生的聲音，遠從 3 公里外都聽得到。此外，只要手掌與手指按壓海螺殼開口的方法正確，還能產生出人意料的音階,包括長而尖的高音和隆隆低鳴聲。一定要有一副好耳力,才能聽出海螺音準而吹奏出音符,畢竟海螺沒有控制音階的按鍵或琴鍵。

如果對於海螺象徵敬意卻又震耳欲聾的聲響敬謝不敏,其實海螺殼還能發出另一種神祕的平靜聲音,產生安神的作用。只要將海螺拿近耳邊,你就會清楚聽見彷彿海浪輕拍岸邊的聲音。

3. 地底乾坤:越南古芝地道　P. 018

位於越南胡志明市郊區的古芝,看似一般尋常農村地帶,其實整座城市下方暗藏玄機,形成另一座神祕的地道之都。

站在地面上,很難察覺古芝地道的入口。古芝地道最初建於法國佔領越南時的 1940 年代,並於 1955 至 1975 年越戰期間擴大規模。事實上,250 公里長、錯綜複雜的古芝地道,不過是越南大型地下戰道的一小部分。

對於支持南越共產主義的越共而言,地道是最佳的隱匿地點,不僅能遮風避雨、提供庇護,還可做為伏擊敵軍的有用陷阱。無論是傳訊或供應補給品,均可透過地道送達,大量的糧食武器皆囤積於隱密處。此外,美軍慣用的空襲戰略,雖然會對地面造成毀滅性的破壞,但安然躲藏於地道的人卻幾乎毫髮無傷。

隨著空襲與轟炸次數漸增,越來越多人選擇撤退至地道內。日子久了,地道自然成為他們的安家之處。餐廚水井供應的糧食,可餵飽超過 1 萬名越軍和村民。他們甚至建造醫院來救治傷者,設立學校來教育兒童,有的孩子還是在地道裡呱呱墜地的。這裡成為全民隱居的虛擬城市,而在地面上行進的美軍,渾然不知竟有一座城鎮在自己的腳下。

為了保護地道,越共設置尖銳的竹樁陷阱,目的在於重創或消滅靠近其地下庇護所的任何美軍。不過,美軍亦非省油的燈。當美軍發現越共的地道後,即特訓所謂的「地鼠兵」,以探勘繪出地道路線,並設下美軍自己的陷阱。

如今,古芝地道已是當地紀念越戰的景點之一,同時能讓觀光客體驗到,當時的人民願意付出多大的努力,為的就是在戰爭恐懼下,保有一絲生活常態。

4. 古老機構的新穎學習法　P. 020

科學家指出,我們透過雙眼獲取大部分的感官資訊。有些科學家也說,用視覺來學習能學得更快、記得更多。難怪新推出的系列影片挑戰並改變了許多人原先對於教育的見解。各位先生女士,歡迎進入皇家文藝學會的動畫世界!

英國皇家工藝與商業協會(簡稱 RSA)設於倫敦,已成立超過 260 年,是個現有約 29,000 名會員的協會。任何人皆可申請加入 RSA,但不保證能獲准入會。該機構致力於改變及改善社會,其中一項目標就是以簡單明瞭的方式來教導人們複雜的概念。這就是 RSA 動畫興起的由來。

所有 RSA 動畫影片都有相同的基礎架構。以 RSA 會員講授的課程作為音源,在講解的同時,影片中可看到有一隻手在快速抄寫重點與論述說明。這隻手也能隨著講述的內容繪製圖畫、示意圖、圖表,以及其他輔助圖解——許多看起來就像是自行增加變化的。影片整體的呈現速度極快,讓觀眾整整 10 到 11 分鐘內必須保持全神貫注,而這也是大多數影片的長度。

值得一提的是,RSA 動畫影片涉及的是抽象的概念,而非特定時事。影片討論的主題涵蓋了動機的特性、不斷改變的教育重點,以及語言與人性的關聯等。唯有當特定人物與個別情況和這些更廣泛的概念有關時,才會受到討論,但這種情形極少發生。

除了 RSA 動畫系列之外,RSA 也發表文章、演說及其他一般影片,包含動畫與真人實景,並在世界各地舉辦各種活動。該協會聲稱其目標在於創造 21 世紀的啟蒙運動,志向確實遠大。然而,沒有人是完全客觀不偏頗的,因此問題就變成了 RSA 的政治理念能否不損及其教育價值。

5. 黃金香料　P. 022

　　現代生活中，我們習慣將事情視為理所當然。以香草冰淇淋甜筒為例，在享用時，我們只會想到它有多美味，卻不曾想過，香草這種口味其實來自世界上最奢華的一種香料。

　　香草大多萃取自一種原生於墨西哥的蘭花。數百年前，歐洲列強將這種作物引進各個殖民地。香草在 1793 年時首次由法國帶到馬達加斯加。這種作物也開始在印尼、大溪地、印度，當然還有墨西哥等地栽種。現代香草的生產仍然集中在這幾處。光是馬達加斯加和留尼旺小島就出產了世界上 80% 的天然香草。

　　簡單來說，香草是一種很難製作的香料。這種植物需要兩年到四年的時間才能熟成，而且一年當中的花期只有一天，這就表示它們必須透過人工授粉。在花朵收成後，還必須經過好幾個月加工處理才能出口。言而總之，六百朵花只能產出一公斤的香草豆。

　　漫長的生產過程讓種植者難以應付全球需求的轉變，造成目前所見的價格大幅波動。自 2011 年以來，一公斤香草的價格已上漲近 20 倍。2018 年，一公斤香草比一公斤的銀還貴。現在天然香草已經值錢到黑市為此而生。

　　有一種人工合成香料可替代天然香草；事實上，你在享用冰淇淋甜筒時所品味到的，可能就是它。它叫做「香草醛」，用在 95% 以上的香草口味食品中。香草醛可以從許多種材料中提煉出來，但大部分你應該不會想吃下肚，例如廢紙、松樹皮、肉桂，甚至是柏油。若你覺得這聽起來令人作嘔，你可不是唯一一人。香草價格高漲的部分原因，便是人們避免使用人工合成香精、偏好天然香料的趨勢。其結果便是香草需求竄升，而種植者仍難以滿足此需求。

1-2 找出支持性細節

　　一篇好文章，一定會以事實、統計數據和其他證據為基礎，堆砌出作者想要表達的主旨。這就是「支持性細節」，因為此類資訊能「佐證」作者的論點。因此，倘若你想撰寫敘述俄羅斯嚴寒程度的文章，最佳的輔助細節資訊就是氣溫統計數據。

6. 高速快感：重型機車　P. 024

　　有一種機車類型稱為「superbike」（重型機車），俗稱「crotch rocket」（胯下火箭）。也許你會納悶此名稱的由來。因為此類機車馬力強大、車體輕盈，車手必須以前傾姿勢騎乘，才能達到極速效能。騎乘重機的感覺彷彿坐在火箭上奔馳穿梭，故俗稱為「crotch rocket」。

　　以火箭來比喻重機再恰當不過了，因為重機的時速可高達 400 公里。Honda Fireblade 等某些車型，能在短短三秒內加速至時速 100 公里。在此車速下，一定要配戴專門設計的安全帽。如果沒有安全帽的保護，車手很容易因為迎面呼嘯的強風而分心。

　　任何高速競技賽事皆廣受歡迎，重機賽車也不例外。世界重型機車錦標賽於 1988 年創辦，每年均於各國舉辦國際賽事，例如葡萄牙、義大利、印度與澳洲。與名氣略勝一籌的世界摩托車錦標賽（或簡稱 MotoGP）不同，世界重型機車錦標賽只允許僅稍微改裝過的市售重機參賽。因此，觀賽者可自行在外購得與場上專業賽車相同型號的重機，滿足競速的欲望，或純粹滿足購物欲。

　　重機特技表演亦十分熱門。重機引擎的最大馬力，能讓車手表演各種特技，例如讓重機後傾、前輪抬離地面的「翹前輪特技」；或是在高速情況下剎車，利用重機的動力抬離後輪，以前輪維持車體平衡的「翹後輪特技」。如果仍嫌單調，車手還可嘗試「反向騎乘甩尾特技」，也就是車手面朝車尾方向坐在前輪檔泥板上，以高速催油的方式帶動後輪而原地甩尾轉圈。

　　無論是玩命特技或疾風車速，都不算是安全行為，因此重機車手發生車禍的機率比一般機車騎士高出四倍之多，亦不足為奇。如果你仍想加入全球上千名重機粉絲的行列，還是要謹記慢慢騎的原則，儘管不太可能做到。

7. 動漫旋風　P. 026

　　日文「Manga」意指日本漫畫，其悠久歷史可追溯至 19 世紀。日文「Anime」意指衍生自日本漫畫的動畫卡通，來歷可追溯至 20 世紀早期，當時的日本畫師開始繪製動畫短片。動漫於日本大受歡迎並不奇怪，畢竟動漫從日本文化發跡。更了不起的是，動漫竟成為風靡全球的現象。

　　早年有許多動漫作品，成為動漫跨出日本、流傳至海外市場的開山始祖。手塚治虫的《原子小金剛》就是元老之一。1952 年甫出版《原子小金剛》漫畫，當時日本仍處於第二次世界大戰激進民族主義延燒的情緒中。原子小金剛天真又無所不能的性格，征服了日本人的心，亦獲得海外市場的青睞。1960 與 1970 年代，各種原子小金剛的連載漫畫與卡通片席捲全球各地。

　　以動畫而言，在海外市場大放異彩的作品非《光明戰士阿基拉》莫屬。《光明戰士阿基拉》是以大友克洋的連載漫畫為背景，故事講述一場失控科學實驗所帶來的不堪設想後果。此部動畫於 1989 年發行海外後，瞬間吸引大批粉絲，至今仍是動畫史上公認的最佳動畫長片之一。

　　初試啼聲的《原子小金剛》與《光明戰士阿基拉》所帶來的動漫熱潮，到了網路時代，更展現出猶如文化運動般的純熟爆發力。現在的海外日本動漫粉絲，均紛紛在網路論壇熱烈討論、自行翻譯最新動漫內容，甚至在當地成立俱樂部和舉辦觀影活動。Crunchyroll 等新興動漫發布網站也提供動畫影片分享服務，讓動畫卡通能更無遠弗屆地放送。

　　如果你還不相信動漫有多麼夯，翻閱美國最新一期的《御宅族》雜誌就知道。《御宅族》裡介紹許多即將舉辦的「cosplay」（角色扮演）特展資訊，讓粉絲裝扮成自己喜愛的動畫角色參展。某些「角色扮演達人」甚至在展覽前數月就開始精心準備自己的服裝，由此可見他們的熱衷程度。

　　轉眼之間，動漫已從標新立異的日本奇幻風潮，搖身一變成為全球性的主流文化。

8. 染紅食物的昆蟲　P. 028

　　假設你問別人：「你會吃蟲子嗎？」他們可能會回道：「才不呢！」他們不知道的是，自己可能一直都在吃蟲子。噢，每當你食用或飲用某些紅色的食品時，你也在吃蟲喔。

　　本文介紹的是胭脂蟲的故事。胭脂蟲是一種白色小蟲，數百年來不斷為我們提供紅色的奢侈品。胭脂蟲原生於墨西哥，雌蟲既沒有腳也沒有翅膀，大半生都在仙人掌上度過，食用紅莓果維生。當它們被採集、風乾、磨碎、和水混合後，就會產生出一種絢麗的紅色。這種顏色可用來染衣服，還有——你已經猜到的——將食品染色。

　　這些小蟲背後有一段漫長又迷人的歷史。幾世紀以來，墨西哥原住民用胭脂蟲來染衣服。西班牙人來到墨西哥後，發現當地人的染色技術比自己的還要好。他們很快就開創了一個新產業，並壟斷了全球胭脂蟲染料市場將近 250 年。後來在 1777 年，一位法國人將一株仙人掌偷運出墨西哥，不久後，人們便在大溪地、葡萄牙與印度製造胭脂蟲染料。

　　隨著 20 世紀合成染料的發明，胭脂蟲的使用就減少了。然而，由於最近人們對人工色素有健康上的疑慮，使得這種昆蟲再度復出。現在許多消費者喜歡天然的食用色素，更勝於負面報導不斷的人工合成色素，比如紅色 2 號，一些研究便發現其與癌症息息相關。

　　大家可能不希望自己的食物裡有人工合成食用色素，但知道了胭脂蟲背後的真相後，仍讓人感到噁心不已。星巴克在 2012 年吃了一頓苦頭才學到教訓。當時爆發了一則醜聞，指出他們在草莓星冰樂中使用胭脂蟲，群情激憤迫使這家全球咖啡連鎖產業改用另一種食用色素。

　　如果你擔心自己會吃到蟲子，只要檢查一下成分表就知道了。胭脂蟲通常標示為「胭脂酸」、「胭脂紅」或「胭脂紅萃取物」，大多使用在冷凍肉品、汽水、酒精飲料、罐裝湯品、水果罐頭與糖果中。不過請記得，多數科學家認為胭脂蟲對人體完全無害，況且如果我們這麼久以來都一直在吃蟲而不自知，也許牠們也沒那麼糟……。

9. 地中海飲食　P. 030

　　在這個充斥速食和反式脂肪食品、現代人又缺乏運動的年代，營養學家開始將注意力轉移至歐洲地中海沿岸，他們發現到當地居民上千年來均過著延年益壽的健康生活。營養學家發現，地中海居民的飲食習慣能降低許多疾病的罹患機率，包括第二型糖尿病、高血壓、阿茲海默症、肥胖症和心臟病。最棒的是，你不用住在歐洲，也能享受到「地中海飲食」帶來的益處。

「地中海飲食法」意指衍生自義大利和希臘料理的特定營養攝取方式。遵循此飲食法的人，應盡量攝取豐富蔬果，並且限制紅肉攝取量。亦需減少食用其他種類的食品，包括加工食品、鹽、奶油，當然還有速食。關於飲品的部分，地中海飲食法建議以白開水取代含糖飲料，並且鼓勵大家用餐時搭配兩、三小杯的紅酒。總之，地中海飲食的黃金法則就是多樣化。遵循此法的人應自行混搭各類蔬果、雞肉和魚肉，盡可能讓身體吸收豐富養分。別忘了還有初榨橄欖油！某些營養學家認為，此液體黃金是地中海飲食的靈魂。

想要擁有地中海生活習慣帶來的健康益處，遵循飲食法則還不夠。以往地中海沿岸的居民均於戶外工作，運動量亦十分充足。如要將此原則套用於現代生活，則可藉由每天走路上班或至公園慢跑的方式來實踐。

地中海飲食法並非短短幾年內曇花一現的潮流，因為此法確實有效，而且多數人亦認同此料理方式十分美味。這就是為何地中海飲食一直是北美最受歡迎的飲食習慣之一。全世界似乎開始認同地中海沿岸居民長期以來已知的事實：維持營養的飲食習慣與健康的生活作息，能有助於減重、遠離疾病且延年益壽。

10. 免費素食者的生活觀 P. 032

為了拯救地球，你願意做到什麼程度？你願意賣掉你的車，或者夏天不開冷氣嗎？對許多人來說，這是兩個偏激的手法。但對免費素食者來說，那還不夠極端。

免費素食主義是一種藉由提倡完全另類的生活方式，力圖拯救地球的運動。此名稱是「免費」（free）和「純素食者」（vegan）（不吃肉類或動物製品的人）的複合字。免費素食者認為資本主義制度造成氣候變遷、農地破壞與海洋汙染等環境問題。因此，免費素食主義者只要一有機會，便設法削弱資本主義的思維與行為。

以食物浪費為例，免費素食者拒絕接受每日丟棄大量可食用食物的「一次性文化」。因此，

他們到外面尋找被浪費的食物，而不上超市購買食品。免費素食者常從大垃圾箱及垃圾桶裡翻找還可以吃的食物，這種作法稱為「垃圾桶尋寶」。以目前丟棄的數量來說，要找到還不錯的東西根本不需要花太長的時間。根據一項研究指出，在美國大約有 40% 的食物遭到浪費。

「垃圾桶尋寶」是免費素食者最廣為人知的作法，但還不僅於此。都市公共空間的社區菜園是另一個顛覆現代食物制度的常見方法。免費素食者在城市公園裡耕種菜園，利用廚餘作為肥料。作物收成後，他們會自己食用或是分享給最需要幫助的社區住戶。

「分享」是免費素食者的重要特點，不論是分享技術、食物或是交通工具。免費素食者會把握任何機會，在不用到錢的情況下進行個人對個人的交易。舉例來說，你幫人修理腳踏車，而對方則幫你縫補冬衣外套作為交換。這些交易的焦點始終放在公平、在地社區以及環境永續上。

對許多人來說，免費素食者的生活方式過於極端，「垃圾桶尋寶」尤其令人覺得噁心。但有鑒於我們目前所面臨的嚴重環境危機，難道不該考慮採取一些更激進的方式嗎？

1-3 分辨事實或意見

多數文章的內容均含有事實和意見，因此分辨兩者間的差異相當重要。只要是能透過測驗、紀錄或文件來證明真實度的資訊，即屬於「事實」；「意見」則代表作者的信念或主觀評判。有時候「意見」看似「事實」，倘若無法證明其真實性，該資訊還是得歸類為「意見」。

11. 如果一張照片勝過千言萬語，你的照片說了什麼呢？ P. 034

心理學家說，人們通常僅憑一眼就評定他人的性格。在這個時代，許多人在網路上的朋友比真實的朋友還多，這表示我們放在社群媒體網頁上的大頭照非常重要。如果研究者的說詞可信，那些照片傳達出來的個人訊息遠遠超乎我們所能想像——或想要的。

有一項研究針對 66,000 張推特頭像照片，將用戶分成五種性格類型，研究結果與這五大個性異常吻合。不出所料，外向的人往往發布色彩繽紛的個人照，展現出正向的感覺。他們也比其他人更常張貼團體照。反之，神經質的人則幾乎不會露臉。就算露臉，也可能只會面無表情地盯著相機，或是用眼鏡掩飾情緒。

一絲不苟的人通常大頭照會面露微笑，照片大小適中，畫質極佳。這反映出他們對秩序和規畫的渴望。親切友善的人通常會在網路照片中表現出正面積極的情緒。但比起其他人，他們的照片多半沒那麼清晰，色彩也較豐富。最後，勇於嘗試的人往往具有創意，他們的大頭照通常不會露出臉孔，或是以比較有創意、特別的方式露臉，讓他們從人群中脫穎而出。

另外還有其他與大頭照相關的研究。根據某些研究發現，張貼貓或狗而非本人照片的人，多半比較沒那麼外向、認真，較不平易近人，也更神經質一點。抱歉囉，寵物愛好者！

性別上的較量在大頭照的世界中也占有一席之地。相較於女性，男性在臉書上的照片穿著較為正式且較少露出笑容。他們也喜歡在照片上展示所有物，像是車子和手錶。相對來說，女性較常張貼家人的照片。有些研究者相信，這反映出臉書成為一種配對與約會平台的狀況。

就像其他我們所提供的個人資訊，大頭照也提供了他人我們公開和隱藏的線索。對於經由照片傳達的一切訊息，我們應該更加謹慎視之。

12. 為何我們不接受拒絕　P. 036

對所有人而言，被拒絕很痛苦，正因如此，絕大多數人會極力避免受到拒絕。對於為何遭到拒絕會讓人如此痛苦，科學為此提供了一些強而有力的見解。腦部研究顯示，大腦對遭人拒絕時的反應與對身體疼痛的反應，基本上一模一樣。也就是說，在經歷身體和情感上的傷痛時，腦部活躍的區塊完全相同，就像是大腦分辨不出這兩者之間的差異。

另一項研究則提供了更多證據證明這兩種疼痛的關聯性。事前服用過止痛藥的受試者，受到要求回想遭拒的痛苦經歷時，比起服用糖丸安慰劑的受試者，較少感到情緒不佳。因此，問題不在於遭到拒絕時我們為何會感到情緒上的痛楚，而是該如何好好調適心態。所幸，對於如何處理被拒時所產生的傷痛，心理學家為大家提供了一些相當不錯的建議。以下是一些絕佳的方法：

其中一項最重要的處理方式，就是避免對自己太過嚴苛。遭到拒絕已經夠傷自尊心了，人不該再因他人負面的評價而自我批判或自責，這麼做只會加深痛苦，且久久無法平息。

同樣地，老是沉溺在被拒絕的負面情緒上，並不會給自己帶來任何好處；反而應著眼於更正面的事物上，最好是未來能如願以償的方法。

遭到拒絕後可別完全壓抑所有情緒。專家表示，拒絕承認傷痛只會讓情況更糟。許多心理學家相信，承認並接受傷痛很重要。他們認為將失敗視為一種學習經驗是比較健康的方式。

或許上述建議可以總結如下：受到拒絕後，應該對自己好一點，這種態度有助於更快走出傷痛，並減緩被人拒絕的痛楚。

13. 澳洲原住民　P. 038

澳洲原住民文化是世上最古老且從未斷層的文化。現今澳洲原住民的祖先於超過 4 萬年前、海平面仍偏低的時代，跨越陸橋或滑著獨木舟穿梭島嶼之間而抵達澳洲。

對於老一輩的原住民而言，當年占領的土地雖為不毛之地，但是他們自有一套應對其惡劣環境的方法。他們採用所謂的「火棒耕作」技巧以改變地貌，燃燒不必要的草木來創造出草坪綠地，以便可捕食的物種在此生生不息。

雖然探勘寬廣大陸的任務艱鉅，但是原住民以特殊歌謠保持良好的方向感，甚至能藉此穿越數百公里的沙漠。在原住民的信仰裡，人類與其居住的土地，均誕生於遠古的「夢世紀」。在夢世紀的年代，造物主的靈魂漫遊於大地，沿途造物，並將路徑與所創地貌，化為嵌入歌謠中的音符代碼。原住民長途旅行時，僅需邊走邊唱歌，跟著所謂的歌之徑，就永遠不會迷路。

事實上，歌謠與故事是原住民文化的精髓。在沒有字母或書寫制度的情況下，並無任何證明其存在的文字記錄。但是他們以口傳歷史的方式代代相傳，不僅對原住民本身極具意義，人類學家亦覺得非常實用。

英國於 1788 年殖民澳洲以前，澳洲原住民一直遵循著幾乎亙古不變的生活方式。殖民時期後，許多原住民因體內無免疫力而死於外來疾病，倖存的原住民則飽受多年的種族歧視之苦，他們被迫捨棄自己的家園和傳統。澳洲歷史甚至有一段黑暗時期，強迫原住民子女離開原生父母，生活於非原住民的家庭。不過，從 1960 年代開始，澳洲政府和原住民社群之間的關係大幅改善。2008年，澳洲政府為過去的不當對待，正式向原住民道歉。

14. 神奇的療癒植物 P. 040

植物入藥的歷史已有上千年之久。老祖宗曾運用在地植物療癒眾多疾病。現今許多非工業國家仍以植物做為天價現代藥物的替代品。

植物天然形成的許多化合物稱為植物化學物質，進入人體後則可產生有益療效。藥商藉由分離與加工這些植物化學物質，創造出廣泛且有效的複合療法。事實上，有 25% 的現代處方藥是以植物化學物質為基礎。

許多植物具有抵禦重症的成分物質。舉例而言，毛地黃所含的化學物質，用來研製心臟病藥物已行之有年。罌粟則用以製造嗎啡，也就是全球公認止痛效果最好的藥物之一。

那麼，為什麼草藥常遭受無效或令人存疑的批評？最主要的因素之一可能是，儘管植物有某種程度的療效，卻往往被誇大，令人覺得言過其實。毛地黃就是一個例子。人們曾經以毛地黃治療許多疾病，包括癲癇在內，但毛地黃根本拿癲癇沒轍。分佈廣泛的薊狀牛蒡也是一樣，牛蒡雖然能有效舒緩蕁麻和毒藤刺傷所造成的輕微皮膚敏感症狀，但是治癒癌症、愛滋病和糖尿病的效果則完全未經證實。

草藥類的植物亦可能產生患者不清楚的副作用或危險。中藥和印度藥學數世紀以來均廣泛運用日日春，不僅以此治療各種疑難雜症，還用以改善糖尿病和便祕，但日日春其實含有劇毒。此外，相同品種的草藥，生長在條件不同的環境裡，效力也可能各異。因此，在難以推敲的情況下，可說是以碰運氣的方式，驚險判斷正確的用藥劑量。

本文並非否認草藥療法的功效。就如同使用處方藥的情況，服用任何藥物之前，一定要先請教專業醫師的建議。

15. 風箏衝浪運動 P. 042

到公園放風箏通常是孩童在悠閒夏日的活動；衝浪通常是喜好追浪的酷男靚女，於海灘舉辦狂歡派對前進行的運動。有誰想得到，這兩種八竿子打不著的娛樂，竟能如此合拍？

現今的風箏衝浪運動發跡於 90 年代初期，是當時隸屬波音飛機製造商的航空動力學家比爾・羅斯勒與其子柯瑞，共同發明將風箏裝設於滑水板的一種水上運動。

接下來幾年，其他設計師開始精進裝備的風格與外形，讓此項運動融合衝浪、風帆、飛行傘和體操的元素。玩家必須具備高超技巧和絕佳運動細胞，才能駕馭風箏衝浪。

風箏衝浪的原理十分簡單。風箏利用風力拉動衝浪手，而衝浪手的雙腳則繫於衝浪板上，滑行馳騁於海浪之間。銜接風箏線的把手能讓衝浪手控制風箏，而衝浪手的腰帶則連接至把手，讓衝浪手不需費盡雙臂力量來帶動風箏。風箏衝浪手一旦能夠完全掌控滑水板和風箏，就能開始學習特技，例如翻滾、跳躍以及抓板動作。

風力條件良好的時候，有些風箏衝浪手可到達時速 100 公里左右的高速，跳躍高度可超過 9公尺，在空中停頓的時間甚至能長達 22 秒，簡直就像在空中飛行一樣。不過，在捉摸不定的疾風地區，風箏衝浪具有潛在危險性，經驗不足的新手尤其要格外小心。

我們強烈建議有志嘗試這項運動的人先參加課程，學習安全駕馭風箏衝浪的技巧，以免置自己和他人於危險之中。優良的課程內容應包括基本操作、風箏裝設、器材保養、氣候規劃，以及（最重要的）緊急降落等教學。只要是盛行風箏衝浪的地區，就一定找得到此類課程。風力穩定強勁、水域面積寬敞的任何地方，都會吸引風箏衝浪愛好者聚集。你或許可在距離最近的海灘，看見風箏衝浪手的身影！

1-4 明瞭作者目的和語氣

作者寫作皆有目的，可能是提出論點、呈現重要議題，甚或只是想娛樂讀者。為了達到寫作目的，作者會調整文中的字彙和資訊，來符合文章所欲呈現出的語氣。

16. 潛水艇的歷史　P. 044

人類一直希望探索海洋的深度，儒勒・凡爾納的經典之作《海底兩萬哩》，更精彩呈現出人類對大海的嚮往。不過，在世人於 1870 年認識此科幻鉅作的主人翁尼莫船長與其潛艇「鸚鵡螺號」之前，已有許多人致力於打造能帶領人類深入海底的真實機具。

首度嘗試建造潛艇的是美國人大衛・布什內爾，他於 1775 年建製「海龜號」。海龜號呈圓弧堅果狀，其功能在於讓潛艇船員趁機將炸藥裝設在停泊於港口的英國船艦。僅管經過多次嘗試，海龜號卻從未順利炸沉船隻，最後在 1776 年的運輸途中遭到摧毀。雖然海龜號的設計不完全防水，但幸好從未有人溺斃！

另一艘不完全防水的潛艇就是「美國海軍鱷魚號」。1862 年正式啟用的鱷魚號速度驚人，時速可達 7.4 公里。服役時間將近一年，直到一艘船隻因為氣候不佳必須捨棄船上運載的鱷魚號，才結束了它短暫的服役生涯。

人類對潛艇的研究，從好奇心轉變為於第一次世界大戰中使用的致命武器。當時德國海軍以所謂的「U-Boats」潛艇擊沉供應敵軍補給品的商船。戰爭初期，U-Boats 潛艇在攻擊前會先浮出水面，讓乘客有逃生的機會。但此政策維持不了多久，U-Boats 潛艇就開始在沒有事先警告的情況下開火。其中一次的攻擊還擊沉了露西塔尼亞號客船，慘無人道地謀殺了 1,198 名無辜民眾。擊沉露西塔尼亞號的不義之舉，導致美國加入協約國的行列參戰。

如今，潛水艇是世上最高科技的機具之一。美軍維吉尼亞等級的戰艇配備核動力引擎，可乘載 134 名船員，並以戰斧巡弋飛彈捍衛戰艇，最遠可攻打 2,500 公里外的目標。顯而易見，現在的潛艇科技已與海龜號時代大相逕庭！

17. 獻給逝者的藝術　P. 046

有一種東亞藝術形式終於獲得了應有的關注。它有許多名字——紙藝術、紙紮、紙雕。你可能很快就會聽聞其名，因為它正風行藝術界。

紙藝源自於中國民間宗教，特別是道教。道家認為，人死後會到另一個境界，在世的人可以燃燒紙製品來供養在另一個世界的摯愛親友。紙品可以做成各種樣貌：金錢、器具，甚至是房屋。它們通常格外華美，有著鮮豔的顏色和許多複雜的折法。

為往生者燃燒紙品的習俗由來已久，可追溯至漢朝。從前製作紙紮的人都是畢生奉獻給這項手藝的大師。現今，在台灣、香港及東亞其他地區所使用的紙紮品多由少數幾家工廠生產。然而古法依然完好留存。有些年輕人繼承家業，日益精進紙藝技術。在台灣，有些人家在治喪期間，全家人會接連數日圍坐摺紙紮品。

紙藝得以悠久流傳，其中一項原因是它能與時俱進。所有你能想到的現代產品都可用紙呈現出來：筆記型電腦、平板電腦、跑車，甚至是 iPhone 手機。還有些大師能做出更複雜、客製化的物品。舉例來說，有位工藝師受家屬所託，為一名在演出時意外身亡的樂手做了一把紙吉他。

藝術界現在開始注意到了紙藝。2016 年，羅浮宮舉辦了國際設計展，特別展出台灣藝術家的作品。是時候發光發熱了！東亞紙藝之美不僅在於它精細的技藝，也在於其稍縱即逝的特質，以及這些動人作品注定要獻給火焰的意涵。因為如果藝術的存在是為了傳達人類的經驗，還有什麼主題會比死亡更崇高呢？

18. 健康殺手──厭食症 P. 048

我們沒人能預料到，會在寂靜的醫院度過小妹伊莉莎白的 22 歲生日，就這麼看著她瘦弱的身軀躺在病床上。她厭食症的惡化速度快得驚人。短短六個月，一個年輕女孩居然從活蹦亂跳的健康狀態，變成虛弱到連一階樓梯都爬不了的地步。

她的初期症狀相對輕微許多。和多數年輕女孩一樣，她花很多時間攬鏡自照，而且除非仔細查詢每道飲食的卡路里，否則不願吃下肚。

但不久後，她的症狀開始每況愈下。每當爸媽試著讓她多吃一點的時候，她就開始和爸媽大吵。等到她終於再次和家人一同用餐後，體重卻持續下降。我們後來才發現，原來她每次吃完飯就跑去廁所催吐。

當她因為暈眩和疲憊問題而在大學翹課時，我們開始警覺到事態嚴重。任何人都看得出來她是病態的紙片人模樣。連她自己都意識到不對勁。她從爸媽的眼神察覺到他們的恐懼和擔憂，卻對自己弱不禁風的樣子無可奈何。僅管我們不斷三催四請，希望伊莉莎白尋求協助，她也保證會聽話，但她還是繼續讓自己餓肚子。

我真的不曉得我妹妹對體型的審美觀怎麼會變得如此扭曲。罹患厭食症以前，她怎麼看都很正常，正常和朋友交際、一樣保有嗜好、照常看電視，體重也很標準。但我知道的是，如果她會得厭食症，厭食症同樣會找上任何人。

我在醫院病房裡，握著妹妹的手，看著她極力抵抗病魔的樣子，真的很難讓人不去正視，厭食症居然是一種致命的疾病。不過厭食症患者仍然看得到曙光。等伊莉莎白甦醒，我們會開始著手進行全家心理諮商的計畫。我們將幫助她重新認識她曾遺忘的觀念，那就是：擁有健康幸福的人生，才能真正散發美麗氣質。

19. 食羊樹 P. 050

能讓綿羊恐懼的事物可說是寥寥無幾。打雷、閃電和火光根本起不了作用。有些農人甚至目睹，綿羊在大地震發生時仍冷靜地打著呵欠。即使讓人類操之於股掌而面對無法避免的屠宰命運時，綿羊還是靜默地保持臨死前的尊嚴。對於注定餵飽人類五臟廟的動物而言，綿羊的反應還真是奇妙。

不過，還是有令綿羊聞風喪膽的剋星，那就是：智利普亞菠蘿，俗稱食羊樹。智利普亞菠蘿是一種原生於智利的植物，擁有蔥鬱翠綠的色澤，可生長至兩公尺高，最重要的是（對綿羊而言），智利普亞菠蘿滿佈長型尖刺。

這就是讓人覺得可怕之處，智利普亞菠蘿的尖刺如刀片般鋒利，它會以此誘捕綿羊和其他小動物。一旦獵物誤觸尖刺，越掙扎就會越深陷其中。最後，困在智利普亞菠蘿上的這些動物，不是餓死就是失血過多而亡。

想當然爾，這就是智利普亞菠蘿打的如意算盤。科學家相信，智利普亞菠蘿是為了利用動物死屍與其鮮血做為肥料，而逐漸演化出尖刺。因此，智利普亞菠蘿基本上是一種能分解家畜屍體的嗜血植物。也難怪綿羊如此驚恐！

想在智利以外的地區看到智利普亞菠蘿盛開，可說是一大挑戰，因為智利普亞菠蘿需要大約 20 年才會開花。英國有一株智利普亞菠蘿於 2013 年 6 月開花，距離英國皇家園藝學會當初引進培植的時間，相隔整整 15 年。英國皇家園藝學會溫室的工作人員表示，雖然他們以液體肥料灌溉智利普亞菠蘿，但還是很有可能有行為不妥的工作人員，偷偷餵食「綿羊點心」。無庸置疑，所有當地綿羊鐵定對此花展避之唯恐不及。

20. 手語 P. 052

手語意指以手勢與手部動作取代說話來表達意思的語言，而口語則是較常見的人類溝通方法。世界各地的聽障人士均慣用手語，因為他們無法聽見口語文字。

數百年來，手語的發展受到阻礙，原因在於古希臘所傳出的某些流言蜚語。西元前 364 年，知名哲學家亞里斯多德誤稱聽障人士沒有學習能力，因為人類必須透過聽覺才能有效學習。就是這個謬論，讓數世紀以來的歐洲人認為聽障人士生來駑鈍。

到了 18 世紀的法國，人們看待聽障人士的態度開始轉變。天主教神父查爾斯・米歇爾・德雷貝看見兩名聽障流浪兒互以手勢溝通，覺得很有趣。他創辦一所學校，讓聽障人士免費受教育。德雷貝神父鼓勵學生們展現自己在家使用的手語，並且整合所有手語，形成一套標準系統。他以此系統教導自己的學生，以及來自其他國家的手語教師。世人因此將德雷貝神父譽為「聽障之父」。

數十載過後，一位名為湯瑪斯・霍金・高勒德的美國醫師希望教導其聽障鄰居如何與人溝通，因此他前往歐洲請益。與德雷貝的眾多子弟諮詢過後，他返回美國，成立美國聽障學校，他的鄰居亦成為該校的第一屆學子。

如今，世界各地已發展出繁多不同的手語。由高勒德創辦的學校所發展出來的美式手語（簡稱 ASL），是目前最廣為流傳的手語方言，全球約有 25 萬至 50 萬名的使用者。美式手語有點像中文字，手勢通常會與想要傳達的概念相似，但又不盡相同。此外，美式手語不是只有單一字母的比法，這是常見的誤解。從亞里斯多德的時代至今，聽障人士已走過風風雨雨，這些改變均需歸功於為聽障人士著想的德雷貝神父若干人等，以及手語等教育工具的演進。

1-5 釐清寫作技巧

作者通常會想盡辦法呈現妙趣橫生與主題清楚的作品。例如運用各種技巧、文字和措詞，編排出起承轉合的文章結構，吸引讀者的注意力。為了辨識出此類技巧，你必須要能夠有系統地解構分析文章，以便看出作者寫作風格的巧思。

21. 基金投資 P. 054

你希望不費吹灰之力就能荷包滿滿嗎？投資就是一種以錢滾錢的方法。問題是很多人不知該從何開始。

投資到底為何物？簡單來說，投資是一種以金錢達到獲利目標的行為。你可以將投資試想為賭馬。某些投資穩賺不賠，但利潤不高；某些高風險、高獲利且大小通吃的投資，雖然可能讓你一夕致富，也可能使你跌到谷底。

那麼，什麼才是最佳投資理財術？你可以投資股票，但股價常呈現不穩狀態，彷彿溜溜球般上下波動。也可以投資債券，保證幾乎可回本又賺得利息。但是，配息金額實在不多。

此外，必須精通市場經濟，才能獨立操作投資。萬一錯綜複雜的金融知識讓你一個頭兩個大，或許共同基金會是最好的選擇。

共同基金意指在理財專員的監督下，所集結的一筆投資資金。當你進場投資共同基金時，等於將自己的資金匯整若干投資人的資金，再由投資經理人代為操作。共同基金的投資風險較低，因為匯集而成的資金比一般投資更能選擇較多投資標的，進而分散風險。

共同基金的種類繁多。「股票型基金」意指幾乎以股票交易的基金，目標在於透過資金成長的方式來加乘投資額。「平衡型基金」意指兼顧股票和債券的混合式投資，能以性質穩定的債券平衡股市潛在的賠錢風險。「生命週期型基金」剛開始以高風險且高獲利的股票為主，隨著投資人的年歲增長，會調整選擇風險越低的投資標的，較適合退休人士。當然還有其他許多基金類型，族繁不及備載。

那麼該選擇哪一種基金呢？其實沒有正確答案，重點在於選擇符合自己的需求與個性的共同基金即可。

22. 亞馬遜雨林 P. 056

亞馬遜雨林於南美洲佔地 550 萬平方公里，充滿茂密叢林與險峻惡水。彷彿多樣生物的大本營，上百萬種動植物均以此為家，至今仍有科學未知的雨林物種。此地亦為全球規模最大的供氧來源，更是醫學研究人員心目中的瑰寶，因為亞馬遜雨林的多元植物群，可能蘊含治癒癌症和愛滋病等疾病的解藥。

然而，生態豐富的雨林，卻因為伐木工人、農人和殖民行為所造成的濫砍爭議問題，面臨消失殆盡的風險。自 1970 年代開始，已有 20% 的雨林遭到破壞。為了讓大家更能清楚體會濫墾的規模，請想像一下：光是 1991 年至 2000 年這九年期間，遭受砍伐的雨林面積已相當於一個西班牙這麼大。

以作物維生的農人，利用「火耕法」清除草木。此農耕法必須以砍伐樹林、焚燒土地的方式，讓林地適合務農。但是，在亞馬遜採用此法，會導致土壤豐沃度不足，因此無法多次收割作物。一年過後，土壤中的養分所剩無幾，使得曾經欣欣向榮的雨林之地一片貧瘠，農人則遷移至他處，繼續燒墾更多土地。

不過，農耕並非亞馬遜雨林所面臨的最大威脅，畜牧業才是元兇。與作物不同的是，牧草可以生長於荒蕪的亞馬遜土壤，因此自 1970 年代開始，已有 91% 的土地做為放牧用途。

亞馬遜雨林本是吸收二氧化碳的地球之肺，能回收廢氣再排放出人類賴以維生的清淨氧氣。但是亞馬遜持續遭到破壞的情況，大幅增加了全球暖化的風險。保護亞馬遜不受威脅，人人有責。大家務必徹底拒買在原雨林土地上耕種的食物，並且施壓政治領導人採取果決的措施，以避免發生環境災難。也許你認為你的發聲會被忽略，但 2011 年的數據顯示，亞馬遜雨林的濫墾率已維持在最低標的狀態。

23. 奇幻電影 P. 058

大家小時候一定都幻想過前往遙遠的魔幻國度冒險，與巫師對戰，或邂逅古怪奇特的生物。即使是成年以後，我們仍從未放棄幻想探索天馬行空世界的刺激。或許正因如此，奇幻電影得以在大銀幕活躍數十載的時間，並且創下空前的票房佳績。

充滿想像力與夢幻元素的奇幻電影，情節大都有跡可循。傳統的奇幻電影故事，通常以近似中古世紀的時代為背景，主角多為半獸人、精靈與妖精。此類奇幻電影又稱為「傳統古典奇幻」，通常會將謙卑或其貌不揚的人物，塑造為內心天人交戰而必須對抗邪惡力量（例如闇黑巫師或惡毒君王）的英雄。《魔戒》三部曲可算是最忠實呈現此奇幻概念的作品，而《哈利波特》系列則將傳統古典奇幻元素跨足現代與現實世界。

不過，某些電影會融合奇幻片與科幻片、驚悚片或冒險片的題材。以《阿凡達》為例，雖然故事背景位於遙遠的星球，充滿外星種族與未來科技，卻仍在架構編排完整的世界裡，演繹奇幻元素以及正邪拉鋸的情節。無庸置疑，奇幻電影主題還可無限衍生出奇幻冒險、浪漫奇幻以及超級英雄奇幻等子類型。

雖然奇幻電影到了 1980 年代才開始廣受歡迎，但是從電影工業誕生開始，奇幻電影即已問世。早期膾炙人口的此類作品就是《綠野仙蹤》，這部電影描述桃樂絲前往陌生奧茲國的冒險故事，以及沿途遇見的各種人物。

電影特效開始於 1950 年代蓬勃發展後，雖然讓奇幻電影擁有更多發揮空間，但是誇張的演技與低成本的拍片預算，常讓早期的奇幻電影流於廉價粗糙。電腦合成影像技術（CGI）於 1990 年代發明後，奇幻電影的品質突飛猛進。電腦合成影像技術的推波助瀾之下，不僅能安全完成特效場景、預算相對低廉，更重要的是能呈現栩栩如生的畫面。看來，唯一能限制奇幻電影發展的阻礙，只剩下電影人的想像力了。

24. 花道奧義 P.060

你可能認為插花不算是一種藝術，但日本人卻不這麼認為。日本花道（賦予花卉生命）或花道（插花的方式）是日本最古老、也最流行的一種藝術，在日本國內及世界各地都日漸風行普及。

據信，花道的歷史可追溯至西元 6 世紀，當時中國僧侶將佛教傳到日本，這些僧侶將鮮花作為儀式供品獻給佛陀。日本僧侶受到啟發，開始用花卉裝飾寺廟。幾世紀後，插花本身成為一種藝術，獨立於宗教組織之外。1462 年，第一所花道學院在京都成立，傳授仍盛行至今的正規「池坊流」花道。

但日本花道究竟有何特別之處？嗯，與西式花藝不同的是，西式花藝著重在大量色彩鮮豔的花卉上，而日本花道則表現出極簡的抽象藝術型態。日本花道可能只單獨插一支花，甚至完全沒有花；枝葉和其他素材與花卉本身同等重要，且必須仍鮮活具生命力。隱藏的莖梗、金屬絲、劍山以及其他工具，皆可用來固定花材。花朵和葉子會裁成奇特的形狀，甚至是上色。木頭浸水泡軟，以便彎折成形。上述作法的重點在於創造出比素材本身更美的作品，這樣既展示了素材本身的特質，也展現出藝術家的內在本質。

傳統的日本花道「生花」奠基於宗教的象徵意義。在插花的配置上，上層最高的枝椏象徵的是「天」。第二層枝椏略矮三分之一，代表的則是「人」。第三層還要再矮一點，可能是一朵花、一段枝梗或其他素材，則象徵著「地」。至今，幾乎所有日本花道家在創作花藝造型時仍會留意這些規則。

但是，就如許多其他藝術一樣，日本花道在20 世紀也發生了極大的變化。外國花卉植物引進日本，藝術家開始打破舊規則。「草月流（現代風格）」形成，挑戰傳統的「池坊流」花道。同時，花道也傳出日本，外國人開始學習花道，嘗試原先唯日本獨有的插花方式。因此，花道現已是一種國際藝術形式，擁有無限學派和風格。

25. 新加坡的大寶森節 P.062

雖然新加坡看似現代化的繁華都市，摩天大樓林立且生活水準高，不過華人、印度人與馬來人此三大族群奉行的古老傳統和習俗，仍於新加坡大行其道。最受人矚目的節慶之一，就是印度大寶森節。不過話先說在前頭，心臟不夠強健的人，可別輕易觀禮。

大寶森節於泰月（西曆的一月中旬至二月中旬）滿月的時候舉辦慶典，目的在於向攻無不克的印度戰神沙巴馬尼亞致敬。信徒帶著牛奶鮮花等祭品，以繞境遊行的方式獻上敬意。雖然聽起來還不賴，但某些信徒會以極端的方式表達自己的誠心。

透過誦經和冥想讓自己進入恍惚狀態後，這些信徒會自殘，將鋼棒穿過兩邊臉頰或將鉤子刺掛於背部、腿部、舌頭或其他身體部位，並且使用這些鉤子拖曳裝飾精緻的重物，藉此向神明表達自己的虔誠信仰，旁觀者與擁戴者則敲鑼打鼓、吟誦經文，維持遊行隊伍的士氣。有些信徒甚至會背負稱為「卡瓦地」的行動祭壇，以上百支鋼絲刺穿皮膚加以固定。信徒宣稱沙巴馬尼亞神會於儀式過程中保護自己，確保信徒身上幾乎毫髮無傷。

信徒於一個月前即開始準備，並且投入許多時間齋戒、禱告和冥想，目的在於鍛鍊堅強的意志力，以便經歷大寶森節的苦行過程。遊行結束後，撐過自懲行為的信徒，表示獲得觀見神明的殊榮，因此接下來的一年，可於當地印度族群裡享有特殊待遇。

雖然此靈修行為對多數人而言看似極端，卻是新加坡印度族群最為重視的宗教儀式。對於觀禮的外來者來說，剛好可以見證印度人認知的神聖習俗。

1-6 進行推論

「推論」技巧意指運用已知資訊來猜測未知的人事物。舉例而言，如果朋友開門時看起來怒氣沖沖，你會猜測事有蹊蹺或有事發生。作者同樣會以推論方式，來提點讀者相似的情境。

26. 設身處地，為無家可歸者著想 P. 064

花點時間想想你曾聽過所有關於街友的事。通常都是負面的，對吧？也許家人說他們太懶了，不願意工作。或許你還記得曾有新聞報導指出，有的街友私下其實身家不斐。這些傳聞在全世界都一樣：街友並非受害者，而是他們咎由自取。

當然，這些傳聞幾乎皆不正確。現實中，無家可歸可能發生在任何人身上──甚至是你身上。

事情可能就像失業這麼單純。我們從未預料到會被開除或裁員，當事情發生時，可能需要很長一段時間才能找到新工作。倘若你又失去了公寓或房子，你也就失去了永久地址，這對求職來說是個危險信號。

也許最令人驚訝的是，許多街友其實都有工作。他們擁有全職工作，卻仍買不起房子。根據估計，全美國無家可歸的人口中，有三分之一到二分之一的人都有工作。街友人數眾多，光紐約市就有約 63,500 人。

個人或家庭的悲劇也可能導致無家可歸。離婚、醫療費或大筆意外支出都會造成家庭財務崩潰。某些案例中，有人為了自身安全被迫逃離暴力傾向的配偶或家人，最後只能在全然陌生之處落腳，人生地不熟，不但失業，也無任何支援網絡提供生活協助。藥物也是一大問題，尤其是類鴉片藥物成癮。起初可能只是用這類藥物來緩解運動傷害造成的疼痛，最後卻成了賠上工作和家庭的惡習。

事實上，無家可歸有許許多多不同的成因，責怪受害者對解決問題毫無幫助；我們反而應當在朋友、家人及社區成員最需要幫助時伸出援手。早期及時的援助，對一時面臨無家可歸的人而言，可以大大改變他們的命運。

在不確定實際情況下，我們應該避免對人太快下定論。下次當你路過街友時，謹記這句俗諺：「評斷他人之前，先設身處地想想對方的處境。」

27. 南美印加帝國的興亡 P. 066

歐洲水手於 16 世紀左右發現南美洲時，發現自己踏上一塊有著眾多不同語言、文化，以及政治團體的土地。印加帝國就是這樣一個族群，其國土於南美洲西岸佔地 200 萬平方公里，擁有 600 萬至 1400 萬人民。

印加帝國的故事始於西元 1200 年左右的庫斯科，位於現今的祕魯。當時由勢力龐大的貴族帶動經濟與行政結構的雛形，為印加社會奠定基礎。1432 年，帝王帕查庫特開始征服庫斯科周遭國家，印加帝國就此而生。此後，印加帝國繁榮昌盛，直到 1532 年，慘遭不到兩百人的西班牙兵團滅國。

如不論及軍力層面，印加帝國可謂文化涵養與行政制度成熟的超級強國。印加帝國統一人民溝通的語言，其國教推崇膜拜太陽神。印加金屬製品和醫藥技術更是先進。四通八達且晴雨無阻的遼闊道路長達 39,900 公里，方便帝國內的人民長途通信。印加帝國亦設立勞工制度，人民藉由為帝王建造道路和其他公共建設的方式，換取糧食衣物。此制度應該算成效顯著，因為多數道路鋪設品質十分良好，仍沿用至今。

印加社會最了不起的事蹟，非富麗堂皇的城堡與神廟莫屬。印加帝國盛產金銀礦，人人家中均金碧輝煌。造訪庫斯科的第一批西班牙探險家紛紛表示，到處都是黃金古物、雕像、缸甕以及瓶罐，並且鑲有珍貴寶石。

印加帝國令人津津樂道的話題，即是勢單力薄的西班牙兵團何以戰勝一個宏偉帝國。而原因就在於叛變和晦運等複雜因素。西班牙兵團冷酷無情，在雙方休戰期間綁架印加帝王，印加帝王即使支付了自己的贖金，仍慘遭撕票。再者，當時爆發嚴重的天花疫情，1520 年開始於南美洲肆虐，奪取無數人的性命。

28. 資源回收創舉 P. 068

你可能早已聽過資源回收再利用是怎麼一回事，但是並非所有的資源回收計畫都齊頭並進。隨著環保意識抬頭與科技不斷進步，有些國家已經開始在反對浪費的行動中拔得頭籌。

某些資源回收計畫極具雄心壯志，以所謂「零廢棄物」思維為基礎，呼籲個人及公司透過減少消費、重複使用和回收再利用的方式來停止製造垃圾。資源回收單位在零廢棄物的計畫中舉足輕重，因為可回收再利用的物料越多，垃圾掩埋場裡與焚化爐中的汙染物就越少。

台灣就是個絕佳典範。1980 到 1990 年代，全台各地垃圾掩埋場裡的垃圾堆積如山，台灣當時因而被戲稱為「垃圾島」。1993 年，台灣的垃圾回收率竟只有 70%！最後人民實在是受夠了，迫使政府在 2003 年採取零廢棄物的政策。從那時起，台灣成為其他國家效法的楷模。台灣政府運用資源回收基金，付費給私人與公司收集可回收再利用的物料，然後將這些回收材料送往具先進設備的工廠，分解成可再利用的物質後，再販售給有其原料需求的公司。台灣資源回收基金中最重要的層面，可能在於其資金均來自國內販售消費品中所徵收的處理費，治根治本，讓製造商為自家產品造成的環境影響負責。物品越難處理，處理費就越高。

德國亦為成功執行資源回收計畫的榜樣。就像台灣，德國人必須自行將資源回收垃圾分類。社區設有色彩繽紛的垃圾箱，以顏色來區分塑膠製品、紙類、玻璃和廚餘等，讓居民據此分類。此分類垃圾箱計畫相當成功，幾乎不再有垃圾運往德國的垃圾掩埋場。

德國消費者還須支付玻璃瓶與塑膠瓶的押金，待他們把瓶子退還給當初消費的商店後，就可以取回押金。

資源回收甚至可以促進國內經濟，對抗失業問題。德國約有 5 萬人受雇於資源回收產業，而德國資源回收技術的全球市佔率為 24%。這對拯救地球來說，也算是不錯的獎勵！

29. 獻給亡魂的奇觀盛宴 P.070

搶孤活動可追溯至兩百年前的台灣。這個慶典的意義在於追思當時渡海來台過程中客死他鄉的先人。搶孤儀式用意在安撫先民的孤魂，因為人們認為客死異鄉的孤魂無法安息。

搶孤活動在農曆七月（也就是鬼月）的最後一天舉行。當天，全台各地的人紛紛來到宜蘭的頭城鎮。有些參觀者從祭祖開始，有些則是參加特殊的宗教儀式。群眾會聚集在稱為「孤棚」的巨大建物四周，整座建物高聳入夜空。孤棚分為上下兩個部分，較低的那層有 12 根將近 20 公尺高的粗柱，上層則是一座大型平台，支撐著 13 座竹編孤棧。整座結構高得驚人，足足有 43 公尺高。而在每一座孤棧頂端都插著一面稱為「順風旗」的小紅旗。

鬼月的最後一個時辰一到，比賽就可以開始。五人一組的隊伍衝到孤棚的底座，開始攀爬棚柱。因為棚柱上塗滿了牛油，想往上爬可不是件容易的事。一旦參賽者到達平台，他們會暫停片刻，繫上安全繩，緊接著開始爬上竹編孤棧，孤棧上繫滿了祭品、隨風搖擺。第一位摘下紅旗的人贏得比賽，預期一整年的好運。但這還沒有結束。在最後一個習俗中，參賽者會從平台上將袋裝食物拋給底下的群眾。

自從這個活動在 2004 年解禁後，與會者日益增加。原本旨在安撫鬼魂的當地宗教儀式現已轉變成吸引觀光客的旅遊盛事。事實上，許多人認為，搶孤活動現在已成為台灣最大的其中一項傳統盛會。

30. 世界最深潛水紀錄 P.072

對某些人而言，潛入伸手不見五指的深黑海洋，能帶來腎上腺素激增的快感，也有某些人避之惟恐不及。端看你站在什麼角度，也許有朝一日，你也會想嘗試看看水肺潛水。而且，如果夠勤快練習，說不定還能創下最大潛水深度的世界紀錄！

水肺的原文「Scuba」，是用以形容水肺潛水員探索海洋深度所使用的裝備縮寫語。當然，有些潛水員會潛至較深的海底。一般休閒水肺潛水員皆持有下潛深度至多 30 公尺的執照，超過此深度均屬危險的潛水行為。然而，最大潛水深度的世界紀錄，讓 30 公尺相形見拙。2014 年 9 月，阿梅德 · 加布爾以 332 公尺的深度，成為最大潛水深度的金氏世界紀錄保持人。在精密設備的協助下，人類還可能突破上述潛水深度。美國海軍潛水員使用大氣潛水系統裝備,即可下潛至 610公尺。

想要在深潛世界紀錄榜上有名,不只極為艱難,還非常危險。多數的潛水危險性均來自於人體對極端海水深度的反應,「潛水夫病」就是其一。潛水夫病是指血液中產生氮氣栓塞。症狀輕則頭痛和反胃,重則引起威脅生命的心臟病和肺病。潛水員下潛越深,罹患潛水夫病的風險越高。氧氣量也是一個問題。潛水深度越深,潛水員仰賴的氧氣就會因為水壓而壓縮,因此耗氧速度更快。而深度超過 66 公尺時,氧氣還可能產生毒性,導致潛水員失去意識。

雖然只有意在突破世界紀錄的專業潛水員會面臨多數潛水風險,但從事任何水肺潛水運動時,一定要謹記循序漸進以及聽從教練指示的原則。

1-7 理解因果關係 ————————•

事出必有因,所導致的行為或事件就是一種結果。因果之間的關係有時顯而易見,有時卻幾乎不著痕跡。為了更清楚理解因果關係,請仔細觀察具有因果意味的用字,例如「therefore」(因此)、「as a result」(所以)或是「consequently」(因而)。

31. 和綠藻一起綠化 P. 074

游泳客討厭水藻,但是水藻這種滑膩的綠色有機體,卻有望成為一種替代能源。這種看起來既噁心又黏糊糊的東西,幾乎在任何水體中都能生長。它只需要陽光、水和二氧化碳就能欣欣向榮。最重要的是,從能源的角度觀之,水藻含有植物油,可轉化為生質燃料。加工後,這種油性物質可以作為各種車輛、甚至是飛機的燃料。水藻作為生質燃料,比石油燃燒得更完全,這是它最吸引人的主要原因。

這就不難理解,開發水藻作為能源有多振奮人心了。有些研究員認為,水藻的產油量比其他植物高上近百倍。數年來,投資者、企業與政府單位已傾注數百萬元開發藻類生質燃料。然而,對某些投資者來說,成果卻相當令人失望。這主要是因為使用水生物質作為能源所帶來的挑戰以及技術上的阻礙。

大規模生產藻類能源的困難之處,在於養殖水藻、提煉油質以及加工處理。要培育出所需的水藻數量需要大量的水。此外,也需要大片土地,而這些陸地原本可另作他用。至於提取天然油質有許多方式,但全都所費不貲。其他成本還包含將水藻乾燥以及將油質轉化成可使用的能源。

雖然有些評論家基本上已經放棄這種替代能源,但其他人卻更加樂觀。美國大型石油公司艾克森美孚,在藻類燃油的研究上取得了重大突破。艾克森美孚和一家生物科技公司合作,找到了能加倍產出藻類燃油的方法,只要稍加改變藻類中的一個基因,就可以實現。艾克森公司相信,到了 2025 年,一天就可以生產出 1 萬桶藻類生質燃料。與現今上千萬桶石油的產量相比,這只是滄海一粟。但是,對於確保世界擁有更健康且低汙染的未來,這卻是很重要的一步。

32. 無國界料理 P. 076

過去數十載以來,全世界儼然成為巨大熔爐,全球即時通訊讓文化隔閡幾乎不復存在。隨著人們對更優良環境的需求,大家逐漸背起行囊,為了工作、婚姻或單純追求更高生活品質而離開家鄉。

國際間的文化遷移與移民趨勢大行其道,無國界料理也因而成為越來越常見的現象。人們到了新環境安身立命後,經常會帶入某些文化色彩。所以,某地特有的飲食文化與烹飪方式和其他料理風格融合的情況也就不足為奇。

經過一段時間後,混搭過的新式料理甚至可能成為主流。沒有使用番茄食材卻又宣稱自己是道地義大利料理的餐廳,鐵定會被指責呼攏消費者。事實上,番茄並非歐洲土生土長的植物,直到 16 世紀才從南美洲引進。

許多西方國家的亞洲料理餐廳,以無國界料理的方式,烹調出整合次大陸地區風格的佳餚。以專攻東南亞美食的餐廳為例,可能會活用越南、泰國、中國以及該區其他國家的食材、香料和烹飪技巧,打造不完全越式、中華或泰式風味,卻又獨一無二的東南亞料理。這種菜色風格融合得渾然天成，常見於兩國交界之處。由於地緣關係，自然產生文化交流的結晶。例如德墨料理就是兼具德州與墨西哥菜的混搭美食。

不過，有些餐廳業者還會試圖結合不同大陸的料理風格。1970 年代，結合亞洲與法式料理的做法，在美國廚師圈裡蔚為風潮，跨洲料理成為許多餐廳試水溫的特餐。然而，由於跨洲食材和烹飪風格過於迥異，因此這種無國界料理很難生存。而「混淆料理」一詞就是在形容嘗試師法「混搭料理」卻東施效顰的菜色。

33. 哺餵母乳的優點　P.078

新手爸媽必須在短時間內做出許多可能會對寶寶影響深遠的艱難決定。新手媽媽面臨的第一個艱難抉擇，就是是否該哺餵母乳。對許多人而言，哺餵母乳與否應該不會導致什麼嚴重後果。畢竟，美國有極大比例的成人幼時並未攝取母乳（嬰兒配方奶廠商大肆廣告所造成的現象），也沒有什麼負面影響。然而，近期研究顯示，哺餵母乳會影響孩子的生活，甚至是成年以後的一生。

哺餵母乳的首要影響層面就是健康。因為嬰兒的身體尚未發育完全，較容易患病。母乳具有幫助嬰兒抵抗感染的特性，因此攝取母乳的嬰兒較不容易產生耳朵發炎、呼吸道疾病、過敏、腹瀉與嘔吐等症狀。

雖然配方奶能夠仿效母乳所含的眾多營養成分，但母乳仍然無可取代。母乳是極佳的營養來源，成分會隨著寶寶成長而改變，為不同成長階段的寶寶確切提供所需的綜合養分。事實上，以母乳及早提升寶寶的發育狀態，還能降低寶寶往後罹患糖尿病、心臟病與癌症的風險。

近年來最令人驚訝的發現之一，就是哺餵母乳對孩子未來的社會地位能產生正面影響。英國針對三萬四千人做了一項研究，將每位長大成人的受試者與自己父親的社會地位做比較，結果發現小時候攝取過母乳的人，比攝取配方奶的人，社會地位較可能超越自己的父親。

此項研究似乎證實了母乳養分能大幅改善腦部發育的早期報告。攝取過母乳的人，童年產生的情緒壓力較低，原因可能在於早期哺餵母乳時，肌膚之親所產生的安全感，而長大後的成就亦可歸功於母乳。

34. 「普普藝術教父」——安迪‧沃荷　P.080

你是否曾納悶過，是誰繪製康寶濃湯罐頭上的知名圖像？又是誰在畫布上呈現色彩鮮豔的瑪麗蓮‧夢露名人肖像？這些赫赫有名畫作的背後推手，就是「普普藝術教父」——安迪‧沃荷。

沃荷對於藝術融合廣告的表達方式著迷不已，他將可口可樂罐、康寶濃湯罐、美金鈔票等家喻戶曉的美國物品以及名人肖像，幻化為充滿自我風格的藝術作品。以大眾流行文化的主題與傳播技巧為基礎，所產生的實驗性質「普普藝術」風格，在往後廣受其他畫家仿效。雖然現在已是司空見慣的表達手法，但在 1960 年代時可說是十分前衛，改變了人們對藝術的看法。

沃荷生於 1920 年代的賓州匹茲堡，小時候常臥病在床。在家養病的他，以畫畫、聽收音機，還有收集電影明星照片的方式充實自己。沃荷表示，童年階段是培養他人格特質、作風，以及對流行文化產生興趣的關鍵。

除了畫家身分以外，沃荷還是一名熱衷商業的生意人。他與其他畫家不同，完全不會因為銷售創作獲利而感到不好意思。沃荷執著於量產策略，他想成為一部不斷重製相同圖像的機器。也因為這股熱情，讓他從繪畫轉戰網版印刷（譯註：又稱絹印），此技術能讓他大量重製相同的作品。經過一段時間後，他甚至不再事必躬親，而是雇用助理負責絹印量產的工作。對沃荷而言，印刷事業等於在畫布作畫，也是一種藝術形式。他在自己的著作中表示：「賺錢是藝術，工作也是藝術，而會賺錢的生意是藝術的最高境界。」

沃荷的作品彷彿有先見之明，呈現 21 世紀風靡的現象，例如名氣、媒體，以及大眾對量產商品貪得無饜的胃口。因此，縱使沃荷當時遭到批評，指稱他向消費主義妥協，他的普普藝術仍從未退流行。

35. 溫馴的龐然大物：鯨鯊 P.082

　　鯨鯊長度可超出 12 公尺、重量可超過 20 噸，是世上最龐大的魚類。雖然名稱容易產生誤解，但鯨鯊並非鯨魚，牠的命名來自於其碩大體型與覓食習慣，和有些鯨魚品種雷同。鯨鯊擁有厚達 10 公分的深灰皮膚，皮膚表層還擁有各異的獨特白斑紋路。彷彿指紋般的鯨鯊斑紋，讓科學家得以辨別每隻鯨鯊，並且精準計算其數量。

　　鯨鯊與牠們好鬥又有食人嫌疑的表親不同，屬於性格溫馴的生物。牠們泰然自若，浮潛者與潛水員可恣意游繞與觸摸牠們，甚至可抓緊鯨鯊魚鰭，一起乘風破浪。鯨鯊是濾食性動物，意指牠們不會像鯊魚咬碎食物，而是吸入充滿成千上萬微小浮游生物的一大口海水，再從魚鰓過濾掉海水，以濾食片留住食物。雖然鯨鯊擁有 350 排細小牙齒，卻不具覓食用途，因為鯨鯊捕食微生物的習慣，加上上百萬年的演化，已經讓牙齒無用武之地。不過，潛水員遇到鯨鯊時應留意的唯一危險，就是被鯨鯊整個生吞。2011 年就有一名潛水員在墨西哥海域差點被鯨鯊吸入嘴裡。

　　偏好溫暖水域的溫馴鯨鯊，於熱帶和副熱帶海域出沒。通常可於沿岸地區以及熱帶島嶼的潟湖發現牠們的蹤影。每年春季，都會有大批鯨鯊遷徙至澳洲西岸，因為該區珊瑚礁附近豐沛的浮游生物，實在令鯨鯊難以抗拒。另一個鯨鯊偏愛的遷徙地區，就是菲律賓小漁村董索附近的海域。每年一月至六月，鯨鯊會群聚於充滿浮游生物的董索岸邊。遊客為了一睹驚人鯨鯊的風采，紛紛湧入董索，帶動了這座小漁村亟需的發展。看來，人類似乎對於這悠然自得的海洋巨擘百看不膩。

1-8 瞭解譬喻性語言

　　作者會運用**譬喻性語言**來觸動讀者的感受或令人在腦海中產生畫面，讓讀者留下深刻印象。本單元會呈現下列幾種譬喻性語言。

　　明喻會以「like」（像）、「as」（如）或「than」（比……還……）等字比較兩者，例如「她的心比石頭還硬」。**隱喻**會更直接比較兩者，並且將兩者畫上等號，例如「她有一顆鐵石心腸」或「全

世界就是一座大舞台」，因此表達效果比明喻更強烈。

　　擬人法意指將無生物的物體賦予人類特質，例如「太陽漫步於天空」。**成語**屬於不能照字面意思解讀的片語，其意義與拆解各字來看不同。例如「To let the cat out of the bag.」和貓一點關係也沒有，真正的意思為「洩漏祕密」。

　　最後，**誇飾法**意指加油添醋的誇張表達方式，例如「我已經告訴過你一百萬遍了！」

36. 柏拉圖的思維 P.084

　　柏拉圖是最偉大的西方哲學思想家之一。生於西元前 428 年的希臘雅典，柏拉圖捨棄政治前途，踏上追尋知識之路，也讓他在探求過程中，推出倫理道德學、政治哲學以及公平正義題材等著作，在他逝世後仍猶如一盞智慧明燈，影響後世達千年之久。

　　柏拉圖雖然是多產的作家，但是他的著作並非枯燥乏味的哲學論文，反而妙趣橫生。柏拉圖以對話語錄的方式寫作，內容架構為若干人物辯論某主題、互相答詢，彼此推翻和提出不同的論點和歧見。或許看似混亂，但事實上卻能讓讀者瞭解所有辯論觀點，並且在心中自行產生最中肯的見解。

　　柏拉圖語錄中最重要的人物就是蘇格拉底。蘇格拉底並非虛構角色，而是真實存在的人物。事實上，他是當時最受敬重的思想家。年輕的柏拉圖是蘇格拉底的學生。柏拉圖語錄中所描寫的蘇格拉底為人謙遜，且思想充滿邏輯與批判性，又能一針見血。

　　歷經蘇格拉底殉道的悲慟後，柏拉圖離開雅典，周遊歐洲超過十年，造訪不同導師，求知若渴般地吸收知識。旅行期間，他開始撰寫聞名遐邇的語錄。雖然柏拉圖語錄主要以蘇格拉底為智慧泉源，但仍難以得知有多少良言真正出自蘇格拉底的想法，以及有多少錦句是柏拉圖藉其啟蒙恩師的身分發言。

　　柏拉圖最著名的語錄非《理想國》莫屬，內容在於質疑個人正義以及整體社會正義的層面。

他表示，其所處年代的領導者以自我和權勢而非邏輯與智慧治國。再者，他論道國家必須由「哲人王」以邏輯而非貪念來統理天下，如此才能讓百姓安居樂業。對柏拉圖而言，邏輯與理性是做人處事的成功原則。

37. 盧安達大屠殺事件 P.086

當不同族群因種族、宗教、文化或政治立場相異而欲殲滅對方時，就會發生大屠殺事件。1994 年，東非國家盧安達胡圖族屠殺圖西族的悲劇，就是近年來慘絕人寰的大屠殺事件。僅僅三個月的時間，將近百萬名男女老少，如待宰羔羊般，於家中和街上遭到砍殺。

人們普遍認為，大屠殺的導火線在於胡圖族總統哈比亞瑞馬那搭乘的飛機，遭到圖西族帶領的盧安達愛國陣線所炸毀。但是胡圖族和圖西族之間的衝突，其實早已因為種族仇恨而根深蒂固許久。

雖然圖西族自 15 世紀開始統治盧安達，但是盧安達境內人口絕大比例卻是胡圖族（84–85%）。胡圖族一直被視為粗人，與圖西族統治階級相較下可謂相當貧窮（「圖西」一詞的原意為「擁有大量牛隻」）。隨著圖西族不斷增強權勢，他們分配土地的方式開始因人而異，通常直接分配給其他圖西族人，而不是延續數世紀以來土地代代相傳的傳統。

此舉使得胡圖族心懷不滿，因為圖西族逼迫胡圖族必須以勞力換取居住於自有土地的權利。無可避免的情況終於發生，1959 年爆發社會大革命，胡圖族人掌權成為總統，造成許多圖西族人逃離祖國。對於圖西族而言，簡直是風水輪流轉。

儘管胡圖族已統治盧安達數十年，兩族仍互看不順眼。許多胡圖族人均認為，要讓盧安達成為穩定國家的唯一辦法，就是驅逐或滅絕圖西族。而總統哈比亞瑞馬那的飛機炸毀事件，點燃了導火線。屠殺行動的安排迅速展開，政府單位向胡圖族人發佈廣播，呼籲族人砍殺圖西族鄰里。胡圖族成功滅絕 75% 的圖西族人口，而盧安達大屠殺事件則成為人類史上最黑暗的慘劇之一。

38. 猶太教 P.088

猶太人屬於民族宗教的族群，也就是因為相同宗教和種族背景所凝聚的民族。全世界大約有 1,400 萬猶太人，居住在以色列或美國。他們源自中東，爾後於以色列安身立命。自西元前 6 世紀開始，因為受到征服、壓迫與驅逐，迫使他們顛沛流離而遷徙至世界各地，多以東歐、中東、非洲為主，近期則逐漸湧入美國。1948 年，以色列重建為猶太國之後，全球上百萬名猶太人返回祖國，齊心協力建國。

猶太人的向心力來自其信仰的猶太教。即使本身種族非猶太人，一旦皈依為猶太教徒後，同樣具備猶太人的身分。猶太教屬於一神論的宗教，意指僅信仰唯一的真神——耶和華。

猶太教與基督教息息相關。事實上，基督教衍生自猶太教——最悠久的宗教傳統之一。基督教聖經裡的〈舊約〉，算是略為重新編排過（且經常遭到誤譯）的猶太聖書《塔納赫》版本。不過，雖然基督徒認為耶穌為上帝之子（希伯來文為彌賽亞），但是猶太教卻相信耶穌為一介凡人，彌賽亞尚未降臨人世。

兩個宗教的差異包括猶太教的安息日（希伯來文為 Shabbat）為星期六，而非星期日。正統猶太人十分看重安息日，絕對不允許在此日進行任何違反安息意義的活動，甚至是打開電燈、煮飯或開車都不行。

此外，猶太人遵循許多獨特的節日儀式，例如節慶為期八天的光明節，時間大約與聖誕節相去不遠。入夜後，家家戶戶都會點燃宛如繁星般閃爍的蠟燭，吟唱聖歌、交換禮物，齊聚一堂享用美味炸物。但是，如果要鉅細靡遺地解說如此古老的宗教文化，恐怕亦需費時千年。希望這樣的簡介能先滿足大家對猶太教的好奇。

39. 全球娛樂首都：拉斯維加斯 P.090

在美國何處能讓你飽覽艾菲爾鐵塔、埃及金字塔，以及砲聲隆隆的海盜船呢？哪裡能讓你在同一天乘坐雲霄飛車、觀賞 IMAX 電影、參加演唱會、欣賞馬戲團、漫步於博物館、在泳池畔悠閒休憩、享受美容 SPA、大啖美食、在賭場贏得百萬獎金，還有舉行婚禮？如果你追求的是娛樂行程，拉斯維加斯絕對是你的不二選擇。

拉斯維加斯喧囂、五光十色、金碧輝煌的程度完全不假修飾。拉斯維加斯位於莫哈維沙漠，屬於典型的沙漠氣候，夏季炎熱乾燥，冬季氣溫微涼。一年四季陽光普照且降雨量稀少，不斷吸引遊客湧入。大張旗鼓主打觀光的風格，讓希望擁有美好度假時光的眾多觀光客每年不斷回流。

拉斯維加斯在西班牙文裡意指「綠蔭之地」，此命名由來是因為拉斯維加斯附近的河谷地帶曾經碧草如茵，讓酷熱沙漠中的旅人有個歇腳之處。墨西哥於 1848 年承認該地屬於美國領地之後，摩門教徒遷移至此處，試圖將其轉化為派尤特印地安區。不過短短幾年後，摩門教的殖民政策失敗，殖民地亦遭到遺棄。有誰想得到，假使當年摩門教徒成功落地生根，現在的拉斯維加斯會變成什麼模樣？

1931 年，內華達州合法開放博弈事業，而拉斯維加斯聞名遐邇的賭場飯店則如雨後春筍般蓬勃發展。1940 年代、1950 年代與 1960 年代期間，群眾紛紛湧入拉斯維加斯遠觀鄰近沙漠所進行的核子彈試爆，而開發商（以及不少黑幫）大力投資拉斯維加斯的賭場度假村，讓拉斯維加斯彷彿一顆耀眼聖誕樹，每天都像是一座不夜城。因此，長時間下來，拉斯維加斯逐漸成為了大家公認的世界娛樂首都。

拉斯維加斯的觀光客只需謹記一件事：觀光此地時無需矜持，豁出去就對了，拉斯維加斯保證讓你度過難以忘懷的愉快假期！

40. 爭妍百花：可口抑或致命？ P.092

一提到花卉，你會想到什麼字眼？香氣、五顏六色……可口？我想你一定納悶：「等等，花卉怎麼會可口？我又不是牛！」

事實上，花卉常進到我們的五臟廟。我們以茉莉花與洋甘菊增添茶飲的風味，以酸豆的花苞調味食物，以葵花油煎煮炒炸。某些花卉甚至被當做蔬菜，例如綠花椰菜、白花椰菜和朝鮮薊，均為含苞待放型的花卉，掩人耳目的功力真是一流！

一旦你開始習慣這個看似怪異的想法，你會發現可食用花卉其實唾手可得。花園就像是自家廚房，草地就像是超級市場，花卉博覽會簡直是吃到飽的西式自助餐！鬱金香、秋海棠、洛神花、康乃馨等花卉，均可直接食用花莖，且擁有獨特風味，例如蜂蜜般的香甜氣息，至強烈的酸甜柑橘味。當然，這些花卉不過是冰山一角，還有數百萬計的可食花卉生長於田野、森林甚至是鄰近的河床。

但一定要小心，某些花卉雖然芳香無比，卻暗藏致命的食用危機。例如原生於歐洲的毒堇此綠葉植物的小白花不甚美觀，亦看似毫無殺傷力。但是，古希臘人卻以毒堇做為執行死刑的毒藥。最著名的受刑者就是偉大的哲學家蘇格拉底。記載蘇格拉底事蹟的柏拉圖描述蘇格拉底服藥後，雙腳開始產生冰冷麻痺的感覺，接著往上蔓延至軀幹，最後襲擊心臟。

曼陀羅花屬於具有惡臭的灌木植物，花朵外觀狀似號角，數世紀以來均作為治療氣喘的草本藥物。不過，只要稍微超出醫療劑量，就會有致命的危險。民間形容曼陀羅花致死症狀的俚語是這麼說的：曼陀羅花讓心臟驟停之前，「會滿臉通紅、皮膚乾如柴骨、盲如蝙蝠，極盡發狂之能事」。

但是，別因為花卉裡的害群之馬而卻步，可食花卉還是能點綴襯托任何餐飲，只要記得在食用前做好功課即可！

1-9 分析寫作偏見

作者有其本身的歷練、看法和信仰。混為一談的時候，就會形成偏見，或是特定觀點。雖然有時難以看出作者的偏見，但可從作者的用字以及是否公平陳述雙方論點來窺見端倪。

41. 社交焦慮症 P.094

你知道有 7% 到 13% 的人口，深受某種「疾病」之苦，此疾病會讓群眾形成一種渲染恐懼氣氛的危害嗎？這就是所謂的「社交焦慮症」（Social Anxiety Disorder，簡稱 SAD）。社交焦慮症會讓患者感到無地自容，且時常感覺被同儕評頭論足。罹病者也會產生心因性的生理症狀，例如心跳加速、面色潮紅與發抖，有時甚至還會汗如雨下。

且慢，不是很多人都這樣嗎？我們都會在社交場合感到緊張，誰能斷定這樣一個常見現象，其實是一種疾病？專家一定會說，社交焦慮症的症狀程度因人而異。有些患者的症狀十分輕微，例如開商務會議做簡報時容易冒汗。有些人則因為強烈畏懼社交場合而無法正常生活。但是有沒有可能只是這些人的個性較為孤僻呢？或許社交焦慮症根本不是一種疾病。

最常見的社交焦慮症療法稱為「認知行為治療」，主要在於突破患者的心防。例如患者會將使用公廁聯想為很尷尬，此療法會將這樣的聯想取代為更合理的想法。瓦解所有負面聯想的心防後，患者就能跨出障礙，參加以往所避免的社交活動，例如公開演講、至公共泳池游泳、參加烹飪課程或跟朋友聚餐。倘若經過認知行為治療後仍未改善，那麼這名患者可能純粹只是一個扶不起的阿斗。

有些人會告訴你，社交焦慮症是美國第三大心理疾病，僅次於憂鬱症和酗酒，其實此說法過於誇大。老一輩的人對於社交焦慮症一詞頗有微詞，他們認為那其實只是「害羞」的表現。畢竟，誰說社交焦慮症患者如果願意直接走出戶外、面對自己所有的社交恐懼，不會達到與認知行為療法一樣的效果呢？或許這樣也能幫助自己停止怪異舉止！

42. 消炎食物　P. 096

發炎是人體抵禦病毒、細菌和其他敏感源等有害刺激物質的自我保護反應。但有時候此自然反應會變本加厲，為人體帶來弊大於利的結果。慢性發炎或極端發炎症狀，均為若干疾病的成因，例如花粉病、類風濕性關節炎以及氣喘。

幸好有其解決之道，而且在當地賣場超市即可尋得。含有各種維他命與養分的特定食物，能有益改善發炎問題。鮭魚、鮪魚和鯖魚等脂肪豐富的魚類就是其一。研究顯示，富含 Omega-3 脂肪酸的魚類能大幅改善發炎問題。事實上，

Omega-3 的神奇效用，讓多數人直接天天補充維他命營養食品而省略吃魚的步驟。

這還只是冰山一角，消炎的食物多如繁星。鳳梨蘊含高單位的維他命 C、E 與 A，亦含有改善發炎的鳳梨酵素；蔓越莓與藍莓則是具有抗發炎功效的水果；堅果與全穀類則為有益健康的食物。如果你喜歡拌炒的烹飪方式，別忘了加入大蒜和生薑，因為經過研究證實，兩者均含有消炎化學物質。假使大家都願意攝取此類食物，世上就不會出現那麼多病痛問題。

當然，也有些食品有害無益，還會造成發炎問題。也就是所謂的「3P 食品」，意即加工（processed）食品、包裝（packaged）食品和熟食（prepared）。3P 食品實在不應吃下肚，不只是為了避免體內發炎，還為了讓自己朝健康人生的目標前進，因為此類食品傷身匪淺。

某些自命不凡的人認為，醫藥的效力比飲食更為強大。舉例而言，醫生常會為發炎感染患者開立消炎藥。醫師大都不會提及抗發炎飲食的益處。最糟糕的是，處方藥通常具有比患者發炎症狀更不堪設想的副作用！如果醫師多瞭解水果和堅果的療癒效用，開立處方藥前一定會三思而後行。

43. 自淨水泥　P. 098

別被這個複雜的名稱困惑了，其實光觸媒水泥是史上最偉大的發明。這個由義大利公司研發的新型態水泥，能像吸塵器般吸附煙塵與空氣汙染物。

光觸媒水泥的發明者原意在於生產可自淨的人行道。然而，測試產品初期，卻發現出乎意料的結果。能破壞灰塵汙垢的自淨二氧化鈦，曝曬陽光時不僅能清淨人行道，還能帶來空氣清新效果！而且，做為光觸媒水泥的二氧化鈦永遠不會有用罄之虞，因此理論上，可以維持數十年清淨空氣的成效。這絕對是一項改變世界的發明。

光觸媒水泥仍為前衛發明，因此僅用於某些試營運專案。芝加哥為首度率先試用此材質的美國城市，而義大利與荷蘭早已使用光觸媒水泥來鋪設人行道。這項革命性的科技，往後將用於建

設世界各地的高速公路，有效綠化都市叢林，達到更永續的居住狀態，兼顧用車和清淨空氣的優點！

儘管光觸媒水泥擁有絕佳的優點，還是有某些傻子對此材質躊躇不已。他們發牢騷的原因在於，光觸媒水泥的費用可能過於昂貴且難以保養。有些人甚至抱怨任何綠化科技的發明，反倒認為大家應該停止用車，返回山頂洞人時代什麼的。

幸好，沒有人認真聽進去這些愚蠢的片面之詞。有智慧的人都知道煙塵是一項重大問題，會造成氣喘、癌症與心臟病等健康威脅。如果我們能使用光觸媒水泥來鋪設道路，進而改善大都會的空氣汙染，何樂而不為呢？畢竟，我們真的捨得讓下一代的健康為此付出代價嗎？

44. 十二星座迷思　P. 100

你今天查看星座運勢了嗎？理想的情況下，星座運勢分析會說：「你單純的個性和相信魔法的傾向，讓你容易受騙」。別擔心自己到底是何時出生的，因為這樣的分析其實適用於任一星座。

十二星座學確實由來已久。星相學或研究行星與恆星如何影響我們生活的學說，是由西元前3000年的印歐民族興起。占星業因而從印度傳播至中國等世界各地。發展尚未成熟的天象觀察行為，演變為以十二星座為基礎的「極簡科學」。

17世紀是迷信歷史的重要轉捩點。當時的天文學開始衍生出制度粗糙的占星學。天文學屬於精準科學，以經得起考驗的證據建立宇宙的物理法則。占星學則是一廂情願的幻想。最奇怪的是，占星學曾是一門廣受研讀的學術。儘管已過了上千年，現在仍有許多人視星座運勢為精準預測人生大事的工具。我想我們真的沒有進步多少。

多數西方人因為西方的黃道十二宮而熟悉處女座、天蠍座和摩羯座等星座。星座總共有十二個，個人的星座取決於自己出生當日的特定恆星與行星位置。十二星座不僅以每日星座運勢的方式用於預測未來，有些頭腦簡單的人還真的相信星座決定個性。例如處女座的人（生於8月23日和9月22日）應該很會分析與觀察事物。但是我告訴大家，我就是處女座，但如果我的護照上沒有清楚寫明我的居住地，我根本不知道自己身處哪個國家。所以，星座與黃道十二宮根本是無稽之談。

45. 米開朗基羅　P. 102

米開朗基羅生於1475年的托斯卡尼，是義大利聞名遐邇的畫家。他在小時候即加入藝術坊而非學習經商技能，此舉震驚了他的父親。他在藝術坊耗費多年時間精進自己的技藝，最後專攻人體解剖學與雕刻藝術。米開朗基羅出師後，開始創作西方藝術史上最富盛名的傑作。至今仍有許多人認為他是史上最偉大的藝術家之一。

但米開朗基羅真的實至名歸嗎？以他最家喻戶曉的作品之一為例，《大衛像》於1501年至1504年間的佛羅倫斯雕刻完成。專家會告訴你，這是米開朗基羅大師之作的證據，將人體線條展現得栩栩如生。但你知道大衛像的右手比左手大嗎？雙眼視線亦朝向不同方向。以我的觀點來看，這叫做「馬虎」。但由於這是米開朗基羅的作品，因此大家都寧願忽視這顯而易見的瑕疵。

這還不是米開朗基羅失手的唯一例子。他設於聖彼得大教堂的著名《聖殤》雕像，同樣有失真問題。《聖殤》雕像於《大衛像》之前竣工。此作品呈現聖母瑪莉亞抱著耶穌基督冰冷屍體的模樣。然而，以歷史準確度和可信度而言均為敗筆。《聖殤》所呈現的聖母瑪利亞臉孔過於青春洋溢，歷史上的瑪麗亞面臨白髮人送黑髮人之時已超過40歲。連米開朗基羅時代的人也察覺不太對勁。他的傳記作家問及聖母瑪利亞的模樣為何如此年輕時，米開朗基羅回應那是因為聖母瑪利亞過著蒙主恩寵的人生。事實上，他應該老實承認自己搞砸了。

大家急於讚揚米開朗基羅的現象實在可悲，因為古典藝術界的真正鬼才成了遺珠之憾，那就是李奧納多．達文西。天才、具前瞻性、大師等字眼，都能用來形容李奧納多，但他絕對不馬虎。他甚至早在人類發明飛機數百年以前，就已設計出直升機的雛形。李奧納多．達文西才是真正的大師，米開朗基羅不過是山寨版。

1-10 實力檢測

46. 垃圾食物，說戒就戒！ P. 104

你是否對珍珠奶茶總念念不忘？或者在百般聊賴的時候，覺得只有巧克力甜甜圈才是振作良方？信不信由你，你可能已經是垃圾食物癮君子。

「癮君子」通常會讓人聯想到藥物、酒精或香菸成癮的人。但不只有上述顯而易見的有害物品會產生戒斷反應。密西根大學的一項研究透露了驚人的真相。

該研究結果發現，一旦戒掉披薩和薯條等加工食物，恐出現各種負面症狀，包括情緒起伏過大、嗜食、焦慮、頭痛和失眠。飲食中只要一剔除此類食物，就會出現上述症狀，但五天內即可逐漸好轉並恢復正常。因此，斷然戒掉垃圾食物所產生的戒斷症狀，其實和戒菸或戒大麻十分相似。

此研究進一步指出，越來越多證據顯示加工食品會令人上癮。多項研究顯示，我們的大腦將糖視為藥物。攝取過量的糖，就會改變腦部的化學反應，使大腦渴望更多的糖分。我們一吃下甜甜圈或餅乾，大腦就會分泌多巴胺，產生飄飄然的感覺。最終讓我們上癮的其實不是食品本身，而是那種愉悅的感受。不過最糟的是，如同抗藥性，人體也會累積「抗糖性」。因此，為了達到分泌多巴胺的效果，我們攝取越來越多糖分，進而吃下過多垃圾食物。這種暴飲暴食的惡性循環會導致嚴重的健康問題。

密西根大學的研究幫大家上了寶貴的一課。最重要的一點，就是垃圾食物與危險藥物沒有什麼不同。我們都應限制加工食品的攝取量。顯然，大家或許覺得知易行難，畢竟有誰想受到頭痛或徹夜輾轉難眠的煎熬？不過只需謹記，這些症狀只會維持幾天。當你真正步上正軌，飲食更簡單無糖後，一切都值得了。

47. 埃及文化 P. 106

古埃及是人類歷史上最古老的文明之一。其先進發展和異國商品，吸引了世界各地古國的商人。這些商人通常會留在埃及與當地人打成一片。或許這就是現代埃及文化融合新舊特色的原因。

以埃及人回應需要協助的觀光客為例。如果有人遊蕩於開羅街頭且貌似迷路，當地人主動向前伸出援手絕對司空見慣。不到幾分鐘的時間，可能會有更多當地人前來，一起認真討論最適合觀光客到達其目的地的好辦法。搞不好其中一人會邀請觀光客到家喝茶，甚至請吃一盤埃及傳統美食「埃及豆」，食材包含了蠶豆、洋蔥，有時還會加入水煮蛋。埃及善待旅人的習慣行之有年，當地人皆情不自禁展現十足的人情味！

與古埃及時代不同的一項改變就是宗教。埃及人口約有 85% 至 95% 為穆斯林，許多埃及人的日常文化生活深受宗教信仰的影響。舉例而言，由於穆斯林禁食豬肉，因此難以在餐廳菜單看到豬肉菜餚。埃及人亦不太喝酒，因為穆斯林信仰同樣禁止飲酒。

從埃及熱鬧的國定假日即可看出其多元歷史。埃及的兩大節日就是穆斯林慶祝的開齋節，時間就在為期一個月的齋戒月結束後，還有忠孝節。然而，還有許多傳承上千年的民俗慶典。其中一個節日就是「sham el-Nissim」，或稱「聞風節」。許多埃及人會於這一天出外野餐。埃及的基督徒別稱為科普特基督徒，他們同樣慶祝聖誕節。此類基督徒自西元 451 年即居住於埃及，其習俗包括前往遙遠聖地朝聖，以景仰聖人。

48. 綠茶的神奇功效 P. 108

現代人為了改善健康常倉促行動，反而容易忽略長久以來近在眼前的好物。這是一種茶飲，由中國帝王神農氏率先於西元前 2737 年沏製，延續至今仍極受亞洲地區歡迎。這種飲品平價且產量豐富，科學家每年均不斷發現其帶來的健康益處。此夢幻飲品就是「綠茶」。

綠茶帶來的健康益處博大精深，要想一一列舉實屬不易。研究顯示，綠茶能抵禦癌症和心臟病。某項研究特別指出，高血壓患者飲用綠茶可讓血壓降低 46% 到 65%。其他少數的研究結果顯示，綠茶可降低膽固醇和燃燒脂肪。某些專家甚至相信綠茶能預防糖尿病、中風以及老人失智症。

綠茶的優點不僅止於保健。神奇的綠茶還能讓人容光煥發。想要擁有亮澤秀髮嗎？只要沖泡綠茶，放涼隔夜後，再浸潤剛洗好的髮絲，然後記得再洗一次頭和潤髮一次，即可達到最佳成效。綠茶還能做為無化學物質的染髮替代劑。如果以放涼的綠茶泡腳，還能遠離腳汗與腳臭問題。這是因為綠茶經過證實，具有抗真菌與抗細菌的功效。

綠茶好處多多，大家自然會想問：「到底應該飲用多少綠茶？」最常見的答案是一天大約飲用三杯。這樣的飲用量最能吸收到綠茶的有益抗氧化物。另一個問題或許是：「紅茶和白茶是否與綠茶一樣健康？」專家意見略為分歧。有的專家說，所有的茶飲均擁有類似的保健功效，有些專家則認為綠茶才是首選。無論如何，大家都知道綠茶是最美味的茶飲。

49. 里約嘉年華　P. 110

我永遠忘不了擔任巴西駐外記者時，第一次出勤的經驗。那次是為了歡慶為期一週的里約熱內盧嘉年華。從沒聽說過此節日的我，在抵達巴西之前做了點功課。嘉年華會在復活節前 40 天的星期五舉辦，連續進行五天至星期三結束。有些人說里約嘉年華源自古羅馬的農神節，富人與窮人會交換服飾，然後舉辦數日的狂歡派對。有些人認為此說法憑空無據，嘉年華會的真正起源應該是平民在 19 世紀中葉，打鼓與手搖鈴鼓遊行通過里約而來。無論如何，大家的共識都是：嘉年華是一場盛會。這是巴西規模最大的文化活動之一，每年吸引高達 200 萬名觀光客前來里約。

嘉年華開始的第一天星期五，我在街頭帶著相機和筆記型電腦，準備執行我的任務。身處里約，讓我所有的感官均飽受衝擊。來自四面八方的巴西森巴音樂瀰漫於空氣之中，伴隨著重擊節奏，幾百人高歌手舞足蹈。空氣中還夾雜烤雞、汗水與嘔吐物的氣味。我遊蕩了數小時之久，從某街區的派對續攤到下一個街區。回想起來，好像大約凌晨三點的時候，有人想要用一瓶酒與一支金羽毛頭飾換得我的相機。雖然不太確定為什麼我竟然同意交換，或許是因為受到嘉年華精神的感染吧。不幸的是，我的上司不接受這個說法，我最後必須自掏腰包購買新相機。

不過我還是覺得很值得。我仍留著那支金色頭飾，因為它讓我回想起當時的壯觀景象。每個人有生之年，一定要來一趟里約嘉年華。參加此節慶的經驗，比我家鄉某些陳腔濫調的文化活動還要精采許多。

50. 人類免疫缺乏病毒／愛滋病　P. 112

HIV/AIDS 意指兩種疾病，分別是「人類免疫缺乏病毒（HIV）」以及「後天免疫缺乏症候群（AIDS）」。據說這兩種疾病源自 19 世紀末、20 世紀初西非的黑猩猩或是猴子。無論如何，HIV 後來開始傳染人類，美國則於 1980 年代早期開始出現病例。此後，HIV 成為全球傳染病，現今世界各地患有 HIV/AIDS 的人數約 3,690 萬人。

接觸病毒帶原者體液的人，就會感染 HIV。一旦感染 HIV，病毒即開始破壞人體的 CD4 細胞，而此類細胞的功能在於幫助人體抵禦疾病。人體一旦流失特定的 CD4 細胞數量，就會確診為 AIDS 患者。AIDS 患者的免疫系統不堪一擊，他們屬於伺機感染疾病的高危險群，等於被宣判死刑。

HIV/AIDS 在 1980 年代與 1990 年代屬於絕症，僅能存活不到 13 年。如今，HIV 已成為可控制的慢性病。被診斷出 HIV 的 20 歲年輕人，可望再活 53 年。感染率亦急速下降。根據聯合國統計，全球 HIV 新感染案例已從 1996 年的 340 萬件，降至 2017 年的 180 萬件，足足減少了 47%。多虧阻擋 HIV 變異的新型抗病毒藥物，才能有此捷報。各國衛教宣導亦協助終結常見的誤解，並且教育民眾如何自保，避免感染。不過，還有很長的一段路要走。抗病毒藥物的價格對於多數患者而言仍不堪負荷。至今仍有許多 HIV/AIDS 的誤導訊息，例如因為馬桶座椅而感染 HIV 等莫名其妙又傷人的迷思。

HIV/AIDS 帶來的警惕與啟發，就是人類能戰勝此可怕疾病。只要多一點合作、衛教、研究，以及最重要的同理心即可。

Unit 2 字彙學習

英語單字如此繁多（據估計將近一百萬字），要記住每個單字的意義幾乎是不可能的任務。隨著英語知識增長，我們會發現其實很多單字的字義都相近。除此之外，我們也可以從前後句子或段落中，判斷出單字的意義。

在學完本單元之後，任何艱深的單字都將難不倒你。能夠辨識並運用這些單字之後，你不僅能閱讀無礙，亦能流暢地寫作和說英語。

2-1 同義字

同義字是意義完全相同或非常相近的單字，例如 huge 和 gigantic 就是同義字。英語擁有將近一百萬個字彙，其中許多單字的意義相近。如果能夠辨識這些同義字，將是增進閱讀理解能力的一大利器。

51. 此袋鼠非彼袋鼠？——澳洲大袋鼠
P. 116

動物的命名方式有千百種，有的因叫聲而得名，例如嘰喳柳鶯（一種嬌小的歐洲鳥類，叫聲嘰喳嘰喳的）；有的因外觀而得名，例如駝豹（長頸鹿的舊稱，早期認為長頸鹿很像是駱駝和花豹的雜交種）。而大袋鼠的例子和駝豹很類似，牠是一種澳洲的有袋動物，因為外型介於小袋鼠和袋鼠之間，所以被稱為「大袋鼠」。

有袋動物屬於哺乳類動物，幾乎是澳洲特有的品種。雌性的有袋動物身上有育幼袋，可供幼兒初期成長。雌性大袋鼠的幼獸出生時還無法視物，也沒有毛髮，身長小於 1 英吋，必須在母親的袋子裡面生活 237–269 天。袋鼠、小袋鼠和大袋鼠囊括了澳洲有袋動物的三大品種。

大袋鼠的毛色取決於棲息地。生活在澳洲東部岩石山丘地帶的大袋鼠，通常是黑色或暗灰色；住在西部沙漠地區的大袋鼠比較偏紅色，方便牠們融入環境。除此之外，大袋鼠也是唯一一種口鼻部位沒有毛、呈黑色的有袋動物，很容易和其他兩種區別。

白天時，大袋鼠喜歡躲在巨大的花崗岩下避暑。水在澳洲惡劣乾燥的沙漠環境中是奢侈品，所以大袋鼠不是躲著避暑，就是在地上挖洞找地下水喝，這些洞可深達一公尺。大袋鼠身手敏捷，毛茸茸、厚實的腳掌讓牠們在布滿岩石的崎嶇地面上穿梭自如，盡情享用沿途的青草和灌木。

大袋鼠多為獨居動物，牠們會避開其他動物，尤其是人類。如果你看到一隻長得像小袋鼠或袋鼠的動物在挖洞找水源，或是在岩石下打盹兒，牠可不是小袋鼠也不是一般袋鼠，而是大袋鼠！

52. 讀唇術
P. 118

讀唇術是指「解讀說話者的唇部活動，來理解說話內容的技術」，主要是聽障者用來與不諳手語的人士溝通的工具。聽障者藉由分析說話者唇、口、舌的活動、形狀和位置，可以推測對方的發音，進而組合出每一個字。

事實上，沒有聽力受損問題的人，也隨時都在使用讀唇術，只是沒有意識到而已。當我們與人交談時，會觀察對方的臉部表情和嘴型，幫助我們理解，尤其是周圍環境特別嘈雜的時候。

然而，光靠讀唇取得視覺線索仍有一大缺點，就是許多音的發音唇型非常接近。事實上，只有 30% 左右的英文發音能夠僅靠視覺清楚辨識。正因如此，有效的讀唇極度仰賴對話的前後脈絡。舉例來說，meat、beat、peat 這三個字從視覺上看起來是一樣的，不過如果套用在「The Chicago Bulls ＿＿＿ the Knicks last night.」（昨晚，芝加哥公牛隊 ＿＿＿ 尼克隊。）就只有一個字符合條件。

不用說，天生耳聾的人學習讀唇術，所面臨的挑戰遠大於早已熟習這些發音的人。儘管如此，讀唇術還是不好學，即便學會，一點小障礙，像是鬍子或陰影，都會讓讀唇的效果大打折扣。

如果你有興趣學讀唇術，這裡有一些小技巧：在他人說話時，練習注意看他們的嘴唇。看新聞對這種訓練特別有用，因為播報員比一般人說得更清楚，你比較不容易讀錯。當你看新聞駕輕就熟之後，就可以開始用靜音模式看你喜歡的電影或電視連續劇，試著讀唇來理解對話內容。如果電影有字幕，也可以在遇到瓶頸的時候，適時開啟字幕！

53. 樂聖貝多芬　P. 120

路德維希・范・貝多芬於 1770 年 12 月 17 日生於德國波昂，同為音樂家的父親約翰・貝多芬希望他成為一位神童，因此不斷鞭策他培養音樂方面的才華。

約翰堅決栽培兒子成為傑出的音樂家，甚至會在深夜把可憐的貝多芬從床上拉起來，督促還是小男孩的他練琴直至清晨。

貝多芬 11 歲時，在波昂跟隨宮廷裡的琴師，接受專業的鋼琴和作曲訓練。到了 1790 年代中期，貝多芬以精湛的琴藝，在當時的音樂之都維也納小有名氣。18 世紀末時，他已成為當代最重要的作曲家。

貝多芬一生中最大的轉捩點發生在 1798 年，當時他的聽力開始退化，持續性的耳鳴讓他飽受折磨，連音樂也聽不清楚。他因此開始迴避朋友、意志消沈，甚至有過自殺的念頭。

貝多芬一邊對抗著憂鬱和聽力喪失，一邊使用特別改造過的鋼琴繼續創作。他用棍子連接鋼琴的音板，並且咬著棍子感受聲音的振動。而他此時期的創作以表達英雄氣慨與奮鬥為主，日後也成為他的名作。

然而這位傑出的作曲家終究還是不敵失聰之苦，當他演奏完《第九號交響曲》之後，轉過身發現全場觀眾正如癡如狂地為他鼓掌，而他竟然絲毫聽不見，不禁潸然淚下。

久病一場之後，貝多芬於 1827 年 3 月 26 日辭世，享年 56 歲。他的真正死因長期不明，後來有人分析他的頭髮與骨骼，認為應該是醫師開了過量的含鉛藥物，意外造成他鉛中毒而死。不論原因為何，一代樂聖之死震撼了維也納。一共有 2 萬人加入他的送葬隊伍，向當代真正的音樂天才致敬。

54. 人體自焚之謎　P. 122

2013 年 2 月 18 日，65 歲的丹尼・范贊特被發現全身焦黑，陳屍於奧克拉荷馬州穆德洛鎮的自家中。

郡長朗・洛克哈特表示，范贊特的屍體幾乎完全燒成灰燼，詭異的是只留下頭與手、腳掌，並且沒有明顯的外部起火痕跡。更奇怪的是，屋子本身沒什麼受損，沒有家具著火，就連距離屍體僅 3 英尺的物品都毫髮無傷。

為了解釋這次事件，有人提出范贊特應該是發生了「人體自焚」這種奇怪的現象，也就是在沒有明顯外部火苗或火焰的情況之下，人體自己從體內起火燃燒。

過去三百年來記錄的人體自焚案件約有兩百件。案件特徵往往都是軀幹全毀，獨留手、足與頭，同時屋況完好，鮮有火燒痕跡。雖然許多理論咸認這種現象起因於超自然力量，然而在科學上還是有其解釋。

第一個要思考的問題是此人為什麼會著火。大多數人體自焚的案件裡，死者都有抽菸習慣。除此之外，大部分死者不是過重、傷殘，就是酗酒，因此在火災中難以迅速逃生。而現場均未發現明顯的外部起火痕跡，則可以解釋為數小時的燃燒之後，起火點也早已被銷毀。以范贊特先生為例，他本身就有抽菸和喝酒的習慣。

那麼其他奇怪的現象又該如何解釋？例如四肢完好無缺，以及隔絕式的燃燒方式？當人的衣服著火而無法逃脫時，很快地，身體的脂肪受熱會開始溶解，成為燃料。類似蠟燭效應，劇烈而集中的熱度會讓衣服繼續緩慢地燃燒，直到燃料（人體脂肪）耗盡，這個過程可能會長達數小時。這就解釋了為何火災不會延燒到人體身邊的家具，以及手腳（沒有衣服覆蓋）多半完好無缺。

55. 致命的太空垃圾　P. 124

我們常視太空為未經探索的邊陲之地，漆黑無垠又空蕩寂寥。但是，大家知道其實太空中四處漂浮著成千上萬噸的垃圾嗎？

我們稱這樣的物質為太空殘骸，也就是所謂的「太空垃圾」。某些太空殘骸出自太空本身，例如流星體這類大型的漂浮岩石或金屬。但是像老舊人造衛星或不再運作的火箭零件，就是人造的太空垃圾。無庸置疑的是，所有太空殘骸對太空人與人造衛星而言，均十分危險。

風險來自於太空殘骸繞行軌道時的高速。想像一下，一顆漂浮在宇宙中的小螺絲並不會造成多可怕的威脅，是吧？假設這顆螺絲以時速 17,500 英里（約時速 28,000 公里）移動——在這樣的速度下，螺絲便可輕易穿透太空衣，甚至是國際太空站的艙壁。

在天時、地利、人和的情況下，所有太空殘骸都會造成危險，而殘骸量甚至有增無減。美國太空總署預估，環繞地球軌道的太空殘骸中，約有超過 2 萬件殘骸的尺寸大於壘球，另有 50 萬件大於彈珠。根據歐洲太空總署所述，體積小到無法追蹤的太空殘骸尚有 16.6 億件。更糟的是，太空垃圾會自行增生。一件太空垃圾撞擊另一件後，兩者就會碎裂，產生上千片的太空垃圾。

儘管有人已著手開發實驗性質的新方法，但目前清除太空殘骸的簡易方法尚未問世。薩里大學的「清除殘骸」計畫，旨於採用巨型風帆來收集太空垃圾。在清除方案問世之前，美國太空總署會將重心放在追蹤已知的太空殘骸。美國太空總署針對超過 21,000 件太空殘骸，建立定期追蹤的目錄。假使任一件太空殘骸對太空船造成威脅，美國太空總署就會確保該太空船移動位置。

只要仍有尚未追蹤到的太空殘骸，人類在太空活動，均面臨致命風險。世界各地的太空計畫目前仍十分幸運，因為過去數十載以來，僅發生少數撞擊事件。但我們光靠運氣還能撐多久呢？

2-2 反義字

反義字是意思相反的單字，good 和 bad、big 和 small、hot 和 cold，這幾組都是反義字。有時候我們很容易辨別反義字，有時候則需要費點力。記得務必從前後文當中，尋找可能的線索。

56. 好的「肢體語言」是成功的一半　P. 126

我的祖父過去常說：「話能騙人，但身體騙不了人。」他深信肢體語言的重要性，我們的每一個姿勢、動作和臉部表情，無不反映出我們的情緒和性格。一開始，我覺得這些肢體語言之說實在無聊，然而多年之後，我才明白這些話的珍貴。

我第一次參加重要的工作面試，就證明了肢體語言的重要性。我記得坐在等候區時，看見旁邊的競爭對手坐姿懶散、雙手交叉在胸前。要是祖父也在場，他一定會婉轉地告訴他，這種肢體語言已經說明了他懶惰、反社會的性格。輪到我面試的時候，我奉行了所有正面的肢體語言規則：保持良好的眼神交流和體態，以展現自信，同時手腳不要動來動去。於是我的面試進行得很順利，我也立刻獲得錄取。

後來我把祖父的肢體語言理論，運用到生活的各個層面。出去約會時，我一看就知道這個女生對我有沒有意思。如果她總是向我靠近，雙手自然敞開，面帶微笑並且與我眼神接觸，我就知道這個人值得我追求。反之，如果對方總是把身體後傾，左顧右盼，或者把玩自己的手，就不太值得把感情投注在她身上了。

甚至有一次，我在數個月前就察覺了分手的先兆，只因為我發現對方說謊的種種跡象。根據我祖父的理論，一個人說謊的時候常會摸臉或手，不自覺雙手交叉，身體也會遠離對方。就算我再怎麼不願意相信，他說的實在是千真萬確。

祖父教我洞察肢體語言，讓我獲益匪淺。好的肢體語言可以為我們開啟職場和人生的大門，錯誤的肢體語言則會成為人生路上的絆腳石。

57. 冥王星究竟是不是行星？　P. 128

對於全球的自然科學老師和星象儀迷而言，2006 年 8 月 24 日是一個教人難忘的日子，因為這一天，冥王星正式從行星中除名，他們必須緊急修改教學計畫、更新教科書，並且修正繁瑣的試題解答。

冥王星之所以被重新歸類，起因於科學界重新界定了行星的定義。國際天文聯會（負責太空命名的國際組織），針對是否要採行認定行星的新標準，舉辦了一次投票。經過無數次的激辯之後，多數會員投票支持新的行星標準。他們最後將行星定義為：繞行太陽運轉的天體，必須能夠自己產生足夠的重力，並且清除鄰近軌道的其他天體。

冥王星雖然符合前兩項條件，卻不符合第三項，冥王星並沒有清除鄰近的天體。事實上，冥王星正位於一大片由太空碎片組成的古柏帶之中。古柏帶位於海王星之外，內部還有幾個與冥王星大小相當的天體。假如在國際天文聯會 2006 年的爭辯中，另一方的論點能夠勝出的話，這些天體會和冥王星一起並列為行星，太陽系就會有 12 個行星。

不過顯然事實並非如此，冥王星被踢出行星之列，並且設立了一個新的類別，叫做「矮行星」。只要符合國際天文聯會所制訂的前兩項條件，但不符合第三項的天體，就被稱為矮行星。如今，矮行星若要重拾其天文地位，唯有二途：一是必須被幾個小行星或岩石撞擊，增加它們的整體質量，才能重回行星地位；二是等待國際天文聯會的科學家們再次修改行星定義。屆時，冥王星將是唯一一個經歷過躋身行星的高峰，也嚐過被拒於門外的低谷這兩種大起大落的天體。

58. 世界文化遺產：吳哥窟　P. 130

全世界最大的宗教建築，既不是義大利的梵諦岡，也不是麥加的克爾白聖殿，也不是拉薩的大昭寺，而是柬埔寨的吳哥窟。第一位造訪此地的西方人，曾留下了這麼一句最佳寫照：「它的卓越工法已非筆墨所能形容，尤其全世界沒有其他建築能與之相提並論。」

吳哥窟最初是為了紀念印度神明毗濕奴所建，後來才演變為佛教聖地。吳哥窟建於西元 1113 年到 1150 年之間，為柬埔寨國王蘇利耶跋摩二世所建。廟宇的最高處有一座 65 公尺高的寶塔，四周伴隨四座較小的寶塔，最初的建造者用這樣的設計，來象徵印度神話中神明的居地須彌山。廟宇的四周圍繞著一條大約 4 公尺深的巨型護城河。吳哥窟結合了一幅美景所該具備的所有重要元素：雕工細緻的建築、茂盛的植被、映照山光水色的護城河。也難怪觀光客經常選在日出時分湧入吳哥窟，用相機捕捉最美麗的畫面。

有人形容吳哥窟為「叢林中的廟宇」，因為吳哥窟位於大片的古蹟群之中，許多古蹟正逐漸長滿高大的榕樹。這片佔地 400 平方公里的古蹟群被稱為吳哥古蹟，包含了西元 802 到 1431 年間，雄霸東南亞的古高棉帝國歷代都城。每當一位新的統治者即位，就會建造一座新的國都。在當時高棉帝國的全盛時期，這些都市的人口甚至可達上萬人。

如今吳哥窟已是亞洲最熱門的觀光景點之一。有意參觀者可以搭機前往吳哥窟南方 5.5 公里處的暹粒市，再從這裡安排吳哥古蹟群的參觀之旅。別忘了：這裡還有許多古蹟值得參觀，可以多安排幾天的行程。

59. 國家公園保育員　P. 132

收件人：吉兒

寄件人：吉姆

主旨：最愉快的假期！

我知道我下週二就回家了，但就是想和人分享我的假期。你也知道，原本來美國拜訪莎莉阿姨之前，我還有點擔心。可是到了這裡的第一天，我就知道這會是一趟愉快的旅程。她先生的家人多半是懷俄明州人，比我還熱衷戶外活動。馬克叔叔和他的小孩，幾乎每個週末都會去黃石國家公園，在漫漫荒野中健行。

不過這還只是一部分而已，我還發現了全世界最棒的工作，現在我知道大學畢業後要做什麼了。馬克叔叔的妹妹貝蒂在黃石國家公園擔任保育員，我從來沒有聽過這種工作，很像野外警察和科學家的綜合體，他們在全美各地的國家公園執行各式各樣的任務。貝蒂說，上個月她循線抓到了幾個覬覦瀕臨絕種生物的惡徒，她和當地警察一起跳下車，大喊：「把手舉起來！」你說酷不酷？

國家公園保育員也要做一些與自然相關的工作。貝蒂有時候會被派去察看一些瀕臨危險的棲地是否確實執行保育工作。甚至臨時要為觀光客導覽、介紹地方生態。我覺得國家公園保育員有時是警察，有時是科學家，有時還是老師！

貝蒂說，要成為國家公園保育員的唯一條件，就是要熱愛大自然。我說沒有這麼好的事吧，她才笑了笑，然後更具體說明。據說，最好能夠取得科學或環境領域的學士學位。我聽得一清二楚，所以我已經搜尋了一些當地大學的科學課程，我下定決心要成為一名國家公園保育員！

60. 復活節島 `P. 134`

遼闊的太平洋中有一座孤島，大約位於南美的智利與玻里尼西亞的大溪地之間，該島的歷史是人類文明興衰的寫照。你可能聽過這個地方，它叫做復活節島，已被聯合國教科文組織列為世界遺產。

復活節島最早有人定居是西元 300 年左右，居民是僅有石器時代技術水準的玻里尼西亞人。他們稱之為「拉帕努伊島」，在這裡發展文化、與世隔絕，直到 1722 年歐洲人抵達。島民的由來也是個有趣的問題，據推測，復活島的原住民來自玻里尼西亞，為了追求更好的生活移民至此。這些早期的探險家乘著小獨木舟，航行數千公里才抵達這裡。

復活節島最享譽盛名的當然就是島民所建的石像群。島上四處可見人形「摩艾」雕像，專家們對於原住民如何有能力搬動如此沈重的石板，依然意見紛歧。他們最初也不確定這些石像的用途，不過大部分的人認為這些石像應該是用於某種宗教儀式或祭典。不管他們最初建造石像的用意為何，摩艾石像永遠是一大創舉。

然而，復活節島史上也有過幾段紛亂的時期。其中在 16 世紀時，島上曾經歷一次環境的劇變，造成這場災難的原因誰也說不準。有人認為是人口過剩和環境破壞的結果，有人認為是入侵種的引進，造成島上的植被枯死。這次的危機使人口一分為二，其中一個族群最後把島上的摩艾石像全都推倒。所以當歐洲人抵達的時候，發現這裡是個只有兩三千人的荒島，遠遠低於前一世紀估計的 15,000 人。

2-3 依上下文猜測字義

英文單字可能有很多不同的意思，以形容詞「fine」為例，既可以指「可接受的」、「纖細的」，也可以指「有吸引力的」。當你遇到可能有爭議的單字時，一定要讀完上下文再決定字義。萬一遇到完全陌生的單字，也可以從上下文來推斷字義。

61. 蒙特婁塔姆鼓節 `P. 136`

蒙特婁發展進步的高原區周邊有個公園，每到星期天下午，總有數千名來自不同年齡層、國籍和經濟背景的人，齊聚在這裡演奏樂器或載歌載舞。這項夏季舉辦的活動，每週都在皇家山公園的雅克・卡帝爾紀念碑前面舉行，被稱之為「塔姆鼓節」（一種非洲鼓的名稱），這個節日在蒙特婁的頹放派圈內已經蔚為傳統。

鼓手們群聚在雕像周圍，交換各自創作的節拍、詳細說明彼此的拍子，他們即興表演一些爵士樂句，讓現場觀眾聽得如癡如醉。鼓手前方會空出一塊圓形的空地讓舞者表演，通常是一些嬉皮，在舞蹈上很敢表現。出人意外的是，就連非常保守的觀眾，沒多久也會隨著節拍渾然忘我。

高原區是加拿大文化最多元的地區，這裡的公寓和工作室租金低廉，因此吸引許多藝術家、音樂家和作家到這裡居住。六〇年代時，高原區發展成蒙特婁的前衛區，店家為了迎合居民的喜好，紛紛開始販售前衛時尚的服飾、音樂和書籍。

到了七〇和八〇年代，皇家山公園成為藝術家和音樂家聚集、共進午餐或共享午後時光的地方。音樂家們（也就是鼓手）帶著他們的樂器，最後自然而然開始即興演奏。隨後詩人們也受到吸引，伴著樂聲朗讀他們的作品。

聚會的事情傳開之後，吸引了更多人聚集，最後發展成每週日下午的固定集會。與會的人們縱情享受，音樂家們也藉此機會彼此交流，進一步相約碰面，討論音樂合作事宜。

塔姆鼓節現已成為蒙特婁的一種習俗，週週吸引數千名人潮，是自由與創作的象徵。活動於每週日正午左右展開，到傍晚才結束。塔姆鼓節歡迎任何人參加，不過能夠自己帶樂器來更好，因為唯有群眾的熱情參與，才使得每一次的塔姆鼓節如此獨一無二。所以來吧，跟著感覺走，隨著音樂搖擺，節奏絕對會讓你舞動起來！

62. 惱人的嗡嗡聲　P.138

仔細聽，你聽得到一種持續而有節奏的低鳴聲嗎？如果你聽得到，那可能就是所謂的嗡嗡聲，據說那是一種類似電鑽或汽車引擎聲的嗡嗡聲，頻率低、持續不間斷。紐西蘭也好，蘇格蘭也好，世界各大城鎮都市的居民都可能聽到這種聲音。但並非人人都能聽見這種聲音。出現這種聲音的地方，也只有 2% 左右的人能夠察覺。聽得到的人聲稱，這種聲音不但擾眠、害他們頭痛，有時候還會引起流鼻血。

耳鳴也被認為是造成這種嗡嗡聲的可能原因，如果患者耳邊不斷聽見高音頻的聲響，就是耳鳴的症狀。但是嗡嗡聲的頻率偏低，並非高頻的聲響。此外，有些人也只在特定地點才會聽到，像是自家中。有人說這種聲音在室內聽起來比室外大聲，還有人聲稱他們能夠感覺到聲音在他們體內「振動」。

不過許多質疑者堅稱所謂的嗡嗡聲，只是交通工具、電力線路、風力發電廠或者類似的來源所發出的一般背景噪音而已。發電廠、飛機、工業風扇，甚至夏威夷火山，都是嗡嗡聲的來源，一旦它們停止運轉，數百人就得以喘息。同時，嗡嗡聲屬於低音頻的聲音，這一點也很重要，因為相較於高頻聲響，低頻聲響可以傳遞更遠、穿透更多物質，遇到牆壁或密閉空間，比如房子，甚至會有擴大的效果。

但是當周遭找不到噪音來源的時候，嗡嗡聲又是從何而來（這種案例佔了大約三分之二）？英國劍橋阿登布魯克醫院的大衛・巴古力醫師認為，嗡嗡聲可以解釋為人類本能的防禦機制：聽覺過度敏感。

人類聽力演化，在遇到極度危險或壓力的時候，會變得特別敏感。這種現象在某些人身上造成惡性循環，他們越是留意正常的背景噪音，就越是焦躁，當他們越焦躁，耳朵又下意識放大這些噪音。這麼說或許很好笑，不過治療這種症狀的良方或許就是放輕鬆。

63. 新世紀的發明：合成肉　P.140

漢堡肉是很好的療癒性食物，美味多汁，令人滿足，但是沒有人會認為漢堡肉是健康食品。不過，或許在不久的將來，既美味、脂肪含量又和鮭魚相等的漢堡肉將會問世！21 世紀肉品的供應，將可能由實驗室合成而非殺生取肉，且漢堡肉只是其中之一。

環境的破壞威脅著地球生態的穩定，而肉產業正是當前環境破壞的主因之一。全球所釋放的溫室氣體有 18% 來自於肉產，預估到了 2050 年，全球人口將暴增至 98 億人，各地科學家紛紛表示，為了因應可能發生的全球糧食短缺，研發合成肉可能勢在必行。

動保團體也樂見該領域近來的發展，認為這是減少動物虐待和保護環境重要的一步。投資者似乎也大為贊同，紛紛投入資金協助新技術的研發。就連最大間的雞肉生產商——泰森食品公司也加入行列。

合成肉是將幹細胞浸在高養分的液體內，培養出肌肉組織。目前已成功合成出雞肉、鴨肉和牛肉，但對於口感的意見因人而異。

說也奇怪，科學家面臨的一大問題，竟然不在於合成，而在於口感不對。真肉由無數種組織構成，能正確地刺激味蕾。舉凡血管、脂肪含量、帶筋的肌腱，都是肉品好吃的關鍵，也讓科學家傷透腦筋。

荷蘭一個科學團隊算是幾乎達成這個目標。他們培養出兩萬條肌肉組織，再煞費苦心地一條條組合，根據一名成員的說法，製造出的漢堡肉「相當好吃」。

研製出的漢堡肉，在 2013 年當時造價高達 32 萬 5 千美元。現在價位已降至不到 12 美元。無論合成肉何時會出現在餐廳裡，滿足飢腸轆轆的肉食主義者將不成問題。

64. 青少年的部落格：一笑解千愁 P. 142

嗨，大家好，歡迎回到我的每日部落格，我會在這裡分享每日趣聞和網路軼事。今天的文章有點偏科學，總之希望你們會喜歡。相信大家對「一笑治百病」這句話一定不陌生，我一直以為它不過是句名言罷了，直到今天上網看到一篇文章說明，開懷大笑真的有療效。

不過，首先我要講一些關於笑的知識。顯然我們在襁褓時笑得最多，長大之後笑容就少了。嬰兒平均一天笑 300 次，成人一天才笑 17 次。說到我的數學老師雷金納德「咯咯」薩維奇先生，大概一輩子只笑 17 次吧！

此外，手機上的百科全書應用程式說，人在獨處的時候比較少笑。事實上，假如有伴，發笑的機會幾乎是 30 倍以上。下次一個人看連續劇的時候，留意自己大笑了幾次——我是說捧腹大笑的那種（會把洋芋片噴得到處都是的那種），然後再比較跟朋友一起看電視的大笑次數，保證你和好朋友一定比自己一個人笑得多。為什麼呢？因為笑聲會讓兩人更有共鳴啊，是不是？

好了，剛才只是暖身而已，現在開始進入主題：一笑治百病。好，沒有人會主張把醫生都換成小丑吧，或者有藥不吃，反而去買一套《辛普森家庭》。我們看待事情還是得正確。研究顯示，大笑會讓血管擴張，增加血流量，降低心臟疾病的發生。大笑也會刺激腦部分泌腦內啡，一種會引發快樂感覺的天然化學成分，可有效抒壓並舒緩身體疼痛。最重要的一點，大笑能刺激對抗傳染病的抗體生成，增強抵抗力。所以以下次身體感到些許不適的時候，就看看漫畫或是個人幽默脫口秀吧，保證很快就沒事了！

65. 海上的勇士——維京人 P. 144

維京人是凶猛的勇士和侵略者，在 8 到 11 世紀間征服了大部分的歐洲。他們居住在現在的斯堪地納維亞半島，素以殺人凶殘聞名。他們的戰鬥技巧無人能敵，航海天分同樣無人能出其右。

維京人是十分堅毅的民族，他們吃苦耐勞、不畏飢寒的性格，可歸功於高北緯的國家地理位置。在如此嚴峻的天候之下求生存，養成他們敢於面對大自然一切挑戰的能力，即使在漫漫寒冬的海上遇到狂風暴雨也毫無懼色。不怕危險的並不只是維京的勇士們，由於維京人不願意與家人分離，因此總是攜家帶眷，航向未知的海域。

維京人以其高超的航海技術聞名於世，他們乘著優美、靈活的長船，在海上乘風破浪，這種船不僅能容納充足的糧食以應長途旅行之需，同時又能維持輕巧敏捷，便於作戰。他們憑藉著冒險犯難的勇氣與精神，發現了冰島、格陵蘭島和法羅群島，甚至西行遠達美洲。第一位踏上美洲的歐洲人，正是維京人李夫・艾瑞克森，於 11 世紀達成。據說他在前往格陵蘭的途中偏離航道，才意外發現了新大陸。當時他看到美洲遍地種滿了葡萄，便稱之為「文蘭」（葡萄酒大陸）。

那麼維京人今日的情況又是如何呢？以維京人不服輸的精神，維京文化不可能被區區的時間打敗。假如你看過 2011 年的賣座強片《雷神索爾》以及一系列漫畫原著，你一定對揮舞戰槌的雷神索爾、擅於變身離間的洛基，還有許多來自維京神話的人物並不陌生。維京人對我們的影響不僅止於此，很多人並不知道，有些週間日就是以維京神祇命名的。星期四是索爾日，星期三是眾神之父奧丁日，星期五是維京愛神弗蕾亞日。

2-4 實力檢測

66. 阿克巴大帝 P. 146

阿克巴是蒙兀兒帝國的統治者，他所領導的帝國幾乎橫跨了整個印度次大陸。阿克巴統治期間戰功彪炳、文化成就輝煌，他對人民寬宏，政策包羅廣泛，也讓他贏得「阿克巴大帝」的美名。

阿克巴的成功並非一蹴可幾。1542 年阿克巴出生的時候，他的父親正處於貧窮與流放生涯，1555 年重掌政權之後沒多久便過世了，由 14 歲的阿克巴繼承王位。當時，蒙兀兒仍是個微不足道的小國，不久之後，阿克巴和他的攝政王開創了新局面。他們合力策劃了一次成功的軍事行動，從阿富汗手中奪下印度北部。到了 1560 年，阿克巴解散攝政王，獨攬大權。

隨後的幾項改革，才真正奠定了阿克巴在歷史上的地位。阿克巴旋即重組軍隊，並且建立了一套稱為曼薩布達爾制的軍事系統，提昇軍事效率，並且按照軍階定薪俸。阿克巴也擅於利用新技術，例如：加農炮、防禦性建築和大象。這些革新技術加上阿克巴的天生將才，使得蒙兀兒帝國戰無不勝、攻無不克，版圖不斷擴張。

除了開疆拓土，阿克巴還強化管理機構。由於領地內的人民大多數不像阿克巴一樣為穆斯林，於是他一改以往對非穆斯林加重徵稅的方式，採取全國公平稅率。同時阿克巴也指派印度教徒擔任重要官職。有些人甚至相信，阿克巴所展現出的寬容，正是現代印度文化多元發展的根基。

此時期也是藝術蓬勃發展的時候。阿克巴在位期間發展出蒙兀兒式建築，結合了波斯、印度教和伊斯蘭教的元素。他本身也是藝術的支持者，他的宮廷經常是藝術家、詩人、哲學家和音樂家雲集之處。阿克巴真不愧是一位才華洋溢的統治者。

67. 科技 VS. 民主 P.148

民主制度的出現可上溯至古代，已有數千年的歷史。在時間洪流裡，唯一不變的，就是政客依舊需要運用才識和機智來預測支持者的意向。假使猜錯或忽視了選民的心聲，恐怕掌權不久。

不過時代變了。科技能讓政客免於推敲的麻煩，世界各地的民主政治因而產生轉變。這樣的轉變主要是由兩大科技所推動。首先是臉書等平台的問世，能夠掌握龐大的公眾相關資訊量。還有，新形態人工智慧與機器學習科技的發明，足以處理上述資訊。

這些工具能讓政黨掃描大規模的資訊量，找出行為與投票模式。舉例而言，某政黨可利用此類科技來確認潛在的支持群眾。接下來，他們即可運用社群媒體平台，針對這樣的同溫層投入廣告資源，並略過其他族群。由於多數選舉的勝敗取決於些微差距的選票，目標式的選舉戰略可左右選舉結果。

新科技已經對全球選舉結果產生影響。2016年，劍橋資訊分析公司透過一項測驗，在臉書搜刮選民數據。該公司藉此資訊建立出上千萬美國選民的心理特徵資料庫，此資料庫協助川普的競選團隊將宣傳火力集中在支持者。2016年的英國脫歐公投同樣運用此策略。在上述兩例中，採用先進人工智慧科技的那方均順利勝出，然而新科技卻對2017年的法國總統選舉起不了作用。競選期間，有人以上千名推特假帳號，散播抹黑候選人馬克宏的消息。但馬克宏仍大獲全勝。

顯而易見的是，現今的民主制度面臨新科技帶來的挑戰。然而，我們應謹記，科技本身並無害，而是取決於如何運用科技。人工智慧或許會摧毀民主，卻也能為選民提供一個與政治人物互動的新管道，進而復興民主。最終決定權仍操之在己。

68. 至聖先師孔子 P.150

孔子生於西元前551年，當時正值中國暴君當政、社會紛擾的時期。動盪不安使得社會制度開始崩解，孔子發現人民道德日漸淪喪，而身為動盪社會的一分子，他認為自己有責任鞏固仁慈與律己的傳統思想。孔子最有名的一句教誨「己所不欲，勿施於人。」在英文裡也是待人處事的金科玉律。孔子認為，假如統治者都能把這句話奉為圭臬，必能慈愛他的人民，百姓也會彼此友愛。孔子終其一生都在實踐他的理想，他抱持著寬大的胸襟，對學生不分階級和社會背景，一律有教無類，因此後來獲得「至聖」和「先師」等尊稱。他往往不以說教的方式教學，而是鼓勵學生藉由推理領悟偉大的真理。

孔子認為一個社會若要正常運作，必須有適當的階級制度，而孝道是維繫人人各司其職的關鍵，也就是說，子女必敬愛父母、晚輩必敬愛長輩、人民必敬愛君主，君主自然會以智、德待民。然而，不能為了一己之私而濫用或利用孝道，子曰：「君子喻於義，小人喻於利。」換句話說，君子會注意自己的社會角色，盡到自己的責任，而小人只想到自身的利益。重要的是，居上位者若是行為失當，一樣要接受指責。總而言之，孔子認為人類演化的過程就像是一面拼圖，如果每一片都拼對了位置，就能達到大同世界。

69. 搖擺樂 P.152

搖擺樂是 20 世紀美國新興的著名樂風之一，它的興起要追溯到 1930 年代初期的經濟大蕭條。在這段高失業率、一片清貧的時期，非裔美國人組起了大型的爵士樂團，其中一些樂團開始嘗試用各種節拍和樂器編曲。低音號和五弦琴被吉他和低音提琴所取代，節拍也從四二拍改為四四拍。樂團團長原本只擔任指揮的角色，此時也改由傑出樂手來領導其他團員。

這些轉變默默持續到 1935 年，班尼・古德曼和他的樂團開始攻佔全美各大電台。隨後幾年，古德曼一共獲得了「搖擺樂之王」和「節奏之王」的封號。1938 年，班尼・古德曼進入紐約市傳奇的卡內基音樂廳演奏，成為首位登上這個殿堂的爵士團長。此次演奏的成功也開啟了美國的搖擺樂年代。

搖擺樂年代從 1935 年延續到 1946 年，全美的青少年經常齊聚一堂，欣賞大型爵士樂團表演。許多人會隨著音樂舞蹈，一些舞步在當時蔚為風潮，例如：林迪舞、巴波亞舞、學院沙格舞、吉特巴舞。一些爵士傳奇人物也在搖擺年代崛起，例如：路易斯・阿姆斯壯、比莉・哈樂黛和艾拉・費茲潔拉。

搖擺樂在二次世界大戰期間開始式微，其中一項原因在於一些大型爵士樂團有許多團員赴海外征戰，使得樂團難以經營。1942 年之後出現好幾項錄音禁令，戰時的交通管制也讓樂團難以巡迴全國各地。最後搖擺樂終於退出了舞台，由另一種爵士——波普樂接手，風靡 1950 到 1960 年代。

70. 凍結命運的「冰手指」 P.154

一想到許多動物物種能在幾近冰點的北極海和南極海生存，實在令人不可思議。畢竟，如果沒有特殊衣物和配備的萬全準備，人類絕對無法在極區存活。但即使是酷寒深海裡的堅韌物種，對於號稱「死亡冰柱」的海底鐘乳石，都會聞之色變。

極地到了冬季，水分子就會形成海冰，結冰過程中會失去鹽分（鹽分自然而然降低水的冰點，這就是大家在結冰路面撒鹽的原因）。水結冰後所殘留的鹽分，會在固體冰裡面形成濃鹽水囊。而濃鹽水比一般海水的鹽分濃度更高。

也因為濃度很高，濃鹽水的溫度遠低於海水也不會結冰，且重量和密度亦高於海水。因此，海冰崩裂後，冰層裡的濃鹽水會迅速竄入海水。低濃度的水分子會吸水，而高濃度的水分子又有往低濃度水分子移動的自然特性。因此酷寒的濃鹽水會使海水立即結冰，進而形成一路延伸至海底的冰柱。

鐘乳石般的冰柱觸及海底後，會開始蔓延形成冰毯，可怕的情景就此展開。棲息於海底、移動緩慢的海星與海膽等生物，均無法倖免於冰柱的吞噬，直接被冰封於冰柱內部。綿延距離如果夠長，光是一個冰柱，就能讓成千上萬的動物喪命。

不過別擔心，海底冰柱對於人類等體型較大的物種並不至於造成威脅。即使有風險，又有多少人會去南極海深潛？不過，海底冰柱仍是一個謎，因為我們近期才發現此現象。誰知道在地球最嚴寒的海底深處，還有什麼樣的現象在蟄伏，等待下一個獵物？

Unit 3 學習策略

本單元將介紹兩種重要的閱讀技巧：如何**解讀影像圖表**和**利用參考資料**。影像圖表是將統計資料和數字等以**圖表**呈現，讓我們更容易理解。參考資料則是可以幫助我們迅速有效地找到資訊的**工具**。本單元將同時訓練你這兩種技巧，讓你能有效分析圖表資料，並且迅速找到資料。

讀完本章節以後，你將不僅能讀懂、解釋和評論文本，亦能有效地探索浩瀚的資訊世界。

3-1 影像圖表

資料有許多種形式，有些難以用文字來表達，這時候就需要使用影像圖表來輔助說明。影像圖表運用了圖片和圖表來傳達資訊，包括了**圖表**、**表格**和**地圖**。運用得當的話，可以化繁為簡，使資料容易理解。

71. 地圖：利用谷歌地圖尋路 P. 158

以往迷路可謂司空見慣。沒有網路與智慧型手機的時代，我們只能仰賴紙本地圖。現在尋路再也不成問題了！無論要造訪哪個新去處，我們都有實用的工具協助找尋路線。

請看下一頁的谷歌地圖，地圖內含括眾多實用資訊。舉例而言，右下角是比例尺，能讓你判斷地圖所代表的距離。每條巷弄街道均清楚標示，亦以圖標顯示博物館、餐廳、飯店、商店與加油站等重要地標，並以小小的「M」符號來代表捷運站點。

請運用下頁地圖回答以下問題。

72. 行事曆：加拿大的體育活動 P. 160

冰上曲棍球是在冰上進行的競賽運動，兩隊要設法把「冰球」打進對手的球門。選手們必須配備溜冰鞋、護具、控制冰球的曲棍球棒，以及安全帽。這項運動起源於 19 世紀的加拿大，現已普及全世界，在寒帶國家尤其受到歡迎。

在下面的行事曆中，列出了一項冰上曲棍球錦標賽。行事曆是用來安排時間的圖表工具，典型的行事曆將一個月劃分為一天一格，方便記錄重要約會、查詢某天是星期幾。所以養成使用行事曆的好習慣，每天早上查閱行程，才不會錯過任何重要活動。

現在就用以下的行事曆來回答下頁問題。

73. 表格：搶救貧窮大作戰 P. 162

第二次世界大戰結束後，聯合國（簡稱 UN）力圖改善世界的景況。西元 2000 年，189 個聯合國會員國一致通過一系列降低貧窮的目標，這項計畫稱為《千年發展目標》，原先預計在 2015 年達成。他們針對全球貧窮問題訂出幾個發展方向，例如：教育、健康、飢餓和環境永續發展。

下列表格羅列出九年間，這些目標最大宗的個別捐款以及受贈國。表格將資料以容易分類和閱讀的方式呈現，是非常好的視覺輔助材料。

大部分的表格以垂直和水平的欄位來區隔各項資料。辦公室簡報、個人記錄和預算編列時，也都常使用表格。請用下頁表格回答以下問題。

74. 長條圖：瑜珈──尋求心靈的平靜 P. 164

瑜伽是一種風行全球的心靈養生風潮，它是一套源於古印度的身心修行法門。不同時代的人對瑜伽有不同的詮釋，過去的瑜伽修行者往往遠離塵囂，過著持戒、自律、純樸的生活。然而到了現代，練瑜伽的人駕著新跑車，隨手把喝完的咖啡杯往窗外一扔，也不足為奇。

下頁的長條圖追蹤了 2014 到 2018 年間，古瑜伽學院的男女招生情形。長條圖這種圖像工具，非常便於顯示一段時間內的數據變化。垂直軸通常代表數量，水平軸則代表時間，某個項目在一段時間內的數量變化情形一目瞭然。有時，同一張長條圖上也會並列多組長條圖。請用下頁長條圖回答以下問題。

75. 圓餅圖：生活的調味料 P. 166

多采多姿可說是現代生活的奇蹟，過去人們對於飲食、購物的選擇性很少，然而現在卻五花八門，這都要歸功於全球貿易的興盛，和製造技術的進步。以飲料為例，踏入便利商店的大門，面對架上一望無際、色彩繽紛的解渴飲料，你難道不曾嘆為觀止嗎？可能不會，因為我們早就習以為常，但是總勝過數千年前人們用手盛河中髒水喝的窘況吧。

下頁圓餅圖顯示了各種飲料的熱賣程度。圓餅圖和折線圖、長條圖一樣，都是視覺輔助工具，但是圓餅圖不適合表現時間的推移，它們專門用來表達物品的成分，極適合用來將複雜的概念或系統，分解成較小的元素。現在請用下頁的圓餅圖回答以下問題。

3-2 參考資料

我們生活在資訊無垠的世界。百科全書、旅遊指南、網際網路、報紙、食譜等，這些都是知識的寶庫。但是，要在如此巨大的寶庫中找到特定的資訊可是件棘手的事。此時，索引、搜索引擎、節目表等工具就派得上用場了。只要學會如何瀏覽這些資料，知識的寶庫不久將垂手可得，任你遨遊！

76. 電視節目表：英國的地下寶藏　P. 168

「地下寶藏」這詞彙令人想起了獨腳的海盜、消失的島嶼，以及畫個叉的藏寶圖，可是幾乎沒有人會將這麼浪漫的字眼，跟位於英國中部翰莫維區某個寂靜村莊附近的一塊農田聯想在一起。然而，2009 年 7 月 5 日，名為泰瑞·賀伯特的男子，僅以一具金屬探測器便找到了一座寶藏。這是一批 3,500 件盎格魯撒克遜時期的金、銀物件，深埋英國郊區地下超過一千三百多年。這批寶藏的價值預估為 530 萬美元，是迄今發現最大宗的盎格魯撒克遜寶藏。

若想知道這批寶藏從何而來，又是誰將其埋藏在地下，可觀賞與之相關的電視紀錄片。請查閱下頁的電視節目表，找出各節目播出的時間與頻道。

77. 地圖索引：暢遊澳門　P. 170

澳門曾被葡萄牙統治過，如今是中國的特別行政區。澳門以博奕產業聞名於世，其規模與富麗堂皇的程度甚至超越了拉斯維加斯。

如果到澳門遊玩，你可能會需要一張地圖來指引你找到旅遊景點、餐廳、飯店與賭場的方向。地圖索引的目的就是為了方便你找到路，地圖通常會以座標方格的樣子呈現，上方標有字母（A、B、C 等），側邊則標有數字（1、2、3 等）。地圖索引會列出知名景點的名稱、代表該景點的數字或符號、以及其座標（A1 或 C3 等），以指引你找到該景點所在的方格。

現在請用下方的地圖索引和下頁的地圖來回答以下問題。

78. 食譜：美味鬆餅　P. 172

鬆餅因作法容易，故世界各地隨處可見。鬆餅有甜的、有鹹的，可以當早餐，也可以當點心，而且鬆餅上的配料多得令人難以置信。

不同國家的鬆餅作法與口味也各異其趣。例如在歐洲，鬆餅通常煎成薄餅，搭配水果或冰淇淋一起食用；然而在南美洲，最受歡迎的餡料卻是絞肉跟蔬菜。

不過，大家最熟悉的鬆餅或許是北美的厚煎鬆餅。這種鬆餅的餅皮蓬厚鬆軟，一般是灑上糖粉或糖漿當早餐吃。

想學會做鬆餅很容易，上網或是從烹飪書裡找食譜即可。食譜會列出食材（包括每種食材所需的份量），以及烹調的步驟。不知不覺間，便有一盤剛煎好的美味鬆餅正等著你享用。

現在，請用上頁提供的食譜來回答以下問題。

厚煎美式鬆餅

份量： 4-6 人份

材料： 麵粉 135 公克
　　　　泡打粉 1 茶匙
　　　　鹽 ½ 茶匙
　　　　糖 2 湯匙
　　　　牛奶 135 毫升
　　　　大雞蛋 1 個，略打散
　　　　融化奶油 2 湯匙，額外準備一些，煎餅用

可搭配： 奶油
　　　　　楓糖漿

作法：

1. 將麵粉、泡打粉、鹽、糖放進一個大碗裡，混合均勻。

2. 在另一個碗裡放入牛奶跟蛋，輕輕拌勻後，再倒入融化的奶油。

3. 將作法 2 的牛奶混合液倒進作法 1 的麵粉調和物裡，然後用叉子將麵糊打至順滑無粉粒為止。

4. 以中火加熱平底鍋，放入一些奶油。

5. 奶油融化後，倒入一勺麵糊。

6. 待鬆餅上面開始起泡後，翻面煎另一面，煎到兩面金黃，鬆餅上升約 1 公分厚為止。

7. 重複上述步驟直到用完所有麵糊。

79. 搜尋引擎：相撲　P. 174

　　兩個大力士在土俵內相撞。兩人幾乎赤身露體，身上除了有條絹帶遮羞外，別無他物。他們抓著彼此，用力將對方推攘向土俵的邊緣，最後終於有人失足，絆倒在土俵外。這場相撲賽在短短 10 秒內便結束了。

　　相撲是日本特有的摔角比賽，十足刺激。兩位相撲力士交鋒的那一刻，榮耀或失敗立見。但是，相撲帶給觀眾的不只是刺激感。我們還可從相撲的起源、歷史、傳統等看到日本文化引人入勝的一面。

　　你可以在網路上找到與相撲有關的各種資訊。只要在搜尋引擎上輸入「相撲」兩個字，就會發現眾多搜尋結果條目。每個搜尋結果都包括了標題、網址、一段摘要或者是一段節錄自網頁的文章。請利用下頁搜尋結果，來分辨哪個網站最可能擁有你正在尋找的資訊。

80. 註腳：「神槍手」安妮・歐克利
P. 176

　　安妮・歐克利是蠻荒西部的一名神槍手，她的槍法神準到有人稱她為美國第一位女性超級巨星註 1。她能從 90 英尺遠的距離射穿紙牌的邊緣註 2，能擊中拋向空中的硬幣，還能射中香菸頭的菸灰註 3。

　　安妮很小的時候就開始學射擊。她八歲時便已是非常出色的獵人，靠著獵殺販售野生動物奉養寡母註 4。1885 年，她加入「水牛比爾西部綜藝團」註 5。在接下來的 17 年，到世界各地巡迴演出，為皇帝、國王與皇后表演槍法註 6。

附註：

1. Connie Fields, *The Legendary Annie Oakley* (New York: Penguin, 2009), 12.

2. 她會在紙牌落地前射出更多洞。

3. T. J. Stone, *Annie Oakley: Sharpshooter Extraordinaire* (London: Random House, 1998), 71-73. 安妮曾擊中德國威廉二世嘴上叼著的香菸頭的菸灰。威廉二世後來引發了第一次世界大戰。

4. Phyllis Mathews, *Little Sure Shot: The Early Years of Annie Oakley* (New York: New York University Press, 1994), 89.

5. 當時該團的冠軍神射手波嘉達斯隊長離開綜藝團僅一年的時間，安妮才幸運有了出線的機會。

6. Jeremy Wilde, *Buffalo Bill's Wild West Show: A History* (Cambridge: Cambridge University Press, 1987), 123. 當綜藝團於 1887 年到倫敦巡迴演出時，連深居簡出的英國維多利亞女皇都到場觀賞安妮的表演。

　　撰寫這類充滿資訊的文章時，作者通常會在該章或該書的結尾加上附註，說明引用資料的來源。章節附註也讓作者有機會為讀者提供他們覺得有趣，但與本文沒有直接關聯的補充資料。請試著用上方的註腳來回答以下問題。

Unit 4 綜合練習

　　既然各位現在已經熟悉各種閱讀與字彙的技巧，以及一些重要的學習策略，那麼該是測驗的時候了。本單元與前幾個單元不同，不再是一篇文章只有一種技巧。現在，你面臨的挑戰是，必須在每篇單獨的文本上，運用數種不同的閱讀技巧。

　　利用這幾篇複習的單元，看看自己有多大的進步，從之前的單元中又學到了多少。試著在模擬考試的情境下進行本測驗，接著分析自己的優缺點。這麼做能讓你知曉自己將來需要在哪方面下更多的功夫。

4-1 綜合練習（I）

81. 科技紋身　P. 180

　　想像一下，如果手指在手臂上滑動就能在音樂播放器選歌，或是將智慧型手機靠近手背，就能閱讀最新影評，該有多麼方便。如今，這樣的情境已真實上演，最棒的是，此科技還能讓你酷炫有型。

歡迎來到 DuoSkin 的世界，這項科技不僅顛覆傳統，還兼具時尚外觀。

由麻省理工學院研發的 DuoSkin 其實不是一項產品，而是一種科學原理。幾乎人人都能以低成本的方式，輕鬆自創獨一無二的電子紋身。科技從未如此個人化！

DuoSkin 的神奇材料在於金箔，具有導電、價格低廉、強韌又能安全用於皮膚的特性。以繪圖設計軟體描繪圖案後，使用者運用電腦割字機，在紋身貼紙裁切出此圖案。再將金箔直接附著於紋身貼紙，按壓至皮膚即可形成暫時性的紋身。聽起來不難吧？真的就是這麼簡單！

DuoSkin 電子紋身目前共有三種型式。第一種主要藉由觸覺達到輸入功能。這種紋身猶如觸控式面板或螢幕，可控制電子裝置。某間小學甚至製作出一觸摸就能自拍的電子紋身！

第二種主要用於顯示或輸出。貼附皮膚的加熱元件能讓此類電子紋身感應到體溫改變而變色。有的電子紋身甚至會在使用者出現強烈情緒時，亮起 LED 燈。此類電子紋身是 DuoSkin 問世前的始祖，但僅作為醫療用途。

最後一種電子紋身則可用於儲存和傳輸資訊。採用近距離無線通訊（簡稱 NFC）晶片，就能和鄰近電子裝置互動，原理類似房卡與門鎖的通訊方式。不過與房卡不同的是，此類電子紋身可接收與傳送資訊，彷彿配戴式的迷你硬碟。

DuoSkin 的科技原理雖然十分了不起，不過 DuoSkin 的發明者——來自台灣的高新綠，對於此紋身的時尚外觀則更加自豪。DuoSkin 的穿戴式控制不但兼具外型和功能，更以嶄新的方式實現人機合一的概念。若電子裝置都能裝設於皮膚，未來又會往什麼方向發展呢？

82. 伊斯坦堡——橫跨兩大洲的古老城市
P. 182

土耳其的伊斯坦堡無疑是世界上最有活力的一座城市。在伊斯坦堡，古老與現代儼然水乳交融，歐亞亦交會於此。熱情好客、慷慨大方且魅力四射的當地人，總有說不完的故事。

伊斯坦堡是世上唯一地跨兩大洲的城市。博斯普魯斯海峽是世界上最繁忙的航道之一，它將這座城市一分為二：西邊是歐洲，東邊則是亞洲。因為城市裡有許多名勝古蹟以及其他有趣的事物，故乘船沿著博斯普魯斯海峽而行，是遊覽伊斯坦堡的最佳方式。

要在最短的時間內遊覽這座城市，就是租艘雙體船，這是一種有著兩個船體的高速帆船。若是租不起雙體船，也可以在雙體船的導覽中訂位。搭乘雙體船，你就能從博斯普魯斯海峽，逛到黑海或馬爾馬拉海，將伊斯坦堡所有美景盡收眼底。雙體船是很方便，但它有一大缺點：你沒辦法與當地居民交流，但這或許也是伊斯坦堡最有趣的地方。若要感受當地文化，你應該捨棄雙體船，改搭更經濟實惠的大眾運輸工具——渡輪。渡輪走的路線雖然沒有雙體船那麼遠，但你還是能看到許多重要的旅遊景點，而且搭乘渡輪還能讓你跟土耳其人打交道，看看他們是怎麼過日子的。

渡輪一大早就開始營運，會定時從伊斯坦堡西邊艾米諾努主城區的碼頭開船，全天都有航班，直到晚上才會收班。坐在渡輪中間的茶館裡，看著如珠寶般耀眼的托普卡匹皇宮和聖索菲亞大教堂蕩漾而過，是很難得的體驗。身穿繡花天鵝絨外套、頭戴土耳其氈帽的服務生，會為你送上一種叫做「çay」的土耳其茶，茶杯是鬱金香形狀的玻璃杯，旁邊還放著一塊方糖。一邊啜飲著茶，一邊欣賞博斯普魯斯海峽的風光，是見證伊斯坦堡之美的奇妙方式。

83. 道歉語的各種用途 P. 184

在 10 個東亞國家旅居超過 26 年的我，自認對此地區的文化瞭若指掌。不過，我至今仍會不時對兩件事感到吃驚，那就是亞洲人的道歉方式，以及道歉的頻繁程度。而遠東地區的「道歉文化」究竟從何而來？

日本大概是最容易道歉過頭的國家，我們不妨先從此國談起吧。日本至少有 20 種不同的道歉用語，以及眾多道歉姿勢，日本人隨時處於幾乎任何事都能說聲抱歉的狀態（他們也的確這麼做）。無論是否發自內心，至少看似如此。

目前最耳熟能詳的日文道歉用語就是「sumimasen」，意思是「不好意思，請容我……」，而不是「對不起」。這樣謙卑的措辭適用於各式場合，包括在公車上請他人「借過」，或是遲到五分鐘等各種情況，甚至比日文的「arigato」（意指「謝謝」）更常用來表達謝意，表示你意識到自己或多或少麻煩到對方。所以下次身處日本，有人替你開門的時候，別謝謝他，先說聲不好意思才對！

而日本的道歉文化，隨著日據時代流傳至台灣亦不足為奇。在台灣，「不好意思」等同「sumimasen」，但用途更為廣泛。除了可以用來道歉、致謝、請求許可等情況，此一靈活用語甚至可打開話匣子。

台灣文化和日本文化雷同，均重視禮節、謙卑態度與和睦的氣氛。團體的重要性大於個人，社會期待每個人以大局為重。而多數台灣人和日本人處於極度擁擠居住環境和高壓的生活條件之下，更突顯上述風氣的重要性。因為幾乎任何互動方式都像闖入對方的空間，必須先獲得首肯，方能繼續互動。

然而，太習慣表面上的道歉，也許會讓人感受不到發自內心的歉意。我和許多旅居亞洲的外國人一樣，多年來已聽過太多無心脫口而出的「對不起」，包括沒寫作業、踩到我的腳等各種情況。道歉用語可能已演變為一種口頭禪，而不是真心感到歉意才說出口的用語。

84. 京都的寺廟建築 P. 186

京都是日本中部的一座城市，以寺廟之美名聞遐邇。京都在 794 年至 1868 年間曾是日本的首都，現在則是主要觀光景點，亦是探索日本寺廟、園林、傳統文化的絕佳地點。這些景觀在日本其他大城市裡有時難以見到。

日本寺廟不像中國寺廟雕樑畫棟，其寺廟更加簡樸，且使用自然的色調。但日本的寺廟還是很美，而且更為人所知的是它的典雅，而非裝飾。到京都，絕對不能錯過的景點是延曆寺寺廟區。該寺在西元 788 年興建於比叡山山頂，共包含了 120 座寺廟與 3 座佛塔。這座寺廟群提供人們

健行的地點，讓人一觀全京都令人驚豔的美景。若還想一睹活生生的歷史，那就到根本中堂來，這裡有已經燃燒一千兩百年之久、不曾熄滅的法燈！

另一個值得觀賞的景點，是位於京都市中心的西本願寺。這座寺宇由五座建築物組成，俱是安土桃山時代最美麗的藝術作品與建築成就，當時整個日本都在京都的統治下。現在這座寺廟仍然是淨土真宗教學院的總部。淨土真宗是佛教禪宗的一個派別，在全世界擁有超過 1,200 萬信徒。

南禪寺位於京都的東山山腳下。該寺曾經是龜山天皇退休後居住的別墅，現在則是世界最著名的禪宗寺廟。如果你到這裡參觀，會看到有人在打坐、禮佛。三門就位於寺廟的入口處，牌樓型的大門莊嚴巨大，門頂上是美麗的雀鳥與天使的手繪壁畫，在在令人印象深刻。

在京都，逛園林是另一種消遣。跳虎園是座古典日式庭園，亦是遊覽的好去處。庭院裡有瀑布可供觀賞，也有草席讓人席地而坐，是參與日本茶道的理想場所，尤其在看了一整天的寺廟後，茶道是沈澱內心的絕佳方式。

85. 量子物理學 P. 188

物理學的先鋒尼爾斯‧波爾曾說過一句名言：「不為量子論所震撼的人，是因為還不懂量子論。」量子物理學是研究原子層次內的物質與能量理論，自生成以來造成廣大的爭議，因為量子物理學的理論架構，不僅挑戰物理學的古典定律，還提出科學的新可能性與重大突破，而這些理論一度被認為只會出現在科幻小說中。

量子物理學是相對較新的研究領域，發展於20 世紀初期，目的是為了解釋幾個與物理學的古典定律不符合、甚至相左的實驗結果（物理學的古典定律是指包括由牛頓、伽利略等人於數百年前提出的物理法則）。

對於量子論的學生來說，要真正掌握量子論的原則是個極其困難的任務。因為量子論幾乎執拗地違悖常理。量子論旨在闡述次原子世界的運行法則，這種運行法則與我們日常生活的物理世界（也

就是基本粒子具有粒子性與波動性）迥然不同。我們無法同時準確測得粒子的位置與動量。次原子粒子，如電子，是以機率表示存在，只有在測量時才會瓦解變成現實。即使是對量子論發展有極大貢獻的愛因斯坦，也對某些量子論的主張提出強烈的懷疑，多年來試圖予以反駁，卻徒勞無功。

量子論是非常複雜的領域，許多對量子論的詮釋都是有可能的，每位物理學家都有各自支持的說法。有一種詮釋認為次原子粒子可以來回時間之流，能同時出現在所有可能的地方。另一種詮釋則表示在每個時刻，宇宙會分裂成億萬個平行的宇宙，意思是存在著無限個版本的你。還有另一種詮釋提出我們的意識會影響次原子粒子的行為，甚至它的存在。

被弄糊塗了嗎？嗯，別太難過。讓我們引用另一位知名的量子理論家查德‧費曼的話：「如果你自認很懂量子力學，那表示你並不懂量子力學。」

86. 耀眼奪目的馬祖螢光海灘　P.190

在智慧型手機、飛行機器人和網路充斥的年代，每個人似乎已見多識廣。但令人驚歎的大自然奇景，仍舊能喚起我們童心未泯的一面。而我們何其有幸，不需千里迢迢，就能親身體驗罕見又奇特的景致。

其中一個自然奇觀就在台灣管轄的小型馬祖群島。馬祖的海灘到了夜晚，會散發螢光般的光芒。此現象稱為「藍眼淚」，螢光出自無害的夜光藻。有時整座海岸在夜裡受到神秘的藍色潮汐團團包圍。對許多遊客而言，這嘆為觀止的難忘經歷，成為風靡社群媒體的打卡勝景。

大家可能會納悶，海水發出藍光的原因為何？首先，海水裡聚集許多夜光藻。一滴海水就能含有上千隻微小夜光藻。科學家相信，夜光藻之所以發光，是為了嚇阻天敵所產生的本能反應。

不過，想要目睹藍眼淚的螢光盛況，需要碰點運氣。雖然四月至九月都能欣賞得到藍眼淚，但四月至六月是最佳賞景月分。氣候亦為關鍵因素。一定要在漆黑炎熱的夜晚，才能看到最絢麗的藍眼淚效果。此外，海面越平靜，一睹藍眼淚的機率越高。理想情況是，浪高需低於 20 英吋，且不能有任何白浪。

而藍眼淚出沒的地點遍布馬祖的所有小島，包括東引、南竿和北竿。然而，光害越少的地方，越容易看得見藍眼淚。而當地飯店和旅行團業者就能幫上大忙。他們能協尋較鮮為人知的觀景暗處，甚至能預測何時觀景條件最佳。

前往馬祖觀光的遊客，一定要做好可能無法看見藍眼淚的心理準備。但藍眼淚只是馬祖群島自然奇景的其中一環，大家還是可以盡情遊覽探索這座群島！

87. 把玩食物　P.192

對熱愛烹飪的人而言，變出可口料理的過程，與畫家或雕塑家的創作過程十分雷同。他們熱衷於實驗各種風味與口感，並仰賴創意、直覺和食譜完成創作。不過，「分子料理學」的追隨者則側重從科學方法入手。這不代表分子料理學缺乏原創性；反之，分子料理開啟了通往驚人料理新境界的大門。

何謂分子料理學？簡言之，主要是從科學的角度實驗烹飪結果。更確切來說，分子料理學的重點在於烹飪過程所產生的物理和化學變化。「分子料理學」一詞是由尼可拉斯‧庫提與哈維‧提斯這兩名牛津大學科學家於 1988 年所創。他們聯手研究食物的化學結構與交互作用。哈維‧提斯甚至設計出一套數學公式，幫助人們依據分子料理學的原理來分析食物。食物科學並不是新的概念，但過去僅限於大規模的食品製造業，例如在超市購得的品項。但分子料理學卻推出了另類的食物科學，並介紹給新的愛好者，即餐廳主廚和追求極致的家中掌廚者。

庫提和提斯的研究，激盪出許多令人震驚、甚至古怪的食物組合。有誰會想到，蝸牛粥或煙燻培根冰淇淋會如此美味？以分子料理學觀之，上述料理包含的成分配比均恰到好處。再者，將此創新原則學以致用，就能呈現出意想不到的全新料理。包括完全沒有用到魚卵的「蘋果魚子醬」，用注射筒將蘋果汁注入混合劑，形成魚卵口感的晶球顆粒。還有一道蘋果料理，運用分子料理的科學原理就能產生肉的味道與口感。要是想在家製作美味綿密的冰淇淋呢？有液態氮就不成問題！

對分子料理感興趣、想一飽口福的人有幾種選擇。勇於嘗試的廚師可上網搜尋食譜，在家試做。另外，有興趣的饕客也可找尋供應此獨特（且超級昂貴）料理的餐廳。不過，多數人可能會發現，上述選擇若非太難實踐，便是所費不貲。欣賞眾多分子料理照片的「視吃」方式，或許是最容易滿足此口腹之慾的捷徑。

88. 節目表：音樂劇　P.194

2013 年，奧斯卡金像獎頒獎典禮上所演出的音樂劇《悲慘世界》成績斐然，讓全新一代的粉絲認識了音樂劇。雖然音樂劇主要是舞台劇的形式，但自從電影業興起，許多舞台音樂劇即陸續被改編成電影，如《媽媽咪呀》、《真善美》、《悲慘世界》，有些電影甚至也被改編成舞台音樂劇，例如：《獅子王》、《比利・艾略特》。

大家容易將音樂劇與歌劇混淆。雖然這兩種表演形式都是以歌曲傳達故事內容，但兩者間還是有本質上的差異。歌劇通常沒有對話，而音樂劇的某些片段是以對話的方式呈現，而非演唱的方式。音樂劇有舞蹈，也有各種不同的音樂風格，跟歌劇比起來，旋律較為輕快。

如果有機會到美國或英國度假，想看一場音樂劇，那麼就到紐約的百老匯區，或者是倫敦的西區。你可以查閱報紙或網路上的音樂劇節目表。節目表會提供當地的文藝表演資訊，在每個節目名稱下方，會列出表演日期、地點、票價，以及節目簡介。

現在利用下頁的節目表，來回答以下問題。

89. 心碎而死　P.196

每個人或多或少都有過痛徹心扉的經驗。也許是變調的校園戀情，抑或好友的背叛。當下心情猶如世界末日降臨，彷彿經歷撕心裂肺的痛苦。但你終究撐過來了，日子照樣過下去。

當然，這是幸運的版本。

但在某些情況下，我們比喻的「心碎」感覺，真的會導致心臟病、重度憂鬱、中風甚至死亡。這就是萊斯大學新研究得出的結果。他們發現了極具說服力的證據，也就是重大的悲慟經歷會對健康造成不堪設想的後果。該研究追蹤喪偶不久的鰥夫，研究結果令人憂心：走不出傷痛的人，身體發炎指數比正常人高出 17%。而發炎指數上升會導致多種健康問題，包括糖尿病、癌症和心臟病。

接著談談神秘的「心碎症候群」。此病症又稱為「章魚壺心肌症」，因為發病時的心臟狀似日本人用來捕捉章魚的壺籠。醫界於 1990 年首次發現此新形態的心臟缺陷。醫師進一步注意到，許多患者的共同點，便是在不久前痛失摯愛，於是將這個病症另取了「心碎症候群」的別名。「心碎症候群」症狀包括胸痛和呼吸急促，因此常被誤認為心臟病。某些醫師甚至懷疑，在極端情況下，心碎症候群可能會使患者病危。他們認為，患者幾乎在喪偶後驟逝，就是一大證據。有些人相信，2016 年，《星際大戰》女星嘉莉・費雪的母親黛比・雷諾就是在女兒過世後，因為心碎症候群而撒手人寰。

目前尚缺乏心碎症候群的正式研究。不過，生心理健康之間的相互影響，是否讓你稍感驚訝？在醫界前線接觸病患的醫師倒是司空見慣。他們的經驗是，慢性病患者可說是衍生心理健康問題的高危險群。他們同樣看過心理健康連帶影響生理健康的病例。我們的身心終究無法分而論之。因此，如果你正在經歷分手的煎熬，切記平常心以對，別太苛責自己。

90. 長條圖：旅居海外　P.198

每個人一生中的某段時間，都應該要到國外居住。完全沈浸在不同於自己國家的生活方式，是一段建立人格的過程。但是搬到國外居住不是件簡單的事。在語言不通又無親友在旁的異國，獨自生活是很艱難的。

那麼，搬到他國居住的決定就應審慎以待。先到那個國家旅遊，看看自己是否適合搬到異國居住，或許是個不錯的作法。也許先到你考慮移居的國家度個假，看看工作好不好找？氣候合不合適？食物好吃，還是會讓你倒胃口？你能不能想像自己長期居住該地？當然，住在異國的理由有一籮筐。請看下頁的長條圖，該圖記錄了一千名外國人移居台灣的原因，接著回答以下問題。

受過蒙特梭利教育，後來功成名就的例子，比如亞馬遜（Amazon.com）的創辦人傑夫・貝索斯。但是，如果瑪麗亞・蒙特梭利現在還在世的話，她很有可能會強調她的教育體系是培養終生對學習的熱愛，而不是為了擁有銀行帳戶的鉅款。

4-2 綜合練習（II）

91. 瑪麗亞・蒙特梭利　P. 200

1870 年 8 月 31 日，瑪麗亞・蒙特梭利誕生於義大利。瑪麗亞的母親受過高等教育，熱衷閱讀，對其成長過程影響深遠。這或許是為何在涉及到自己的教育問題時，瑪麗亞會拒絕妥協。起初，她想讀工程學，這在當時社會是頗有爭議的選擇。而後，她轉讀醫學，這對那群誤以為女人就該待在家裡的人眼中，更具爭議。最後，瑪麗亞的努力沒有白費，她成為有史以來第一位就讀羅馬大學醫學院的女性。

無可否認的是，瑪麗亞・蒙特梭利是位聰慧、勇敢又能幹的女性。但是，這些令人欽佩的特質並不是她讓人懷念至今的唯一原因，教育領域才是她留給世人最偉大的遺產。

瑪麗亞之後的人生開始從事與孩童有關的工作，她於 1907 年成立第一個「Casa dei Bambini」，即「兒童之家」。她深信，只要給孩子一個適合的環境，孩子就會在自己的教育之路上引領向前。換句話說，他們會開始自主學習，並不是因為有人要他們這麼做，而是因為他們自己想這麼做。在她眼中，真正的挑戰在於如何提供合適的教育環境。

瑪麗亞的教育理論直到現在仍廣受歡迎，世界各地的學校實施「蒙特梭利教育」。這些學校試圖考慮人類心理的某些要素，例如溝通、工作、秩序、抽象等。他們的目的是讓學生建立自己的觀念並自我激勵，而不是由權威人物來告訴學生他們做錯事情。說到實際的教學，實施蒙特梭利教育體系的學校所採取的教學法運用到五種感官，而不是只是聽跟看而已。

蒙特梭利教育理念的倡導者認為，其教學法能培養學生克服成人生活會面臨的挑戰，不論是在情感上、學術上，還是職業上。也有好幾個曾

92. 貫通古今中外的《孫子兵法》　P. 202

孫子出生於西元前 544 年，是中國重要的軍事戰略家。他因撰寫《孫子兵法》而聞名於世，這是一本闡述如何打勝仗、征服敵國的兵書。《孫子兵法》共 13 篇，每篇著重於戰爭的某個面向，其中包括了〈作戰篇〉、〈軍爭篇〉、〈九變篇〉等。

雖然孫子的戰術針對的是古代的戰爭，可是現今仍然有人從他的兵法中得到指點。例如，孫子寫道：「兵者，詭道也。」在孫子的時代，這是事實，現在也依然如此。事實上，在第二次世界大戰時，盟軍有個叫做「堅忍計畫」的戰略，可說是一場騙局。盟軍成立了實際並不存在的軍隊，連充氣式的坦克車都出動了，就是要讓敵軍以為他們即將發動攻擊。最後，孫子的觀點是正確的，「堅忍計畫」成功了。

《孫子兵法》中另一句備受青睞的引文是：「故進不求名，退不避罪，唯民是保，而利于主，國之寶也。」在現代，收音機、電視、網際網路等傳媒，使得這句話更形重要，因為有太多人會從旁推測軍方幕僚的一舉一動，使他們很難按戰略行事。

世界各地的商人也求助於《孫子兵法》，想要找出能勝過同行的優勢。他們認為孫子斷言理想將軍該具備的特質，同樣也適用於經理人。例如，孫子認為臨陣畏縮、肆意妄為、性情暴躁易怒等都是身為一個將領不該有的缺點。這些無疑也是商場上不該有的缺點。商人還特別喜歡引用兩則孫子的言論，分別是「知己知彼」與「避實擊虛」。

孫子在兩千多年前就已經有這麼多既充滿智慧又貼切的看法，顯然是個真正的天才。但若孫子知道他的智慧結晶如今出現在《以孫子兵法挽救婚姻》這等無用的自助書籍時，即使孫子這個偉大的兵法家，也可能會瞠目結舌吧。

93. 芬蘭的教育體系 `P. 204`

芬蘭的優質教育體系，在全球排名裡，向來居高不下，這項成就令人激賞。但讓人更感興趣的是，芬蘭是怎麼名列前茅的，特別是芬蘭採用與大多數國家相反的教學法。

芬蘭傑出的教育體系，在某些方面很值得稱許，其中一項是他們對待教師的方式。芬蘭的教師必須取得碩士學位，而且排名前 10％的畢業生才能入選。這表示芬蘭所有教師的素質都很高。此外，老師被視為是專業人士，在制訂自己的教育策略上能發揮的空間很大。這包括每日授課四小時以外，每週還有兩小時有薪的「專業發展」時間，從而在必要時，能有時間私下輔導有學習困難的學生。

這讓我們看到另一個有趣的事實：在芬蘭的教育體系下，很少會有被忽視的學生。學生並不是分成「聰穎」、「學習緩慢」這兩類，而視為處於不同的發展階段。如果有學生在課堂上的學習成效不彰，老師會以適性教學來解決問題。這種情況在芬蘭很常見，因為將近 30％ 的學生在小學入學後的九年間得到老師專業上的協助。這種制度肯定很有用，因為芬蘭學生的畢業率傲視全球。

大家覺得最令人震驚的其實是芬蘭的考試方法。大多數國家最愛採用「早測試、常測試」的方式，然而芬蘭卻非如此。芬蘭的學生一直到十幾歲為止都很少寫作業、很少考試。學生啟蒙的前六年竟然連小考都沒有。除了上述情形外，學生在校每天總共有 75 分鐘娛樂休息的時間，而美國的學生平均才只有 27 分鐘。

總之，芬蘭的教育體系似乎是「質」勝於「量」。芬蘭教育強調的是「人」，而不是「數字」——不管是考試的分數，還是學生入學的人數。而其教育下的成果亦不言自明。

94. 人腦如電腦硬碟？ `P. 206`

人腦有時被認為是生物科學最後的未知領域。雖然科學家對人體其他部位的知識不斷增加，但是對他們來說，大腦的功能仍然是個謎。不過，有鑑於現今對大腦的研究逐漸增加，也許大腦真正的本質不久就能明朗。

威斯康辛大學麥迪遜校區的心理學家朱利奧・托諾尼提出了一個新理論，不僅可能改變我們對人腦的看法，還可能改變我們的睡眠。托諾尼教授認為，睡眠時大腦會「重新組合」，切斷現有的神經元連結，以便能夠形成新的神經元連結。

他的理論有助於回答困擾科學家許久的問題：為什麼大腦在我們睡覺時還這麼活躍？它正在做什麼？人體其他部位在我們睡覺時幾乎處於癱瘓狀態，唯獨大腦不同，它會維持與清醒時相同程度的活躍度。

直到現在，科學家認為大腦在我們睡覺時會忙著建立新的神經元連結。這些神經元的連結是通過經驗的學習或記憶形成。但是，托諾尼教授表示，真相有可能恰好相反。他認為不斷建立神經元連結會消耗太多精力，而且這些無意義的細節會壓垮我們的大腦。所以，大腦在我們睡覺時反而會切斷這些連結，空出來的位置正好可以讓我們第二天在學習新知識或體驗新事物時，形成新的神經元連結。

如果在我們睡覺時，大腦跟電腦硬碟一樣會刪除記憶，以便新記憶能夠妥善地儲存，那麼有趣的問題來了。例如，我們的大腦是怎麼「知道」哪些記憶無關緊要，所以是值得刪除的呢？或許科學家再多做一些研究，就能發現我們是如何控制這個過程。如果哪些要記得、哪些要忘記，都由我們說了算，這不是很棒嗎？如果是這樣的話，我們絕對能夠輕易地通過英文測驗。有創傷記憶的人也能夠有機會忘記創傷，然後繼續向前邁進。

95. 內線交易 `P. 208`

企業有兩種類型：上市公司（股份上市公司）與有限公司（股份不公開公司）。如果一家企業是有限公司，那麼這家公司是屬於少數人擁有的獨資企業。反過來說，如果一家企業是上市公司，那麼任何人都能夠投資這家公司，而投資者要做的，就是在證券交易所購買這家公司的股票。

股價的漲跌取決於市場現狀。或許這家公司公布的收益高於眾人預期，股價因而飆升。但也有可能是收益減少，導致股價下跌。無論如何，重點是大家在同一時間取得敏感性資料，以便決定是否購買或出售股票。

但是，若與這家公司有關的某些人比一般大眾還要早聽到某些資訊時，又會發生什麼事？也許他們發現公司的利潤下降，所以在其他人有機會做出反應前，且股價還很高時，就賣出手中的股票。這就叫做「內線交易」，亦即利用非公開資訊來決定買賣股票的作法。這不僅僅是公不公平的問題，內線交易在大多數的國家都屬於非法行為。

不一定是公司的高階主管才有可能從事內線交易。連你無意中聽到某家公司的主管談到即將合併的公司，而去買了該公司的股票，你就有可能會因內線交易而被逮捕。形成內線交易的關鍵條件是利用非公開資訊進行交易，而不是跟這家公司是否有任何的私人關係。

因內線交易而被逮捕的案件通常都是大新聞，因為涉及內線交易的人往往很有錢、人脈也很廣。2004 年，美國電視圈名人瑪莎・史都華從朋友那兒得到內部消息後，隨即賣出所持有 ImClone 公司的股份，之後因共謀罪罪名成立而被判入監服刑五個月。2003 年，名為雷內・瑞弗金的澳洲銀行家則因內線交易入獄服刑九個月，而他從中僅獲利不到 3,000 美元。每年都會爆發數百件內線交易的醜聞，其中有一些會成為新聞頭條。

96. 左翼（左派）與右翼（右派）　P. 210

只要你看報紙或是聽收音機的政論談話節目，一定會聽到那些名嘴提到「左派」、「右派」政黨。可是，這些詞彙是什麼意思？又是從何而來？

答案就在法國的歷史中。早在 1789 年法國大革命初期，國民議會的議員按照固定的座位入座。當時，擁護君主的議員通常坐在議長的右邊，而支持改革的議員則坐在議長的左邊。最後，媒體習慣以國民議會的位置來辨別各黨派：即「左」、「右」黨派，這個現代政治詞彙的重要性就此誕生。

雖然這些政治標籤是在兩百多年前發明的，其原義與現代用法仍舊相關。以左派或左翼為例，這些人在法國大革命期間主張徹底改變法國的政治制度。在他們眼中，舊的政治結構不公不義且毫無作用，故要全部予以消除後，國家才可能有所進步。如今，左翼人士認為，要改善社會，就要嘗試新的施政方針。他們也偏好將財富重新分配給窮人與弱勢團體，施行高稅收與社會福利政策。左翼人士亦強調和平與非暴力政策，然而相對於他們在法國大革命後期所造成的混亂來說，這簡直就是諷刺。

國民議會的另一端是右翼人士。這些人緊抓著傳統不放，即使這個傳統意味著無數人民正活活餓死。右翼政客已經有了金錢跟權力，所以他們害怕變革，因為他們會損失最大。如今，右翼人士依舊支持傳統。他們認為一個人的成敗基於個人特質，而不是來自政府的任何幫助。不過，他們覺得費解的是個別情況下的差異。撇開優缺點的問題不談，當某人為了生存而不得不輟學時，是很難功成名就的。

97. 百科全書：人類與貓的友誼史　P. 212

科學家如今相信貓跟人類已經一起生活了將近一萬兩千多年。這段時間也是人類首次開始大規模從事農耕的時間。農耕意味著要為過冬儲備糧食，貓就是在這個時候走進人類的歷史。貓會幫忙消滅偷吃穀倉儲糧的老鼠與其他動物。貓與人類從一開始的互助關係，最後演變成了生活在同一屋簷下的同居關係。

但是，這樣還不足以讓貓依賴我們人類。貓不像狗，狗在經過一段時間後逐漸失去賴以維生的技能，可是貓仍舊保有大部分天性。許多養貓的飼主可以證實這一點，因為貓還有外出獵物，把獵物帶回當作「禮物」獻給主人的習慣。

請利用下頁與貓有關的百科全書內容節錄，回答下列問題。

98. 植物的戰鬥力　P.214

你是否曾因為踐踏植物而感到內疚？答案應該是「不會」。畢竟，多數人視植物為裝飾品或食物，而非生物。植物無法移動或感知疼痛；因此，我們將植物定義為「物體」。

但萬一我們錯了呢？

威斯康辛大學麥迪遜校區科學家提出的一項驚人發現，可能會顛覆我們看待植物的方式。此實驗將麩胺酸鹽——一種改善神經元訊號傳導的物質——塗抹於植物上。接下來，科學家使用會發光的綠色蛋白質來追蹤該植物的鈣質流向。最後，他們剪下一部分的葉片，並以顯微鏡觀察植物的反應。結果令人震驚：發光的鈣質輸送至整株植物，彷彿因為受到威脅而發出求救訊號。

此研究結果顯示，植物擁有與人類相似的神經系統。有別於人類的神經傳導，植物以體內鈣離子傳送訊號。而人體中，心跳和肌肉收縮等部分生理機能，同樣透過鈣離子調節。就植物而言，此類訊號可用於啟動防禦機制。最耐人尋味的是：鈣質分泌量取決於植物受損的程度。小範圍的割傷會產生少量鈣質；但如果整片葉子遭輾碎，鈣質分泌量就會激增。

大家也許會納悶：植物能採取何種防禦措施？其實手段可多了。舉例來說，某些植物會分泌酸性物質傷害昆蟲的消化道，讓昆蟲逃之夭夭。有的植物則會硬化自己的細胞壁，讓潛在天敵無法吞食。有時植物的防禦機制甚至足以致命。例如含有茉莉酮酸的植物遭受攻擊而受損時，就會分泌有毒化合物。

威斯康辛大學麥迪遜校區的實驗僅證明了我們早已確知的事實：那就是人類和植物細胞擁有相似的生物學構造。我們面對「綠色朋友」時，或許應時時牢記這點。下次外出健行時，請記得腳下留情！

99. 禿頭掰掰──同時還能香氣怡人！
P.216

新研究讓科學家開始相信，治癒禿頭已非遙不可及。更棒的是，該研究指出，鼻子以外的人體部位同樣具有「嗅覺」。是否覺得摸不著頭緒呢？別擔心，雖然細節十分複雜，但還不至於難懂到讓你搔破頭的程度！而且即使你還沒有禿頭的徵兆，一樣受用無窮。

為理解該研究的來龍去脈和影響，須先知道何謂受體與人工合成檀香。鼻子具有四百種不同的受體，能讓我們察覺 1 兆種氣味。而人工合成檀香，顧名思義，是效仿檀木香氣的人造化學物質。如果你從沒聞過檀香的氣味，請試聞看看。檀香具有十分宜人的木質調與幾分花香香氣。

由曼徹斯特大學科學家瑞夫・伯斯所領軍的研究團隊，將頭皮組織浸泡於人工合成檀香。在很短的時間內，頭皮組織的毛髮出現驚人且顯著的變化。人工合成檀香不僅能減緩落髮速度，還能在短時間內促進毛髮增生。研究人員表示，此物質能使頭皮的賀爾蒙增加 30%。意料之外的結果簡直超越了研究人員的期望。伯斯向記者透露：「老實說，我沒料到會有這樣的成效。」優於預期的研究成果，意味著有效治療落髮的產品，或許近在咫尺。相關產品遲早會上市，因為此研究已進入自願者接受人體試驗的階段。

倘若上述內容還無法讓你刮目相看，請聽聽以下重點。研究人員之所以有此發現，是因為他們早已知悉某種有助於傷口癒合的特定嗅覺受體。他們推斷代碼為 OR2AT4 的受體亦能促進生髮。此外，嗅覺受體並非侷限在鼻子內部，事實上，人體全身上下都有嗅覺受體。理論上，我們能刺激嗅覺受體以協助治療其他人體部位，而非僅止於頭皮。因此，這項研究不僅為有落髮困擾的男女帶來福音，更開啟了嶄新的皮膚研究領域，將來甚至可用來預防疾病。

100. 折線圖：人民幣疲弱的原因 `P. 218`

　　曾經升值長達十年之久的人民幣，從 2014 年起兌美元的匯率卻開始疲弱，此趨勢甚至延續至其後幾年。原因何在？首先，中國國內生產毛額已開始下滑，不復 2000 年時代的驚人雙位數成長率。另一項因素則是美國總統川普於 2017 年年底發動的貿易戰。中國向來出口眾多商品至美國，因此關稅壁壘恐重創中國的經濟。

　　下頁列出的折線圖顯示 2005 年至 2018 年人民幣兌美元的匯率走勢。左側的 Y 軸意指 1 美元可兌換的人民幣金額。橫向的 X 軸則代表時間。此圖表讓我們一覽人民幣的長期走向，並顯示出即使人民幣仍處於疲弱狀態，但貶值幅度仍遠不及 2005 年的慘況。

ANSWERS

Unit 1 Reading Skills

1-1 Main Idea

1	1. c	2. d	3. a	4. c	5. a
2	1. b	2. a	3. d	4. c	5. a
3	1. b	2. c	3. c	4. a	5. d
4	1. c	2. c	3. b	4. a	5. c
5	1. c	2. a	3. b	4. b	5. d

1-2 Supporting Details

6	1. d	2. d	3. a	4. b	5. c
7	1. d	2. b	3. c	4. d	5. a
8	1. c	2. a	3. b	4. c	5. a
9	1. c	2. d	3. c	4. a	5. a
10	1. c	2. c	3. c	4. a	5. d

1-3 Fact or Opinion

11	1. c	2. c	3. d	4. a	5. b
12	1. b	2. c	3. b	4. a	5. c
13	1. d	2. b	3. b	4. a	5. d
14	1. a	2. c	3. b	4. d	5. a
15	1. b	2. b	3. b	4. d	5. b

1-4 Author's Purpose and Tone

16	1. b	2. d	3. b	4. a	5. a
17	1. a	2. d	3. b	4. b	5. a
18	1. c	2. b	3. b	4. a	5. c
19	1. d	2. a	3. c	4. a	5. d
20	1. b	2. d	3. b	4. a	5. c

1-5 Clarifying Devices

21	1. d	2. b	3. a	4. b	5. c
22	1. a	2. b	3. c	4. a	5. c
23	1. a	2. c	3. c	4. b	5. a
24	1. b	2. d	3. c	4. d	5. a
25	1. b	2. a	3. d	4. a	5. c

1-6 Making Inferences

26	1. b	2. a	3. c	4. d	5. b
27	1. b	2. c	3. d	4. a	5. c
28	1. c	2. a	3. c	4. b	5. a
29	1. c	2. a	3. c	4. c	5. b
30	1. c	2. b	3. d	4. b	5. a

1-7 Cause and Effect

31	1. d	2. c	3. a	4. c	5. b
32	1. d	2. a	3. b	4. c	5. b
33	1. a	2. b	3. d	4. c	5. b
34	1. c	2. d	3. a	4. b	5. c
35	1. a	2. c	3. c	4. d	5. b

1-8 Figurative Language

36	1. d	2. a	3. c	4. a	5. b
37	1. b	2. d	3. a	4. c	5. b
38	1. c	2. b	3. d	4. a	5. c
39	1. d	2. a	3. d	4. b	5. c
40	1. b	2. c	3. a	4. d	5. b

1-9 Finding Bias

41	1. b	2. b	3. c	4. a	5. d
42	1. c	2. b	3. a	4. d	5. c
43	1. c	2. c	3. a	4. d	5. c
44	1. d	2. c	3. a	4. a	5. d
45	1. d	2. b	3. d	4. b	5. c

1-10 Review Test

46	1. b	2. b	3. a	4. a	5. d
47	1. a	2. c	3. d	4. c	5. b
48	1. c	2. d	3. a	4. c	5. d
49	1. b	2. a	3. b	4. b	5. d
50	1. c	2. a	3. b	4. c	5. a

Unit 2 Word Study

2-1 Synonyms

51	1. c	2. a	3. d	4. b	5. c
52	1. c	2. a	3. c	4. d	5. b
53	1. b	2. a	3. c	4. c	5. d
54	1. c	2. d	3. d	4. a	5. b
55	1. b	2. c	3. b	4. a	5. d

2-2 Antonyms

56	1. c	2. b	3. a	4. b	5. d
57	1. d	2. b	3. d	4. d	5. b
58	1. c	2. c	3. a	4. c	5. c
59	1. a	2. c	3. b	4. b	5. c
60	1. c	2. a	3. c	4. d	5. b

2-3 Words in Context

61	1. b	2. c	3. a	4. d	5. b
62	1. a	2. c	3. c	4. b	5. d
63	1. c	2. c	3. d	4. a	5. b
64	1. c	2. c	3. d	4. b	5. c
65	1. c	2. a	3. b	4. b	5. d

2-4 Review Test

66	1. b	2. c	3. b	4. a	5. d
67	1. c	2. a	3. d	4. a	5. b
68	1. c	2. b	3. b	4. d	5. a
69	1. d	2. c	3. a	4. a	5. b
70	1. d	2. b	3. b	4. a	5. c

Unit 3 Study Strategies

3-1 Visual Material

71	1. a	2. b	3. d	4. b	5. a
72	1. a	2. d	3. c	4. c	5. a
73	1. b	2. c	3. a	4. d	5. d
74	1. a	2. b	3. b	4. a	5. b
75	1. d	2. b	3. b	4. b	5. c

3-2 Reference Sources

76	1. d	2. b	3. c	4. a	5. b
77	1. b	2. d	3. a	4. c	5. c
78	1. c	2. c	3. d	4. a	5. c
79	1. a	2. b	3. d	4. b	5. c
80	1. b	2. c	3. a	4. d	5. c

Unit 4 Final Reviews

4-1 Final Review (I)

81	1. b	2. c	3. a	4. b	5. d
82	1. b	2. b	3. d	4. a	5. b
83	1. d	2. b	3. a	4. c	5. c
84	1. c	2. a	3. b	4. c	5. a
85	1. b	2. a	3. c	4. d	5. b
86	1. b	2. a	3. d	4. c	5. a
87	1. b	2. d	3. a	4. c	5. a
88	1. d	2. c	3. c	4. c	5. c
89	1. b	2. c	3. a	4. b	5. c
90	1. d	2. d	3. d	4. a	5. c

4-2 Final Review (II)

91	1. a	2. d	3. c	4. d	5. c
92	1. c	2. b	3. a	4. b	5. d
93	1. c	2. a	3. b	4. d	5. c
94	1. c	2. c	3. d	4. d	5. a
95	1. b	2. a	3. a	4. c	5. c
96	1. a	2. d	3. a	4. b	5. d
97	1. b	2. d	3. a	4. d	5. d
98	1. c	2. b	3. c	4. b	5. d
99	1. a	2. c	3. c	4. b	5. a
100	1. a	2. c	3. c	4. a	5. b

英語閱讀技巧
Success With Reading
完全攻略

3

二版

作　　者　Zachary Fillingham / Owain Mckimm
協力作者　Richard Luhrs (4, 11, 24, 28, 63, 70, 81, 83) /
　　　　　Brian Foden (12, 31, 87, 99)
審　　訂　Treva Adams / Helen Yeh
譯　　者　劉嘉珮／丁宥榆／黃詩韻／林育珊
企畫編輯　葉俞均
編　　輯　呂敏如／丁宥暄
主　　編　丁宥暄
校　　對　黃詩韻／申文怡
內頁設計　鄭秀芳
封面設計　林書玉
製程管理　洪巧玲
出 版 者　寂天文化事業股份有限公司
發 行 人　黃朝萍
電　　話　+886-(0)2-2365-9739
傳　　真　+886-(0)2-2365-9835
網　　址　www.icosmos.com.tw
讀者服務　onlineservice@icosmos.com.tw
出版日期　2023 年 10 月二版三刷 （寂天雲 Mebook 互動學習 APP 版）

郵撥帳號　1998620-0 寂天文化事業股份有限公司
訂書金額未滿 1000 元，請外加運費 100 元。

國家圖書館出版品預行編目 (CIP) 資料

英語閱讀技巧完全攻略 (寂天雲 Mebook 互動學習 APP 版)
/ Zachary Fillingham, Owain Mckimm, Richard Luhrs, Brian Foden
著 ; 劉嘉珮 , 丁宥榆 , 黃詩韻 , 林育珊 譯 . -- 二版 . -- [臺北市]
: 寂天文化 , 2023.10-
　　冊 ;　　公分
ISBN 978-626-300-220-3 (第 3 冊 : 平裝)
1. 英語 2. 讀本
805.18　　　　　　　　　　　　　　　　　112016399